Acclaim for Elaine Coffman's wonderful novels

So This Is Love

"[A] heartwarming and humorous tale of awakenings and new beginnings."
—*Romantic Times*

"A battle of wills and emotions that will keep [the reader] enthralled and wondering."
—*Rendezvous*

Heaven Knows

"Coffman has crafted a smoothly milled romance."
—*Publishers Weekly*

"An emotionally intense and poignant tale ... A love story to cherish."
—*Romantic Times*

Also by Elaine Coffman
Published by Fawcett Books:

HEAVEN KNOWS
SO THIS IS LOVE

A TIME FOR ROSES

Elaine Coffman

FAWCETT GOLD MEDAL • NEW YORK

A Fawcett Gold Medal Book
Published by Ballantine Books
Copyright © 1994 by Guardant Inc.

Library of Congress Catalog Card Number: 94-94651

ISBN 0-449-14862-9

Manufactured in the United States of America

First Edition: January 1995

10 9 8 7 6 5 4 3 2 1

For my sister, Suzanne

Although the world is full of suffering,
it is full also of the overcoming of it.
—Helen Keller, *Optimism* (1903), 1.

❧ PROLOGUE ❧

England, 1815

They say it is better to be blessed with good fortune than to be a rich man's child.

She was neither.

Misfortune seemed to smile upon her, yet she never doubted she would survive. She was like a cork. Nothing would sink her. Not the loss of parents or country. Not the death of her benefactor. The will to survive was strong within her—after all, she was Russian.

Her benefactor, William Weatherby, the sixth Earl of Marsham, was dead and laid to rest. And now, the funeral was over. Lord William's death meant Natasha's life had changed—changed, but it was by no means over. The future was all questions and uncertainty.

Throughout Marsham Manor, mirrors and pictures were draped in crepe. A wreath of rosemary hung on the front door. Inside the stately country house of the recently departed, the earl's ward, Natasha Simonov, came slowly down the stairs.

The striking of the great hall clock seemed to herald a descent that was soft and silent, save for the rustle of

1

black bombazine. She was young and pale, and the sight of her was enough to raise the protectiveness in the most manly of hearts.

At the bottom of the stairs she paused, looking around the dimly lit interior, where signs of mourning lay everywhere. How strange these traditions seemed, how hollow, for she found little solace in them. But it did not matter. She needed no mirrors draped in crepe, no black-bordered writing paper to serve as a reminder. The pain in her heart was enough.

The Earl of Marsham is dead. How final it sounds. Her beloved benefactor was gone, and Natasha could not help wondering if his death was an ending or a beginning. What would happen now? Her head down, her footsteps solemn, she lifted the black veil from her face. A moment later she went outside to sit upon the stone bench in the garden just beyond the hawthorn hedge.

Winter was just around the corner. Already the horse chestnuts along the lane blazed with color and the cardinal willow was showing off its bright red bark. The air was filled with the smell of burning apple wood. Fat pumpkins were stacked in a wagon by the coach house door. Withered lobelia spilled from an old olive jar on one side of the stone bench, a terra-cotta pot of dried geraniums stood on the other. Over near the fountain, red and gold chrysanthemums anxiously awaited their first blanket of snow. The creeper that covered the back of the house flamed scarlet; the trellis drooped with dead black roses. Beyond the hedgerow, ivy climbing the stone arch near the toolshed was beginning to show winter color.

All about her, pale amber sunlight fell across the garden, touching the trees with red and yellow, their colors reminding her, somehow, of summer and her loss. In the beds that ran along the flagstone walk, the bright heads of marigolds turned their faces to the sun, and she found herself doing the same. With her eyes closed, she felt the sun's warmth upon her face. Today was the 10th of October, the Devil's Blackberry Day, and the memory of that, recalled another.

She remembered it had only been a year ago that she sat upon this same stone bench, Luka and Pavel sitting at her feet, listening to the Earl of Marsham tell them, "As legend has it, you must not eat blackberries after this date. St. Michael the Archangel threw the devil out of heaven on October ninth and he landed in a blackberry bush when he fell to earth."

"What did the devil do?" Pavel had asked.

"He was so angry, he cursed the blackberries, making them no good to eat after that date."

Natasha plucked a sprig of lifelong, twirling it in her fingers as she gazed across the garden to the hazy blue of the fields beyond. Autumn surrounded her with the mellow warmth of colors found in the old stained glass in the chapel. The peace of the garden reached out to her. Was there anything more beautiful than the fading rust of summer?

Warmed by the sun overhead, scented with the smells of dry grasses and seedpods, the familiar surroundings seemed more dear to her because of her loss and the mystery of death. Dropping the sprig of lifelong into her lap, she sat with her chin resting on her fists as she wondered about the effect of the earl's will upon their lives—a will being read in the library this very moment.

She knew the earl would have remembered them and kept his promise to provide her and her brothers with a home at Marsham for as long as they needed one. Yet she also knew that in spite of continuing their lives here at Marsham, everything would somehow change. Perhaps it was the child in her—or perhaps it was the woman—that made her wonder just what those changes would be. The biggest question was, of course, just who would be coming to live at Marsham, to live here as the new Earl of Marsham and to manage their lives. . . .

The distant scream of a peacock pulled her attention away from her somber thoughts. She glanced around, trying to imagine how everything could possibly look different than it did now. Then, a glimpse of the sloping roof of the earl's beloved greenhouse caught her eye and she could not help but wonder about it as well. Now that he was gone, what would happen to the Earl of Marsham's exotic collection of plants from all over the world—plants he had spent the greater part of his life collecting and studying?

She thought of the boxes of aged and yellowing papers stacked in his study, of the botanical books filled with notes and colored drawings, and felt a twinge of guilt that she had not given the greenhouse and gardens the attention they needed during the earl's illness. With a sad smile she remembered how he had such a fondness for using funds that were needed for the running of Marsham to purchase yet another plant species he had longed to own. Even now, a deadly machineel sapling was on its way from the Caribbean. She wondered what would become of it once it arrived, just as she wondered what would become of the other treasured plants the earl had left behind in his greenhouse. The future of his botanical collection was as uncertain as her own.

Soon, she thought. *Soon it will be over and the earl's wishes will be known.* What would happen to her and her brothers then she had no way of knowing. *Oh, Papa. What will happen to us now?* She paused, turning her head to listen, for indeed, she could almost hear the soft lilt of long-forgotten words, lingering like an old haunting melody in the back of her mind.

> *But what am I?*
> *An infant crying in the night?*
> *An infant crying for the light:*
> *And with no language but a cry.*

Natasha let out a forlorn sigh, thinking she had so many questions and precious few answers. Suddenly the full impact of what had happened hit her. The weight of it felt as if it would crush her. Her heart fluttered in her chest like a trapped bird. Her head hammered. Tears, which she did not know she wept, made a slow descent down her pale cheeks. For a moment she let them flow, unchecked, feeling the slow return of her strength. She would not give in.

She wiped the tears from her face. Her grief would be private and unseen, for she did not want her brothers to know just how afraid she really was—afraid and uncertain about their future. But hiding her fear did not banish her uneasiness. What *would* happen to them?

Uncertainty, she decided, was in some ways worse than bad news. At least one could deal with bad news when it came. . . . But uncertainty? Even the word seemed to hover elusively about her. She closed her eyes and prayed, feeling better when she finished. She had seen much death during Napoléon's siege of Moscow. She and her brothers survived the death of their mother and their father. She would be strong through this as well. They would make it. God would not abandon them now. Trembling, but filled with a quiet sort of courage, she came to her feet, glancing down at the watch pinned on her bodice.

It was one o'clock in the afternoon, and the staff of

Marsham was gathered in the kitchen while the will of the Earl of Marsham was being read. Lifting her skirts, Natasha left the garden to stroll down the leaf-strewn path that opened to an avenue of Irish yews.

At half past two, the housekeeper, Mrs. MacDougal, came into the kitchen to find the gardener enjoying a bowl of blackberry-and-apple meringue and Cook up to her elbows in flour. Mrs. MacDougal surveyed her friends with a knowing eye, crossed her arms over her ample bosom, then said, "He left everything to his nephew, Lord Anthony Hamilton."

"Well, that bangs Banagher," Cook said.

While Cook was banging Banagher, the gardener gave Mrs. MacDougal an astonished look. "He left *everything* to Lord Anthony? But why would he leave everything to that scoundrel? He didn't even come to the earl's funeral."

"Well, the earl doesn't know that," said Mrs. MacDougal.

"Heaven knows Lord Anthony is a rogue of the first water, but a likable scamp none the less," Cook added. "I know for a fact the earl was a favorite of his. I am certain Lord Anthony would have been here if he could."

"Well then, where is Lord Anthony? Why isn't he here?" asked the gardener.

"I understand he is in Ireland buying horses," Mrs. MacDougal said. "Word has been sent to him, but no one knows just how long it will take to locate him, or how long it will be before he arrives."

"And Natasha and her brothers? What happens to them?" asked Cook.

"That is entirely up to Lord Anthony, since he is now their guardian," said Mrs. MacDougal, giving Cook a hopeless look and sadly shaking her head. "Poor child. It is bad enough to lose the earl, but now she must wait indefinitely to learn her own fate." Mrs. Mac shook her head. "I have never met Lord Anthony, you understand, but all the rumors I've heard . . . Well, they only serve to make me all the more worried about the outcome of all of this. A distressing thing it is."

"Foolish, too," Cook said. "From what I hear, Lord Anthony has three outstanding talents—cricket, horses, and fornication . . . and not necessarily in that order."

"Dear me," Mrs. MacDougal said. "Poor Tasha. I cannot conceive why the earl—God rest his soul— deemed it prudent to place that reprobate nephew of his as guardian over that poor unfortunate child and her brothers. It's like putting a fox into the henhouse, if you ask me. She's just a child, and innocent as they come. And worried sick, mind you. Have you noticed her coloring? Byron pale, she is."

Harry the gardener nodded in agreement.

Mrs. MacDougal moved to the window to gaze outside. She saw Natasha walking along the path that led to the yews.

"She might be young, and she might be innocent, but she has a strength of spirit not found in many who are older and more experienced," Harry said.

"I hope you are right," Mrs. MacDougal said. "Still, it seems my place to worry about her."

"I worry as well," Cook said, with a shake of her head. "Poor little lamb. An innocent maiden of seventeen—strapped to the sacrificial altar of a notorious scoundrel."

"Aye," Mrs. MacDougal said, "what an odd twist of fate it is that has put such an innocent into Lord Anthony's hands."

"Well, if it's her being so innocent you are worried

about, Lord Anthony will make fast work of that, I'll wager," the gardener said, his mouth snapping shut when Mrs. MacDougal gave him a quelling look.

Cook straightened her aching back, dusted the flour from her hands, and said, "There is no heavier lot in life than finding yourself trapped in the coils of fate." She shook her head wistfully. "You were right, you know. This is an odd twist of fate."

"Well, she is young," Harry said. "And youth has a way."

"Yes, they do," Cook said. "Almost makes me wish I were younger."

Mrs. MacDougal took one last look out the window, catching a glimpse of Natasha sitting on the stone bench. "Lord, Lord," she said. "No wise man ever wished to be younger."

It was indeed—just as Cook and Mrs. MacDougal said—an odd twist of fate that had made Natasha Simonov an orphan in her native Russia. It was that same twist of fate that made the Earl of Marsham bring Natasha and her twin brothers to England as his wards.

Natasha and her brothers were the children of a Russian nobleman, Count Alexi Simonov, who served as an officer in the Russian army at the time Napoléon decided to teach the Russians a lesson for not fully closing their ports to British trade as Czar Alexander had agreed to do.

The Earl of Marsham had been in Moscow for several months, working with the Russian leaders as an emissary of King George. During the thirty-five-day siege of Moscow, the presence of the Earl of Marsham was discovered by the French and a trap was laid. His life was saved by Count Simonov, who took a bullet meant for the earl. Barely escaping the French, the earl took Count Simonov back to his country estate near Moscow, where a short while later, the count lay dying in the arms of his fourteen-year-old daughter, Natasha.

"Don't cry," Count Simonov said. "Don't be sad for me, *babushka*. There is a time for everything, even dying. Be happy, Tasha mine."

"Oh, Papa, I cannot. If this is your time to die, it is my time for sadness," Natasha said.

The count touched her cheek. "I don't want you to be sad."

"How can I be happy without you?" Natasha began to cry softly. "Papa, please don't leave us."

The count coughed and blood rose in his throat, reducing his voice to a gurgling whisper. "*Paslusha-tyeh!* Listen! My time is near . . . and how strange it feels. This should be a time for sadness, yet I feel I am ready to go."

Natasha broke into uncontrolled sobs, and Count Simonov drew her closer.

"It hurts now," he said, "but there will come a time when you will laugh again." He closed his eyes against the pain. "I have only one regret—that I will not see your time for roses."

"There will be no roses without you, Papa. Never."

Count Simonov stroked Tasha's cheek. "Yes there will . . . and what a time that will be. One day you will fall in love, little Natasha, and then you will understand. Wait for it, Tasha. Wait for it. And when it comes, remember to tell me I was right. For you, there will be a time for roses. I promise."

A moment later Count Simonov was dead.

They had only enough time to bury the count before Napoléon's troops arrived. Furious that the count and the Englishman had escaped them, they set torches to Count Simonov's ancestral estate. Their home in flames, the count's children homeless orphans, the Earl of Marsham realized there was little he could do.

Count Simonov was dead—and it should have been him. There was no way to repay such a debt, but he could try. Without a moment's hesitation, the Earl of Marsham did the only thing he could do. He took Natasha and her twin brothers to England with him.

Because of his friendship with the king, the Earl of Marsham had been called to serve his country as a special emissary, but it was because of his work as a botanist that the earl was best known. For three years the earl—who had never married—enjoyed his new life as a father. Although the twins were much too young to be interested in his botanical work, their sister was not. From the very beginning, the earl realized Natasha was unusual because she excelled at the practical and theoretical aspects of gardening—and she possessed the artistic ability to make beautiful and detailed drawings of the plants and gardens at Marsham.

The earl was never able to fully recover from the nagging cough he had acquired that terrible winter in Russia when 500,000 of Napoléon's troops had been so weakened from the bitter cold that they had been easy to kill or capture, most of them escaping that fate by starving or freezing to death.

Once his doctors told him that he was dying, the earl made a change in his will—which passed the title, Earl of Marsham, and all the estate of Marsham to his sister's youngest son, Lord Anthony Hamilton. To the will he added one stipulation: that the three children of his dear friend, Count Alexi Simonov, be well provided for and given a home at Marsham, as well as an education befitting the children of a nobleman.

Now, three years later, Natasha Simonov was seventeen—a farm-fresh country girl, sheltered, practical, energetic, and wide-eyed with curiosity. Her twin brothers, Luka and Pavel, were twelve—brothers who were both the joy of her life and the bane of her existence. While living with the aging Earl of Marsham, Natasha and her brothers had led a simple country life.

They continued to thrive for six months after the old earl's death. But when blond and handsome Lord Anthony came to the sprawling country estate to live, Natasha's sheltered life abruptly came to an end.

"Venus favors the bold."
—Ovid, *The Art of Love* (ca. 7 A.D.)

PART ONE

CHAPTER
❧ ONE ❧

Six months later . . .

The orchard at Marsham was ancient, and the peach trees, lined up like fluffy clouds in a pink sunset, were just as old. Ordinarily Natasha would not have been in the orchard this time of year, or climbing a ladder to the topmost branches of such a gnarled old peach tree.

It was springtime, and all about her the hills and fields were alive with hues and tints that could only be found on an artist's palette. The fruit trees blushed with color and bees hummed.

But it wasn't the bees, or the peach trees—or even the reminder of pink clouds—that drew her to the meadow on this sunny day. It was simply because no one should stay indoors when the whole world is in bloom and bursting with color.

Only moments ago Natasha had been in the meadow, gathering a bit of nature's bounty for herself, when she spied old Mr. Pottingham's dog happily scattering a herd of sheep in hot pursuit of a kitten he was chasing up the weedy path that led to the orchard. Always a champion of those in need, Natasha dumped her armload of meadow flowers and took up the chase.

By the time she ran Mr. Pottingham's dog from the orchard, she was winded—and the hissing puff ball of a kitten had climbed to the topmost branch of the tallest tree in the orchard, where it stood, trembling and spitting, with its back arched high.

Natasha called to the kitten in her most coaxing voice, but soon realized all the pleading and promises in the universe wouldn't have persuaded that kitten to budge. If it wouldn't be coaxed down, there was nothing else to be done. She would have to go after it herself.

A meadowlark took flight from a nearby tree as she conducted a brief search, which turned up a wobbly ladder that looked decrepit enough to have been used when the two-hundred-year-old trees were first planted.

She braced it against the tree, but the ladder was still rickety enough for her to think climbing it fell somewhere between dangerous and stupid. In spite of her trepidations, she climbed as high as the ladder would allow, but even that was not high enough to reach the kitten, so she had to step from the ladder to a twisting but sturdy old branch.

Just as she had the kitten safely in her grasp, she saw the twins come bounding through the hawthorn hedge. "Luka," she shouted, "climb up here and take this kitten."

. Luka drew up short, took a quick look at Natasha, and whispered something to Pavel.

Pavel nodded his blond head, then laughed.

Natasha looked at the two golden heads whispering together and frowned. If there was anything she recognized, it was thoughts of mischief clouding their reason.

"Luka," she called again—louder this time.

Her shout caused the kitten to dig his claws deeper into her shoulder, and that caused Natasha to forget about the twins' look of mischief. "Come quickly," she said. "My skirts are caught fast. I cannot free them and hold the kitten at the same time."

The twins laughed and trotted over to the tree. Pavel eyed the ladder suspiciously, then motioned for Luka, who apparently had no reservations about climbing it, to fetch the kitten down. Pavel waited at the bottom while Luka climbed up the ladder, stood on tiptoe, and reached for the kitten. Natasha handed him the kitten, thinking he would offer her some assistance, but without wasting a moment, he backed down the ladder, handed the kitten to Pavel, and jumped clear.

A second later he pulled the ladder away from the tree. The next thing she saw was the two of them streaking down the path, dragging the ladder behind them.

"Of all the bounders!" she shouted. "Come back here! . . . Luka! . . . Pavel! Bring that ladder back!" She expended a few more finalities of eloquence upon them, but by the time the words were out, the twins had disappeared through the hawthorn hedge—and the ladder, too.

Not even the kitten remained behind.

Natasha shouted until she was sufficiently hoarse, then she sat down. After a short rest, her resilient spirits adequately revived, she gave her attention to freeing her skirt, tearing a large triangular rip in the worn blue dimity and exposing a goodly portion of the lace on her petticoat.

Ready to find a way down, she leaned forward, bracing her palm against the scaly bark, then carefully rising to her feet. The branch creaked and drooped, sending a flutter of peach-white blossoms to the ground. Holding on with one hand, Natasha lowered her right leg, trying to reach the branch below. Her foot slipped; she grabbed the branch overhead to secure her footing, scraping both her arm and leg and sending another cloudburst of petals downward. With a dejected sigh, she inched herself around and sat down. Perhaps she would have better luck standing on the branches with her shoes off.

Pulling up her skirts to give her better access to her feet, she began to unbutton her shoes—which was devilishly slow going and difficult without a hook.

It was while she was in this charming position that the new Earl of Marsham, Lord Anthony Hamilton, cantered down the sun-dappled lane that ran along one side of the orchard. Seeing the sudden shower of peach blossoms floating downward—punctuated by the soft thump of a lady's shoe, and then another—Anthony looked up.

He was ever so glad that he did.

For there, nestled among the delicate pinks and whites of peach blossoms, was a rare beauty—a woman in all her inky-haired radiance, the sunshine glorious upon her curls, looking misty eyed and beautiful, virtue just oozing out of her. Coming to a sudden halt, his interested gaze lingered upon a shapely pair of limbs and the daintiest ankles imaginable.

"Hello, sweetness," he said, breaking into a wide grin as his gaze traveled upward to rest upon the goddess with the raven tresses and a face flushed scarlet. " 'A maid yet rosed over with the virgin crimson of modesty.' Alas, I am doomed."

The vision overhead gave him a hot glare but said nothing.

His gaze traveling back down to the lovely limbs she

was frantically trying to cover, he said, "Tell me, pretty maid—are there any more like you at home?"

"No, and will you please stop staring at me in that lecherous fashion!? No gentleman would dare peep under a maid's skirts, much less ogle her."

He laughed. "You are absolutely right, lovely. . . . No gentleman would," he said, looking his fill.

Wiggling back on the branch and sending a sprinkle of blossoms cascading over him, she said, "You could help me down, you know."

The gelding snorted and shied away from the deluge of blossoms. Anthony rode him in a sweeping circle to bring him under control, then riding the mincing gelding back to the tree, he said casually, "Now, what were we talking about?"

"We were not *talking* about anything. I merely said you could help me down. In case you are wondering, this tree is not my natural habitat."

"Help you down?" he said, thinking her natural habitat should be a bed. "Now, why would I want to do that when you make such a fetching picture where you are, garbed in peach blossoms?"

His grin was wider now. "I do believe fortune has smiled upon me." A teasing glint lurked behind the brilliant blue of his eyes as he said, "It has long been my practice to take the advantage when fortune smiles."

He saw her lovely face darken with displeasure, but even then she was uncommonly beautiful. "Past disputing, fair blossom; you must be the favorite of the gods."

"If I were so favored, sir, I would not be out on such a limb."

"Ah, but what limbs," he said, ogling her once more. She sent him a chilling look and wiggled forward.

He knew she was seriously contemplating a jump— foolish though it was, for she was some twenty feet off the ground. By Jove, she was an exquisite creature, looking charmingly bewildered as he dismounted.

He led the black to the hawthorne hedge and tied him, returning to gaze up at the vision in the peach tree. For a moment he was distracted by the contrast of jet black ringlets against the perfect pink-and-white complexion, the sheer innocent beauty of her as she sat there on that limb—as desirable as she was delectable. He gave her a good visual groping, imagining her naked and wet, fresh from her bath. Here was a damsel in distress if he had ever seen one, and he had a sudden vision of seducing a naked and distressed maid at the edge of the meadow where lambs leapt and would-be lovers could dally—a thought that sent blood pumping to his head. And a few other places as well. This, he decided, was an occasion that demanded action, and being as hot-blooded as he was horny, he rose to the occasion.

She shot him a questioning look. "Have you decided to help me?"

A capital notion, seeing as how I am not overly fond of resisting temptation, he thought, but what he said was, "I have decided to rush to your rescue as fearlessly as Dick Dauntless, since I cannot resist a maiden in distress."

"I doubt you resist anything lecherous," she said, giving him a wary look.

"Desire has no rest . . . One look at you and I was helpless. Now, drop into my arms, fairest blossom."

She inched forward, looking down at him. "You are certain you will catch me?"

"Dear heart, a beauty such as yourself is rarer than bird's milk. Only an idiot would dash such an opportunity." With a low-sweeping bow, he added, "A faithful lover of maidens such as myself would never be so idiotic . . . or foolish."

"Humph!"

Holding up his arms, he smiled and said, "Now, push away from your lofty perch, angel face, and fall into the arms of paradise."

"Purgatory, you mean," she said, staying where she was. Her brows narrowed in thought. "Perhaps I am safer here."

"Dainty flower," he said, with a deepening smile, "I would not harm a hair on your lovely head. You are safe with me."

"I am surrounded by poor choices," she said, taking the bait and dropping down into his arms.

"Ah," he said, catching her and making no move to put her down, "light as a feather and as tender as Parnel, who broke his finger in a posset curd."

She regarded him quizzically. "Put me down, or have you forgotten your words?"

"As fair as foolish," he said, laughing. He looked at the velvet peach gilt of her skin, thinking she smelled of almonds and peach blossoms. "Put you down, you say? Now, why would I do a foolish thing like that? By Jove, you've a fair body and a bright countenance. I fancy myself in love."

"And I fancy you are a big philanderer. Now, put me down. You promised I would be safe."

"Alas, distracted as I am by the ringlets of beauty, the fetters of reason seem to fade faster than the daisies of May."

She wiggled and pushed against him. "If you are through playing the poet—and badly done, I might add—will you behave yourself?"

He gave her a wicked grin, for in truth he couldn't remember what she had just said. Frankly, he supposed that was because he was having such impassioned thoughts—thoughts she must have read.

"Oh, you trickster, you! Put me down, I say. This instant, or I shall scream."

He lowered her to her feet, feigning a shocked look. "What? A virtuous milkmaid?"

"Virtue I have aplenty, and I am no milkmaid."

He grabbed at his heart and staggered backward. "*Virgo intacta,* and just my luck. A maiden untouched."

"And I plan to stay that way."

Ignoring that, he picked up her shoes, then walked to where his horse stood, and, untying him, brought him to stand beside her. "Come then, little virgin. I'll give you a hand up."

She snorted her disbelief. "Up what?"

He laughed. "A beauty and a wit. I am becoming more enamored by the minute."

She gave him another hot look. "*Enamored* is not the word I would choose."

He raised his brows. "Oh? And what would your choice of words be?"

"Never mind," she said, turning down the road at a fast pace, walking in the direction of Marsham.

He led his horse around and in front of her, blocking her path. "I have offered you a ride. As a gentleman I cannot allow you to walk. You haven't any shoes," he said, holding her shoes aloft. "Come now. My horse is gentle enough."

"It is not your horse I am leery of."

"Then you have nothing to fear. Now, up with you, pretty maiden," he said, reaching for her, but she shied away.

"If I'm on the horse," she asked, with a suspicious look, "just where will you be?"

He smiled. "Why, I'll be right behind you, of course—and as close to you as I can get. This is not the face of a fool you are looking at."

"Then I will walk, thank you," she said.

"Why would you prefer to walk when I have offered you a ride?"

"I don't trust you."

He stroked her rosy cheek. "Have I harmed a hair on this fair head?"

"You have not, as yet ... But I'll wager it was not from lack of wanting."

He laughed. "*Vae victis.* 'Woe to the vanquished,' and all that," he said, and swept her into his arms, depositing her upon the back of a horse as black as sin.

"I know I will come to regret this," she said.

"Breathe easy, dainty flower of maidenhood. Your virtue is safe for now," he said, mounting behind her.

She turned and gave him a look that said how much she believed that.

Reaching around her, he took the reins. "Upon my oath, it's the truth. I seem to have a catch in my neck."

"From all your ogling, I'll wager."

He looked thoughtful for a moment. "You have an excellent command of the language, but your accent—besides being damnably seductive—is not English. Where do you hail from, little beauty?"

"Russia."

"Russia?" He gave her a considering look. "You don't strike me as an impoverished maid imported to work."

She gave him a blank look. "I am neither impoverished nor am I employed."

"And the other?"

"The other?" she repeated, turning to look at him.

"Are you a maiden, then?"

She blushed beautifully. "Of course I am," she said, noticing he had the gall to look disappointed.

"I might have known. With a face like yours, it is hardly believable, yet just my luck."

She smiled at that. "You have not seen many maidens, I take it?"

He chuckled. "All the virgins in London could dance in an eggshell."

She laughed, but stopped when he nuzzled her neck and whispered low. "A maid that laughs is half taken. *Veni, vidi, vici.*"

" 'I came, I saw, I conquered,' " she said. "I have studied Latin. Are you trying to insult me?"

"It is said that those near the temple insult the god," he said. Then he nuzzled her again and said with a throaty laugh, "I have no desire to insult one so fair, but you must know I am deuced eager to seduce you, rare beauty."

"I think you should put me down. I can walk home, thank you. I think it would be much wiser . . . and safer."

"But not half so much fun. I could not allow such a lovely lady to walk."

"So, I am a lady now. A moment ago I was an impoverished milkmaid."

He smiled. "What you are, matters not, but seduction will have to wait. I find I cannot move my head with this blasted crick. Where do you live, innocence?"

"Just down the lane."

All this and convenience, too? "How bloody fortunate. That happens to be the way I am going. You wouldn't happen to live anywhere near Marsham, would you?"

She smiled and dipped her head. "You might say that."

Handy amusement in the country, no less. This is turning out much better than I thought. Ah, there is

*nothing like a relaxing interlude in the country—
between the thighs of a rosy-cheeked country lass with
a heart-bursting accent.*

"Turn here," she said when they reached a graceful
wrought-iron gate.

He looked down the chestnut-lined drive and gave
her a surprised look. "This is the lane that leads to
Marsham."

"I know."

"You live at Marsham, then?" he asked, not believing
he could be so fortunate as to have this delectable mor-
sel dropped into his lap . . . or better yet, his bed.

"I do."

*By Jove! Smitten by the country life—and on my first
day.* He could not believe things were going so well.
Here he was, the youngest son of a duke, with no title
to inherit, and what happens? He inherits from his
mother's brother both a title and a vast country estate,
complete with resident beauty—and he had never been
in finer tupping form—except for this cursed crick, of
course.

Life was wonderful. "So, you live at Marsham," he
said, as if not believing it himself, "yet you are not employed."

"That is true. I am not."

"Ah, you are the daughter of one of the servants."

"No. My parents were never servants . . . and they
are both dead."

"Hmm . . . A Russian orphan with an intriguing
past," he said, not saying any more, for they turned onto
the drive, where a lavish circle curved in front of
Marsham Manor.

Just at that moment, the twins burst through the
hedge at a breakneck speed, racing over a meadow of

cow parsley, right up to the front door, shrieking and calling for someone by the name of Mrs. MacDougal.

A second later the front door was thrown open and the robust frame of a she-dragon emerged, pausing for a moment in the carved stone entrance, puffing like a winter wind, broom in hand.

All Anthony could think was the twins had apparently witnessed the encounter between the black-haired Russian beauty and himself in the orchard, and fearing the worst, had taken the shortcut, streaking across fields of yellow rape, then bursting through the hedge, their voices dry and crackling.

"Mrs. MacDougal! Mrs. MacDougal! Come quick! There's a highwayman in the lane and he's kidnapping Tasha!"

CHAPTER
☙ TWO ☙

Harry came racing around the corner of the manor house armed with a rake. The moment he did, Natasha knew the handsome stranger she met in the lane was in for it.

Waving his rake overhead and looking ready to smite the intruder, Harry joined Mrs. MacDougal, and the two of them set upon the stranger, who had the misfortune to come prancing into their line of vision, riding a devilish black horse, with his arms around Natasha. He also had the misfortune to be dismounting just about the time they reached him—and had just pulled Natasha into his arms.

Before he could put her down, he was set upon.

Joining in the attack were the twins and Marsham's three resident beagles, Winkum, Blinkum, and Nod, who promptly turned upon Anthony with great vigor and many teeth. It was a dreadful row, Anthony dropping Natasha in an unceremonious heap on the ground and single-handedly fighting off Mrs. MacDougal's broom, the twins' attempts to trip him, and dodging Harry's rake—while having the legs of his smart trousers shredded by the sharp teeth of the beagles.

If Natasha had had her wits about her, she would have put an immediate stop to it, of course, but her in-the-nick-of-time intervention was hampered somewhat by her jovial nature. Above the thrashing of rake and broom, the Russian curses yelled by her brothers, and the shrill yapping of dogs could be heard the bubbling sound of her uncontrollable laughter.

It was about this time that Natasha realized it was just as well that this stranger had dumped her in the dirt, for she was as weak as rainwater and her legs had turned to mush—so she sat there, barefoot and in a fluffed heap of flounced petticoats and tattered skirt, tears of laughter streaming down her face as Mrs. MacDougal, seeing the beagles had the ruffian sufficiently occupied, tossed away her broom and grabbed the kidnapper by the ear.

"How dare you abduct a lass in broad daylight," a winded Mrs. MacDougal said, giving his ear a twist.

This threw Natasha into fresh peals of laughter, for indeed, it did sound to her as though Mrs. MacDougal was implying that abduction was perfectly acceptable as long as it was done under the cloak of night.

Any further verbosity from Mrs. MacDougal was halted when the London dandy suddenly found his voice. Apparently at the end of his patience, he shouted, "Cease this at once!" in an authoritative manner that would have sent shivers down the most aristocratic spine.

With one fell swoop, he tore the rake from Harry's hands and cracked the handle across his knee. Waving the broken pieces, he gave Mrs. MacDougal a blistering look as he said, "One more move from you, my good woman, and your neck will be next." He threw the broken handle to the ground. "This is a lunatic farm," he said, glancing around him. "What in the deuce is going on here?"

Harry, looking a bit sheepish, didn't say anything. He picked up the pieces of his broken rake and called the dogs to his side—about the same time that Mrs. MacDougal found her voice. Turning to Natasha, she said, "Oh, you poor little lamb. Are you all right?"

Natasha nodded weakly—for a weak nod was all she could muster, seeing as how all her energy was expended upon trying her best not to laugh.

Turning to Anthony, Mrs. MacDougal gave him her most fierce Scot's look and said, "What do you think you are about, you scoundrel? You should be ashamed of yourself."

"I thought I was doing the gentlemanly thing and helping a lady in distress," Anthony said. "Apparently you did not see it that way."

"Aye, I didna. You looked to be in the midst of an abduction, you knave. Now, you'd best be away from here before the Earl of Marsham arrives and gives you a good thrashing."

"The Earl of Marsham . . ." Anthony smiled, giving her a look that said he wondered just how long it would take the sheep to realize she was being sheared. "His lordship is quite a bonny fighter, I take it?"

"Aye, that he is," said Mrs. MacDougal. "Quite bonny, and taller than Westminster Cathedral, too. He is . . . due . . . here . . . today . . ." Mrs. MacDougal finished with her last words trailing off to nothing, as if slow awareness had suddenly crept upon her. She gave him a speculative look. "You wouldn't, by any chance, be . . . ?"

"Lord Anthony Hamilton, of God's Hallowed Hamiltons and the seventh Earl of Marsham at your service," Anthony said, making a low-sweeping bow, loving every exaggerated movement. Then turning toward the twins, he grabbed them by the necks as Pavel attempted a swift kick. "Try that again, you little gudgeon, and I'll see that you regret it." He gave the two of them a rousing shake. Then to Mrs. MacDougal, he said, "Are these mischief-makers yours?"

Obviously taken aback, Mrs. MacDougal stammered, "Mine—? Why— Goodness no. My husband has been dead so long I've forgotten what he looked like. Luka and Pavel are the sons of a great and noble Russian count," she said, her chest swelling in harmony, "who saved your late uncle's life and lost his own in the doing of it. They were brought to England under the earl's protection and have been wards of his estate, along with their sister, Natasha."

At this, Anthony released the twins, his interested gaze drifting over to Natasha, who by this time had extracted herself from the dust and was standing nearby. A few steps brought him to stand in front of her, where he lifted one hand and caressed her face gently with his knuckles, speaking in a voice that had softened considerably.

"And now, the lovely Natasha has passed, bed and baggage, into my hands."

Mrs. MacDougal's ample form trembled with outrage, but she was cut off from saying anything when Anthony spoke, his curious gaze never leaving Natasha's face. "I am finding I have more and more to thank my dear departed uncle for," he said.

At that, Mrs. MacDougal swelled with such indignant rage that for a moment it looked as though her bodice would split asunder. As it was, one button popped off and was promptly swallowed up by Winkum, who dashed around the house with Blinkum and Nod in hot pursuit.

Ignoring the lost button, Mrs. MacDougal went on, "Natasha is a decent Christian girl, your lordship . . . and the earl—your uncle—had great plans for her."

Anthony let his eyes travel over the decent Christian girl with slow ease. "Oh, I am certain he did. Selfish plans, I'll wager. That old satyr was old enough to be her father . . . perhaps even her grandfather."

Sputtering and stumbling over her words, Mrs. MacDougal said, "H—his lordship was not like that. Why, he treated these babies like they were his very own. Hired the finest tutor he could afford. It was his wish that the twins go to Oxford. For Natasha, he wanted a good match." She crossed her arms across her ample middle and gave him a triumphant nod. "You will find he put all of that in his will. Why, just before he died, he was making arrangements for her to have a season in London—a season as grand as any earl's daughter. Hired a dressmaker, too. Wanted her to have a fine, fancy gown. Pure silk, it was to be."

She prosed on a bit about the late earl's goodness and

character, but Anthony had already raised his brows and directed his gaze toward Natasha, who shifted uneasily from one foot to the other. "A fine, fancy gown hmm? And pure silk?"

Natasha remained mute.

He took a cursory glance at Mrs. MacDougal. "A pretty maid and a fine body need no fancy trappings. She is as fair as a rose in May," he said.

"It was the old earl's wish," Mrs. MacDougal said, remaining staunch.

Looking back at Natasha and curling long fingers beneath her chin, Anthony lifted her face full into the sunlight. "So, you wanted a season in London, did you? Fancy balls, silk dresses, and a good match as well?"

Natasha returned his steady look, not blinking once. "That was his lordship's wish, not mine," she said. "I never wanted to go to London."

He smiled. "No? And why not? Surely a country lass would have her sights set on marriage to a titled lord and a life in the city."

"I like my life the way it is, thank you."

"And what way is that?"

"Near my brothers."

He frowned, his gaze drifting over in the direction of the twins. "Those imps?" He released her. "Blister it! I cannot understand that," he said, giving the twins a black look. "Two wilder little duffers I've never seen." The hard-set mouth relaxed, and as he looked back at Natasha the intense blue of his eyes seemed to darken. "Perhaps you are better off here in the country . . . and in my"—*bed,* he almost said, and caught himself— "under my guardianship."

Natasha thrust her nose in the air. "My brothers and I can return to Russia. You don't have to be burdened with us."

He smiled. "It is no burden, I assure you. In any case, it would not matter if you were. If what I am told is true and my uncle did outline his wishes for you in his will, then, under British law, when one inherits a title and estates, he inherits the responsibilities and debts, along with the obligations . . . as well as any revenues. Like it or not, you and your brothers are now my responsibility."

"Then I am heartily sorry for the burden we put upon you, your lordship," she said, giving him a mocking curtsy to teach him something about Russian pride.

"Natasha Alexandra," exclaimed Mrs. MacDougal in her most horrified tone. "Such an unladylike outburst, and quite unlike you, I might add. Upon my word, you owe his lordship an apology."

Anthony regarded her thoughtfully, a smile spreading over his mouth. "You will be a burden of pleasure, I am certain," he said, adding as he passed her, "and I am a man devoted to pleasure."

CHAPTER
❧ THREE ❧

Natasha was in the drawing room—studying a canvas screen painted on both sides with pictures of dogs and cockerels—when she heard the commotion outside.

Recognizing the eager yapping of the beagles, she went to sit upon the sofa in the large bay, so she could look out the window.

The first thing she saw was Anthony. She sighed wistfully and crossed her arms across the back of the sofa, resting her head there as she looked her fill— something that would be hard to do, considering she could spend the rest of her life looking at Tony and never grow tired.

Was there ever a more handsome man? Had she ever heard such an infectious laugh? Was there a man anywhere who was kinder, more diverting, more enjoyable to be around? Would there ever be another man who could set her heart to pounding with just the mere mention of his name?

She didn't think so.

The nice thing about being in love, she decided, was that it took up so much of one's time, for literally her days were filled with his presence, and at night he was in her thoughts.

Mrs. MacDougal walked into the room. "What are you doing in here on such a fine morning?" she asked. "Don't you feel well?"

"I feel wonderful," Natasha said. "Truly."

Mrs. MacDougal watched her with new interest, a look of speculation in her eyes. "Then you must be in love."

Natasha smiled, her eyes lighting up at the thought. "Why do you say that?"

"Listen, my wee little one, love and smoke are two things that canna be hidden."

"It is that obvious?" Natasha asked, thinking she was glad, since her feelings for Tony were not something she wanted to hide.

"Aye, though it pains me to say so."

"Pains you? Why?"

"Love, like Ulysses, is a wanderer. A man with love in his breast has spurs on his heels," she said. "No good will come of this. Mark my word."

"Oh, I think you are wrong." Natasha said. "Tony would never deal falsely with me. I know it."

"Love is something . . . well, when it gets hold of you, it's good-bye to common sense."

"Not when it's as great a love as this," Natasha said, her gaze going back to Anthony.

"Great love, great sorrow," Mrs. MacDougal said. "You'd best be remembering that. Through love's eyes, even copper turns to gold. Mind your step, Natasha. You're just a wee, innocent lamb when compared to the earl, and don't be forgetting this is the first time for you. There will be others."

Natasha was about to tell Mrs. MacDougal there would be no others, but she was distracted by the sight of Tony.

Mrs. MacDougal came to stand beside Natasha, looking out the window. "Aye, he is a bonny one all right, but I hear he has a way with the lassies." She turned to look at Natasha. "I don't want to see you with your heart broken."

"I know, but Tony would never break my heart," she said, with great confidence. "I know he wouldn't. This is true love."

Mrs. MacDougal shook her head. "True love rarely comes the first time, child."

"This must be one of those rare times then," Natasha said, with complete innocence.

"Well, for your sake, I hope you are right," Mrs. MacDougal said, placing a comforting hand upon Natasha's shoulder. A moment later she made her departure.

Natasha watched her go, then returned her gaze to Tony and sighed wistfully. Love and eggs are best when they are fresh.

How could love ever be any better than this?

Anthony was so eager to please, so happy, so determined to have her. She was so happy she wanted to shout. She wanted to run through the house calling out his name. She wanted the world to know and share her happiness. How fortunate she was that the first time she had fallen in love, it was with such a man.

About that time the dogs ran out of the hedge and happily discovered Tony on the other side. She smiled. Apparently Winkum, Blinkum, and Nod were ready for a bit of sport, but Lord Anthony was not ready to be the sport they were ready for. A rapt expression came over her face as she watched the dogs' overeager attack— barking and tugging at his trousers as they struggled to enlist his enthusiasm for a game of chase.

Looking at the handsome Earl of Marsham, she thought that even after a whole month around him, she still couldn't believe he was real. Natasha knew she was in love. She had never been in love before, certainly, but she knew this was love as well as she would have known an old friend. Life was indeed strange, for out of a time of darkness and sadness, which came with the old earl's passing, the love of her life had appeared.

For the briefest flicker of a moment, she found herself thinking about the old earl's greenhouse and how she had neglected his beloved plants. Feeling a bit guilty over this, she promised herself she would do better, but even as the idea formed, her thoughts were back on Tony.

As she watched, the earl came to his feet, throwing something that sent the dogs flying down the gravel path and through a folly.

The outline of his body was a sharp silhouette against a pink and orange backdrop, where a flaming sun seemed to call attention to its disappearance over the hedge that ran along the top of the hill. Tall as the trees beyond, and blond as a bloody Viking, Anthony was as charming as he was handsome. She could not see his eyes from where she sat, but she did not need to. Those eyes—so blue and full of promise—were forever etched upon her mind. She smiled, thinking of all the feats and accomplishments attributed to him, then wondered if they were all true.

There were so many tales—tales and stories she had heard repeatedly since he had inherited Marsham. Natasha frowned, thinking of those spectacular feats— some of which could have only been performed by a very limber man capable of twisting himself into more shapes than a sailor's knot—then she laughed at the absurdness, the sheer impossibility of it.

Oh, there was no doubt in her mind that Anthony was a rounder. According to the cook's helper, who had it straight from a cousin in London, "Lord Anthony is a rake *and* a scoundrel." She went on to add he was a notorious despoiler of feminine virtue.

The upstairs maid agreed that the latest gossip from London proved he was all of those things and more, but she was quick to add, "But la, Lord Anthony is so irresistible that one does tend to forget all the other."

Natasha released a pensive sigh. *All time not spent on love is wasted.* She blinked, wondering where that thought had come from and who had said it. No name came to mind, but then, it did not really matter. What was important here was that whoever it was knew what he was talking about.

Anthony was a man devoted to pleasure, but now, after a month of being chased about the grounds and gardens of Marsham Manor, she decided a man devoted to pleasure was not such a bad thing. Rumor had it that such men brought more than one innocent to ruin, but Natasha, Russian-born, country-reared, and city-green though she might be, was no man's fool.

If Tony wanted her as much as he said, then this devilishly handsome, wickedly charming man, who set the most jaded tongues in London to wagging, had two choices: He would either continue with his never-ending string of London trollops, or make her an offer of marriage.

The way she saw it, the distinguished Lord Marsham might be an English earl, but after all, *she* was the daughter of a Russian count.

All these thoughts about marriage prompted a few other thoughts, and before long the pleasant expression faded from her face. She remembered the shattering disclosure he had made to her only last night, right on the heels of a promise of undying love and a marriage proposal—a revelation that set Natasha's Russian blood to boiling.

She remembered, too, the way she had looked at him with such love in her eyes. "Are you asking me to marry you?"

"Of course I am," he said, taking her in his arms. "The sooner the better."

"How soon will that be?"

Tony looked a bit troubled. "I'm not sure," he said.

"You're not sure?"

He kissed her on the nose. "Sweet Natasha, there is one slight problem."

"What problem is that?"

"It's nothing to worry your lovely head about. Every problem has a solution, and I will find a remedy for this one."

"I am sure you will, but tell me what the problem is?"

Looking a bit guilty, he said, "I am affianced to another."

Her heart pounded. Her throat grew dry. Mrs. MacDougal's words crept into her consciousness: *A man with love in his heart has spurs on his heels . . .*

She stared at him in shock, then she felt shock giving way to anger. How dare he. "You've been dallying with me, and all the while you have been in love with someone else?" she asked, her voice trembling with rage.

The more she thought about it now, the more she wished she had drawn back her fist at that moment and punched him in the eye.

How dare he? Here he was, her family's benefactor . . . and assuming such liberties with her—all under the pretense of courtship.

And he called himself a gentleman.

What brass. What cheek. The very idea. Giving her slow, yearning glances, leading her on with his easygoing ways, his breathtaking smile . . . and making her heart flutter with the warmth of slow, suggestive whispers.

And him with nothing but deception on his mind.

If he didn't have all the nerve—waiting until she was limp with desire before telling her he was affianced to Lady Cecilia Stanhope, daughter of the Duke and Duchess of Whybourn and a second cousin to the prince regent.

As if she could compete with that.

Last night she had told him so, but Anthony had merely laughed and said, "Sweetheart, there is nothing for you to compete with, believe me. Lady Cecilia is a meek, timid person who would get the vapors if I so much as ogled her."

"But you are betrothed . . ."

"Something that can be readily undone."

Natasha stared at his perfectly formed features and felt her heart melt. "I would not feel right about that," she said. "A promise is a promise."

He kissed her quickly, before she could resist. "It was my father's promise, not mine. I told you it was arranged. I daresay Lady Cecilia would be as happy about this as I. Really, I fear I frighten the timid little mouse to death. Every time I walk into the same room with her she swoons."

"Perhaps it is because of your divine good looks."

Anthony raised what appeared to be a delighted but curious brow. "Divine good looks?"

She poked him in the chest. "And you know it, so do not feign surprise with me. I am certain every nanny you ever had cosseted you shamefully. I daresay that once you were in britches you had to beat the women away. Why, the first time I saw you, I—"

She stopped suddenly, snapping her mouth shut. She glanced up in time to see that Anthony was regarding her with a fascinated air.

"Pray continue," he said, a wide grin stretched lazily across his mouth.

She turned away from him with a sassy flip of her skirt. Crossing her arms in front of her, she said, "I have given you all the compliments I intend for one day."

As she swept from the room, Anthony reached out and caught one of her bouncing black ringlets, giving it a good-natured yank.

"There will be other days," he said, "for I intend to marry you."

Any further thought was interrupted, for outside, the sound of her brothers' laughter drew her attention; she turned to watch them fly around the corner faster than boiled asparagus. They were trying to get a kite aloft in the gusty spring wind and having little luck. The dogs, seeing fresh opportunity, seized it, taking off after them, barking and jumping at the kite, which rose in the air, where it hovered for a moment before diving back to the ground and catching on a mulberry bush.

Not far from where Luka and Pavel ran with their kite, Anthony sat on the top step of an outdoor staircase overgrown with cotoneaster, moss, and alchemilla, giving a naked statue the eye, while a vision of Natasha Simonov danced—in a similar state of undress—before his eyes.

No doubt about it, she was incredibly lovely— enchanting even, with hair as black as the devil's soul and eyes as blue-violet as a harebell. A month ago, when he had first seen her in the top of that peach tree, he had thought her the most exquisite creature he had ever laid eyes upon. Now, after pursuing her for the past four weeks, he was absolutely certain of it.

And she had come damnably close to being all his. With a ragged curse, he thought about last night. All would have gone well, except for the fact that he was a bit too swept along with the moment—and quite forgetting of a fiancée he had left in London.

Not that it was all his fault, for in all honesty, Lady Cecilia *was* a woman a man could forget. She was as brainless as a feather duster, and being the daughter of a controlling father and a domineering mother had made Lady Cecilia meek as a mouse. There just wasn't anything exciting about her. Even the way she looked was unexciting—golden blond hair, usually hidden beneath a ridiculous bonnet, pale blue eyes, pale skin, even paler clothes. She had none of the country-fresh look, and compared to the black-haired, violet-eyed Natasha, who scampered about Marsham barefoot and speaking English with a heart-thundering accent, Lady Cecilia didn't fare too well.

Well, to be perfectly truthful, she did fare considerably well in one area, and that was money. Cecilia didn't have a brain in her head, but she had plenty of money in the bank. Lady Cecilia Stanhope was England's greatest heiress ... and therein lay the snag.

Anthony wanted Lady Cecilia's money, but he did not want Lady Cecilia.

What he really wanted was the inky-haired goddess who spent each night under his roof—and he wanted her enough to marry her, for he had already learned that Natasha was not the kind to allow him so much as an ardent fondle or a gratifying grope without it. He could have kicked his backside to Whitechapel and back for allowing his father to push him into this arrangement with Lady Cecilia. He was in a royal fix for certain, but there was nothing to be done about it—save allowing Cecilia to discreetly discover he was smitten with Natasha. In her wounded anger, she would cry off ... and he would be free to marry.

Anthony frowned, for it suddenly occurred to him that he would have to be most circumspect around Natasha in order to protect her reputation. Fortunately Mrs. MacDougal was as suspicious as a nun and as fiercely protective as a watchdog.

"Natasha, come and help!" The twins' cry interrupted his thoughts, and Anthony looked up in time to see Natasha come outside.

He watched her send the dogs to the kennel with Harry, then quietly observe her brothers attempt to launch the kite. With a wry grin of amusement, Anthony leaned one shoulder against a cypress tree and watched Natasha make a couple of runs with the kite herself. Then, without giving any thought to the fact that someone might be watching, she hoisted her skirts and began tearing strips of ruffle from her petticoat. A moment later she was tying these strips to make a tail on the kite. One last run across the green and the kite went shooting upward.

Watching her, Anthony felt a certain determined, hurried resignation toward making Natasha his. Pushing away from the tree, he contemplated with cheerful amusement the unexpected—but delightful—turn of fate.

After years of wenching and seducing—always diligently avoiding the most carefully laid matrimony snares—he had finally settled upon the idea of marriage . . . purely for financial reasons, of course. And what happened? The moment he found himself betrothed to the wealthiest woman in England, he wished he weren't. Such were the ironies of life, he thought, pushing away from the tree.

Natasha must have noticed him walking toward her, for at that moment she looked up and waved.

"Hullo, Tony," she called. "I didn't know you were here."

"I'm here, sweetness, and feeling lost without you." With a sigh, he realized that was the truth. He also realized about the same time that it did not matter if Cecilia was the richest woman in England *and* the world. Natasha was the woman he wanted, and he would stick by his decision to marry her. He would just have to find another way to make money.

It suddenly occurred to him that although he had been at Marsham for a month, he had not, as yet, taken a look at the account books. Anthony frowned. That sort of thing held precious little appeal for him, as did the greenhouse filled with those hideous plants his uncle had such a fondness for. At that moment Natasha looked at him and smiled.

Necessity had a way of making the account books more attractive.

Tomorrow he would look at the accounts and find a way to make Marsham profitable. If he wanted Natasha, he had no choice. He pushed away the reminder that it was not only himself who depended upon Lady Cecilia's fortune but his parents as well.

Natasha caught up to him, taking his arm. "Come walk with me," she said. "I want to show you what I've done in the water garden."

Tony went with her, but his mind wasn't on water gardens.

In spite of his inheriting Marsham from his uncle, it was his brother Trevor who was the only member of the Hamilton family of secure financial means. Several years ago, Trevor had inherited a considerable sum of money from his maternal grandmother, and, after buying a ship, was making quite a fortune for himself as a privateer during the ongoing war with Napoléon.

Unbeknownst to Trevor or Anthony at the time, their father, the duke, had made considerable investments— all of them unwise and unprofitable. The duke's finances were at best shaky, and on the verge of collapse, when he finally chose to reveal the sad state of his affairs to his sons.

"You mean we are penniless?" Tony asked.

"Soon to be, I'm afraid," the duke said. "Unless we are blessed with a miracle."

They had gotten their miracle; it had been a godsend when the wealthy and powerful Duke of Whybourn had given his blessing to the engagement of his only child and heir, Lady Cecilia Stanhope, to the duke's youngest son, Lord Anthony Hamilton.

Tony might not be a man of figures and account books, but he was no fool. He realized that not only would his crying off and breaking his engagement to Lady Cecilia be something that would ruin the Hamiltons socially, but their father, without the Stanhope dowry—which was already partially spent—would be financially ruined as well.

"Tony, are you listening to me?" Natasha asked, interrupting his thoughts.

Tony looked at her. "Of course. You were showing me the water lilies."

She laughed deliciously. "I was showing you where I planted the white violets."

Tony cursed under his breath. "Forgive me, love. I seem to have some pressing business on my mind today."

"It's all right. I shouldn't be disturbing your thoughts with all my flowerpot chatter."

He gave her an adoring look. "All of your chatter delights me . . . Flowerpot, cooking pot, chamber pot . . ."

She laughed and took his hand. "Come on, we'll take a stroll instead." With an impish grin, she looked at him and said, "I promise to be quiet."

He smiled down at her and gave her hand a squeeze. "I'm glad you understand," he said.

"Of course I understand," she replied. "I often find myself occupied about a plant I need to prune or a packet of seeds I need to plant, completely forgetting what is being said around me. Why, when I have my mind elsewhere, I can be in a room full of conversation and not hear one word."

Thinking that he felt the same way when he was around her, Tony smiled. Truly, she was as distracting as she was delightful.

They passed a stand of foxglove swarming with bees,

and Natasha said absently, "The honeybees are in the foxglove." Then she blushed, as if embarrassed to be caught thinking out loud. She gave him a radiant smile and asked, "Do you know where they got their name?"

Enchanted, Tony shook his head.

"The wicked fairies gave these flowers to the foxes, so they could slip their paws into them and prowl quietly around the chicken runs." She plucked a stem of foxglove covered with rosy pink blooms. "See these marks?"

Anthony looked down at the tiny speckles on the inside of the blooms and nodded.

"They are the fingerprints of the mischievous elves," she said. "Some people think they are there to warn of the poison within."

He watched as she tucked the blooms into her sash, her attention suddenly taken by something else. "Look. The cornflowers are blooming. I must remind myself to come back and pick some. The juice from the petals, mixed with alum-water, makes a delightful shade for watercolor painting. And there is columbine," she said, pointing to another bloom. "Years ago it was unacceptable for a gentleman to give columbine to a lady, as it was associated with loose morals."

"Then I will take care to see I never give you columbine."

She laughed. "It's an old legend."

They passed a hawthorn hedge. " 'And in the warm hedge grew lush eglantine. Green cow-bind and the moonlight-coloured may.' Shelley must love flowers," she said.

He took her hand and turned her toward him. "But not as much as I love you. You are delightful, you know that? You have completely bewitched me. Completely and without mercy."

She laughed and drew him away. "Come on," she said. "This way." They came to a weedy path. "I really must tell Harry to tend this path. It is frightfully over-grown."

Then, as if aware she was talking again, she smiled and looked off. "I talk too much," she said.

They walked on in silence, and before long, thoughts of Natasha began to drift to the back of his mind as Tony's attention, once again, centered upon money.

Although he did inherit a title and a large estate, there was precious little money that went with it. He knew this was due mostly to the old earl's penchant for ordering exotic plants that he had no means to pay for. As it now stood, the estate did not make enough to pay the taxes and afford the owner and staff anything more than the barest bones of a modest living. Perhaps if they closed the greenhouse and he found a buyer for all the plants, that would give them enough to tide them over until he could think of something else.

Suddenly he remembered how much she loved the plants. Perhaps he could find a way to keep them. Even selling his uncle's plants, Tony knew he could never raise enough money to support them in anything but a modest style.

Marsham was an impressive country estate, but it was a bit crumbly in places, and, if one looked closely enough, they could see it was somewhat tattered about the edges. Simply put, it was in need of repairs, and marriage to Lady Cecilia had been the only hope of restoration.

Well, Tony thought, *I'll live without hope, then. For I will break my engagement with Lady Cecilia and I will have Natasha . . . my father and Lady Cecilia's money be damned.*

CHAPTER
❧ FOUR ❧

The patriarch of the esteemed Hamilton family was Charles Hamilton, the fifth Duke of Hillsborough, who was nothing more than a frustrated lepidopterist who never quite forgave the world for thrusting the title Duke of Hillsborough upon him—and thus forcing him to abandon his lifelong dream of living the life of a scientist-adventurer—compelling him to pursue the study of butterflies, moths, and skippers as a hobby, instead of a profession.

In this, he was perfectly suited to the duchess, his wife.

The duchess, Sophia, was a granddaughter of the famed botanist, Sir Edward Fitzhugh, and a sister to the late botanist of some notoriety, Lord William Weatherby, the Earl of Marsham.

Although she was not the eminent scientist her grandfather and brother were, the duchess had managed to become enraptured with anything of the family Rosaceae, and spent her days digging in loamy soil and leaf mold—when she wasn't concocting a new spray to try on the thirps on her beloved roses.

As Trevor once said to his father on the occasion of

being called strange, "If I am strange, sir, there is little wonder for it . . . having grown up in a house that always reeked of alcohol, bug spray, and whale oil. It's a wonder we all did not end up at Bedlam."

"There is still a chance for that," was the duchess's dour comment.

"Come now, Trevor," Anthony said. "You will have to admit that the strange occupations of our parents kept them at home and made them quite easy to find."

"Oh, they were easy to find all right. You could never miss Father's butterfly net protruding over the tops of the shrubbery, and Mother could always be located by following a trail of damp humus through the house."

When word of Anthony's latest infatuation and his intention to marry his Russian ward reached his mother, the Duchess of Hillsborough went immediately to the residence of her dear friend, the Duchess of Lanshire—not because she wanted to see her friend, but because she wanted a word with a visiting relative of hers. The Duchess of Lanshire had as her houseguest an elderly aunt—several times removed—who was a Russian noblewoman by the name of Countess Irena Kropotkin.

It was from this ancient old countess that Tony's mother wanted to glean as much information as she could about the family of this Russian girl who wreaked such havoc in their lives. Perhaps getting rid of her would be as simple as locating some of the girl's relatives in Russia and sending her back. Her brother, the Earl of Marsham, might have owed this Count Simonov a debt, but in the Duchess of Hillsborough's opinion, *she* did not.

After being presented to the white-haired old countess and exchanging a few pleasantries, the Duchess of Hillsborough made her inquiry.

"Simonov," the Countess Kropotkin repeated, as if searching her mind for some recollection of the name. "It is a common enough name," she said at last. "I am afraid my memory has become as bad as my eyesight. I don't think I can be of much help. There is nothing in my memory that stands out about the name. I'm sorry."

The duchess wasn't about to give up so easily. She wanted to know about the background of this Russian girl Tony was so taken with, and she was determined to find some way to stir the old countess's memory. "Supposedly the girl's father was a count," the Duchess of Hillsborough said. "He was an officer in the military and died during Napoléon's invasion of Moscow."

"Ah, *Count* Simonov . . ." the countess said, as if the name stirred a long-forgotten memory. Suddenly the eyes of the old countess seemed to grow brighter, as if they were fired by a spark of remembrance. "Yes . . . yes," the old woman said. "From what you have said, it sounds like it could only have been Count Alexi Simonov," she said. "Poor dear man. But we thought the family dead," she added a moment later. "When Napoléon invaded Moscow, Count Simonov's home was burned to the ground. It was my understanding that he and his family perished in the fire."

"The count didn't perish in the fire. He saved my brother's life and was killed doing so. My brother buried him, but he didn't know what to do with the children. He brought them to England."

The countess nodded slowly. "From what you have said, it must be Count Alexi," she said.

"Did this Count Alexi have twin sons?" the Duchess of Hillsborough asked.

"Yes, although I cannot recollect anything about them. I saw them only once, you understand, when they were quite young. The girl I remember seeing only a few times." The countess shook her head. "And all this time we thought the family dead."

"Do you know of any other family members still living in Russia?"

"No . . . at least no close relatives. The count had two brothers, one who died young. The other was killed early in the war with Napoléon. His wife was an orphan, and although of noble breeding, her family was not one of social importance."

"And the count?"

"The count was known more for his military genius than being a powerful member of the Russian aristocracy."

"I see," the duchess said. "You mentioned the count's home was burned. Was he a man of considerable property?"

"He was not a man of tremendous wealth, but I have no knowledge of his holdings . . . not that it matters. I am certain whatever lands he owned have been seized by the crown."

"Yes," the duchess said absently, "it would have happened that way in England as well."

When the duchess returned home and told her husband about Tony and her meeting with the Countess Kropotkin, he shook his head sadly. "It sounds like we'll get no help from that quarter," he said. Then he inquired as to the whereabouts of his eldest son and heir—and, in the duke's words, "Hopefully, the son with more sense."

The duke's eldest son, Lord Trevor Hamilton, the Marquess of Haverleigh, was busily engaged in privateering during the Napoleonic Wars and could not always be located with ease. However, upon this occasion, the duke was fortunate. After a brief inquiry, the duke was happy to learn Trevor was indeed in London, having put into port only a few days before. Without wasting a moment, the duke dispatched an urgent summons to his son.

Trevor, meanwhile, had been trying for some time to arrange an assignation with the tantalizing Spanish actress, Lita Perez, and that was difficult, considering his own busy schedule of chasing and plundering Napoléon's ships and the fact that Lita Perez was currently the mistress of the powerful Duke of Northrup.

When his father's summons reached Trevor, the Duke of Northrup was in Brighton and Trevor was at Lita's town house. He had her breasts out, his pants down, and was about to give the rapturous Lita what she wanted most when the maid pounded upon the door.

"What is it?" Lita called out.

"A message . . . for his lordship," the maid said through the door. "His valet is downstairs. He said it was urgent."

"Bloody hell," Trevor said, looking down at Lita's rosy breasts.

"What shall I tell his lordship's valet?" the maid asked.

Lita was studying the broad, muscular shoulders, the narrow waist, with regret. Then her gaze dropped to the part of him that seemed to interest her most. She sighed. "You might as well go see what your message is about," she said, taking his shrunken penis in her hand. "You seem to have lost your concentration."

His manhood wilted, Trevor cursed and stomped to the door, jerking it open with such force that the maid was almost sucked inside. Seeing Trevor's angry scowl, his naked state, the maid gave a terrified yelp and thrust the note at him before fleeing down the hallway.

Without even bothering to close the door, Trevor

opened the note, reading his father's frantic summons. With a quick appraising look back at the bed—and a parting thought that without the summons he would have been between Lita's willing thighs at that very moment—Trevor swore, then dressed with true military dispatch.

A moment later, a disappointed Lita Perez lay back in the bed and sighed as she watched Trevor tuck his linen shirt into his tight-fitting riding breeches. Without so much as a good-bye, he departed for his father's town house, leaving Lita to think he was every bit as arrogant as she had heard he was.

"Perhaps Anthony is in love with this Russian chit," Trevor said to his father upon his arrival at his parents' town house and being greeted with the news of his brother's dual engagements.

The Duke of Hillsborough grunted. "He *cannot* be in love with her," he said. "He is pledged to Lady Cecilia."

Trevor laughed. "As if *that* makes any difference to Tony. You of all people should know how Tony is. He never does anything according to convention."

"What say?" asked the duke. He was staring out the open doors to the terrace, his mind occupied at the moment with a perfect specimen of the family Nymphalidae.

"We were talking about Anthony, I believe," Trevor said.

"Oh, right," said the duke.

" 'Oh, right'?" the duchess said, coming to her feet and sounding remarkably like her canaries in the morning room. She gave her husband an exasperated look. "Is that all you have to say, Charles? *'Oh right'*? You have been distraught for days and called Trevor away from his pirating—"

"Privateering, Mother."

"Well, whatever," the duchess said, with a wave of her hand; then she went on. "Charles, you know Anthony's marriage to Lady Cecilia is our only hope for rescue, and now he is smitten by a penniless girl my *benevolent* brother brought back from Russia—a girl we know nothing about, save her name—and all you can say is *'Oh, right'?*"

The duke pulled his gaze away from the garden and looked at his wife. "When you come up with a better reply, my dear, I will be happy to use it," he said.

The duchess nodded, apparently satisfied with that. "I will give the matter some thought," she said. "Then turning to Trevor, she added, "Your father and I had hoped you would go to Marsham and speak to your brother."

"What the deuced good will it do for Trevor to go all the way to Marsham just to speak to Anthony?" the duke asked, turning back to look at his wife. "He can speak to him anytime. He better try talking some sense into the featherwit."

"Don't go calling Tony a featherwit," the duchess said. "He is a bit confused, that is all. Don't you remember what it was like to be in love?" The duchess looked at her husband and frowned. "No, I am certain you do not," she said, "but never mind. I am certain that Tony can be made to see the way of it. He was ever a bright child."

The duke shook his head, giving the duchess a doubtful look. "You think Tony is simply confused? Dash it all, Sophy, any man who would affiance himself to two women at the same time is past confused."

Trevor was about to say something here, when his

thought was interrupted by the duke, who made a dash for his butterfly net and charged through the door shouting, with true fervor, "By george! It's a *Vanessa cardui.*"

The duchess looked after her husband and sighed. "I am the only woman in the whole of England who does not send for the hartshorn when her husband rushes out the door pursuing a painted lady."

"You recall the species with remarkable ease," Trevor noted.

The duchess gave him an appraising look. "I remember a time when you were guilty of as much," she said.

Trevor laughed. "Thankfully, I was rescued from a lifetime of swallowtails and hairstreaks. One does tend to forget."

"I pray for the day," the duchess said, holding up her arms and casting a beseeching look heavenward.

Once the family talk was ended, the first thing Trevor did—after his father had successfully bottled, fumed, and pinned the unfortunate painted lady—was to offer to pay his father's debts out of his own funds, since that seemed far easier than going all the way to Marsham and trying to talk sense into Tony . . . something he had little faith in his ability to do, since Tony rarely listened to anyone anyway.

His father didn't see much chance of salvation in Trevor's proposal. "Our finances are in dreadful shape, Trev. While your generous offer to pay off our debts is a capital idea, I fear it will only serve to rescue your mother and I from debtors' prison. It won't get us out of debt."

"Debtors' prison? Dash it all, Father! You aren't in such dire straits as all that . . . are you?"

The duke shook his head. "No, at least not yet, but

we are uncomfortably close. Unfortunately . . . And as I was saying, there are considerable other things at stake here besides a few pounds," he said.

"Hell and damnation! What other things are you talking about?" Trevor asked, feeling his irritation rise with his temper. He wanted this business of Anthony's foolishness to be over, so he could get back to Lita, or better yet, so he could get out of London altogether. War was never this complicated.

Trevor realized he had suddenly lost his taste for anything connected with London, and that included Lita Perez. He wanted to return to his ship. Tormenting Napoléon was more important—and certainly a lot easier—than wasting time trying to talk Anthony into anything.

"I am speaking about our family name," the duke went on to say. "There are other roads to ruin besides taking a wrong turn down Financial Street. The Duke of Whybourn isn't a man to be taken lightly, you know. As the king's cousin, he is most influential. Anyone who crosses him can count on a visit from some of the duke's unsavory friends, if you get my meaning. If angered—as he most assuredly will be if the engagement is broken and his only child humiliated—he is in a dandy position to ruin the entire family . . . for about five generations hence."

Trevor was about to play that down when he remembered Lady Cecilia's father and the Duke of Whybourn were the same person. It had been the Duke of Whybourn who had authorized *his* request for a letter of marque—which granted Trevor the right and the authority to arm his ship and seize French goods, plundering the enemy at will.

Trevor was staggered. With all his attempts to stay out of this bloody mess, he was in the middle of it, and in it deeper than he would like. If Anthony cried off and offended the Duke of Whybourn, the duke would take Trevor's letter of marque and probably hand him over to Napoléon himself!

Thoughts—horrid thoughts—began to form in Trevor's mind. He had visions of the unsavory dockside scum—the types the Duke of Whybourn had in his employ—and shuddered at the thought of having those fellows coming upon him in the dark to rough him up . . . maybe even to press him into service on some greasy ship bound for God knew where. It was a sobering thought.

How the deuce was he going to get out of this bind? Trevor wondered, knowing there was no way out.

Once the Duke of Whybourn heard of this latest coil of Tony's, he would not waste any time in coming to look for certain members of the Hamilton family to ruin, in any way he could—physical, political, financial, or all three combined. Trevor had heard stories about the far-reaching arm of the Duke of Whybourn. He couldn't spend the rest of his days lurking around London, jumping at the sound of his own voice and keeping his eyes peeled for the duke or his ruffians. Trevor wanted no part of it. Cowards, after all, lived to fight another day.

He stood there, thinking it all over like a man dazed. He thought about his brother, dashing into yet another amorous entanglement like a young idiot, dragging the entire Hamilton family with him, giving little or no thought to what that might mean.

Suddenly Trevor realized Tony was stepping on *his* toes, and it required no abundance of intelligence to realize there was little to do but agree with his parents. Tony had to be stopped—and soon.

Trevor knew positively that he did not want to go to

Marsham or to become involved in this mess, but when it came to Anthony's marriage to the Russian chit, or his own letter of marque, there was little doubt where Trevor's interest lay.

Anthony had to be made to see the way of it.

"You see now, do you not, that we have no choice?" the duke was saying. "We must go to Marsham with all due haste and put a stop to this nonsense, once and for all. If Lady Cecilia or her father get wind of this, we could all be ruined."

"Well, if we're going, we might as well leave tomorrow," Trevor said. "If Tony has been under the same roof with this girl for over a month, he may have taken her virtue already. If he has not, the Archbishop of Canterbury wouldn't be able to hold him off much longer."

Just about that time, Trevor noticed his father's attention was focused upon a moth sitting on the windowsill. "We haven't time for that," he said rather snappishly. "Your butterflies will have to wait."

The duke sighed wistfully. "Moth," he said. *Thetidia smaragdaria.* It may be the last Essex emerald I will see this season."

Trevor released an irritated sigh. "If we don't get to Marsham and stop Tony, it may be the last season you see, period."

He looked around the room. "Where is Mother?"

"Probably up to her elbows in seed hips by now. She is propagating in the greenhouse," the duke said.

"Hmm," Trevor said, looking suddenly thoughtful. "Propagating in the greenhouse . . . That is one place I never thought of."

"Dashed uncomfortable it would be," the duke said, "fighting for space among rose thorns, orange trees, and hygrometers . . . inhaling bug sprays and rose dust."

Trevor laughed. "It was always just as bad in the library, for there Tony and I had to contend with clap nets, collecting jars, the smell of alcohol, and bolts of muslin."

Up went the Duke of Hillsborough's brows. "The library, you say? You mean you and Tony . . . ?"

Trevor nodded. "Frequently."

"In the library, by Jove! That is first rate," he said, clapping Trevor on the back. "Fornicating in the library," he said, then added, "how old were you?"

"Old enough to get a lady's mind off bugs and butterfly nets," Trevor said.

"The deuce, you say!" The duke's chest puffed out. "Get that from me," he said. "Had a way with the ladies, I did."

Trevor's look turned serious. "I think Tony is the one who inherited that trait," he said.

"Tony," the duke said absently. "Dash it all, I almost forgot about that bind." Then his face brightened. "Well, there is always a bright side to everything. This is, after all, a jolly time to be going to the country. Marsham was ever a collector's paradise. Perhaps a few days in the country is what we all need. I'll go pack my butterfly net and my collecting jars. You go tell your mother."

Trevor looked at his father, thinking he wished he had inherited the trait of looking at everything in such simple terms, then he nodded and went to the greenhouse to find the duchess.

She was watering her rose trees.

"To Marsham?" she said when Trevor told her they were going. "Why of course I want to come, Trevor. I have long wanted to get my hands on the rosebushes at Marsham."

"That is Tony's concern now," Trevor said.

"Yes, but we both know how Tony feels about horticulture. I really should make some arrangements about all of poor Willie's plants. I am certain Tony has not set foot in the greenhouse, or for that matter, made any arrangements for anyone to water and look after them." She shook her head sadly. "A lifetime of work shriveling on the vine."

"Yes, that would be a real shame," Trevor said, thinking they had much more important things to worry about than Uncle Willie's plants.

Apparently his mother did not see it that way. "Your uncle Willie was quite advanced with his studies, you know."

"Yes, I know," Trevor said, with much sarcasm. "If Uncle Willie did anything, he did botanize charmingly."

"Yes," the duchess said with a meditative air, "*charmingly* is just the word ... and it is the reason Willie was such a favorite of the king." The duchess frowned. "And Willie's closeness to King George is what allowed him to be persuaded to involve himself in all that espionage jumble with the Russians. If it had not been for all his charm, dear Willie would still be alive." She looked at Trevor. "He never did recover from that horrible winter, you know."

"Yes, I know."

Now the duchess's meditative look was back. "Poor, dear Willie. He was in a constant state of decline since the day he returned with those poor, unfortunate children."

Trevor stared at his mother, thinking she looked to be lost somewhere between rose bushes and Russian winters and not on the matters at hand.

"You know, I never did really understand why Willie persisted with his love and devotion to all of those strange plants. It wasn't as if there weren't enough lovely plants right here in England. If it hadn't been for his fondness of traipsing about the world gathering seedlings and seed pods, he might have married and had a family of his own. For years I tried to interest him in roses, but he always preferred those strange, foreign plants of his."

"They were strange plants, weren't they?" Trevor said. "I do recall that he seemed to have a special fondness for the poisonous varieties. I remember them well."

"So do I," the duchess said. "Monkshood, poisonwood, wild parsnips . . ."

"You left out the worst of the lot."

The duchess gave a start, looking suddenly thoughtful, and then smiled. "Oh, yes. I remember now . . . You and Tony did have a terrible bout with one of Willie's pets. Neither of you ever went near the greenhouse again after a bout with that vine as I recall. From one of the Americas, was it not?"

Trevor nodded. "North American poison ivy. I will remember the name until I die."

The duchess laughed. "For a while I thought it might be sooner than I expected. It was the only time I could ever remember having the two of you sick at the same time. What a time you had of it."

"I cannot speak for Tony, but I never spent a more miserable two weeks in my entire life."

"Well, dear William is gone now, and I fear his beloved plants will not be far behind. It isn't likely that Willie made any provisions to have his plants looked after."

"Then that should make it easier to be rid of them," Trevor said. "As far as the poisonous varieties, I think the lot of them should be destroyed."

"It may not be just the poisonous varieties, I'm afraid. You know Tony is not the sort to cosset plants."

Trevor frowned. "Yes, Tony only cossets . . ." He caught himself, realizing just in time what he had been about to say in front of his mother, and immediately snapped his mouth shut.

The duchess raised her brows and gave him a questioning look. "He only cossets what?"

"Never mind," Trevor said, knowing full well his mother knew all about Tony's amorous escapades.

The duchess looked amused, as if she read Trevor's thoughts, then she began collecting things she might need, loading them into a shallow rush basket. "Oh, dear me. I almost forgot. I invited Lady Cecilia and her parents for dinner on Saturday. I will have to send her a note telling her we have been called to Marsham," the duchess said, heading for the house.

Trevor was about to say something, when the duchess's voice reached his ears. "Finish watering that rose tree for me, will you, Trev?"

Trevor nodded and picked up the watering can. He felt like a complete fool and prayed to God no one saw him standing here like this, watering his mother's roses like he didn't have anything better to do. He shuddered to think what would happen if his crew ever got wind of such.

When Trevor finished watering the rose tree, he went inside, where the duchess handed him a note. "I must go see to my packing, or Elise will have my trunks stuffed with ball gowns, which will be perfectly useless at Marsham." The duchess was halfway out of the room when she called back to him over her shoulder. "Will you have that note sent around to Lady Cecilia for me?"

Trevor took one look at the envelope. "Mother, you cannot send this note."

She paused just inside the door and gave him a puzzled look. "I would like to know why I cannot," said the duchess.

"Look at it," Trevor said, holding the envelope up for her to see. "It has dirt smudges all over it."

"Oh, posh," the duchess said. "No one will notice that. If they do, they will simply think your father's valet smudged it. Now, be a dear, will you, and find Hector and give him the note. Tell him to deliver it to the Duke and Duchess of Whybourn, immediately."

Hector must have done just as the duchess said, for the very next morning, just as Trevor and his parents were discussing the plans for their departure to Marsham, a note arrived from Lady Cecilia.

Opening it, the duchess exclaimed, "Fudge and stuff!"

"What is it?" Trevor asked.

" 'Pon my word, we have trouble," the duchess said. "Lady Cecilia writes that it is such a good fortune that things have worked out as they have."

"Good fortune?" the duke said. "What does she mean?"

"It seems Lady Cecilia and her parents are leaving for Marsham today," the duchess said, handing the note to Trevor. "She finds it coincidental that she was about to write us to cancel our dinner plans just about the time our note arrived. Seems she has a cousin who lives near Marsham—you remember Sally Mayfield, the wife of the Earl of Marwood?—well, they plan to visit her after spending a few days with Tony."

"They are going to Marsham?" Trevor asked. "Are you certain?"

"Yes." She handed the note to Trevor.

He took it, opening the note and cursing softly when he read the last line.

"Hope to arrive ahead of you." Lady Cecilia wrote in her perfectly executed note.

This is so exciting. Why, it will be like a race to the country. Perhaps I can persuade Father to offer a small purse to the party who is first to arrive.

The duchess smiled. "I don't suppose Lady Cecilia thought about the possibility that her father might be the first to arrive and therefore would win his own purse."

"Lady Cecilia never thinks that far ahead," Trevor said. "I swear that woman's head is filled with sawdust. Every time she opens her mouth I expect some to fall out."

"Now, Trevor. You must learn to curb your thoughts. Lady Cecilia is soon to be a member of the family and your sister-in-law."

Trevor scowled at that reminder, but he did not linger there with his thoughts. He was too busy thinking that if Lady Cecilia's words proved true and she arrived before, or about the same time as Trevor and his parents, then, Trevor realized, there wouldn't be enough time to talk sense or anything else into Anthony—or the Russian girl, either, for that matter. And if the duke and duchess arrived with Lady Cecilia in tow *before* he had a chance to talk to them . . . Trevor cursed silently at the thought. But the absolute worst fix would be if they arrived and found Anthony in his finest fornicating form, locked in a mad embrace with the Russian.

Then what?

The Duke of Whybourn would call off the marriage and that would be the end of the Hamiltons *and* Trevor's letter of marque—*that's* what.

As a last desperate measure, Trevor arranged for his parents to take the family coach to Marsham, while he elected to take his smart new carriage, which was smaller and faster.

As far as plans went, this one went fairly well—that is, until Trevor reached the tree-shaded lane that led to Marsham Manor.

CHAPTER
❧ FIVE ❧

Morning drove the mist away, but long before it did, Natasha was up and off to the stables for her morning ride. The groom, Ned Hughes, was just outside the stable door, brushing a sorrel gelding, but when he saw Natasha approach, he stopped.

"Good morning, Ned," Natasha said, putting a little more briskness into her stride and wishing that just this once he would leave her be and let her saddle her horse herself, thereby avoiding having to be around him at all. She didn't know why, but she was uncomfortable with him. Whenever she saw him, he would look at her in a lecherous way that made her think his eyes capable of stripping away her clothing. He never said anything out of line, but the way he looked at her made her skin seem to shrink and a cold shiver would ripple down her spine.

Just as she reached the stable door, Ned said in his surly way, "I'll get your horse." He laid the brush on the fence, and giving her a tainted look, disappeared into the stable's dark interior.

While he was gone, she stroked the neck of the young gelding, telling him just how beautiful his satiny coat was, laughing when the gelding shook his head up and down, as if he agreed with her. She was still laughing when Ned brought her horse out, but when she saw him, the laughter died away.

He said nothing, giving her a leg up. As always, Natasha felt him lean against her, his shoulder brushing against her leg. Once she was seated, he kept his hand on her boot, not familiar enough so that she could verbally reprimand him for it, but lingering a bit too suggestively to be proper. When she gave him a look of reproach, he returned it with an expression that made her feel he knew things about her no one else knew. Just as she was about to tell him he could release her boot, he dropped his hand and stepped back, dipping his head in a slightly mocking manner, one that insinuated disrespect.

Ned, the old earl had said, was Romany—a Gypsy lad who was abandoned upon his stoop when he was a young boy and deathly ill. The earl had brought Ned into his home and sent for the doctor. Once he was well, Ned never talked about his past, but seemed content to make caring for the horses at Marsham his future.

He wasn't very old—not more than twenty-five by Natasha's guess. He dressed in that colorful manner Gypsies seem to have a fondness for, a bright purple shirt, open at the neck, where a gold chain glittered. He wore an orange sash about his waist and light brown breeches. His skin was dark, both naturally and from the sun, and that made his teeth flash white upon the few occasions she had seen him smile. His eyes were dark brown, as was his hair, which was long. It was only when Ned tied it back that one could see the gold earring that flashed in his ear. The earl had said he doubted that Ned Hughes was his real name. "As long as he is honest and puts in a full day's work, then I have no quarrel with him. A man has his right to his privacy."

Natasha wanted to give him all the privacy she could. She did not find Ned to be like most Gypsies, for most of them were prone to lengthy discussions and much gaiety and laughter, but in one way his Gypsy blood stood out. He was very bold.

Once, when she was dressing, she heard a noise outside her bedroom window; as she looked out, she saw him standing in the garden, just a few feet away. He watched her in a manner that made her shiver. She made a point to make certain her draperies were always closed when she changed clothes after that.

In many ways, Natasha felt sorry for Ned. He was, after all, homeless and without a family—something Natasha could understand. She knew he needed his job, for it was his only source of income. For that reason, she never mentioned his strange ways to anyone, but his crude brand of familiarity—and the way it made her feel—had prompted her to tarry in his presence no longer than necessary.

She looked down at him, thinking he was handsome in a rough sort of way, but his handsomeness couldn't override his attitude. He might be pleasing and normal on the outside, but inside . . .

Simply put, she did not like the man.

Anxious to be away, she guided her mare into a wide circle and broke into a canter without looking back. She did not need to. She could feel the heat of his gaze boring into her back and knew it followed her until she rode out of sight.

* * *

At first Natasha intended only to ride as far as where the lane met the main road that led to the village, but once she was there, she decided to ride a bit longer and extend her outing all the way to Applecore.

Applecore. Even now, after living near the little village for three years, Natasha still could not help smiling at the quaintness of its peculiar name. If words could paint pictures, Applecore was a tapestry. It wasn't a famous town, nor was it known for anything in particular, but what it lacked in notoriety it more than made up for in charm. Remembering the cozy tangle of streets that lay sleeping below the remnants of a stern Norman castle, the old clock tower, the tall steeple on the church, the row of apple trees that lined the river, she decided it could be called nothing but Applecore.

She turned off the main road and rode alongside a sunlit field of buttercups, catching shimmering flickers of the river between a fine, straight row of lime trees, before passing the wilting plumes of a weeping willow drooping over the water like a green umbrella. On the outskirts of town, three fat brown ducks waddled in a line, and she pulled up to watch them, smiling when a well-trained row of ducklings joined the parade. A moment later she passed a small thatched cottage dozing in the warm sunshine and saw Mrs. Goodperson beating her rugs, her twelve children lined up like stairsteps at the well where they washed their porridge bowls.

"Hullo, Mrs. Goodperson," she called out.

Mrs. Goodperson paused just long enough to wave and then returned to her chore.

The scent of narcissi and wild roses perfumed the warm spring air as Natasha rode through town, waving and nodding her head to those she knew, returning an occasional, "Good morning."

about the village green, thrushes were busily employed in their never-ending search for food, while the blackbirds seemed content to sit on their lofty perches and scold everyone who passed by. The sycamores that dotted the green were bursting with yellow color, and the tight buds on the elm trees were splitting to show a coiled mass of pale leaves.

A short while later Natasha rode out of town, catching sight of the parson in his shiny black carriage, turning up a cloud of dust. Hoping to avoid the dust, she waved at him and turned from the road, guiding her mare on a different route to Marsham, having decided not to take the road this time, but to go by the shorter route, riding across the meadow filled with buttercups and yellow rape she had passed on her way into town.

As they customarily did whenever Natasha was not about, Luka and Pavel were primed for a bit of mischief, but after an hour or so of exploration—and not turning up one speck of mischief to get into—they decided to try their second favorite pastime, which was finding some unsuspecting soul about Marsham they could pester.

Outside for most of the morning, Luka and Pavel heard Lord Anthony the moment he stepped out the door. They also heard when he called them, but they hid in a small bellcote until Mrs. MacDougal came out to see what all the ruckus was about.

"I was looking for Luka and Pavel," Anthony said.

Mrs. MacDougal gave a quick look about the garden. "Did you check the stables? Perhaps they went for a ride with Natasha."

"So, that's where she is," Tony said. "I've been looking for her everywhere. I thought the twins might know her whereabouts."

Mrs. MacDougal gave him a smug look. "I have a suspicion they would know," she said. "There isn't much that goes around Marsham that the twins don't know about."

Tony looked around. "How long has she been gone?"

"Over two hours now, I would guess."

Anthony started toward the stables. "Did you notice which way she went?"

"Last I saw, she was headed down the lane," Mrs. MacDougal called.

"Good. Perhaps I will meet up with her. I am taking the coach into town. I have a meeting with my solicitor. I won't be back until late afternoon."

Mrs. MacDougal nodded. "I wonder where those boys are," she said to no one, then turning, she went back into the house.

Luka and Pavel watched Mrs. MacDougal. They also watched Lord Anthony leave for town. It was a unanimous decision that Lord Anthony was the chosen one—and well deserved it was. Since coming to Marsham, Lord Anthony had taken it upon himself to introduce the twins to the cruelest form of torture—a morbidly savage hideosity known as obedience.

There was a short dramatic interchange, a plaintive discussion of the horrors they had been forced to endure at Lord Anthony's hands—things like keeping their shirttails tucked in, washing their faces and hands before dinner, keeping their hair combed, asking permission before they could leave the table, and the worst one of all, being forced to endure countless hours of extreme and cruel torture with a tutor brought all the way from Edinburgh . . . for the sole purpose of their oppression. In the twins' opinion, the old, malleable tutor hired by the former Earl of Marsham was much more to their liking.

After a short, one-sided review of their grievances, Lord Anthony was found guilty of all aforementioned crimes. It was all downhill after that, for inspiration and action were almost instantaneous.

Once his carriage disappeared around the corner of the house, Luka and Pavel forgot about past injustice and concentrated on future punishment, their attention diverted to happier interests in planning a bit of adventure.

First they went to the barn and led their fat pony outside, then they made their way to the carriage house. A moment later, the pony was hitched to their cart. Making one more trip back inside, they reappeared almost instantly, carrying a large pane of glass—the kind used to replace those occasionally broken in the greenhouse.

Carefully loading the glass pane into their pony cart—along with two shovels—the twins then proceeded down the lane at a merry clip, the perfect picture of innocence.

At just about the midway point between Marsham Manor and the gate at the end of the leafy lane—where it met up with the main road—they pulled the pony to a halt, tying him in the shade of a sweeping oak. A moment later they unloaded their shovels and set to work.

After an hour or so, perspiring and grunting, their arms tingling with fatigue, they managed to dig a large rectangular hole in the middle of one of the two wagon ruts running down the center of the lane. They rested a moment, panting and catching their wind before moving to the second phase of their plan, which was nothing more than placing the pane of glass over the hole.

Once the glass was in place, they covered it with dirt, applying a few finishing touches by sweeping the rut with a tree branch. That done, they began to scatter rocks and leaves and bits of wood along the well-swept rut, tossing a few small clods across it for good measure.

Another critical going-over and they decided their tampering was impossible to detect. Returning the pony and cart to the barn, they hurried across the meadow to the lane and climbed a large chestnut tree—one that had long, leafy branches extending far out over the place where they had concealed the hole. Secreted in its lofty bowers, the twins patiently awaited Lord Anthony.

Lord Anthony did not come along.

However, the Marquess of Haverleigh did, driving his smart new carriage and admiring the spectacular gait of his well-bred carriage horse as he mused about how he was going to save Lady Cecilia's betrothal in true hero fashion, while thinking such a thing could only be called Christian charity.

Right in the middle of this bucolic scene something went afoul. Glass shattered. The horse screamed and reared. The carriage made a jarring thump, then jerked to a halt. Trevor found himself unseated. For a moment he sat there in stupefied silence, then the horse screamed and reared again.

Trevor burst forth with a loud curse. "Bloody hell!" he said as he fought the high-spirited gelding, bringing him under control, still unaware of what exactly had happened.

A moment later he climbed down to see his smart hickory carriage wheel wedged up to the hub in a deep hole. Then he saw the glass. That was when he exploded with a furious outpouring of words not fit for the human ear.

Even the rooks in the trees took flight.

In the midst of this furious red haze he saw the two boys hiding in the trees overhead, and any earlier feelings of Christian charity he might have had went out the window.

He furiously ordered the boys out of the tree.

The twins climbed down and had the presence of mind to flee, but Trevor descended upon them before they went ten paces. Stunned and frightened speechless by the towering giant who looked angry enough to kill, they were wrestled to the ground before they found their voices and began to use them.

It was one of the few times in their lives that anyone had threatened to spank them. Twins, being twins, have a tendency for both of them to squeal, even when only one of them is in jeopardy. In true twin fashion, they were both howling before a blow was struck.

Trevor was having a hard time holding the two squirming and kicking boys down, but in spite of not being spanked as yet, the twins were wailing as if they were. The noise was so terrible that over in the meadow a handful of sheep were huddled in a corner of the fence, bleating and trying to jump over one another.

Trevor was in the middle of trying to give the two misbehavers a good thrashing when he heard a horse approaching. Looking up, he saw the loveliest creature alive trotting up the lane wearing her best blueberry riding suit and plumed hat, and looking so fetching he could do nothing but stare.

He forgot the boys. He forgot the smart hickory carriage wheel buried up to its hub.

What he did remember was to look her over with interest just before she hurled herself off her horse and went at him with both fists.

"How dare you!" she said between snatches of breath and fist-pounding. A second later the twins gleefully joined in. Soon it was a free-for-all. Trevor hadn't seen anything like it since his mother persuaded him to take her to a charity jumble sale a few years back.

The moment Trevor got the situation under control, with one twin pinned beneath his foot, Natasha and the other twin secured—one under each arm—he made them promise to behave. "Or I won't release you," he said.

The twins agreed readily enough, but the ebony-haired beauty looked as if she would rather fight to the finish.

"Who the devil are you?" he asked, unable to take his gaze from her.

She was panting hard, but between pants, she managed to say, "Natasha Simonov, you brute—and besides behaving criminally, you, sir, are trespassing."

"The devil I am," he said, releasing them. "In case you haven't been so informed, Lord Anthony has a brother, and—"

"*You?*" She paused to catch her breath. "You are Hellfire Haverleigh? You are Tony's brother?"

Trevor frowned at the ease with which she used his reputed name without so much as a tinge of a blush. Even the biggest trollops in London *feigned* embarrassment. This violet-eyed goddess, however, delivered the same punch with her words as her fists. This, he decided, was a woman to be reckoned with.

Uncertain as to how to proceed from here, he chose to divert the attention from himself. He growled at the twins.

The twins bolted, but Trevor, suspecting such, anticipated their move and grabbed them easily by the collars before they had gone two paces. Giving them a good shake, he said, "Since you two little gudgeons are the reason my carriage is stuck, and since you are in such a hurry to leave, you may go for help. And to make certain you attend to the matter promptly, I will hold your friend here hostage. Now, off with you before I change my mind and hang both of you by your heels . . . from this very tree."

Without a parting word, the twins shot across the meadow like two flaming arrows fired from the same bow.

Never one to waste time, Trevor took advantage of the time the twins were gone. While he was marveling over the exquisite creature and grinning foolishly, it occurred to him that besides being his hostage, this had to be the woman his brother was so taken with—and understandably so.

He let his gaze move over her at his leisure, following the rounded curve of generous breasts, the nipped-in waist, the flare of gentle, feminine hips, visualizing the things he could not see, like the line of her leg and the tips of her breasts, hard and pointed. He noticed, too, his own aroused interest.

Remembering the reason he was here, he tried to cool his lusty response by thinking of himself sitting naked on an iceberg in the polar region, but that didn't help. One look at her generated enough heat within him to melt the entire polar cap. She was simply too fetching and felt too damn good in his arms to release.

Then he thought about the letter of marque. That was enough to get his mind back on his mission.

Without so much as a caressing hand out of place, he released her, deciding he would spin a tale for this lovely creature his brother was so taken with—a tale about propriety and Christian duty, as well as a reminder of the effects her infatuation with Anthony would have upon the rest of the Hamilton family. He ended with a plea for her to think about what this would do to poor, innocent Lady Cecilia.

For emphasis, he hooked his thumbs in his pants and squinted at her wisely, like a drowsy owl, and said, "So, you see, it would be most unchristian, most unwise, and most unkind of you to allow this thing between you and Tony to go any further."

"Yes," she said. "I am sure what you say is all very true, and while I do feel for Lady Cecilia, I know, too, that no woman wants marriage with a man who loves another. So you see, while I do understand your motive, I cannot possibly refuse Anthony's offer of marriage."

He stood stock-still for a full minute, then something fizzed inside his head, like a gun when its powder is wet and it won't fire. He could feel his face turning purple. His hand came up to his throat. Were those his veins bulging out? He sputtered and went into a black rage.

He saw his hopes dashed and his future ruined. He saw his parents ruined as well. Then he saw the duke and duchess forced to move in with him, his lovely town house littered with rose clippings and butterfly nets.

Panic, hate, and rage gripped him. He wanted to grab this inky-haired goddess and shake her until those glossy black ringlets of hers lost their bounce. He wanted to set her on that stump over there and lecture her until those purple eyes of hers closed from exhaustion.

He fixed his most frightening look upon her and swallowed in horror as his gaze was met by a determined violet stare. He knew then and there that his chances of talking this chit out of anything she had her mind set upon would be as easy as catching a bullet fired from a pistol.

"I would like to know why not," Trevor said in a voice that positively shook with outrage. "Even in Russia there are taboos against this sort of thing. A lady—no matter what country she is from—does not dally with a betrothed man. It simply isn't done."

"I know that."

"Then why do you persist?"

"Because I love him," she said quite simply. "And he loves me."

"Listen, my lovely innocent. Tony has been falling in and out of love since he saw his first female. The average length of his affairs is two months."

"This time it's different," she said, with a stubborn tilt to her chin.

He gave her his bored look. "Yes, yes, I know ... They all say that," he said. Seeing that did not work, he tried again. "Why, pray tell, is this time different? Because it's you? Are you so naive as to actually believe that *you* are any different from the legions of beautiful women—*rich English women*—who have come before you?"

She remained stubbornly silent, but even in her silence, he could see he wasn't getting anywhere with her. Russian stubbornness, he decided, was rigid, dedicated, and resolved, and *this* Russian, in particular, was as unbending, close-minded, and obstinate as they came. Small wonder Napoléon gave up the siege of Moscow.

It was the first time since England had gone to war with France that he actually felt pity for Napoléon.

What was it Napoléon said, *"Scratch a Russian and find a Tartar"*?

Trevor narrowed his eyes in speculation. That was precisely what had happened here. This girl was no Russian. She was a bloody Tartar. Hell and damnation, she was even Tartar-nosed—if that snub on that beautiful face could be called a nose, so small it was.

He looked at her as determined blue eyes met adamant violet ones, and for the first time in his life, Hellfire Haverleigh found a woman he could not charm. There wasn't so much as a twinkle of capitulation in those odd-colored eyes that stared back at him with such spirit and strength. He had never in all his born days seen anything so small possess so much dogged resolution. She couldn't weigh more than seven stone, but he was willing to bet at least three-fourths of it was heart—something he admired in horses but abhorred in women.

Couldn't she see what was happening here? Didn't she understand what she was doing? Was there no way she could fathom that she was forcing his hand? Suddenly Trevor had a vision of never again having the luxury of going to the best shops and clubs, caring not a fig for the total of the bill.

He saw his elegant town house disappear. And his new carriage—as well as the custom clothes, the imported cigars, the best tins of food, the fine liquors, the best tailors, the prestigious clubs, the well-trained staff he employed.

And then he saw the shredded letter of marque.

Trevor threw up his hands. Faced with more than just a formidable opponent, he was going to have to regroup and think this one through. She might be a young, innocent girl, but she was as unbending and obstinate as they came. This was definitely not going to be as simple as he'd first thought. He needed some time to think.

Unfortunately, time was precisely what he did not have.

Lady Cecilia could come clipping down the lane at any moment, causing worse problems for him than a stuck wheel. Truly he had a wolf by the tail this time;

he couldn't hang on to it, and he was afraid to let go. Frustrated beyond endurance, he lit a cheroot.

"You won't convince me, no matter how many of those you smoke."

He glanced at her and almost swallowed his cheroot. The blind, flaming impudence of her was staggering— for there wasn't the slightest doubt in his mind that she was challenging him. He cursed the Tartar blood that circulated through those Muscovite veins, remembering how many times he had read that a Russian is often defeated but never beaten.

Defeated? Hell and double hell. He would settle for that. Defeat was exactly what he had in mind.

"Here they come," she said, interrupting his line of thought.

He looked up the lane to see a wagon approaching. Spying the two blond heads of the twins, he suddenly felt as if he had been granted a reprieve. Later, when his carriage was functional and he had gotten over his indignation, he would be able to think in a rational manner. Then he would figure out something—some way to sway her to his way of thinking.

An hour later the carriage was free. Seeing his hickory wheel was ruined did not put Trevor in his best humor or set him to thinking in a rational manner. Suddenly all his thoughts centered upon one question: How had he come to this?

Fact was, it was hell playing the saint, the angel of deliverance. He wished he had never returned to London. The trials of the high seas were nothing compared to this. Suddenly he was spitting mad at his parents for dragging him into this, angry at Tony for causing the problem in the first place, and furious with this Russian baggage for making it so bloody complicated.

Why has this happened to me?

It was something he did not understand. He thought of all the hours he had spent with his childhood tutor, the years at Oxford, the way he had been groomed for the role of a duke from the day he was taken out of his child's dress and had his dimpled legs thrust into their first pair of breeches. He remembered being expelled from Eton for drinking and wished he had stayed expelled. He could have been so many things—a dashing soldier in one of the lancer regiments, a smuggler, a pirate even. But what did he end up with?

A title.

And what did that mean? That you spent your life being taught responsibility, duty, and adherence to the rules. And for what? So you could stand around waiting for someone to die, so you could inherit your title. Not a very comforting thought, and not one Trevor was enamored with.

He could have been so many things . . .

It shouldn't happen to a man such as he—a man with a sure talent for playing the rogue, the villain. Not that he was such a bad chap. It was simply that he was a lover of adventure who would rather privateer and wench his way to prominence than run to the front of a battle when the sabers rattled. Playing the champion was a bloody bore. If it hadn't been for Napoléon throwing Europe and Britain into war, he didn't know what he would have done. As it was, he worried about what he would do once the war ended and his privateering days were over. Surprise attacks. Flying false colors. Sneaky forays in the dark. Plundering and taking booty. Playing the coward and being called a hero. *Those* were the things that made life worthwhile.

And now, to preserve his letter of marque and his one

tie to adventure, he was thrust into this bloody complication.

He looked down at the girl, the obstacle in this dilemma. What to do? Turn tail and run and let things run their course? Throttle the chit? Throttle Tony? Offer her money? Offer Tony money? More concerned about his letter of marque than any family ruin, he made a desperate decision. Since she refused to do the honorable thing and break off with Anthony, there was no other choice.

The girl would have to be kept away from Marsham until Lady Cecilia and the Duke and Duchess of Whybourn had departed. Question was, how was he to do that? Strangulation was out. And judging from the looks of her, she didn't seem open to a nice vacation about now. Out of unsurpassed desperation, he groaned and cursed, wishing someone would kidnap the chit and give him the easy way out.

Wait a minute . . . Did someone say kidnap?

For a twinkling of a moment even he was appalled—but only for the twinkling of a moment. There was no time to waste, for Natasha's presence when Lady Cecilia arrived would be more fat than the fire could handle.

As soon as he arrived at Marsham, Trevor learned Tony was due to arrive at any time. And so, he remembered, was Lady Cecilia *and* her parents.

Consequently he did the only thing he could do.

Without a moment to waste, he left Tony a note, telling him if he so much as thought about Natasha while Lady Cecilia was in residence, he would never see his Russian flame again. To this, he added a note under the heading of POST SCRIPT.

*Once your affianced and her parents have de-
parted, I will verify your irreproachable behavior
with Mother and Father. If your conduct passes their
approval, Natasha will be returned to you. If not, I'll
give her to the first bloody Frenchman I see.*

That done, he set out immediately to find the Russian
chit. A short search and he found her feeding the fish in
a pond near the water garden.

He had intended, at first, to take her back to the stables where a horse awaited her, but catching sight of a
cloud of dust from a carriage coming down the lane at
a merry clip, he knew there was not a second to be lost.
Even from this distance, he recognized Lady Cecilia's
shrill laughter.

He kidnapped Natasha that very moment, throwing
her over his saddle, cossack fashion—which he thought
was rather considerate of him, since she was Russian—
and riding away with her.

The feat wasn't as easy as it sounded, and although
she weighed no more than seven stone, it was damnably
difficult hoisting her up with one arm and tossing her
over his saddle while at a gallop.

He didn't know how a bloody kidnapper did it.

All was not lost, however, for even in a moment of
haste, he found his hand in the softest place imaginable,
just before she bit him on the knee. He smiled at
that, and pulling his hand away, he pushed her head
down.

"What do you think you are doing?" she shouted
from her upside-down position. "This is England, not
the Ottoman Empire. You cannot go around kidnapping
people."

"Watch me," was Trevor's only reply.

CHAPTER
❧ SIX ❧

The last thing Natasha had a glimpse of was the shadowy, lurking form of Ned Hughes standing in the darkness, just beyond the stable door.

As soon as they had cleared the stable yard, she thought no more about the groom, putting her thoughts instead to the predicament she was in. She was able to reflect with some chagrin that she had not had the intelligence and forethought to scream. She had simply allowed this brute to abduct her without so much as a chastening word.

Even from her upside-down position she could tell they rode in the opposite direction from Applecore. She supposed it was because he knew she would be recognized at any inn nearby, but the realization did nothing to relieve her discomfort. Whatever possessed her to think being abducted on horseback was romantic?

It was dreadfully uncomfortable and quite humiliating, and there was absolutely nothing titillating about dashing across the countryside in an upside-down position, having her ribs cracked with each step the horse took, breathing dust, and struggling for each breath she drew, only to have it immediately slammed out of her.

Her head spinning, her ribs aching, she squirmed and kicked, and when that had no effect upon him, she tried biting his leg.

"Bloody hell!"

Thankfully, that at least got his attention enough so that he pulled her upright, wedging her in the small space in front of him and ordering her to be still and quiet, "In that order," as he so succinctly put it. She let out one last muffled squeak of defiance and then settled down.

It had been dark for over two hours when he stopped at a remote inn on an out-of-the-way road that looked as if it was seldom used. Although Natasha had been riding upright and in front of him for quite some time now, her legs were stiff and she crumpled like a folded fan when he pulled her from the back of the horse and stood her on her feet. Holding her upright, he chuckled as she wobbled and rubbed her posterior.

"Numb, is it?"

She had had about all she was going to take from this barbarian. She drew back and kicked him on the shin. When he winced, she said, "Hurts, does it?"

He scowled at her but said nothing.

The inn was old and questionable-looking, but they were both too hungry to do much questioning. After a meal of mutton and potatoes, which they ate in a deserted room, Trevor moved from the table to speak to the innkeeper, standing far enough away so that Natasha could not hear what he was saying, but close enough to grab her if she tried to flee.

When he returned and motioned for her to follow him, she came wearily to her feet. She might have been exhausted and weak, but her voice was loud and strong. "I am not going to spend the night here with you."

Then, giving the matter some thought, she added more softly, "Without a chaperone."

"You are right in part. You are not going to spend the night here. I have hired a coach for the rest of our journey," he said, holding the door open for her to pass through.

Ramming her excuse for a nose in the air, she swept past him in her blueberry riding outfit, the feather on her hat slapping him in the face.

"How is it your hat managed to stay on?" he asked, pulling his head back in an attempt to dodge the feather when she turned to look at him.

She gave him a hateful look, ignoring his question by asking one of her own. "Where is this absurd abduction going to end up?"

"What?"

"Where are you taking me?"

"I have no idea."

"Wonderful," she said, throwing up her hands as she began to pace back and forth. "I am abducted by a lunatic who has no destination in mind. That is just what I need, thoughtless execution."

"I would be careful, if I were you. Mention execution again and it may give me ideas," he said, wondering if that was a shadow of fear he saw in her eyes, but before he could decide, the look was gone, replaced by one of defiance.

"At least I would not have to wonder about where *I* was going," she said, "unlike you."

"I am warning you," he said.

"Warn all you like. You are the one in the wrong here, not me. Any idiot knows the first rule of abduction."

The first rule of abduction? He gave her an appraising eye. Maybe this was going to be more of an adventure than he had first thought. The girl had a way about her. Damn if she didn't. She was outspoken and independent as hell, and on top of that she seemed in possession of a fair amount of knowledge and wit. He could have done worse, he supposed.

He could have abducted Lady Cecilia.

At that thought he cringed and gave Natasha an indulgent look, his lips twitching in spite of himself. "And what is the first rule of abduction?" he asked.

She actually looked amazed. "You mean you don't know?"

He shook his head. "No, I don't. So why don't you enlighten me?"

"No wonder you have never married. You cannot think that far ahead," she said, then gave him a knowing look. "The first rule of abduction, as any schoolboy knows, is to have a destination in mind *before* you do your kidnapping."

"Listen, you babbling tower of misinformation, I did not have a destination in mind because I did not have *kidnapping* in mind. It was as simple as that. You may not believe this, of course, but it was a spur-of-the-moment decision and a hasty one, let me assure you."

She crossed her arms in front of her and said, "Haste comes from the devil."

Trevor did not say anything else. He knew what she was thinking, and perhaps she was right. After all, it *was* a bit ironic that Hellfire Haverleigh, who was widely reputed for having a way with the ladies, suddenly had a lady that he did not have the remotest idea what to do with. Unable to think of anything else to do with her at the moment, Trevor paused, giving the old coach the once-over, then calling up to the driver. "Point this contraption toward London," he said, "and pray like the devil we can make it that far."

"London," she repeated. "You're kidnapping me and taking me all the way to London?"

He nodded and opened the door, grasping her arm to help her up. "You wanted a destination, did you not?"

She gave him a nasty look. "What I wanted was to be left alone."

"What? Leave you alone? Out here and unchaperoned?" With overemphasized drama, he brought his hand up to his chest in an expression of horror. "Why, I could never call myself a gentleman if I left you to that fate."

"I daresay you can't call yourself one in any case," she said, stopping halfway into the coach and turning back to glare at him.

He gave her his most devastating smile.

She hardly noticed. "Listen, you bloody pirate, this is not necessary. If you want me away from Marsham for a few days, you don't have to take me all the way to London."

He gave her a look that implied he thought he was dealing with an idiot, then dismissed her. "I will take you wherever I decide, and you have no say in the matter. I am the bloody kidnapper," he said, poking himself in the chest, "and don't forget it. Now, act the part of the simpering virgin and be quiet."

She frowned at him. "Are you sure you are Anthony's brother?"

He laughed. "I'm sure. Why would you ask a thing like that?"

"You are not being very kind."

"Haven't you heard? To the kidnapper goes the advantage," he said, placing his hands on her backside and giving her a shove. "Now, be quiet. A coach is no place for bleating."

She toppled inside, mumbling something about a goat having to bleat where it is tied.

The coach made it as far as London, and by the time they reached there, Trevor still did not have any particular destination in mind. He ruled out his town house because of his staff, knowing it would soon be all over London that there was an unchaperoned lady in his keep, and knowing, too, that when the ton learned the identity of the *lady* he had taken . . .

It was the closest to remorse he had felt in all of this. After all, he did have her reputation to worry about, and if word got around that she had spent time alone with him, it would be ruined. It did not take an inordinate amount of intelligence to know what happened to a man who ruined a lady's reputation.

Marriage.

His lip curled with disgust at the thought. He might be forced to abduct her to save Tony's hide, but he would be damned if he would marry her. . . .

Brotherly love went only so far.

The more he thought about it, the more he figured the only place he could take her—where no one would see her and he would be surrounded by loyal followers not prone to gossip—was his ship. With a clean conscience and uplifted spirits, he decided to take her aboard the *Mischief Maker.*

When the coach pulled to a stop at the wharf, Natasha looked out the window. "The *Mischief Maker.*" She scoffed. "That's an absurd name for a ship."

Blue-white flames flickered in his eyes. He was not accustomed to having the name of his ship maligned. In two shakes he was out and around the coach, opening her door.

"Be quiet," he said, "or I'll change it to the *Missing*

Maidenhead ... and see that it earns the reputation. Then you will be in a fine fix, won't you?"

She didn't say a word, so he took her by her upper arm, drawing her from the coach.

"Thank you," she said, with such sarcasm that he laughed. He was a foot taller than she was, so she had to lean her head back to look into his face. The effect seemed to add water to her words, weakening them. "You have me at your advantage, for now," she said.

"A soft answer to turn away wrath. Now, that is more like it."

"Say what you will, but there will come a day when our situations will be reversed and I shall take great pleasure—"

"Save it for later," he said. "Whatever things frighten me, it should be obvious to you or anyone around that feminine threats are not among them." He looked toward the ship, nodding at a man who had come to stand at the railing. He started in that direction. "Let us be aboard and under sail."

She balked at that, coming to a stop. "Under sail?"

He gave her a dumbfounded look. "Under sail," he repeated, with a nod. "That is generally what transpires on a sailing vessel, is it not?"

Her face paled. "You cannot mean you intend to take me away from England ...?"

He did not understand this woman. Why couldn't she make this kidnapping easier for both of them and simply shut up?

"I asked you a question," she said.

He gave in with a sigh. "Look, there would be no reason to take you aboard my ship if I intended to remain in England, now would there? Besides, by now you should be aware that I am in the habit of doing virtually whatever I please, and that includes handing you over to Napoléon, if I so choose."

She must have believed that, for her voice quivered as she said, "You are as mad as the baiting bull at Stamford."

"Fresh country wit," he said, looking down at her. "How charming." He pushed her ahead of him, guiding her up the plank, taking her arm when she stepped onto the deck.

Once on board, she stopped, turning to look at him, but she remained silent.

"What? Nothing to say?"

"I have learned it is ill-advised to argue with the master of thirty legions," she said simply, while casting her gaze about the ship, where all hands suddenly appeared to be on deck.

"Cast off," he said to the first mate.

The first mate nodded. "Where to, Captain?"

That was something Trevor had not thought about, and caught off-guard he could only stare at the first mate. He blinked in confused frustration. There was no greater terror than making a split decision . . . only to be caught with your pants down.

His staring blankly at the first mate must have given her ideas, for she made a dash for it. He caught her by one arm and the hood of her cape, yanking her back against him. "You have more petticoats than brains," he said. "Try that again and I'll lock you in your cabin." Then to the first mate he said, "I thought I told you to cast off."

"Aye, sir, you did. But you did not say where we are going."

Angered and ready to throttle her, Trevor said, "Anywhere, as long as it isn't in enemy-patrolled waters." Then giving her a nasty look, he said, "Although the more I think about it, the more I am convinced that it might not be such a bad idea to turn you over to Napoléon."

"You wouldn't dare," she said, backing away from him. "Anthony would never forgive you."

"As if I care," he said, and with that, the handsome Marquess of Haverleigh threw back his dark golden head and laughed. "Mark a course for the Hebrides," he said, allowing his warm gaze to travel over her at his leisure. His mouth twitched as he added, "Miss Simonov has ample fire and brimstone in her ... she should feel right at home in Scotland."

CHAPTER
❦ SEVEN ❦

Trevor stood at the helm. He took one look at Natasha standing next to the ship's railing and congratulated himself. He couldn't have pulled off a better kidnapping if he had planned it. Considering the haphazard start, things hadn't turned out so bad after all.

True, the Russian was in a pique, but that wouldn't last long. Not if old Hellfire Haverleigh had anything to do with it.

He was, after all, the object of many a woman's matrimonial quest, and come to think of it, he had quite a bit to offer a woman. After all, he was handsome, and he was titled. His confidence returning, he knew he would do all right. He had romanced his way out of worse predicaments than this before.

It was at that moment that Natasha must have felt him watching her, for she turned her head toward him and gave him a don't-you-dare-lay-one-overimpassioned-finger-upon-me look.

He laughed. It was amusing to him to see her pluck up her courage and give him such a visual dressing down. Without blinking an eye, he gave her a cocksure salute. He had seen the kind of looks she gave him. If he wanted her to, he was sure she would be writhing and begging in no time at all.

As if sensing what he was thinking, she gave him a when-hell-freezes-over look and turned her head away.

Feeling quite optimistic and decidedly cheerful, he turned the helm over to the first mate and crossed the few feet that separated them, coming to stand at Natasha's side. "I see no reason why we cannot make the rest of this voyage as pleasant as possible. Do I have your word you won't try anything foolish?"

She turned her head to look up at him. "Why? Is that privilege reserved only for you?"

When he didn't reply, she went on to say, "What's the matter? Don't you consider kidnapping me to be foolish?"

Trevor looked at her. *Typically Tartar,* he thought. She would argue with a block of wood. In spite of all he had done to make her comfortable, to keep her as safe and merry as a ninepence, she seemed determined to stick to the issue of kidnapping.

Didn't she know just how many women in London would give anything to be in her place right now? Didn't she understand that there were kidnappings and then there were kidnappings? Where was her sense of the romantic? Of adventure? And if not those two, then at least her appreciation of an educated and titled male in prime physical form—perfectly agreeable to doing whatever necessary to get her mind off kidnapping.

He couldn't understand her. He was not accustomed to women who were not easily distracted, or women who did not seem to find him attractive. He didn't know why he bothered with her.

Yes, he did.

Her hair was black as Vulcan's hammer; she had a body that would shame a belly dancer, eyes that rivaled Scotland's heather, and a mouth that had perfected the innocent pout. It was her mouth that made him think about yanking her into his arms and kissing her right on the spot—which he was confident would lead to other, more pleasurable things—things which he also knew were something he had no business thinking about.

One Hamilton panting after her was enough. Well, maybe he would indulge in a few distractions—just for the diversion, of course. What else was there to do to pass the time aboard ship?

But first things first. He couldn't allow her comeliness to distract him. He was, after all, a man with a mission, and right now, his objective was to put her mind at ease concerning her safety and to talk her out of her foolish infatuation with Tony. "If you understood the situation better, you would realize kidnapping you was by far the most humane choice," he said, congratulating himself for phrasing his words so eloquently.

"Humane? How dare you even speak the word." She clamped her hands on her hips. "Tell me, just *what* could have been worse? Murder?"

"I would not have gone that far," he said. "Believe me." One look at her expression and he grinned. "All right, don't believe me. But believe this: I could have compromised you any time I liked."

She stamped her foot. "Are you insane? You *have* compromised me, you dull-witted lout. When word of this gets around, my reputation will be in shambles."

He shrugged. "No worse than it would have been when the ton learned you were the reason for Tony's breaking his engagement with Lady Cecilia . . . and that all this time you have been living under his roof."

She opened her mouth to speak, but he held up his hand, cutting her off. "What is done, is done," he said, then paused. "I did the only thing I could think of under such pressure. There was very little time, you know."

When she gave him a skeptical look, he took her hand in his—in what he considered to be a most fatherly way—and said, "My dear Natasha. When word of this attraction between yourself and Tony reached my parents, things were turned upside down. My father did not so much as *look* at a moth for days—and Mother's roses were dying on the vine. In a moment of desperation, they called upon me for help."

She made a doubtful sound and snatched her hand away.

He gave her his profile and his best melancholy air, not shamed in the least to be fishing for her sympathy. "They are, after all, my parents. What would you have me do? Spit in their faces?" he asked, catching a sideways glance at her out of the corner of his eye.

One look and he knew she was softening. She was too romantic minded not to. He stood there, majestically posed, looking every bit the tragic hero as he inched closer. Taking her small hand in his once more, he asked softly, painfully, "Do you hate me so much?"

Poor girl. She sighed and looked up at him. He realized she had about as much chance of escaping his advances as a mouse under a cat's paw.

"I do not hate you," she said at last, "but I cannot say I like you, either."

"Well, at least you should be able to tell me you un-derstand what family loyalty and obligation means."

She didn't say anything, and taking this for a good sign, he went on. "I know you understand. I clearly re-member you coming to the rescue of those two brothers of yours."

She stared out over the water, lost in contemplation, and he knew he had her. At last she said, "Family is family. I suppose I cannot chastise you too severely for being loyal. Devotion is an admirable quality in anyone. I suppose I would have done the same thing."

He had her going now. Get her to feel remorseful, and he was almost there. He feigned gratitude and pat-ted her hand. "Thank you for your forgiveness," he said.

She snatched her hand back and gave him a swift glance. "I said I understood. I never said I forgave you. You are still a bloody kidnapper."

There was a time in his budding youth when the thought of being called a kidnapper—much less a bloody one—would have had him protesting to the hilt, but now she had done no more than put a flea on his conscience. If his years at privateering had taught him anything, it was that there is a time to feel remorse and a time to protect one's interests.

This was definitely the latter. Besides, he was work-ing on *her* remorse, wasn't he? His spirits rising, he put on his most sincere face and said, "Can we at least call a truce?"

She seemed to stiffen at that. "I will consider it once you have returned me to Marsham. Until that day, there will be no forgiveness and no truce, but only this warning: I will do everything in my power to thwart you. I will use every wile at my disposal to extract myself from your clutches, and rest assured that the moment I return, I will tell Tony . . . *everything*."

His look softened. "Even if it meant Tony would challenge me to a duel?"

"Nothing would please me more at this moment than to see Tony put a bullet square between your kidnapping eyes."

With that, she whirled around, walking briskly away. Deuced fetching, it was, too, for there was a certain distracting, swaying rhythm to the action of her hips, as well as—well, there was, simply put, something about the way she moved that enchanted him. She reminded him of a cat, quick and light upon its feet.

He grinned. "Miss Simonov," he called after her, "your cabin is the other way."

"I am taking the long way," she said, not breaking stride.

He cupped his hands around his mouth as he called out to her. "I would be honored if you would have dinner with me later . . . in my cabin," he shouted.

Without turning around, she shouted back, "I would rather starve than share one bite with a bloody Barbary corsair."

So much for gaining her sympathy, he thought as he watched her walk away, the feather on her hat whipping in the breeze. He wondered what was in store for him after such a threat.

Later that afternoon he discovered she had planned a new line of attack and regrouped, for the moment he saw her, she announced that she wished to be returned to England. "And if I am not, then let this serve as a declaration of war."

"Miss Simonov, Russia and England are at war with France, not each other."

"Don't try to distract me and gain my sympathy. It won't work a second time. You have been warned," she said. "God is on the side of the persecuted."

He wanted to laugh at the drama in it, but he merely dipped his head in a mocking gesture of recognition. "Forewarned, forearmed," he said, fighting back a smile.

"That is precisely the kind of response I would expect from dolt stupidity," she said, and disappeared down the hatch.

After she was gone, he whistled a little sea ditty as he returned to the first mate's cabin—since he had given her his own. In excellent spirits, he was not overly concerned. She was doing precisely what women did best—making hysterical cries of impotent rage and dislike while threatening him with biblical wisdom, vows of revenge, and all the customary preliminaries to doing nothing.

He had enough troubles without worrying about threats from her. Compared to his, her problems were no more important than the skip of a flea. He thought about his brother, remembering that Tony was the culprit here—affiancing himself to two women and leaving the family to suffer the consequences.

Was Tony so infatuated with Natasha that he was willing to make himself and his family poverty-stricken social outcasts forever?

Trevor shook his head. He couldn't understand it. *No* woman was worth that. The more he thought about it, the more he knew that he would have never considered such—not for Natasha and a bottle of smuggled French cognac, not for Helen of Troy and a seat in Parliament. It never occurred to him that he might have done it out of love, simply because the Marquess of Haverleigh had never been in love.

In Trevor's mind, he was the sensible brother, the one filled to capacity with brotherly love, parental devotion, and concern for others. He paused a moment, thinking he liked the ring of that, for it did make him sound rather orthodox, if he had to say so himself.

Full of self-satisfaction, he went to his bunk, and, stretching out, he closed his eyes for a short nap—without so much as a smudge upon his conscience.

In spite of his euphoria and smudgeless conscience, the trip to Scotland wasn't altogether what he would call a pleasant one. In fact, it was a journey like no other, with that Russian baggage spewing fire and brimstone and breaking every valuable in his cabin. In her defense, he would have to admit she had settled down somewhat when they reached the Hebrides, although it didn't matter by then—since everything in his cabin had been smashed, broken, or removed. As a result of Natasha's excesses, he had a raging headache and a dandy hangover.

By the time they arrived, she must have been madder than Bedlam and bursting with spirit, for she took full advantage of his delicate condition to dive overboard the moment they dropped anchor.

Standing on deck, Trevor was so taken back by what he saw, he could only stand there, his insides heaving, his head pounding. He could not believe what was happening—his captive was swimming to shore with sure, swift strokes. He knew he looked damnably ridiculous, gaping and gawking like an idiot when he should be taking command of the situation, but he seemed unable to do anything about it. All he could think of was that a woman who could swim like that must have tremendous leg muscles.

And then that thought led off onto another line of thinking altogether.

"Want me to send someone after her?"

Trevor was imagining those strong legs wrapped around him when a voice interrupted. He gave a start. "What?" he said, turning to see the first mate standing beside him.

"The girl, sir. Want me to send someone after her?"

The girl. He couldn't believe she had made such a fool of him. For a moment he was tempted to tell the first mate to set sail for England, leaving Natasha to her own resources. The thought warmed him. It might take her months—years even—to return to Marsham. By that time, Tony would have come to his senses and married Lady Cecilia, their parents' finances would be secure, and he would be free to pursue his own interests.

But what if word got out that he had kidnapped the chit and then promptly lost her? Why, he'd be the laughingstock of England, that's what. He, Hellfire Haverleigh, the same man who teased and taunted Napoléon by capturing his ships and their cargo. He gritted his teeth and regretted the day he had ever heard there was such a person as Natasha Simonov.

"Lower the boat, Farnsworth. I'll go after her myself."

True to his recent run of luck, the absolute worst happened. By the time he reached shore and set his sights upon her, she had managed to find two burly Scots— who apparently wanted total revenge against the English for Culloden—as protectors.

Getting back to his ship was foremost on his mind when Trevor took her by the arm.

"What do you ken you're doing, lad," one of the

Scots said. "The lassie doesna want anything to do with the English. Now, take your hands off her."

For a moment Trevor wondered who gave this highlander the right to stand there acting like he was a mixture of God and Rob Roy. A moment later he questioned his sanity in taking on this whole idiotic kidnapping.

It beat belief, but those two beefy Scots wouldn't listen to reason—not even when he explained to them that she was his runaway sister, that he was simply returning her to their grieving parents. Two more insolent barbarians he had never encountered. The moment he finished telling them the story, they were telling him to leave the lassie be and return to his ship, or all that would be left of him was fish bait.

They seemed quite ready to prove it, too.

In an overexuberant frenzy, they came at him like a typhoon, and it took him only a minute to learn Scots do not fight like gentlemen. One minute he had been standing there with his hand on her arm, and the next instant he had a flashing glimpse of himself flying through the air. A moment later he was lying on the ground, looking up at the two brawny Scots with their bums showing beneath their plaids.

Coming to his feet, his first thought was to throw Natasha at them and to run for all he was worth. Any man who wanted a woman bad enough to fight for her was too desperate by half—especially when so many women could be had with no exertion whatsoever.

But before he could act, he felt something grab him around the chest, crushing him and hurling him to the ground a second time. He was up in an instant, and just as instantly, he regretted it.

The whole of Scotland must be inhabited by brutes, savages, and lunatics who take delight in launching themselves with the greatest vigor upon the unsuspecting English, for a wilder pair he had never encountered.

All gentlemanly behavior abandoned, Trevor went at the two Scots with all the vigor he had used in fights at Oxford, after a cricket match.

Knocked down once more, he saw that his first mate had come to his rescue—that, at least, would make the odds a little better. Back on his feet now, he and his first mate went after the Scots with true military dispatch, with Trevor hoping Farnsworth had the same thirst as he for getting even.

CHAPTER
❈ EIGHT ❈

It was some time later, while nursing a busted lip, goose bump the size of a football on his head, and what he was certain was a busted nose, that Trevor had ample time to think.

Here he was, his body bruised and battered, his cabin in shambles, and his crew doubled over with laughter, and what was Tony doing? Right this very moment, he was probably playing the country earl and hosting a lavish dinner party for his London guests. Tomorrow he would play the role of the besotted betrothed to Lady Celilia and her parents, while Trevor had to second-guess the enemy and wonder where the next battle lines would be drawn.

In Trevor's mind, there was nothing like the dread of another battle for making a man of peace see reason. If Marie Antoinette had taken the time to think things through, she would be eating that cake she was so famous for right now. Having no desire to end up like Marie Antoinette, he came up with yet another plan—and having no desire to be beat and battered again, one that was safer.

Although it was still his hope that during Natasha's absence, Anthony would either come to his senses or be talked into them by their parents, Trevor was not too optimistic this would happen. He pulled his tattered shirt off, wincing at the sudden pain in the vicinity of his ribs.

Hellfire and damnation. If she persists in fighting like this, I'm backing out.

What a bloody pickle ... He was caught up in this whether he liked it or not. There was no other way out. If his parents should fail in persuading Anthony to give up this madness of marriage to this Russian chit—pretty though she might be—he would have to resort to more drastic measures.

Trevor thought about that for a moment. The most drastic measure he could come up with that was both pleasurable and painless, was to make the young—and hopefully, vulnerable—Natasha Simonov fall in love with him.

It was as simple as that.

Make her fall in love with me, he thought. *Perfect. Absolutely perfect,* he said to himself, with a proud swelling of his chest. *Luring her into loving me will be as easy as drinking tea.* After all, it was a well-proven fact that he, Hellfire Haverleigh, was a man women fell in love with quite naturally.

Thinking back over the legions of women who had tried unsuccessfully to lure him into marriage, he was confident he would have no trouble enticing the lovely Natasha to do just that. Rubbing his once beautiful— and now busted—nose, Trevor smiled, thinking of all the satisfaction he would get from beguiling the Russian troublemaker into falling in love with him, then luring the virginal Miss Simonov into marriage.

He chuckled. Of course, there would be no marriage . . . but by the time the unsuspecting Natasha discovered his duplicity, she would be on her way to Russia.

Alone.

He was thinking the whole thing would be as neat as a ninepence when he had a vision of a coil of raven hair, a pouting mouth, lavender eyes, and a warm, husky breath. Dear God, he could hardly blame Tony. She was lovely.

It further occurred to him that he might as well enjoy himself, and if that meant taking a tumble or two, it would be worth the effort. Without a regret, he figured since she had already accused him of behaving like a bloody Barbary corsair, he might as well earn the reputation.

Starting with wine and savory lamb chops, Trevor put his plan into action. His heart beating faster than ever, he decided she had been right. This *was* war.

He would go after her like William the Conqueror— with coals in his drawers.

It took some doing, but he managed to get her into his cabin for dinner. Sitting across from her at the table, he tried to interest her in a little friendly conversation— thinking a distracted mind was an unwary one.

As far as conversation went, Natasha was determined

to speak of three things, and three things only. Tony. Getting off the *Mischief Maker*. Returning to England.

"If you know your brother at all," she said, "you would know that Tony loves me—and that taking me away won't change his mind. 'Absence makes the heart grow fonder,' you know."

"And here I had been told saltwater was a certain cure for love."

"Not true love," she said, feeling every word of what she said was as true as her love for Tony.

His lips twitched. "True love, is it?"

It was said with such mocking cynicism that Natasha gritted her teeth. "I don't expect someone as provincial as you to understand."

"You are speaking to a man who has been in love with women since he was old enough to know what a woman was," he said, and gave her a weary, bored look. "I have been in love more times than I can count."

"You could not have been *truly* in love—not if you have experienced it as many times as you say. True love comes once in a lifetime."

"Thank you for telling me about my feelings," he said. "However did I manage so long without you?"

"I am not telling you how you feel; I simply think you confuse lust with love," she replied.

"And you think what darling Tony feels for you is true, once-in-a-lifetime love?" he asked, his voice shaking with amusement.

She wasn't about to be undone by this brute, and in defiance, she held her head up proudly. "I do," she said.

"Then you are as naive as you are young and inexperienced," he said, with a chuckle. "You know about Lady Cecilia and my brother being betrothed—not to mention Lady Cecilia's vast wealth—so you must know that the best you can possibly do is to come in second."

"I would rather be second with Tony than first with you." The gall of him infuriated her; she leapt to her feet, throwing her napkin into her plate.

He smiled at that, leaning back in his chair with confident ease. "What if I told you there was no way you could have either?"

She ignored that and began pacing the room. "When are we going ashore?" she asked, giving a direct stare. "Or have you decided to keep me on this leaky tub forever?"

"If you must know it was never my intention to keep you on board this long, but since you so cleverly jumped overboard the other day, I realized I could not trust you, Miss Simonov. If you are miserable, then it is your own fault."

"How long are we going to sail Scottish waters? Do you ever intend to return me to England?"

"Of course, but only when you are in your dotage," he said.

She did not laugh at his joke. "You are not being clever," she said, making her way to the door.

Coming to his feet, Trevor crossed the room, intending to stop her, but when he reached her, she dashed through the door and slammed it in his face.

One thing Natasha could say about Trevor and that was he never did what she expected. He was a man who was full of surprises. And surprise her he did, the very next morning, rapping smartly upon her door at the first peep of dawn.

"What is it now?" she asked in her most hateful tone, without opening the door.

"If you can be dressed and on deck in half an hour I will take you ashore . . . on a picnic. A real, honest to Kate, picnic."

She leapt out of bed and came to stand next to the door, opening it just a crack. "A picnic?"

"Aye, as bonny a picnic as you will ever see. We have a basket filled with cheeses, mince pies, and sausages, complete with a bottle of wine."

"Are you lying to me?"

He blinked at her. "Lying? Me? Of course not. Upon my word—as true blue as a Methodist," he said.

"Your word is worth about as much as . . ."

He smiled. "Are you coming, or do I picnic alone?"

"It is indeed a blind goose that comes to the foxes' sermon," she whispered; then speaking louder, she said, "I suppose I will come . . . only because I cannot bear another day on this ship, you understand."

He chuckled. "What I understand is this is the first time you have displayed anything that resembles wisdom."

She slammed the door.

Half an hour later she was on deck, looking as fresh as an angel over a new inn door—in spite of the fact that she was wearing a loose, faded dress the first mate had purchased from a fisherman's wife in Scaloway. Seeing how lovely she looked, Trevor was reminded that she had only one other dress to wear—and that was the blueberry riding suit she had on the day he abducted her.

The island was a place of high hills and bare moorlands, where windswept trees seemed to cling desperately along water-battered cliffs. Trevor did not put the ship to anchor here, sailing instead to the southwestern part of the island, where the beaches were made of fine sand backed by green *machair* lands, covered with short grass and a carpet of blooming color.

Once Trevor rowed them to shore, Natasha found she

was unable to walk steadily after so many days on a ship, but after a few tries, she was running along the sandy beach, finding sea pinks and bladder campion growing in the rocks. Her heart pounding, her legs trembling, she stopped to gaze out over the water, inhaling the scent of salt and grass, taking no mind of her hair, which had fallen from its careful plait to billow in a glossy dark cloud about her face.

She turned to watch him as Trevor approached, a blanket tucked under one arm, a basket swinging from his hand. "Unless you have persuaded one of the mates to pilfer some food from the galley for you, you must be hungry. Have you found a suitable place to spread this feast?"

Her gaze moved away from him to the blue flowers of the lungwort, where it spread a carpet around the cove. "There," she said, pointing to a lushly flowered place between two smooth rocks.

Trevor nodded, and a moment later he had the basket down and the blanket spread. Trembling from exhaustion and confinement, Natasha dropped wearily onto the blanket. She propped her elbows upon her knees and leaned forward, watching him sit down across from her as he began to remove food from the basket. Reaching in one last time, he extracted a bottle of wine. Abruptly, he looked up, and their eyes met.

Natasha leaned back and tried to act as though she had not been watching him so intently, but she knew the blush of color to her face gave her away.

"Hungry?" he asked.

"Very."

"Good. We'll start with a drink, then we will eat." He poured her a cupful, handing it to her.

She was so hungry she would have accepted anything he gave her, and without thinking what she was about, she drank half the cup before she realized her throat and stomach were on fire.

"You tricked me," she gasped, her hand coming up to pound her chest as she collapsed in a fit of coughing. Weakly, she managed to say, "That isn't wine."

He gave her a surprised look, then poured a cup for himself, taking a sniff before he smiled and said, "Unfortunately, you are right. It isn't wine. It's whiskey."

Seeing the expression on her face, he added, "I had no idea. I thought it was wine. I requested wine when I sent Farnsworth into town last evening."

Her look told him how much she believed that.

He glanced around and sighed. "Considering where we are, he probably couldn't find wine. The people here are poor. They cannot afford smuggled goods. Scots' whiskey is all they want and all they have."

In spite of the fiery burning in her throat, she managed to nod and say weakly, "I suppose I will live."

He smiled. "As far as I know, no one has ever died from half a cup." He watched her take another sip. "But I would be careful if I were you. Scots' whiskey can take you by surprise."

"I've had spirits before," she said. "Your uncle always allowed me a glass of wine with dinner."

He laughed. "Wine and whiskey are not exactly the same thing."

They looked at each other for a moment, neither of them saying anything, neither of them looking away. At last, she put her hand to her forehead. "Goodness," she said, wedging her cup into the sand and leaning back, "the sun is certainly warm here."

"That's the whiskey talking. It hits you faster when you have not eaten. Here," he said, handing her a wedge of cheese. Then he tore off a hunk of bread and placed it on the blanket beside her, following that with a link of sausage.

She polished everything off without saying a word, and then, before he could warn her, she drained the cup.

"I cautioned you to go slow," he said. "You'll be lucky if you don't get drunk."

She smiled sweetly. "But, I want to get drunk," she said, handing him her cup. "More, please."

The humor left his voice. "You've had enough."

She shrugged and leaned back, closing one eye and looking at him with the other. "You should never contemplate marriage," she said. "You're too bossy, by half."

"It might surprise you then, if I said I was married."

She was looking at him with both eyes now. "No, it would not—because I know you are not."

"How do you know that?"

"Tony told me about you . . . *all* about you. Hellfire Haverleigh and everything."

"That is not a name I fashioned for myself," he said. He thought about adding that Tony didn't have such a high-polished past, either, but thought better of it.

After all, he was trying to get her mind off Tony.

"It might surprise you, but I was very awkward and shy when I was a boy," he said.

"I know. Tony told me. He said *he* was the charmer—that you always had your studious little head wedged between the covers of a boring book."

Trevor scowled. "That was because I was the oldest son, the heir, the one to inherit our father's title."

"Inheriting a title does not make one awkward and shy."

"Well, I outgrew it, so it doesn't matter now," he said, looking off in what he hoped was his most forlorn expression. When he looked back at her, he could see the compassion in her eyes. She even smiled at him. He poured her another half cup, smiling at the way she drank it. A moment later, rolling over to her stomach, she began writing her name in the sand.

" 'Natasha Alexandra,' " he read. "It's a beautiful name. Do you always go by Natasha?"

She looked at him, studying his features. It was the first time she allowed herself to really notice what he looked like. Before, she had been too angry, but now that the opportunity presented itself, she looked him over good. She would have to admit that he was devilishly handsome by either Russian or English standards. He had a beautifully shaped head and dark blond hair that lay close to a smooth, wide forehead. His nose was straight and classical. His brows were arched over what she called English blue eyes. His mouth was wide and well formed, his lips full and sensual. A strong chin seemed to balance the refinement and perfection in the rest of his face, something that made him quite masculine. Indeed, he was a superb specimen.

But he wasn't Tony.

He was, however, Tony's brother.

Bearing that in mind, and seeing the almost melancholy expression on his proud face—an expression that hinted at deep sorrows nobly endured—she was overwhelmed with a sense of tragic destiny.

"My brothers call me Tasha," she said, glancing at him. Their gazes locked; she could not look away.

He leaned forward, his hand caressing her cheek. "Tasha," he said, "lovely Tasha. What a pity my brother met you first."

Her heart lurched. Something about the way he said that touched her in a throat-catching way. She had never been truly aware of him as a man until now. Before, he was simply Tony's brother and a pest. But now, she was

painfully aware of him, of his being close enough so
that his face held hers in shadow.

Breezes floated over the water, touching them with
salty coolness, causing the grasses to bend and the
flowers to dance upon their fragile stems. Cold water
lapped the shore. Overhead, birds circled and shrieked.
Suddenly she was as aware of her surroundings as she
was of him. He was a physical presence, a man who
aroused feelings in her she did not understand. She felt
confused, finding she was as drawn to him as she was
repelled. She thought about what he had just said and
decided it was absurd, really. This man could not possibly be interested in her.

It was something else that brought his face closer to
hers, something else that made him cover her mouth
with his. *Let him kiss me. He will find out soon enough
that his kisses mean nothing.* She wasn't interested in
him. It was something else entirely that made her close
her eyes when his lips touched hers, something else that
made her kiss him back.

As quickly as it had begun, it was over.

Trevor broke the kiss, seeing the way her startled
eyes flew open, the confused way she was looking at
him, her blue-violet eyes inquiring and puzzled. Her
lips were parted, her breathing slow and easy, yet somewhat disturbed. She was lovely, he thought, and decided
it had not been altogether untrue when he had said it
was a pity Tony met her first. "You are a beauty," he
said, finding himself distracted a moment later by the
sound of her laugh.

What he saw surprised him. Her response was not
prompted by a desire to divert him, nor was it a modest
one. It was a simple, honest reaction—the reaction of a

woman who was completely oblivious to the effect she had upon members of the opposite sex.

For the first time, he realized how different her life was from his. She had been reared in pastoral whole-someness, away from the taint of London society. She was as fresh and pure as country cream. Her entire universe centered around Marsham and a tiny village with an idiotic name.

For the briefest instant he forgot what he was about, what his purpose was. He was simply a man and she a woman. For a time that would be enough. It occurred to him that he wanted to lie down beside her. He wanted to take her in his arms and kiss her again and more slowly. He wanted to explore that enchanting mouth and her exquisite body. He wanted to show her all the things he knew she knew nothing about. He wanted to see those violet eyes of hers darken to purple when he made love to her.

Then he remembered why they were here.

He sighed. It was just as well. She was not ready for him to be that forward. Not yet.

The impulse to drag her into his arms and kiss her again nearly overwhelmed him. God, what would it be like to be that innocent and trusting again? A newly emerging tenderness burned within him and he found himself regretting what he knew would inevitably happen.

It wouldn't just stop with his convincing her not to marry Tony. He knew that now. He was going to have her. He was going to take her to his bed. He had known it the moment she looked at him only moments ago, with her lips parted, her surprise so apparent in the startled gaze of those lovely, lovely violet eyes.

CHAPTER
❧ NINE ❧

Natasha did not know where she conjured up those visions of romantic abductions she had often imagined, for they were nothing at all like the reality.

She lay her cheek against the cool glass of the coach and stared off into space, her mind not upon her return to England, but, as she thought back over the past two weeks that she had spent with him in Scotland, upon the day Trevor had taken her on a picnic.

She sighed. They would be turning down the lane that led to Marsham soon, for according to Trevor, Lady Cecilia and her family had returned to London. She should be deliriously happy to be coming home, but there was something that marred the occasion, something she did not understand. Perhaps she was simply too romantic and too sentimental for her own good. How anyone as kind and gentle as Tony could have a brother as exasperating, opinionated, and headstrong as Trevor was beyond her. Yet, even as the thoughts formed in her mind, she had a vision of Trevor's eyes upon her, the drowsy cadence of his words, the way his mouth felt against hers.

The coach rattled to a stop; she heard Trevor say,

"We're here," and she pushed all thoughts of him from her mind.

She opened her eyes to see he was already stepping down. Beyond him she could see the beloved, if crumbling, walls of Marsham—infinitely more dear to her now than they had ever been. It didn't seem possible that she had been gone two weeks, but it was precisely two weeks and two days after Natasha left Marsham that she returned to it.

Wearily she climbed from the coach, taking Trevor's hand as she alighted. Her legs were stiff; her backside felt as if she had been whipped with a rug beater.

"Thank you," she said in a sweetly musical voice, dipping into a low curtsy—which was no curtsy, really, but simply a way to hide the tired legs that gave way beneath her. Once she steadied herself, her eyes, which had rested upon the immaculately tailored black coat, lifted to gaze into his deep blue eyes.

He smiled down at her and offered her his arm. "Well, my little kidnapped bounty, are you ready to go in with me and face Tony's wrath?" he asked.

She returned the smile. "Perhaps I should be asking that question of you," she said, "for it will not be toward me that Tony's anger will be directed."

He rubbed the back of his knuckles over her cheek. "It is nothing I have not faced before," he said, looking her over once more before his gaze returned to rest upon her face. Natasha blinked, squinting her eyes in the same manner she did when she was in a dark room and someone lit the lamp. She felt dazed. Her heart thundered, yet she did not know why.

She was in love with Tony, wasn't she?

And she was home. Yet how odd it was to find herself feeling a strange mixture of both sadness and joy. Was she happy because she was to be reunited with

Tony at last? And the sadness? Was it, as she feared, because her time with Trevor had drawn to an end?

A few days ago, she would have had no such feelings, for indeed, it had only been in the past few days or so that Natasha and Trevor had called a truce, and she found—strange as it was—that there were times when she even liked the man.

She sighed and looked up at him. "Something tells me it will not be such a simple matter to convince him. We may have the devil of a time persuading Tony he should not skewer you with a sword over this."

"We?" he asked softly. "Surely you don't mean you are feeling a bit protective toward me?"

Natasha knitted her brows in apparent confusion. He had such a way of twisting things and giving them new meaning. "My reasons are honest ones. I have no desire to come between brothers. Because of that, and because I love Tony, I will do all that I can to ease things between you. Do not expect more of me than that."

"Perhaps I won't have to. There is always the chance that Tony will understand my motives and that will be the end of it."

She laughed. "I sincerely doubt that. Tony will be furious at first, but fortunately his anger never lasts very long," she said. "He is like a spark that flashes brightly, then burns itself out."

He cocked a brow and gave her a knowing look. "You know my brother well," he said.

"I feel like I have known him forever."

Trevor grunted his opinion of that, then turning toward the steps, he said, "Come on, wart. Let us have this thing done."

Once inside the house, Natasha paused for a moment in the hallway. The hall candles were not yet lit, keeping her in shadow. The door to the library was open, and the room was empty, except for Tony, slouching in a chair beside a low-burning lamp, one arm dangling a glass of brandy over the side of the chair as he stared morosely into a fireplace that held no fire.

"I have returned," she said, mustering up all her cheerfulness and walking into the room.

Tony glanced up as Natasha and Trevor entered. There was a moment of silence, then the eruption came. He dropped the brandy snifter and sprang to his feet, rushing toward them.

Reaching for her, Tony disengaged Trevor's arm, drawing Natasha against him. "Are you all right?" he asked, a concerned expression on his face as his gaze roamed over her face.

"I am fine, my lord, as you can see," she said happily, doing her best to make light of things by spinning away from him and turning around.

Apparently satisfied, Tony possessively placed his arm around Natasha's waist, then turned on his brother. "Where did you take her?"

She glanced quickly at Trevor, speaking before he could. "He took me to Scotland aboard his ship. I had my own cabin, and the crew could not have been kinder to me. He did everything he could to see to my comfort and keep me safe. And now, I am here."

Tony scowled at her. "Blister it! Why are you defending him? He is a bloody criminal! A kidnapper! A rogue of the first water! Did it not occur to you that I would be worried?"

She was surprised by that. Tony never appeared to her to be the kind of man who worried. "I assumed you would be angry, of course, but not worried. I thought you knew the kind of man your brother was."

"I *do* know," Tony said like a growl. "That is precisely why I was worried."

"Oh," Natasha said.

"If there had been another option—a more favorable one, that is—I would have taken it," Trevor offered.

Tony turned on him. "If you think I believe that, then you are a bigger fool than I first thought."

"And if you think all I have to do is to go gallivanting around the country abducting uncooperative women, then you are the biggest fool of all. Remember, brother dear, that I have been away—doing my best to plague Napoléon—not you. It was not my choice to be brought into all of this, and if you had kept your affairs in order, none of this would have happened."

Natasha's gaze flew from Trevor to Tony. She released a long-held breath when she saw Trevor's words apparently had some soothing effect upon Tony.

"Dash it all, Trev. You had no right to abduct her."

Trevor cocked one brow. "And what would you have me do? Tell her to put on her finest dress and ready herself to meet your other bride-to-be?" He brushed a speck from his sleeve. "Perhaps that would have been the best thing—considering how many things they have in common. What a dandy time could have been had . . . discussing the similarities and peculiarities of your courting habits." Leveling hard, penetrating eyes on his brother, Trevor asked, "Is that what you wanted?"

Tony sighed. "I would have thought of something," he said. "Cecilia is an understanding sort. She would have taken no offense to learn our uncle left me to care for Natasha and her brothers as my wards."

"Perhaps she would have . . . at first, but one look"—Trevor turned toward Natasha—"and that assumption would have been blown higher than a powder magazine on a burning ship. Lady Cecilia may be a bit lightheaded, but she is not a simpleton. Even an understanding sort might find herself just a mite miffed to learn her affianced was affianced to someone else. This is not a simple matter of changing your mind, Tony. There are other people involved in this besides yourself. Powerful people. How long would it have been, do you suppose, before the Duke of Whybourn asked for your head on a silver platter?"

"Ye gods! Whose head are you serving?"

Trevor shook his head at the sound of that voice. *Just what I need,* he thought, as he and Tony turned, in unison, to stare at their father, who had just walked into the room with his butterfly net in his hand.

The Duke of Hillsborough was enjoying his stay in the country, and had, only this morning, declared himself to be in no hurry to leave. Marsham was a place he seldom visited, and he was fascinated to find so many varieties of butterflies and moths that were nonexistent in London did exist in such abundant numbers here. The devoted attention some men lavished upon their mistresses, the duke bestowed upon larva, caterpillars, and cocoons. A simple soul, the duke loved to lead a contingency of guests through his temporary laboratory—where his new collection of local skippers, moths, and butterflies were neatly displayed—with the same show of pride other members of the nobility used to discuss the portraits of their ancestors that lined their hallways and hung in their galleries.

Taking one look at the butterfly net, Trevor said, "Are you coming or going?"

"Going, my dear boy, going. The woods around here are teeming with butterflies this time of year—so many more than we have in London, you know." With that, the duke wandered out of the library, then through the large door that opened into the garden.

Tony waited until the duke had disappeared, then he turned toward Trevor and narrowed his eyes. Seeing his anger toward his brother had apparently been rekindled during the duke's interruption, Natasha took a step backward.

"Did you touch her?" Tony asked.

Taken aback by the peppery outburst and the direction this discussion was suddenly taking, Trevor was momentarily stunned. "Touch her?"

"You know what I mean, you lecherous bastard."

Natasha gasped, and Anthony said, "Pardon, my love."

"Oh, that is dashing good, Tony," Trevor said, ignoring Natasha's scowl. "If you are wondering if Miss Simonov is a virgin or not, you have to ask yourself that question—since you have spent considerably more time with her than I have, and under the same roof, I might add. As for me, I can only say that if she was *virgo intacta* when she left here, then *virgo intacta* she returns."

The fists at Tony's sides clenched, and Natasha put a restraining hand upon his arm. "I still would not put it past you to take a sip or two from the goblet of delight," Tony said, his lips curled into a snarl.

Trevor crossed his arms in front of him and gave his brother a taunting look. Then he made a clucking noise, as he sometimes did when amused. "Goblet of delight, is it?" he said, giving Natasha a considering look, just as she gasped again and glared hotly at Tony.

"Well," Trevor went on to say, "I am sure you should know all about goblets of delight and such." He turned toward the garden . . . just as Tony picked up a teacup from the tea tray and hurled it toward him.

Looking on, Natasha watched as Trevor ducked, laughing as the tiny teacup sailed past him, going through the doorway and out into the garden. The laughter died a moment later when he saw, with a horrified expression on his face, that while Tony had missed him with the teacup, he had not been so lucky with the duchess. With a similar expression of horror, Natasha's hands flew up to cover her face when she saw the cup strike the duchess, shattering into pieces as it struck her bonnet.

"Upon my word," the duchess exclaimed, and plopped herself down on a nearby bench.

Luka and Pavel, who witnessed the entire thing from their hiding place in the hedge, beat a hasty retreat from the garden. Since everyone was prone to blaming them, instinct prompted them to be as far away as possible whenever something was amiss.

Once they were a safe distance away, they collapsed against each other in a fit of laughter. A short while later, they sought the security of a straw-filled stall in the barn, where they began to compose a limerick in tribute to the occasion.

Their singing drew the attention of a new member of their group, a small, shaggy pup fished out of the river by Harry the gardener, who declared the pup had been on the receiving end of a most dastardly deed—an attempted drowning.

As soon as the twins spied the bedraggled pup, they claimed him for their own, responding to Mrs. MacDougal's reminder that there were already three dogs on the premises—namely Winkum, Blinkum, and Nod—by reminding her that those dogs belonged to Lord Anthony. That done, they promptly named their dripping friend Beggar.

It was a name descriptive of his person, for there was little doubt that Beggar was the most recent result of a long series of mésalliances. Small, wiry, and scruffy, he had a grizzled mustache and mismatched ears, and looked very much like the ragged old Gypsy peddler that came Marsham's way twice a year.

Once the twins had their verses composed, they began to sing, so loud and with such spleen, that Beggar flattened himself and put his paws over his ears.

Sometime later, just before afternoon tea, Luka and Pavel made their way to the house to sit on the stairway and wait for Tony. A few minutes later, Tony came down the stairs and tripped over Beggar, who yelped and made a hasty departure.

"Would it be too much to ask to keep that mutt outside?" Tony asked, continuing down the stairs and mumbling something about whoever said there was solace in living the country life had to be the village idiot.

Luka and Pavel wisely said nothing, preferring to wait patiently until Tony had passed; then they began to sing—joined on the second verse by Beggar's mournful howl, which came from the vicinity of the skirted table in the parlor.

The duke was in his laboratory, gazing at his skippers
The duchess was in the garden, pruning with her
* nippers.*
The marquess was in the library, arguing with his
* brother*
When he ducked a sailing teacup, which promptly hit
* his mother.*

Tony stopped and turned, giving them a sour look. "Is that all you two have to do?" he asked. "Because if it is, I will summon your tutor."

That did the trick, sending the twins out the front door faster than a fired shot, Beggar in hot pursuit, the lilting strains of the rhyme—and Beggar's mournful howl—lingering in the air long after they had disappeared.

Hearing a chuckle behind him, Tony turned around. Trevor stood at the top of the stairs, his hands thrust deep into his pockets, a bland expression upon his face. "You never told me the twins were so clever," he said.

"They aren't," Tony replied.

"My, my," Trevor was saying as he came down the stairs. "There is nothing like a bit of relaxation in the country to invigorate one's spirits."

"Go to hell," Tony replied, and disappeared through the front door, followed by the rocking sound of Trevor's laughter.

A short while later, Trevor found his father and mother in the dining room and politely inquired after the duchess's head.

"My head is fine, thanks to my bonnet," the duchess said, "but I simply cannot abide such an outburst of temper from Anthony. That was a perfectly good teacup he wasted—one that had been in my family for years."

"That reminds me," said the duke cheerfully, "of a story of a man who came home late one night, only to be greeted by a flying teacup and an angry wife. 'Where have you been?' his wife asks after throwing the teacup. To which the man replies—"

"Oh, do be quiet, Charles!" snapped the duchess. "I should like to think you see this state of affairs between Anthony and Natasha as a more important topic for discussion."

Then to Trevor, the duchess said, "Did you have any luck convincing her?"

"No," Trevor said, pouring himself a cup of tea. "How about you? Were you able to sway him?"

Trevor was sitting down by the time the duchess

sighed and said, "No. I'm afraid Anthony is as stubborn as he ever was. He fancies himself in love with her."

"And Lady Cecilia?"

"He said if your father was so enamored with her, then *he* could marry her." The duchess sighed. "I suppose he wants to do the honorable thing."

"And what is that?"

"He wants to tell her the truth. He thinks Lady Cecilia is an understanding sort."

Trevor snorted. "All women are understanding until things don't go their way."

After a portentous silence, the Duke of Hillsborough stared out the window, his raptured gaze upon a yellow butterfly sitting on the windowsill, its wings opening and closing slowly. The duchess gazed at her husband and sighed irritably. Trevor, feeling something was expected of him at this point, simply said, "I will speak to Anthony myself."

"And if that does no good?" asked the duchess.

With a wicked smile, Trevor shrugged and said, "Then I will be forced to take matters into my own hands."

"What are you planning, Trevor?" the duchess asked, giving him an interested look.

Trevor smiled. "Perhaps those kinds of things are best discussed between men," he said, glancing at his father.

The duchess nodded and rose slowly, her gaze stern and resting upon the duke. "Your father's thoughts have wandered into the garden to abide with day-fliers," she said, "so he won't hear a thing you have to say."

Trevor looked at his father. "Perhaps that is best," he said. "The fewer involved in this, the better. Tony will not take this sitting down, you know. I think it will be better if he is only angry with me."

The duchess gave him a shrewd smile. "Do you think your mother is too old and decrepit to get the best of a young whelp like Anthony?"

Trevor grinned. "You know better than that. I merely sought to protect you, that is all." He paused, looking at his mother, thinking she was still a beautiful and formidable woman. His curiosity peaked, he could not resist asking, "What *would* you do if Tony was furious with you?"

The duchess chuckled. "Why, I would spray him with my thirp solution," she said, and then her voice turning more serious, she added, "I may anyway."

The duchess stood. Gathering her voluminous skirts, she nodded in Trevor's direction, and, without saying another word, departed.

Trevor turned back toward his father, only to discover that he, too, had left. For the briefest instant, Trevor had a memory of himself as a young boy. It had always been like that—his parents otherwise occupied when he wanted to talk.

After finishing his tea, he stepped outside. It was a fine, fine day, and his spirits were unusually high, in spite of the lack of success his parents had had with his brother. Thinking of Tony, Trevor decided it was the ideal time to have a brotherly talk with him—seeing as how this was such a fine day and he was feeling in excellent form.

He walked down the curving, graveled path, scanning the sweeping lawn, hoping for a glimpse of his brother, when he jerked to a halt. His elated spirits began to sink. He caught a glimpse of Tony all right . . . with Natasha in his arms.

He didn't know why that scraped at his nerves. They *were* in love—at least they thought they were—but knowing Tony as he did, Trevor doubted his brother was any more in love with Tasha than *he* was. As for her . . . *smitten* would be the word he would choose to describe her feelings.

It was inevitable, he supposed, that he would find Tony with her in his arms. It was all very innocent-looking, of course, but Trevor knew Tony was not above taking an enthusiastic squeeze or two in such a situation. He did not know why the thought irritated him—considering he had had similar thoughts regarding Miss Simonov for quite some time now.

He dismissed the thought and continued up the path.

As Trevor was mulling over just how he was going to get Anthony away from Natasha for any length of time, fate dropped the answer right into his lap.

He had just taken a turn through the garden when he came upon Natasha's brothers sitting on a garden bench, looking as alike as two halves of an apple, their towheads bright in the afternoon sun. Stepping behind a tree, he paused to watch them, deciding after a moment that they were weaving a crown and garland out of greenery.

He started to turn away when something caught his attention. He looked back at the boys, his interested gaze resting on the greenery they were devoting so much attention to. He frowned. What was it about that particular greenery that bothered him? Whoa and wait a minute! Swift as lightning it hit him. That was not ordinary greenery they were using, but something he recognized from his childhood—something he had a horrible reaction to. Something he would never forget the name of: North American poison ivy.

Years ago, when Tony and Trevor were just about the same age as the twins, they had come to Marsham with their family for a visit. Upon their arrival, their uncle William had shown them the greenhouse and announced it to be the only place at Marsham they were not allowed to visit.

To soften the command, their mother had explained how her brother was a very well-known botanist who specialized in the study of poisonous plants—and that his greenhouse was filled with samples from all over the world.

"They are very, very dangerous plants," she said.

"And forbidden to both of my sons," their father had added.

Unfortunately, what they said, trying to disinterest them, was the very thing that made Trevor and Tony want to see the greenhouse.

The next morning, Trevor and Tony were up early, sneaking into Uncle William's greenhouse. A few hours later, they were itching and covered with red welts. Inflamed skin and blisters made their skin swell, and the doctor was immediately summoned. Severely lectured and warned never to go near those plants again, Trevor could only ask why Uncle William did not suffer as they did since he spent a great deal of time in the greenhouse with those plants.

"Who is to say," the doctor said, "just why it is that one person can be so affected, while another suffers no ill whatsoever?"

It was a full two weeks before they were completely recovered.

His brows narrowed as Trevor studied that horrible vine Uncle William had imported from North America. There was no doubt in his mind that it was the same vine he and Tony had tangled with as youngsters. He glanced back toward Luka and Pavel, his studious gaze taking in their hands and arms, noticing, too, there were no signs of irritation.

"Have you two imps made garlands out of that vine before?" he asked, stepping into their midst.

In unison, their heads shot up. Pavel scowled, but did not say anything. Luka looked at him for a moment, then said, "Lots of times."

Trevor frowned. *Lots of times?*

If they had ever had the reaction to those vines that he and Tony had, *once* would have been too much. He could only assume these Russians must be made of sturdier stuff than the English, not having the adverse reaction to this vine that he and Tony did.

He stepped closer, careful to keep his distance from the poisonous vine. "Who are you making that for?" he asked, praying it was not for him.

"Tasha," Luka said.

"Hmm," Trevor said, feeling the first hesitant stirring of an idea. "Do you not think something else would suit your sister better?"

The twins were still looking at him, but they said nothing.

Friendly little buggers, he thought. It didn't ride too well with him that he had to stand here humoring two boys barely out of short pants—when what he wanted to do was to put enough fear into them to make them think twice about any more mischief.

Necessity makes a man do strange things. With a cheerful countenance, he said, "There are some flowers growing along the hedge that would be perfect for weaving into garlands."

The twins faces brightened. "Flowers!" they said in unison.

"We could give Tasha flowers," said Pavel.

"And we could give this one to Anthony," Luka added.

Trevor smiled. A capital idea.

"Do you think Anthony will like it?" Pavel asked, holding the crown toward Trevor for him to see.

Trevor took a step back. "Oh, I think he will do more than like it. Much more. Why, I predict it will knock him flat on his back," Trevor said, before adding with a whisper, "for quite some time."

True to Trevor's prediction, within a short time after the crown and garland were placed on him, Anthony was down like a shot rabbit.

Immediately put to bed by the doctor, who covered the upper half of his red, swollen, and itching body with cold plasters, Anthony greedily drank down the opium drops offered him and waited for the blissful moment when he would mercifully slip into a deep and painless sleep.

Trevor, in the meantime, wasted no time in fretting over Tony's distress and declared the lovely Natasha officially under attack. A short while after Tony was put to bed, Trevor was in the garden with her, sitting on the back of the garden bench, one leg braced against the ground, the other idly swinging to-and-fro as he looked at her sitting on the bench beside him. He reached out and picked up a fat black curl that draped itself over her shoulder. He gave her what he would call a provocative smile.

Tears banked in her eyes. "Poor Tony. He is so miserable."

Trevor was unmoved. "He will get over it," he said in the blandest tones he could muster.

Natasha gave him a stunned look, one solitary tear rolling down her cheek. "There are times," she said, "when I think you are the most heartless and inconsiderate man alive. I daresay you would not be so jovial if that were you in there."

But it isn't me, he wanted to say, but instead, he gave her his wounded look and said, "I did not mean to make light of Tony's condition. It is simply that I cannot bear to see you cry. Provoking you seemed the only way." He smiled and stroked her cheek softly. "You see? Your eyes glint with anger now, not tears."

She tilted her head to one side and looked at him, then, without saying anything, she came to her feet and left the garden.

Grinning, Trevor watched her go. He disturbed her. More than she would admit. He felt his spirits soar. Things were going better than he had hoped. If this kept up, he would be back to tormenting Napoléon sooner than he planned.

Natasha walked back to the house. She didn't want to talk to Trevor anymore. He made her feel peculiar, like she was all buttery inside. She didn't understand that feeling, but she knew one thing: Trevor might give her buttery insides, but it was Tony whom she loved.

Once she left Trevor in the garden, Natasha decided to pay Tony a visit, vowing she would not spend another minute alone with his brother.

She stopped by the kitchen, finding Cook peeling turnips. Natasha wrinkled up her nose. She hated turnips.

"They are not for you, Miss Particular," Cook said. "So don't be rumpling up that bit of a nose you have." Cook stopped peeling. "What brings you in here this time of day?"

"I thought I might take Tony a bowl of soup."

"Refused to eat lunch, that one did. Sent the tray back untouched," Cook said, nodding toward the unspoiled tray.

"I'll take it to him," she said, picking it up, "and I will get him to eat it, too."

"I know you will," said Cook. "He would eat splinters if you asked him to."

A few minutes later, Natasha carried the tray into Tony's room, her smile radiant, her voice high-pitched and musical. She forgot all about Tony's odious brother lurking about the garden.

"I thought you might be hungry," she said, putting the tray on the bedside table.

Tony turned his face toward her and said, "I am not hungry, and it's a good thing. I'm too miserable to eat."

"But you must eat, Tony. Please."

He gave her a weak smile, and her heart broke at the sight of those once beautiful lips, now so swollen, cracked, and red. Indeed, his entire face and neck were in a similar state of ruin. "Does it pain you overmuch?"

"Hurts like the devil. I am miserable no matter what position I am in. I can only sleep in snatches. My body feels like it is on fire."

"Can I get you anything?"

"Not unless you can call up a miracle. The doctor left opium drops, but ordered such small doses they hardly seem to have any effect, save making me sleepy." He shifted his position, wincing and closing his eyes. Without opening them, he said, "You could find Trev for me. Tell him I want to see him."

She was startled by that. "Trevor?" she said. "You want to see Trevor?"

"Most assuredly."

"But couldn't it wait until you have rested?"

He opened his eyes to mere slits. "If you knew my brother like I know him, you would not ask that. Time is, as they say, of the essence. I want to see Trev before these drops put me to sleep. Will you find him for me?"

She reached out, intending to caress his hand, but like the rest of him that she could see, it was red and swollen. Drawing her hand back, she gave him a smile that was a little bit too eager and too bright. "Of course I will," she said, and left the room.

"You wanted to see me?" Trevor said, sauntering into Anthony's room a short while later.

Tony tried to hold his eyes open wide, but the drops were beginning to take control. "I sent for you some time ago," he said. "Where in the devil have you been?"

Trevor gave him a sly grin. "Do you really want to know?"

"Never mind. I can imagine where you've been . . . and what you've been up to. That is the reason I wanted to talk to you." He yawned.

Trevor held out his arms in surrender and dropped into the chair next to the bed. "I am all yours, little brother—but from the looks of you, you'd better hurry. Are you sure you don't want to sleep first?"

"Don't be an ass," Tony said. "You aren't being clever, you know. I know what you're up to, Trev, and it won't work."

Trevor raised his brows and gave his most innocent look. "Do you?"

"Yes, I do. It won't work, Trev. No matter how hard you try, it won't work. Natasha is mine and she will stay mine. No amount of meddling will change that. You might as well stop trying."

Trevor feigned indifference, giving a shrug. "Whatever you say, little brother."

Normally that term irritated the spit out of Tony, but today he ignored it, getting back to what he considered more important. "Just what are you planning, Trev?"

Trevor grinned. "I thought you knew."

"I have a pretty good idea," he said, "but why don't you humor a sick man and enlighten me?"

Trevor shrugged. "I am not planning marriage to two women, if that's what's bothering you. You alone have that distinction."

"Bloody hell!" Tony said, raising up on his elbows. He groaned and collapsed back against the bed. "My God! Even my elbows hurt." He sighed, as if willing himself to relax. When he spoke, his voice was calmer, more subdued. "I am not going to marry both of them. I told you that before."

"So you plan to send Cecilia packing and marry your little Tartar?"

"Yes, damn your hide—and it is none of your business."

"And you think Natasha will be happy living a pauper's life here on this crumbling estate?"

Tony yawned. "I do, but that's not my concern at the moment. *You* are. Stay away from her, Trev." He glared at Trevor; it was obvious to him that Tony was fighting to keep his eyes open. "And keep your bloody hands off her."

Tony yawned again, and Trevor saw he was sinking, the fight going out of him. "It might look strange if I bolted every time she came into my sight," he said.

Tony gave a snort. "I have a vivid picture of that," he said.

Trevor laughed.

"I'm warning you, Trev. Keep your distance—and keep your lecherous hands in your pockets."

Trevor was still laughing when he came to his feet. "As much as it pains me to say it, I have *never* had my hands in my pockets. Her pockets maybe . . ."

"Bloody bastard," Tony said.

Trevor laughed. "It runs in the family."

Tony's eyes drooped, taking some of the threat out of his words. "You heard what I said."

"You wound me, brother."

Closing his eyes and apparently no longer able to fight the comfort of sleep, Tony murmured, "Not half as bad as I will if you so much as lay a finger on her."

Trevor grinned. "You should be hoping that a finger is all I lay on her."

"Damn you—"

Trevor laughed. "Sleep well, little brother," he said, and quietly left the room.

CHAPTER
❧ TEN ❧

Trevor soon learned that declaring the lovely Natasha under attack and making any headway with the Russian beauty were two different breeds of cat.

If there was anything he felt he knew, it was women. And he knew them well enough to know that what worked for one woman, didn't necessarily work for another.

It was time to call upon his amorous reservoir, where past events had been organized, classified, hierarchized, and arranged—after all, he was the son of a scientist wasn't he?—if only a part-time one.

Without further thought, he called upon all resources in order to better confront what he named a *lunatic project*, going after Natasha with all the sham eagerness he could muster.

After spending only two weeks with her aboard his ship—and endeavoring to win her favor—he had realized one thing: He hadn't gained much ground.

This was due, he suspected, to Natasha's being a woman whose idea of love was built upon the flimsy foundation of romanticism. For a woman like her, love was the chief reason for existence, as well as marriage, family, and children. Trevor did not have a lot of time here. He had to make her fall in love with him, and fast. The only way to do that was to be what she wanted.

He frowned, trying to gather his wits about this undertaking. He had no experience with women who would rather blush and hold hands than take a tumble in bed. The more he thought about it, the more he knew Natasha was the kind who would settle for nothing less than burning lips, vows of undying love, torture over her beloved's absence, as well as a host of assorted agonies and frustrations. The more he thought about it, the more he realized there was nothing else to be done. He would have to go through with it.

After giving it further thought, he decided the best way to win a woman of this type was to be the tortured hero—tortured heroes being something Trevor felt he could be quite good at. *Love is blind,* he thought, then he snorted. He didn't care if it was blind or not . . . just as long as it put blinders on Natasha Simonov.

The only hitch Trevor found in his plan was that he had to be uncomfortably close to her, and that was the problem. He was as red-blooded as the next man, and being near a woman who looked like her kept his thoughts on things better left alone.

* * *

The next morning he was in a foul temper, but he did manage to mellow out somewhat by the time he saw Natasha at breakfast. After paying his respects to a sleeping Tony, he went to his brother's study to think things through. As any sea captain knew, one had to chart a course before getting the voyage underway.

The more he thought about it, the more he knew he would have to appeal to Natasha's tender side, and he counted on the very hopelessness of their situation to fuel her interest—and hopefully, before too long, her love. His mind at rest, his plan in motion, he came to his feet. *One does what he has to do. . . .*

Without a whit of conscience Trevor went in search of Natasha, thinking *amor ludens*, love is a game.

Natasha spent the morning with Anthony, reading to him from the latest London newspaper and trying to make him laugh when she told him stories about her brothers. When he began to doze off—the effects of a healthy dose of opium drops—she quietly left his room to wander aimlessly around the house and gardens, finding no one about that wasn't otherwise occupied. Luka and Pavel had gone off with the duke to look for butterfly cocoons, and the duchess was instructing Harry the gardener on the finer points of rose fertilization.

For a long while, Natasha sat in the window seat in the parlor, gazing outside, watching the duchess's animated gestures, the way her face lit up whenever she talked about roses. Natasha was wondering if there would ever be anything in her life that excited her as much as that, when she heard someone enter the room.

"What are you doing inside on such a lovely day?"

Trevor. The one person she did not want to see. "I came in here to be alone with my thoughts."

"I'm glad I found you," he said, coming further into the room, but still she did not turn to look at him. "No one should be alone on a day as lovely as this." He stopped beside her, taking her by the hand and drawing her to her feet. "Come on," he said.

Reluctantly she went with him. "Where are we going?"

"For a walk. You need some fresh air and some color on your cheeks. You are far too pale. If you aren't careful, you will give Mrs. MacDougal another body to look after."

She was too preoccupied at the moment to carry on any sort of conversation. He could see that quite clearly. He could also see that her dark-lashed eyes were quite the most magnificent he had ever seen. He led her outside to stroll along a graveled path that wound through a grassy stretch of lawn dotted with wandering ducks. As they walked, the fullness of her skirts thumped against his leg, and he glanced over at her to see if she was as aware of it as he.

Jet black curls escaped the curve of her bonnet, the vivid green of the bow a stark contrast against the milky skin of her throat. The difference of color between her ivory flesh, black hair and brows, the apple greenness of her dress, and the rosy tint of her mouth seemed to draw his thoughts as easily as it drew the breath from his body.

He stole another look at her and felt a twinge of remorse. There was a fragileness to her that made him think she might shatter if he pushed her too much. Then he thought of the letter of marque.

She glanced back toward the house. "How far are we going?"

"Why? Are you afraid to walk with me?"

"No. That is, I don't think so."

He stopped and turned to look at her. "What would it take for you to know?" he asked, stepping closer, backing her against an oak tree, his arms coming up to rest on each side of her head, bracing himself against the tree.

She was breathless and half laughing, as if she did not know if she should be frightened or not.

"Perhaps you should be afraid of me," he said, rubbing his thumb along the contours of her ear, then stroking the sensitive skin beneath it. His hand slipped around, coming behind her neck.

She drew in a sharp breath, her eyes opening wide. "I don't know why you are doing this," she said.

"Don't you?" Without another word, he leaned closer, one of his knees slightly bent, one hand shifting from the tree to join the other, forming a cradle for her head.

"Don't you know, little wonder, what it is that makes a man do crazy things he knows he has no business doing?"

"No," she said, her heart pounding like surf in her ears. Her body seemed to melt against a slow-spreading, intense heat. There was such strength here in this man, in the feelings he evoked. No more could she deny his presence, his existence, or her fascination. He was like no one she had ever known. He both attracted and frightened her. In every other way, he overwhelmed her. She did not know how to behave around him—and found she had difficulty deciding if he was serious, or simply amusing himself.

She gave him a curious look. "I think we should go back now."

"Why?" he asked, the word coming as a warm, penetrating breath that seemed to announce the nearness of his body, which had moved even closer.

This was no game he played, and she pressed herself back against the tree, closing her eyes—as if by doing so she could escape the heat in his gaze, the gentle nudging of his thigh pressing against her legs, the unexpected and strange feeling of masculine flesh touching her. There was promise there. And a warning. She was unprepared for this, unschooled. Indecision had her in its clutch. *Go! Stay!* Her mind gave her no peace. Confused, uncertain . . . she felt the burn of tears against the back of her nose.

His mouth was suddenly upon hers, a feather-light brush, and then it was gone. As slowly as he had come, he drew away. She remained as she had been, breathless and afraid, pressed tightly back against the tree, her eyes closed, the imprint of his hard male body still burning where it had touched her, the memory of his kiss lingering in her mind.

Her knees buckled and she had to fight to keep herself on her feet. How strange that she rarely felt anger, yet now she could only call her feelings just that.

Her eyes flew open. "Is there nothing sacred to you?" she asked, not bothering to mask the anger in her eyes. "Why must you make light of something pure and holy?"

"Is that what I was doing?"

She ducked beneath his arm and stepped away from the tree. "You play with feelings like a cat with a mouse. You tempt and tease with no thought of the consequences." She turned to look at him, to see what effect her words had upon him.

She saw a flare of emotion, something stark and remote, something close to pain but far more lonely and bleak. It was as if her words struck something dark and painful within him. There was so much she did not know about this man, so much mystery that surrounded him.

Pulled away from her own feelings and anger, she was drawn to the fleeting shadow of sadness that seemed to pass over him. She thought for a moment he was warning her, warning that he was going to hurt her, that it was unavoidable, and that he was sorry. *If you are smart, you will run from here and keep on running,* she thought, and she would have done just that . . . if she were smart.

She turned away from him, but he caught her by the arm, turning her back around. "I was not teasing," he said. "Perhaps I wanted you to understand what is going on here. Call it a warning, if you like. Whatever you call it, it is the last one I'm going to give you."

There was a hardness, a determination in his eyes that held her captive, making it impossible for her to pull her gaze away. "Is that supposed to make me feel better? Am I supposed to admire your honesty?"

"You will think whatever you wish to think."

"What I think is that you are like the snake who hisses before he strikes. You give warning only when it is too late."

Her words seemed to have some effect upon him, for his expression softened and his thumb came up to stroke her lower lip. "And is it . . . too late?"

She could not answer, for in truth, she did not know.

As quickly as they had entered upon this foray into sensual madness, he pulled back, his voice taking on a tone of lightness that she found disconcerting. "I have kept you away too long. It is time we went back."

Instead of agreeing with him and making a bolt for the house as she knew she ought to do, she asked, "Why? What made you feel that way all of a sudden?"

"It was a mistake to bring you down here."

"Was it?"

"Yes."

"Why did you?"

"I wanted to talk to you."

"About what?"

"Love."

"Love?"

"Does that surprise you?"

"Yes, it does. You think it shouldn't?"

"And if I do?"

She laughed. "You forget. We had this discussion before. You doubted my feelings for Tony at the time, I believe."

He gave her a look that sliced through all pretension. "I wasn't referring to Tony."

His words seemed to shatter her. She did not understand how he could do it. How could he unnerve her with so few words, or a simple look?

Her heartbeat doubled, pumping anxiety into her veins. "You weren't? If not Tony, then who . . .?" She stopped, pausing in midsentence, then she looked at him, her gaze resting upon his profile. "You," she whispered.

He turned to look at her, his expression cynical, his eyes hard. "Does that surprise you? Do you find it strange that someone like me could feel something as emotional as love?"

"No, you just don't seem like a man who would share such things with a woman. Being a lover and falling in love are not the same thing." She paused, remembering something, and asked, "Why would I find it strange that you might find love?"

He sighed, looking off to stare out across the rolling expanse of green that lay all about them. Suddenly he remembered what he was about. With a flashing sense of regret, a mask settled over his face; the face of the man who looked at her was a stranger. "Perhaps you should because I do," he said, wondering if she noticed that even his voice sounded different.

"I don't believe you."

"It's true," he said. "Love seems to come to everyone, but not to me," he went on to say, raising one eyelid slightly, to steal a quick glance at her, snapping it shut when she looked at him.

"But it will come to you," she said. "I know it will."

"It may come, but it won't stay," he said. "I've been hurt before."

"But, perhaps next time . . ."

"For me," he said, feeling like the vilest blackguard who ever dishonored a lady, "there will never be a next time. . . . I could never love again."

"What do you mean?"

With a dejected sigh, he looked away. "That is part of the agony . . . The knowing—knowing you will never again feel that wonderful sensation."

"You mean you really have loved before?"

"More than once."

"I had no idea," she said. Then placing her hand on his arm, she added, "You must not give up. Love—true love—will come to you. I am certain of it. Why, you are young and quite handsome. Your life is far from over. Any woman would be thrilled to have a man such as you."

He looked at her with a long, sad face . . . and the

faintest glimmer of last hope in his eyes. "Any woman?"

"Of course."

"Would . . .?" He paused, until he thought the drama of the moment was sufficiently stretched, then he went on. "No, never mind. It's hopeless. I know it could never happen. I'm too repulsive."

He heard her indrawn breath of surprise. "Trevor, how can you possibly say that? You aren't repulsive. Not at all. Why, you are a very handsome man. Surely you know that. Now, tell me. What is hopeless about it?"

He looked at her. "Could you have a man like me? *Would* you have me?"

Natasha pulled back, then looking off, she began picking at something on her skirt. "Well, not me . . . I mean, I wasn't—I wasn't thinking of me exactly . . . But only because my heart is already given, you understand."

"I understand." The hope faded from his eyes. He did his best to look even more pathetic than before.

She leaned toward him, placing her hand upon his sleeve, giving it an encouraging squeeze. "Please don't give up, Trevor. You must not."

Now a shot of bitterness to show my wound still bleeds. "Why shouldn't I? It's hopeless. I'm hopeless. I can't even commit suicide."

She gasped. "Suicide? Oh, Trevor. You mustn't even think such a thing."

He gave her a sad, dejected look. "It's too late for that, I'm afraid. You see, I've done more than just think. I've tried it before, you know."

"No!" she gasped, her hand coming up to her throat. "You wouldn't! You haven't!" Her hand was back on his arm now. "Oh, Trevor . . . Tell me you haven't."

He shook his head sadly. "I'm afraid I can't do that. The truth is, I *have* tried it before. More than once."

"More than once?"

"Yes."

"How many times?"

"Twice, to be exact."

Her hand flew to her breast, which was heaving like bellows, and for a moment Trevor was distracted.

"But—but you're still here," she said. "And fit. What happened?"

"The first time the rope broke. The second time the gun misfired. After that I was too much a coward to try again," he said, sounding overly pathetic, even to his calloused ears.

For a moment he wondered if he might have overdone it. He looked away, closing his eyes as if the emotion of recall was too much for him, hoping above all else that she was as naive as he suspected.

It didn't take him long to learn that she was.

"Oh, Trevor. You aren't a coward," she said. "Why, you're the bravest of men. I know you are."

He opened his eyes and looked at her. "How can you possibly say something like that? The bravest of men? Look at me. I am nothing but a shell of a man . . . nothing but a coward."

"You aren't."

"I am."

"No . . ."

"Please," he said, with a wave of his hand. "Whatever you do or say, please don't try to coddle me."

"I'm not. You kidnapped me, didn't you? That is something no coward would do."

Or any man in his right mind, either. "Yes, but that doesn't change anything. My life is over. I know it. I don't even have the right— Oh, never mind," he said, suddenly finding he couldn't bear to look at her face, to see the look of absolute trust there.

"The right *what*?" Natasha asked.

"Nothing. I shouldn't have said that."

"You should talk about what you are feeling, Trevor. That's why you still hurt, because you won't let the pain out. It is like a wound that still festers. You must release it . . . talk about it. Now, tell me what you were going to say. You don't have the right *what*?"

"Feelings," he said, sounding eternally sad.

"Feelings? What do you mean, feelings?"

"There's something wrong with me, Natasha. I don't have those kinds of feelings for a woman anymore."

"What kinds of feelings?"

"*Those* kind," he said, with a look that spoke volumes.

"Oh," Natasha said softly. "*Those* kind." She apparently lost herself in thought for a moment, then her expression brightened. "How do you know you don't?"

How do I know? Good God! No one can be this dense! He felt like throwing his hands up. What did she want? For him to draw her a picture? When this was over, he was going to throttle Tony. He sighed, slipping the mask back into place. "Because I know. I've tried."

"Tried what?"

The usual things . . . the usual perversions . . . fornication . . . he wanted to say, just to shock her. "I've tried kissing a woman."

"And?"

"And nothing . . . I felt nothing."

"*Nothing?*"

"Absolutely nothing. Not even a spark. Not so much as a tremble."

"Oh, dear."

"You see? It's hopeless."

"No, it isn't." She was looking thoughtful again, then she said, "Just how long has it been since you tried?"

He sighed. "I don't know. Two or three years, I suppose. What difference does it make? I try not to think about *those* kinds of things anymore."

"Well, there you have it," she said, with a snap of her fingers. "It's been such a long time, you don't even remember for certain. If it's been that long, things may have changed, you know. You mustn't give up. I think you should try again."

He made a disgusted noise and looked off, picking a small branch from a tree, absently plucking at its leaves. "Who would you suggest I try it with? Mrs. MacDougal?"

She must have had a vivid picture of that, and the reality of it must have been what made her laugh. "Not Mrs. Mac, perhaps, but there are any number of women around here," she said.

"And all of them are either old, ugly, or married," he replied.

"I'm sure there must be someone . . ."

"What about you?" he asked, giving her a soft, woefully pleading look, one that was filled to the brim with hopes and aspirations.

She stopped walking, jerking to a halt. She stared down at the ground. "I—I don't think . . ."

He looked at her for a moment and then turned away from her to stand alone, giving her his best imitation of a rejected man with no hope left. "You see? You're worse than most. You shy away from me, you reject me *before* we even try."

She caught up to him, touching him on the arm. "Trevor, I am not rejecting you, and I'm not shying away."

He turned, looking at her, his voice going suddenly

soft and drowsy, praying there was a glimmer of hope shining in his eyes. "Then you'll kiss me?"

She looked to be having some sort of inward battle with herself, then at last, she sighed. "All right. I will kiss you," she said, "but only to help you, you understand."

"I understand," he said, taking her in his arms. His closeness, his very breath, began to warm her. She stole a quick glance at his face and felt herself undone. Her breath caught in her throat and she felt the beat of her pulse humming in her ears. His lips touched the hollow of one cheek and then the other. She swallowed and swayed against him, unprepared for the rush of feelings the touch of his lips made against hers, full and searching, his tongue touching hers, probing, encouraging.

She gripped his arms, afraid she would fall. The world seemed to fall away beneath her feet. Something warm and liquid suffused her, flowing through her veins and seeming to hum, like the strings of a harp. Everywhere he touched her, she burned, and without thinking she found herself pressing closer, seeking the comfort, the protective hardness of him. *Trevor . . . What are you doing to me?*

She almost whimpered when he pulled away. She could not keep herself from looking at him, but she could not read the expression on his face. Had that kiss touched him? Did it make him feel the same things she felt?

For a long time he stood there, gazing down into her face. The look unnerved her and made her feel suddenly shy—and oh so aware of him as a man.

Suddenly self-conscious, she smoothed her skirts. "Did you feel anything?" she asked softly.

"I don't think so," he said.

Disappointment flooded her. He didn't feel it. She felt so ashamed. She wanted to run from here, to run and keep on running, but she felt the warmth of his hand upon her arm, felt him turning her in his arms. She looked up into that face that disturbed her so.

"Perhaps there was the slightest tremor. Perhaps if we tried again ... ?"

CHAPTER
❦ ELEVEN ❦

It was a mistake.

A big mistake to kiss him. She knew it the moment her lips met his, the moment his mouth invaded hers, sending her thoughts spinning and reeling off in the opposite direction from Tony. The thought filled her with panic. Weakly she pushed at him, trying to break the kiss, to loosen his hold upon her before she was too helpless to resist him at all. But he held her against him, ignoring her protest, as if he knew, more than she, that she wanted this.

She moaned and slumped against him in defeat, not really caring about anything, save the warm comfort of his body, the terrible pounding in her chest. What had happened to her? What had she done? She had been honest. Honest with herself. She had wanted this, had wanted it for some time, and he knew it. *No!* her mind screamed. *No!*

Suddenly, when she least expected it, he broke the kiss and stepped away.

She brought her trembling hands up to her mouth, unable to tear her gaze from his face. Deep blue eyes seemed to stare into her very soul. She knew what he was asking. How could she have allowed this to happen?

"No," she whispered, taking a step backward.

His hand came up to stroke the curve of her cheek. "Poor innocent Natasha. So confused. So afraid. You want me, but you don't want to."

"No," she whispered again. "It's not true. It's Tony I want. Not you."

"You can lie to me all you want, but you can't lie to yourself. You aren't in love with Tony any more than Mrs. MacDougal is. What you felt was nothing more than infatuation—short-lived at that. Even now, that is wearing pitifully thin."

"You are wrong. I do love him. I do!" But the words sounded tinny and not very convincing, even to her own ears. She stared at him. Could it be? Could she be in love with both brothers? No, it was impossible. *I do love Tony!* she thought, as if thinking the words made it so. "I do love Tony."

"So you say. But it's your face that tells me the truth," he said, his arms going around her, drawing her against him. "It isn't love for Tony you're feeling right now, but desire for me. No matter what you do. No matter how hard you try. You won't be able to hide your feelings for much longer. I bother you. I bother you, sweet Natasha, and we both know it."

He stepped back, releasing her. Then he turned away.

She closed her eyes, willing her rapid breathing to

stop. When she opened her eyes, he was gone. For a stunned moment she did not move. Her feelings were on edge; she felt at war with herself. She did not know if what she felt was relief or disappointment. He did bother her, just as he'd said. She didn't want him to leave her like this, but then, neither did she want him to stay. She had never felt so confused.

She leaned back against the wrinkled bark of the oak tree. She knew before she closed her eyes that what Trevor had said was true. She did desire him. She loved his brother, but she desired him. God help her, but she did.

She pushed away from the tree, walking slowly down the narrow path, stumbling along as if she could not see—and in a way, she supposed, she was a bit blind.

Suddenly the full weight of what was happening pressed down upon her, crushing her spirits. Her heart throbbed painfully in her breast. A dull pounding began to punish her head, its steady rhythm stirring her to self-condemnation. How could she? If she loved Tony, then why was she having all these strange feelings about Trevor? Why was it that when she went to sleep at night, it wasn't thoughts of Tony that filled her head but visions of his brother?

All this thinking didn't solve much, but it did help her reach one conclusion: There must be something terribly wrong with a woman who can fancy herself in love with two men at the same time.

She continued to walk for a long time. Gradually the throbbing in her heart subsided, but the throbbing in her head grew worse. Tears she did not know she cried began to splash upon the bodice of her dress. She had never felt so wretched, so worthless. She let the tears flow unheeded as she mulled over what she should do.

Crying must have been good for her, she decided, for

her spirits began to rise as she let the surrounding countryside enchant her, as it always did. All about her fields of buttercups whirled and danced in the warm breeze, while trailing plumes of weeping willow rode the steady ripples of the River Cor.

Sensible, as always, she surmised that she was too rattled now to think straight. A biscuit and a strong cup of Cook's tea would do her more good than all this thinking and crying. With a deep, resigned sigh, she turned her steps toward Marsham, discovering the Duke and Duchess of Hillsborough were preparing to return to London. After bidding them a fond farewell, she went to the kitchen, still feeling she needed the tea.

She found Cook lifting a boiling kettle from the stove. The smell of metal polish filled the room. With one quick glance she saw the emery paper Cook used, and saw, too, the gleaming brass and polished black metal of the stove, the way the knobs and hinges shone. As if waiting for her, a teapot stood on the hob keeping warm.

When Natasha entered, Cook looked up, her strong brown face damp with perspiration, her magnificent bosom heaving from exertion. "Well, bless my buttons! What brings you in here this time of day, looking like you are as lost as last week?"

"I came for a cup of tea," Natasha said.

The lustrous dark eyes beneath prominent gray-black brows fastened upon her. Despite Cook's sixty someodd years, she was a perceptive woman. With a few tut-tuts and several matriarchal words about Natasha's looking "pale as yesterday's pudding," Cook said bluntly, "Two shillings says there's a man involved."

Natasha poured herself a cup of tea. "Would you believe two?" she said, and quickly left the room before Cook could raise her bid and reflect upon that.

A short time later, she was in the old earl's conservatory, surrounded by his beloved plants, a cup of steaming tea in one hand, two crumpets in the other. She placed the tea and crumpets on a nearby table, then pinched a few leaves from a terra-cotta pot filled with trailing vines of ivy before settling herself into an ancient, sagging rocking chair.

After she finished her tea, she placed the cup on the table next to her and began to rock slowly, her gaze traveling around the room, seeing the signs of neglect upon the earl's beloved plants.

I really must see to his plants, she told herself, feeling a sudden urge to lose herself in work. *Tomorrow,* she thought. *Tomorrow, I'll put the conservatory in order, then I'll start on the greenhouse.*

A few moments later, Natasha nodded off to sleep.

When Mrs. MacDougal went to call her for dinner, she could not find her, so she enlisted the help of Trevor and the twins. Trevor, taking charge of the hunt, sent the twins outside to check the garden and stables. After a thorough search of the house, in which he found no trace of Natasha, he remembered he had forgotten to look in the conservatory.

He found her there, asleep in a great rocking chair that was much too large for her. Coming to stand beside her, he looked down, suddenly struck by her youthfulness. Not only her youthfulness, but her innocence, her purity, her trustful nature, the almost artless seductiveness. There was no pretense about her. And because of that, his feelings seemed to go much deeper than he desired.

Seeing her thus, he realized he felt remorse for what he was about. It was the first time in his life that he could ever remember having a twinge of anything remotely related to regret. From an early age on, he, as the duke's son and heir, had been taught to make decisions for the good of the family name, giving no thought to the consequences. It was a code of survival among the peerage, sort of an unsung doctrine of putting the cause first.

She stirred in her sleep, mumbling something incoherent, and his attention was drawn back to her once again. He could not help marveling at the purity of her skin, the milky white softness of a cheek and throat that seemed to beg him to push aside the layers of her clothing to see the glorious texture beneath.

His gaze rested upon the gently rounded curves of her breasts before coming back up to savor her face. There was something about a face like hers, something that made a man want to do crazy things—things that he, of all people, could not indulge.

He had his family to think about, his title, the future of the Hamilton estates. His was a cold world, and cruel. There was no room in it for something as soft as emotion. Soft feelings could destroy a man. It was Natasha's happiness or his. No compromise.

Still, even as he made the decision to go ahead with his original plan of seduction, he could not help thinking it would be something he would later lament.

True, he did regret what he was about to do, but it was an emotion that was not strong enough to deter him. As if wanting to ease his conscience a bit, he stroked the peach-bloom softness of her cheek, his fingers dropping down to rest against the warm cove of her shoulder and neck.

"Little wonder, you deserve much more," he whispered softly.

Without another thought, he turned and quietly left the room, never looking back, for if he had, he would have seen her eyes were open . . . and following him with a gaze that was every bit as violet as it was blue.

Natasha was restless over the next few days. Her appetite waned, and at night sleep was slow to come. As she had done every day since Tony was put to bed, she went to him, sitting by his bed for long periods of time, reading to him, or just talking, telling herself she loved this man and wanted to be his wife, while the most disturbing thoughts of his brother continued to plague her.

Natasha had been in the greenhouse all morning and was returning to the house for a bit of tea when she came across Cook and Mrs. MacDougal, picking herbs in the garden. Such culinary jobs were normally left to Cook, but on occasion, Mrs. Mac could be seen lending a hand. Over parsley and thyme, Cook was giving Mrs. Mac an accounting of the latest gossip from the kitchen help.

Hearing her name mentioned, Natasha drew up short.

"Seems the word is out about our young miss having spent a fortnight in the company of Hellfire Haverleigh. Mark my word, it will reach the village soon . . . if it hasn't already," Cook said.

"Dear me," said Mrs. Mac. "I had hoped to keep it quiet and spare the poor lassie's feelings."

"It isn't her feelings I'd be worried about if I were you," said Cook. "The minute word of this reaches the village, that poor innocent will be branded a hussy."

Mrs. Mac's chest swelled with indignation, and for a moment it looked as if her buttons might not survive the stress. Normally Natasha would have found this quite endearing, but today she hardly noticed. Her brow knitted with worry, she turned away from the garden, her thirst for a cup of tea quenched.

Without making a sound, she left the garden as silently as she had entered it.

Rooks fluttered and called from the elm tree nearby, and from the orchard a dozen or so starlings burst into flight, but Natasha paid them little heed. She was preoccupied with what she had just heard. She knew what damage gossip could do her.

Returning to the greenhouse, she discovered the cats had gotten in, breaking the branches off several geraniums and digging up the anemones. With a weary sigh, she set about putting things to right, pausing for a few minutes to look out the window at her brothers, who climbed up a ladder to the top of the hayrick, then slid down. Life was so simple when you were young.

I mustn't give in to this, she thought. *I must go on as if nothing has happened. I mustn't imagine the worst, just because a few kitchen hands have nothing better to do. Ignore it, and it will be forgotten.*

It was late the next afternoon, when the last rosy streaks of departing sun bathed the countryside in gold, that Natasha discovered the gossip had spread far too wide and too fast to be forgotten. Thinking a ride would do her good, she went to the stables, hoping she would not encounter the likes of Ned.

Entering the dark interior of the stable, she paused just inside the door, feeling a coldness ripple over her, feeling, too, the first creeping apprehensions of fear. It was an instinctual warning that said run. Yet she was paralyzed, unable to move.

She thought she heard something and paused. A swishing sound came to her out of the darkness, a sound like someone walking through tall grass. The sound got closer now, and she recognized it as someone treading lightly on the moist humus floor.

Her mind told her to leave, to run as fast as she could and not look back, but her feet seemed rooted where they stood. A dark shadow passed over her; the sound of raspy breathing reached her ears. Her nostrils flared at the unknown scent of someone standing nearby. And then a man stepped into the fading light, the hollows of his face appearing grotesque and misshapen in the half-light. She stared into the dark recesses where his eyes should be, following the sharp line of his hawklike nose, the thin slash of a sneering mouth. She knew that face. Then he stepped more fully into the light.

Ned.

Her hand flew to her chest and she released a long-held breath. "Heavens, Ned. You frightened me out of my wits!"

"Why should it scare you to be in the barn with me? From what I hear, you have plenty of experience being alone with a man."

She gasped, anger surging through her. So he had heard. This man had always made her uneasy, but now, knowing what he did, it seemed to give him a terrible power. She jerked her head back and looked into his face, seeing a nasty gleam in his eyes. "I think you are speaking out of place. What I do is none of your business. You have no right to speak to me as you have."

He laughed, the sharp sound of it grating across her nerves like a rasp. "No right? Don't be putting on your hoity-toity airs with me. I've got eyes and ears. I've seen plenty, and I've heard even more. The only difference between you and any common trollop is that you prefer to keep it in the family . . . spread your legs for both of them, don't you?"

She drew back her hand and slapped him. Hard.

The look in his eyes was murderous, but he kept his silence.

"You may have eyes and ears, but it's quite obvious you haven't any brains, for if you did, you would know that one word from me and Lord Anthony would have you dismissed."

"But you won't tell Lord Anthony," he said hatefully, "for if you do, he would know the gossip is out and that would mean he would have to do the honorable thing and force a marriage between you . . . or maybe between you and his brother. You don't want that, 'cause you ain't made your mind up. Don't know which one you want, do you?"

She took a step backward. "Stay away from me," she said, her voice trembling. "If you so much as breathe in my presence again I'll tell him . . . even if I have to marry the devil to do it."

Before he could say anything more, she whirled around and ran from the stable, the sound of his mocking laughter echoing in her ears.

As she left the stables and headed toward the gardens, Natasha saw Trevor standing by the statuary. Not in the mood to talk to him, she turned down the path that led to the greenhouse. The moment she stepped inside, Trevor was there, following her through the door, reaching for her arm. "Whoa now. Not so fast."

She looked down at her arm, then at him. "Will you let go?"

"You don't think I'm going to let you get away from me that easily, do you?"

"Leave me alone, Trevor. Stay away from me."

"Can't," was all he said.

She sighed, weariness seeping into her bones. "What do you want?"

Trevor looked down at the lovely face turned toward his, the blue-violet eyes that studied him with such scorn. For a moment he forgot what it was that he did want. "I'm not quite certain," he said. Then with a grin, he added, "But there are several interesting possibilities floating around in my head about now."

"Well, sink them," she said. "If it has anything to do with you, I'm not interested."

Hearing the chilly turndown and seeing the adorable—though irritated—expression on her face, he laughed and said softly, "Don't get angry. I'm not going to have my way with you."

"That is the first truthful thing I have heard you say. Now, leave me alone. Can you not understand that you are not wanted?"

"Can you not understand that a challenge like that draws a man like me?"

"I don't *want* to draw you! I don't want anything to do with you."

She threw him a scorching look, turned away contemptuously, and began stacking a group of scattered clay pots. Why did she allow this man to irritate her? Why did she fall so easily into each trap he laid? Why couldn't she simply ignore him?

She had a mental flash of the way he looked. *That's why*, something in her head seemed to reply.

Bah! she thought. *He does not interest me in the least. His egotism is monumental. He is too swaggering. Too self-assured. His tongue is too loose and too flippant for my taste. What a bore he was to think a few coddling remarks, a few well-placed gropes, would have her simpering at his feet.* But even as she thought this, she knew there was something about him that attracted her as well.

Ruthlessness, perhaps.

* * *

Trevor folded his arms over his chest, his eyes reflective as he watched her slam the pots around. "Careful," he said, "or you'll end up breaking more than you salvage."

"When I want your advice, I'll ask for it," she said.

He smiled, marveling at his luck in being called into this situation between Tony and Lady Cecilia. He had never met anyone like this peppery-tongued Tartar, with her violet eyes and her raven black hair. She was different. Original. Innocently seductive as hell. He wanted her. There was little doubt about that. This realization shook him. No woman had evoked such feelings in him before. He could not help wondering if any other woman ever would.

He stepped around the pots and pulled her into his arms, knowing his grip was too strong and powerful, his mouth too hard and unrelenting. He wanted to master her, and he knew Natasha was not strong enough to push him away, not strong enough to stop herself from kissing him back. And then it did not seem to matter, for her arms went around his neck and she returned each kiss with all the fervor and excitement he aroused in her. He could tell her head was spinning. He knew the minute her knees went weak. He groaned, leaning into her, his knee pressing against her. He had to stop. Now. *Stop, or take her . . .*

When he pulled back, she had to grab his arm to keep from falling. He did not completely release her, but simply took a small step back, gazing down into her face. "What are you doing to me?" he asked, remembering he had come as a seducer, feeling as if he had ended up being seduced instead. He forced himself to remember what was at stake here, what his purpose in coming to Marsham was.

Her look was puzzled and full of confusion. "Why are you doing this?" she asked.

His gaze traveled over her upturned face as if he were committing each inch of it to memory. "I wish to God I knew," he said.

A moment later he turned and walked out of the greenhouse, leaving Natasha standing there among the scattered clay pots.

CHAPTER
❧ TWELVE ❧

Molière said, "Prudence is always in season."

Lady Cecilia must have read Molière.

As luck would have it, it was about this point in time that Lady Cecilia decided to make another jaunt into the country to visit her cousin, who happened to live near the village of Fairfields, which was no more than a stone's throw from Applecore. Once there, her cousin, Lady Sarah Mayfield—whom everyone called Sally—considered it her Christian duty to bring Lady Cecilia up to date on the latest gossip, which included a tidbit or two about the new Earl of Marsham and his obvious infatuation with his ward.

Lady Cecilia was a mild sort, not given to suspicion or jealousy. She was a happy, placid person, a woman whose soft-spoken kindness was too often taken for a lack of backbone—about as much as her tendency to overlook things was taken for lack of mental capacity. There were those who agreed wholeheartedly with Lord Anthony's surmising—that Lady Cecilia was as brainless as a feather duster.

Brimming with trust, Lady Cecilia sat in the garden having tea with her cousin Sally on the afternoon of her arrival. An Albertine rose drooped lazily over the garden wall, and overhead, the sky was bursting with color—pink, gold, lilac, laced with just a pinch of green that made Lady Cecilia wonder if the heavens above didn't reflect the apple green lushness of the world below.

As Lady Cecilia listened to Sally, she nodded from time to time, just to show she was following what Sally said. She was considered to be a most fortunate woman, for she possessed an inordinate amount of wealth. There was something else she possessed as well, but, unlike her wealth, this other blessing went unnoticed. It was an unknown fact all right—but in truth, Lady Cecilia possessed a soft, quiet kind of beauty as well. One look and any passerby could see immediate evidence of her wealth and breeding, but one had to dig a little deeper, look a little harder, to find evidence of any beauty.

It wasn't that Lady Cecilia tried to hide her comeliness, but more that she did it by accident. This was due to the fact that she simply did not know what to do with it. Possessing the typical English beauty—china blue eyes, golden blond hair, skin as white and delicate as thistledown—she was a pale icon, difficult to see on a sunny day. Unfortunately Lady Cecilia's favorite color was yellow, and while she possessed a large number of the most fashionable gowns in London, they were mostly yellow—a color that did absolutely nothing for her, save making her hair look as dull as unpolished brass and her face yellow-cheeked and sallow. Her taste in clothes was as dull as a sermon, and if there was any truth at all to the saying, "Good clothes open all doors," Lady Cecilia would have most assuredly found every one slammed in her face.

Looking as washed out as an old dimity dress, and finding herself still a little weary from her drive from London, she sat nestled in a bower of summer blooms, creaking in a rocking chair, listening to her cousin's suspicions.

When Sally finished the last of her tale, in which she brought Lord Anthony's doings to light, Lady Cecilia discounted the whole of it. "Oh, posh! The girl is his ward, Sally. What would you have him do? Toss the poor, homeless child out on her ear?"

"Child?" Sally said with a croak, almost unseating herself when she shot forward in her chair. "*Child?* Have you met her?"

"Well . . . not exactly. You see, she wasn't at Marsham the time my parents and I called upon Tony."

"How convenient," Sally said. "Then where did you get the idea she was a child?"

Lady Cecilia blinked. "Why, from Tony, of course."

"Of course," Sally said, falling back into her chair and crossing her arms across her middle, a smug, knowing look upon her face. "And, naturally you believed him?"

Lady Cecilia nodded. "Why should I not?"

"Ride over to Marsham and take one good look at this *child* he is being so benevolent toward, and then you tell me," Sally said. "The girl is as ripe as any plum—a full-grown woman if I've ever seen one—and ready for plucking . . . if you get what I mean. She is a rare beauty, and widely discussed because of it."

"Well, whatever she is, I trust Tony." Seeing the disbelieving look on her cousin's face, she added, "I could never go to Marsham to snoop."

Sally looked aghast. "And I would like to know why not?"

"It would not be proper. Tony is my affianced. It is my duty to trust him."

"In love, anything is proper. Besides, it is your duty to look after your interests and to see that he holds to his betrothal. Mark my word—if you don't see to this, you might as well cry off right now. I hear it from the best of sources that your trustworthy Lord Anthony is already contemplating a proposal of marriage . . . and not with you."

If it were possible, Lady Cecilia turned even more pale. Her hands trembled. A sharp pain lodged in her chest. Her eyes began to water. Lose Tony? The man she loved with all her unassertive heart? The man who set her emotions all atwitter with just one glance? *Lose Tony?* Her composure crumpled.

It was time to call in the troops. Meek and mild was fine, as long as it got one what one wanted. Now wasn't the time to wring her hands and bleat like a sheep. Now was the time to become Ares's daughter—Ares being the god of war, and all.

There would be no excuses now. "A good war halloweth every cause," as they say. She had always prided herself in believing a grain of prudence was worth a pound of craft. Well, wasn't it time to be prudent here?

Apparently it was, for at that moment Sally seemed to confirm it when she said, "I think it is time for you to draw out the heavy artillery, my dear cousin. You will conquer more by action in this matter than by passivity or passion. I hear Lord Anthony is bedridden with some sort of rash. It would be the perfectly natural thing for you to pay him a visit, catching a glimpse of this Russian baggage while you are there. You have no idea what kind of tricks this foreigner has stooped to. She is Russian, and they're related to Attila the Hun, you know."

Lady Cecilia looked skeptical.

Sally didn't let that slow her down. "Take it from me. A good general always sizes up the opposition before the battle begins."

"You are right," Lady Cecilia said, rocking forward and closing her parasol with a snap. "Prepare for battle," she said, rising to her feet and waving her parasol like a battle flag. "We go to war with the Russians." Suddenly she noticed Sally was giving her an odd look. "What is it?"

Sally shook her head. "You cannot go into battle looking like *that*."

Lady Cecilia glanced down at herself, seeing nothing out of the ordinary. "Like what?" she asked.

"You look positively insipid. Sometimes I wonder what is in your mother's head. I know my aunt is terribly fond of yellow, and it becomes her . . . But to be perfectly honest, it is simply not your color." Sally came to her feet and began circling Cecilia, eyeing her clothes up and down. "And this dress," she said, giving the lavish ruffle a flip, "the style is all wrong for you. It is bad enough that the yellow makes you look like a sheaf of wheat without the style making you look about as shapely. What else do you have with you?"

"I have a cream-colored morning dress."

Sally shook her head.

"A white one, then."

Sally shook her head.

"There's a lovely gold one with brown trim," Lady Cecilia continued, then seeing the shake of Sally's head, she looked downtrodden. "It's hopeless, then, I'm afraid, for the rest of my things are all . . ."

". . . yellow," Sally supplied, and Lady Cecilia nodded, looking crestfallen.

"Come with me," Sally said, taking her by the arm. "All is not lost. We've work to do."

While Sally and Lady Cecilia sequestered themselves in Sally's dressing room, Natasha was feeling a bit confused. After her last confrontation with Trevor, which ended as all her confrontations with him did of late—with a kiss—she had vowed to stay away from him. But he had a knack for ferreting her out wherever she was, and whenever he found her, it wasn't too long before he had her in his arms. And that was the crux.

She loved Tony, but she had this infuriating habit of kissing his brother—and liking it, too. She was no fool. She knew this infatuation with Trevor had to stop. She also knew she wasn't the one to stop it. *Weak,* she thought. *I am simply too weak.* If only Trevor would leave her alone . . . or better yet, just leave.

Tony, she thought. *With Tony, I will be safe.*

Without wasting a moment of time, she made her way up to the earl's room.

The moment she entered, it was obvious Tony was feeling better, for it was the first time she saw him propped up. "Hello," she said, "you're looking ever so much better."

"I'm feeling better," Tony said, patting the side of the bed. "Come sit by me, my raven-haired angel."

Natasha was about to do just that when the door opened—and in walked Trevor.

"Don't you ever knock?" she asked, with a frown.

That drew Trevor up short. "Not when it's my brother's room," he said, giving her an appraising look. "My, you do look fetching in that pink dress, Miss Simonov. Pink is such a good color on an ebony-haired woman."

"Then I will take care not to wear it again," she said, finding herself more irritated when he had the effrontery to laugh.

Natasha would have said more, but at that time, Mrs. MacDougal came huffing and puffing into the room like a hurricane off course, to announce Lady Cecilia was on her way up.

"On her way up?" Tony said. "Here? You mean Cecilia is *here*? At Marsham?"

"Aye," Mrs. MacDougal said, "and the likes of such you've never seen."

Before Tony could muster a thought about what Mrs. MacDougal meant by that comment, Lady Cecilia called his name from the top of the stairs.

"Tony . . . are you decent?"

Hearing her coming down the hall, Tony glanced from Natasha to Trevor, giving his brother a helpless look.

About that time, Trevor must have realized there wasn't time for him to get Natasha out of the room and away before Cecilia saw her, for he gave Tony a quelling look, grabbed Natasha's arm, and yanked her into Tony's dressing room, just as Lady Cecilia entered.

The door to the dressing room wasn't completely closed, and the moment Trevor released her arm, Natasha had her eye to the crack. She took one look at Lady Cecilia, jerked her head back with a horrified gasp, then went back for another look.

In the pink of prudence, Lady Cecilia floated into the room on a cloud of brilliant blue silk trimmed with green braid, and if that wasn't enough, she had enough cleavage showing to make Tony sit up and take immediate notice. Natasha gasped again, seeing how Tony opened his mouth to speak, but must have found himself unable to do so, snapping it shut.

"Cecilia?" was all he managed to say, and Natasha knew he was completely overwhelmed by what he saw.

She looked at Lady Cecilia, thinking Cleopatra's entrance into Rome couldn't have been more commanding. Nothing about her was what Natasha had been led to expect. There was no severe hairdo pulled ruthlessly back in a manner that made her look like a scraped turnip. In fact, all Natasha saw were glossy curls that were piled high on her head, and with every move she made, golden tendrils floated about a face that was cameo perfect.

And she hadn't been told Lady Cecilia had such lovely skin, such peach-blossom coloring. And those eyes ... Why, they were as blue as the diamond-encrusted aquamarine that glittered between her ample breasts. She looked at Tony, whose gaze seemed frozen on those ample breasts. And he had called her shapeless ...

As he drank in the sight of her, Natasha knew what he was thinking: All this and money, too ...

Before he could recover, Lady Cecilia came to sit beside him, and while he still ogled her breasts, she did something Natasha would only call brazen. Obviously overcome with the moment, she took Tony's face between her hands and kissed him good.

Even to Natasha's unpracticed eye, it was obvious that Tony, the scoundrel, was kissing her back.

When the kiss ended, Cecilia started to apologize, but Tony grinned and said, "Don't. Do it again."

Naturally, she would have to be an agreeable sort, Natasha thought, watching Cecilia kiss him again, this time for a long, long time.

That was when Natasha made an amazing discovery.

Seeing Lady Cecilia kiss Tony didn't bother her in the way she thought it would—or should—considering she was in love with him. She didn't get to think further about that, for at that moment the kiss ended.

Tony frowned. "Where did you learn to kiss like that?"

"You taught me," Lady Cecilia said simply.

His chest puffed out. "I did?"

"Yes, Tony. You did."

"Do it again," he said, looking suddenly pleased with himself.

Before Natasha could blink, she kissed him again, and this time the kiss went on and on.

Another mortified gasp came from the direction of the dressing room, and Lady Cecilia turned in that direction. "What was that?" she asked.

Tony glanced around. "Uh— What?"

"That noise. I heard a noise."

"It probably came from outside."

"No, it came from in there," she said, coming to her feet and walking slowly toward the dressing room.

Hearing her horrified gasp, Trevor yanked Natasha out of the way, and putting his eye to the crack, he saw Cecilia rise from Tony's bed, her gaze fastened on the dressing room. Damnation! This was neither the time nor the place to introduce Natasha and Cecilia. *Bloody hell!* It seemed that all he ever did was make hasty decisions whenever he was around this black-haired Russian.

Trevor frowned. Lady Cecilia was brainless . . . she was not stupid. They would be in a fine pickle if she caught the two of them hiding here in Tony's dressing room. Without a moment to waste, he pushed Natasha into the corner behind a row of Tony's greatcoats and boots, giving her a look that said her life would not be worth a tuppence if she dared to open her mouth. Then he began removing his clothes. He was down to his drawers by the time Lady Cecilia opened the door.

On the verge of challenging him in spite of his threatening look, Natasha was ready to march to the front and tell Lady Cecilia just what she thought of her, but one glance at Trevor and she could only gape. Natasha was as stunned and surprised by what she saw as Lady Cecilia apparently was. With stupefied silence, she could only peek between greatcoats and boots at the naked—or as close to nearly naked as she had ever seen one—man. After giving Trevor the once-over, her gaze locked on Lady Cecilia's face.

Lady Cecilia stood rigid and silent, an expression of absolute surprise upon her face, which soon melted into one of abject delight.

Hussy. Natasha observed the way Lady Cecilia fixed her fascinated blue gaze upon Trevor's person as if trying to memorize it, seemingly in no hurry to beg Trevor's pardon for either the invasion of his privacy or the state she found him in. And that infuriated Natasha. It also made her realize that it upset her more to have Cecilia ogling Trevor than it did to watch her kiss Tony. And if that wasn't an indication that she might not be as in love with Tony as she thought, she didn't know what was.

Natasha looked at Cecilia, then she looked at Trevor. Since the first time he had kissed her, she had wondered what the body that felt so good pressed up against hers would look like, but never in her wildest imaginings had she ever anticipated she would find out. And never would she have imagined a man's body could look so good, or elicit so many responses.

Her throat went parchment dry. Her breathing was rapid and unsteady. And visions of things not remotely connected to sugarplums danced in her head. *This,* she thought with some satisfaction, *is what I call perfection.*

As she watched Lady Cecilia study Trevor, a warm, liquid heat seemed to wash over her. It was a good thing she was not standing, for this was the sort of thing that would have made her knees instantly weak. If Lady Cecilia was so in love with Tony, Natasha would have been hard-pressed to see it, for observing the way Lady Cecilia's chest rose and fell with each rapid breath and the way her eyes seemed to glaze over, it was difficult to imagine her having thoughts about anyone, save Trevor . . . and lewd thoughts at that.

With a lazy, heart-thumping smile, Trevor raised one arched brow and gave Cecilia an elegant bow. "I daresay there is nothing in here that would fit you, Cecilia, but if you are so determined, then you are most welcome to look . . . if you would be so kind as to give me a moment or two of privacy so I might put myself in a more respectable state."

"Oh," said Cecilia, "I—I am so sorry. It was never my intention to gape, but you did take me by surprise."

Apparently, thought Natasha.

"The surprise is mutual, let me assure you, and now, if there is nothing further I can do for you, would you be kind enough to close the door and allow me to finish dressing?"

"Oh . . . Yes . . . Why, of course I would— I mean, I will— That is . . ."

"Cecilia," Tony shouted, "did you come to gape at my brother or to speed along my convalescence?"

Lady Cecilia slammed the door, and the moment she did, Natasha crawled out of her hiding place. "How dare you?" she whispered, poking him in the bare chest and drawing herself up to the height of insulted.

"Shh," Trevor said, then added, "I need to dress."

"Then dress. I have already seen everything," she whispered, and then took another good look, just to be sure she hadn't missed anything.

When she looked back at Trevor, he seemed amused. "Are you certain you've seen *everything*?" he asked in a hoarse whisper.

She nodded.

He smiled. "Sweet Natasha. Have you not heard that a good gambler never shows all his cards?"

"Well, you've certainly shown me enough to know it's time to fold my hand."

His fingers came up to cup her chin, and raising her face to his, he kissed her softly. "I thought you were more of a gambler," he said. "Surely you aren't going to fold now ... before you see what trump I'm holding."

Immediately Natasha's eyes dropped to the one part of him that was covered. She could feel the heat rise to her face. She quickly looked off. "I have a good idea," she said. "There is no need to shock me."

"Shock you? Now that is a strange comment coming from one who has passed the last few minutes ogling a naked man."

"You are not naked, and I did not ogle you."

"I am close enough to the state that it should have offended your sensibilities, and you most assuredly did ogle me, Natasha mine."

Natasha shrugged. He was right, and she knew it. She did ogle him—and once more she enjoyed every informative minute of it. But she wasn't about to let him know that. "I am not yours, and if you did not want to be ogled, you should have kept your shirt on—and your pants, too, for that matter," she added.

He smiled. "I will remember that the next time I have a desire to be ogled by you."

"You will have a long wait."

"We will see," he said, thrusting his long legs into his pants.

"Yes, I suppose we will," she said, inching her way toward the door.

"Come here," he whispered. "You are not going out there to create a scene."

Before Natasha knew what he was about, Trevor, one arm in his shirt and the other out, caught her in his arms, and, pressing her back against Tony's greatcoats, began to silence her in the only way he knew how.

His lips met hers.

"What are you . . .!"

"Shh. Don't talk," he whispered.

"Why not?" she whispered, her mouth up against his.

"Because I can think of something better to do than talk."

"Better?"

"A lot better," he said, his words whispered into her mouth.

She drank in the warm bodily heat of him, shivering at the way his hand was touching the skin at the back of her neck. She leaned into him, her face buried into the cove of his neck as she made little upward pushes, pressing her nose and mouth against him like a calf does when it feeds, and all the while he was talking softly to her, whispering and stroking her with his hands.

While Trevor was keeping Natasha busy in the dressing room, Cecilia was making some startling discoveries. Her brazen behavior did not evoke the reaction from Tony she would have expected. Quite the contrary. Tony was not at all shocked by what transpired; in fact, he seemed quite taken with it—just as Sally had said he would be.

With a satisfied smile, she gave Tony a kiss to cause him some serious reflections, then, with a look that said there was more where that came from, she departed. *Stew on that for a while,* she thought, a triumphant smile on her face.

Some time later, it was a joyous if somewhat dazed Lady Cecilia who returned to her cousin's manor. For years she had been infatuated with Anthony Hamilton, and yet he never paid her any mind, until forced to do so for financial reasons. Always the obedient daughter, Cecilia had shied away from the behavior of her more colorful society sisters—like Lady Caro Lamb and Caro's aunt, the Duchess of Devonshire—behaving in a discreet and dignified manner. She often wondered why the Caro Lambs of the world were married when all her chaste behavior got her was ignored.

But something that happened today was going to change all that. Never had Tony responded to her before. Never had he looked at her like that. Never had his hand found its way to her breast, and never had he kissed her in that glorious fashion. If that was the kind of results reaped from brazen behavior, then brazen she would be.

"Come, Sally," she said. "We are off to your dressmaker's."

"My dressmaker? Why are we going there?"

"We are going," Cecilia said, "for bait."

Meanwhile, back in the dressing room, Trevor and Natasha broke their kiss. Giving her time to compose herself, Trevor stepped out of the dressing room, grinning at his brother.

"Well, well. Who would have thought it? Lady

Cecilia, in dashing good form, swooping in to declare a victory. You gave up without a fight, I noticed," Trevor said.

"When you know you're outmatched, retreat," Tony said, with a grin. "And never let it be said that I am one to tread upon a sore toe."

Natasha stepped into the room.

Trevor turned to look at her. "Speaking of sore toes . . ."

Hurt and humiliated, too proud to listen to Tony's explanation or Trevor's attempts at levity, Natasha was confused by her conflicting emotions. She couldn't think straight, much less talk.

Tony, looking a bit sheepish, said, "Natasha, you know—"

"Don't think you can oil out of this, you ham-fisted buttock squeezer."

"Sweetheart, I can explain . . ."

"There is nothing to explain. I saw you going after her like a rat to a drainpipe. You don't owe me anything, and certainly not an explanation. I don't give a fig for anything you have to say, you—you toadeater!"

Before Tony could respond, Natasha fled the room.

"Beware a donkey's hind foot, a dog's bite, and the tongue of a woman," Trevor said blandly.

"Go to hell, Trev."

"Don't be angry with me," Trevor said. "It could have been worse."

Tony sighed. "I deserved worse."

"Yes," Trevor agreed, "you did."

Running down the stairs, Natasha hurried into the garden before she stopped, taking a seat on the stone bench. Understandably she was disturbed—not so much over Tony's betrayal, but over the fact that it did not seem to matter one whit to her.

If she loved Tony, why did it upset her more to think he had made a fool of her than it did to see him with another woman in his arms? If she loved him, how could she forget he was kissing another woman?

More importantly, how could she kiss another man? Natasha sighed, feeling the strain of confused feelings. What was happening to her orderly life? Well, with so many things going wrong lately, this should be the end of it.

After all, what else could possibly happen?

CHAPTER
❧ THIRTEEN ❧

In the library of his St. Petersburg palace, Prince Mikhail Speransky listened with interest as Boris Vasili gave him a bit of news that was both shocking and quite pleasing.

"I did not believe it myself, at first, so I went to see the countess," Boris said.

"You talked with the Countess Kropotkin yourself?"

Boris nodded. "At length. It seems she learned of the children's existence when she was visiting in England ... from the mother of a man Natasha Simonov is linked with romantically."

Prince Speransky frowned and turned away. Without

saying anything, his face showed his annoyance with what he had just heard. "We cannot allow her to marry a foreigner—at least not until we have her brothers on Russian soil."

"But, if it is only the boys we need, surely—"

"—surely what? Surely we can persuade them to come?"

Boris nodded.

"And how do you think we will persuade them to come to Russia without their sister? Do you think we can simply waltz into England and kidnap them? If what you say is true and they are wards of this Earl of Marsham, then they are protected by the crown." The prince paused, his dark, bushy brows narrowed in thought. "We must have them back, but it must be done properly and with diplomacy."

Boris gave the prince a confused look. "Then what do you plan to do?"

The prince looked thoughtful as he gazed out the window, absently watching the exercising of his wolf-hounds. "I do not know, but I have an idea." Turning back to Boris, he said, "Find my brother-in-law and tell him I want to see him immediately."

Boris found Count Nikolay Rostov at a Gypsy camp with his golden head bent over a mandolin. Sitting before a crackling fire, his strong fingers coaxed from the mandolin a wild song that throbbed with passion. Beside him, and throbbing with equal passion, was a black-haired Gypsy girl, her arms lined with gold bracelets and her feet bare.

It was from such a scene that Boris extracted Niki, as his friends affectionately called him, and sent him to St. Petersburg to answer the urgent summons of his brother-in-law.

Three hours later, Count Nikolay Rostov stood in approximately the same spot Boris had stood earlier, listening to Prince Speransky relate a series of events to him.

The count wasn't too happy about being called back to St. Petersburg in the middle of the night, and even less happy about being called out of the Gypsy girl's bed before he had a chance to get in it. He eyed his brother-in-law angrily.

"Mikhail," Niki said, "why are you telling me all of this? I know Mother Russia has been ruled by conservatives too long, and I know that is the primary reason Masonic lodges and secret societies have begun to flourish. You are telling me nothing I don't already know. If you knew what you called me away from, you would understand that a bit of old news about conspiracies to overthrow the crown was most assuredly not worth it."

"If the news I have received today is true and my plans go according to my wishes, you may change your mind. What if I told you we have located the sons of a man we know to be a direct descendant of Ivan the Terrible?"

Niki stared in disbelief at Mikhail. "What are you saying?"

"Several years ago we discovered documents that proved a certain Count Alexi Simonov was the only living descendant of Ivan the Terrible's son Ivan."

"But Ivan the Terrible murdered his son before he had any children."

"Any legitimate children, but Ivan did father a son before his father killed him, and we have undeniable proof."

"If you discovered this several years ago, why are you calling me out in the dead of night to tell me now—and what does all of this have to do with me in the first place?"

"Because Count Alexi Simonov is dead, and until today we thought his children dead as well."

"And they are not?"

"No. They are living in England." Prince Speransky went on to tell Niki the details of how Natasha and her brothers came to be in England.

"Why can't you go and tell them this story?"

"Because I don't want them to know the story—at least not until I am certain they would return to Russia. If what I am told is correct, the girl is quite taken with a young Englishman. If this is the case, she would be reluctant to leave England, and without her, we have no chance of getting her brothers to come back. I want you to go there, to see for yourself what the situation is." He gave Niki a direct look. "I want the girl and her brothers back, Niki. I don't care how you do it, but bring them back."

"Why are you sending me?" Niki asked. "You have many men at your disposal—men who are well trained in diplomacy . . . men who are more persuasive than I."

"But *not* when it comes to women," Prince Speransky said, lifting a brow. "If she is besotted with this young Englishman, it shouldn't take you long to change her mind. She is bound to be a bit homesick, so that should give you an advantage. Seduce her if you must. Offer to marry her if you have to, but bring her and her brothers back. How you do it is up to you."

"When you have them, what then?"

"We take the Russian crown and put one of her brothers on the throne."

"And the girl?"

"She is yours if you desire her." He winked at Niki.

"It would suit you well, I think, to have in your power the sister of the Czar of Russia."

Niki looked at the prince. "Not as well as it would suit you."

CHAPTER
❧ FOURTEEN ❧

Lady Cecilia became a permanent fixture about Marsham over the next few days, and because of her habit of dropping in unannounced, it was inevitable that she and Natasha would meet.

As it turned out, it wasn't the meeting everyone had been dreading, for instead of arching their backs at each other like a couple of barn cats hissing over the same fish bone, their liking for each other was instantaneous.

Perhaps this was because Cecilia, being a bit older than Natasha and of a more placid nature, felt her heart go out to this lovely orphan the moment she saw her. And then, perhaps it was because Cecilia was such a simple-hearted person.

In some ways Natasha dreaded her first meeting with Lady Cecilia. She knew no one could blame her for being enamored with Tony—half of the women in London were enamored with him. And how could Cecilia condemn her for something she was guilty of herself? To

Natasha's way of thinking, Cecilia probably would want nothing more than to stake her claim—by right of having Tony first.

Before Natasha could think further on the subject, Lady Cecilia walked into the salon where Natasha was having a cup of tea.

"May I join you?" Cecilia asked.

"Of course," Natasha said, picking up a cup. "Sugar?"

"Just a dash of lemon."

Natasha looked at Cecilia's dress, thinking the shimmering, ice-blue fabric was the loveliest thing she had ever seen. "Your gown is lovely. Is it silk?"

Lady Cecilia said, somewhat apologetically, that it was.

Natasha handed her the cup. "I suppose you've come in here to scratch my eyes out."

Cecilia laughed. "I thought about it at first," she said, "but I realized there would be something wrong with you if you did not find Tony appealing. I suppose the logical thing would be for us to be enemies, but truthfully, I would rather have you for my friend."

"You surely have heard the rumors by now," Natasha said sharply. "That Tony and I . . ."

"I distrust gossip," Lady Cecilia said. "Is your heart set on Tony and marriage?"

"Nothing could be further from the truth."

Cecilia smiled. "Good. Now that that is settled, we can get on with things."

Natasha gave her a distrustful look. "I find it hard to believe you would want to count among your friends a woman who almost broke up your engagement."

"If I looked upon every woman who did that as an enemy, I would have no friends—and I would find myself the most unpopular woman in all of England."

"If it makes any difference, I have discovered I was never in love with Tony . . . not really," Natasha said, and found the saying of it surprisingly easy. She had never loved Tony, just as Trevor said.

"Thank you for telling me."

Natasha put her teacup down and sat looking at her hands, which were folded in her lap. "To tell you the truth, it was not so difficult. I don't understand just why it was I ever thought myself in love with him. I don't think Tony and I would have ever gotten on, simply because we are not suited."

Lady Cecilia nodded. "That is because Tony is such a lighthearted person. There is too much fire in you for a man like him. You need a man of intense passions."

Natasha looked up—and seeing the earnestness, the sweet look of understanding in Lady Cecilia's face— she wondered why it was that everyone thought her such a rattlehead. It was obvious to her that Lady Cecilia, with her calm, easygoing manner, understood Tony far better than anyone.

That is because Tony is such a lighthearted person . . .

Lighthearted? He was a rogue. A scoundrel. If she wasn't so relieved that she had come to her senses before too much damage had been done, she would have been even more put out with things. As it was, she could only say she was thankful that Trevor had come along—if for no other reason than to show her how superficial her feelings for Tony really were. She shuddered to think what might have occurred if Trevor had not happened along in time to keep both of them from making a terrible mistake.

She had to admit that her feelings for Tony had been on the wane for some time now, and that it had only taken the timely appearance of Lady Cecilia ogling

Trevor in the dressing room for Natasha to recognize where her affections lay.

"So you see," she said to Lady Cecilia, "I have realized that I was never in love with Tony. I was captivated with the idea of *being* in love, and Tony just happened along. Does that make sense?" she asked, finding herself distracted somewhat by the odd-looking bonnet Lady Cecilia wore. It was of a strange design, but somehow, in spite of its strangeness, it seemed perfectly suitable on her.

Lady Cecilia took a sip of tea and put her cup down. "Of course it does, and do you know why? Because it sounds so much like me. You and I are alike in many ways, you see. Oh, this is wonderful." She came to her feet at the same time Natasha did.

Crossing the room to stand beside her, Lady Cecilia said, "This will be like having a younger sister. I am an only child, you know. Dear, dear Natasha. This is the second most important day of my life." She gave Natasha an apologetic look. "It would be the *most* important, save for the day Tony proposed, you understand."

"Of course I do," said Natasha.

Lady Cecilia took Natasha by the arm. "Come, let us take a walk. We have so many things to discuss. I know you cannot help but notice how taken with you Trevor is. Why, his eyes positively devour you every time he looks your way."

"I think Trevor is the kind of man who devours every woman he looks at. Stories about his escapades have followed him here from London, you know. Even in the country, we are privileged to hear the latest about all the London rakes."

Lady Cecilia patted her hand. "Do not let that worry

you, Tasha— I do hope you don't mind if I call you Tasha?"

Natasha shook her head. "It is what my friends call me."

Lady Cecilia nodded her satisfaction at that. "As I was saying, don't let Trevor's rakish background deter you. It is a well-known fact that the bigger the scoundrel, the better the husband."

"Then Trevor and Tony should both be outstanding," Natasha said, dissolving into laughter at the sound of Lady Cecilia's unladylike snort.

Lady Cecilia came for dinner that night, and it was soon apparent to everyone that Natasha and Lady Cecilia had much more in common than Tony. By the time the main course was served, Natasha and Cecilia had planned a shopping excursion into Applecore and were busily discussing plans for tea the next afternoon at the home of Cecilia's cousin Sally.

After dinner, Cecilia offered to play the piano; Tony invited everyone into the music room, but Natasha begged off, announcing she had a few things to do in the greenhouse.

"Oh, do come with us," Cecilia said. "I was hoping we could play a duet."

"I would love to some other time," Natasha said. "I have been quite neglectful of the old earl's plants. He was in the midst of propagation when he died."

"A most unfortunate state," Trevor said in the driest tones imaginable.

"Propagation," Tony said. "Now, there's a lively topic I'd like to pursue."

Trevor choked on his brandy. Natasha turned red. But Lady Cecilia remained unruffled and quite calmly put

down her cup of tea. "In due time," she said, caressing
Tony's cheek with her folded fan. "All in due time."

At the intensely interested look on Tony's face,
Natasha found herself glancing at Trevor, who gave her
a direct look and raised one brow in question.

Instantly Natasha's throat went dry and her heart
hammered wildly in her chest. Things were happening
too fast. She didn't understand what was going on here
any more than she understood her own feelings.

Trevor nodded at her in a way that made her think he
knew exactly what she was thinking. Embarrassment
and confusion colored her cheeks. She knew she was
suddenly talking, but she had no idea what it was that
she said.

"I—I think I'll be going now. I am sorry I will be unable to hear you play," she said to Cecilia. "I hear you
do it divinely." Giving the three other occupants of the
room a quick glance, she said, "Please excuse me."

She walked only until she was out of the room, then
she lifted her skirt and broke into a run, going down the
long, winding corridor, bursting through the doors that
led from the library to the garden, her feet skimming
over the stones that led down to the greenhouse.

Trevor found her there, standing in the midst of
graceful ivy tendrils that were putting on a brave show
of variegation and pattern, while surrounded by the delicate softness of a pale pink climbing rose in full
bloom.

"Look at this," she said, without turning around, as if
she sensed, somehow, his presence. She picked up a
dangling rope of ivy trailing from a stoneware pot. "I
am ashamed to have neglected these plants as much as
I have. See?" she said, pulling a tendril loose from its
earthly mooring. "The ivy is taking root in this pot of

geraniums and soon it will choke them out." She began to shake the dirt from the roots.

He stepped closer, coming to stand beside her. She turned startled eyes upon him; for a moment he felt as if something had taken his breath away. Both she and the roses were made lovelier by the glossy green mantle ivy interposed between her and the flowers, but it was the bewildered, confused look on her face, the way her eyes glistened, that cut to the heart of him.

"Don't," he said. He took the ivy from her hands, and she looked up at him, then smiled. The overpowering sweetness of it staggered him.

"I am all right," she said. "Truly."

"I know you are," he said, "but it so happens that I am not."

She looked at him, and he realized how alone she was, how isolated out here in the country with nothing but her brothers, his late uncle's plants, and her stubborn, scarred pride. He rarely found himself this considerate toward others, this understanding, and he had difficulty comprehending why he felt that way toward her. Even as he folded her in his arms, he knew the insanity of what he was doing, an insanity that seemed to welcome the inevitability of it all. He justified his feelings by telling himself he only came out here to offer her comfort, that he was going to do nothing more than give it by holding her.

The moment he drew her against him, he knew it was a mistake. He could feel the deep, penetrating warmth of her reaching out to touch him through layers and layers of clothing. He knew the taste of her without touching his lips to hers. The innocent scent of her surrounded him. A legion of painted and perfumed whores could not have produced an ounce of the desire that poured through him now. He dropped his head and began kissing the soft, glossy curls at the side of her face, dropping lower to learn the scent, the curve, of such a dainty neck.

"Why are you here?" she whispered. "Why are you doing this?"

"I wish to God I knew," he said, his mouth moving now to nuzzle the softness behind her ear. He heard the sharp indrawn breath, knew that he had shocked her when he drew her back against him, her back pressed to him, his hands coming around to touch her breasts.

She pulled away, stepping out of his embrace and turning to face him, unable to hide the passion-bright expression in her eyes, not knowing how that look heated his body, or the implications of it. Then she looked away.

"My father killed a wolf once. It was a terribly cold winter, and there was little for the wildlife to eat. At night we could hear the wolves moving about, their frightful howling. My father said they were normally afraid to come so close to civilization, but hunger had made them more daring. One night they were quite close and my father and his men went outside. The wolves were in the pen with the sheep. My father shot one of them. For days afterward, there was one wolf that kept coming back to that same place. He would sit there and howl. The men said it was probably his mate who was killed. Wolves mate for life, you know. One night the wolf stopped coming." She looked at him, seeing his gaze was resting upon her face. "I remember, even to this day, standing in the warmth of my bedroom and looking out at the frozen world below, watching the wolf mourn his lost mate. I found it such a strange feeling that I could look at that wolf and feel both tenderness and fear."

He knew what she was telling him—and he understood then how much depth and feeling there was to her. He reached to take her in his arms again, but she held out her hand to stay him, the expression on her face one he could imagine on her face as she looked at that wolf.

It wasn't exactly fear, but it was a long way from trust.

"You must understand something," she said. "There can never be anything between us. I know why you came here. I know what your life was like in London. I cannot settle for something like that. What you seek from me, I cannot give. I am like that wolf. I mate for life."

Something tender swelled within him, a gentle feeling, an emotion he was a stranger to. It struck him that he was feeling, truly feeling. It was a real emotion, and one he could never remember experiencing before. It was as if something came alive within him, that something long dormant suddenly awoke. The room seemed brighter, the flowers more fragrant, the colors more intense. Everything he saw was something he had seen many times before, but it was as if he were seeing them for the first time.

Everything was the same. Everything was different. Nothing was as it had been before. He knew what she was telling him, that she knew he only had seduction on his mind, that she was neither repulsed nor angered by it, but that she could not be a part of it. He wanted to grant her what she asked. He wanted to leave her as he had found her, innocent and untouched, but he knew it was impossible. This need, this desire for her, was too deep, too profound, too potent. Yet the moment he looked at her, he knew it was not to be.

"I see," he said, fighting the urge to take her in his arms and show her what she would never know. Without another word, he turned away. He'd almost reached the door when he heard her call his name.

"Trevor . . ."

He turned slowly and looked at her. He knew the moment he did that the desire within her was potent as well. One moment she was as staunch as one of the pillars that supported the room, the next moment all the strength and resistance seemed to ebb away from her. Her shoulders slumped in defeat. Her hands came up to cover her face.

He sighed, intending to leave her to her misery, but before he could take a step, her head came up, her eyes wide and bright, looking at him in a way that told of her fear.

"Why did you follow me out here?" she asked, the words flung at him as if she had to force them or not say them at all. The moment the words were finished, she turned away, her hands gripping the edge of the stoneware pot in front of her.

He decided there had been enough lies between them, enough deception. "I came out here because I wanted to be with you, because I wanted to touch you, Natasha—to touch you and keep on touching you until I knew every part of you. You are so lovely. There is so much I could show you."

She squeezed her eyes shut and threw her head back. "Show me then," she whispered.

His heart twisted inside him. "I'm afraid I cannot do that," he said, seeing the way she had turned to look at him. "I don't think I could touch you now, knowing I had to stop. I don't think I would be able to."

"Then don't," she said quickly, closing her eyes. "Touch me, Trevor. Touch me and don't stop."

A moment later she was in his arms.

He pulled her tightly against the fiery heat of his

body, his mouth coming down to kiss her with a touching sensitivity that left her limp and weak.

Wobbly and unsure of herself, she dropped her forehead softly against his chest, feeling the caressing length of his fingers in her hair. Then he lifted her head, pulling back from her ever so slightly, in order to give him access to the row of tiny pearl buttons at her throat.

One by one, he slipped the buttons through, watching the fabric part, revealing the milky fairness of flesh untouched by the sun. He eased the dress further apart, pushing the chemise down until the soft pearly tips of her breasts were bared. He kissed her there, feeling the hard response of her desire. A startled gasp sprang from her lips; he knew it was embarrassment that fueled such an instinctive move, that made her cover her breasts.

He caught her around the waist and lifted her up to sit upon the bench in front of him. "I could spend the rest of my life touching you," he whispered. "I want you, Natasha—so badly I seem to lose sight of all reason."

She drew his head against her, cradling it against the softness of her breasts. "I saw the Alps once, and I remember when I reached the summit and looked out over the world below how in awe I was, how lightheaded and breathless. For a moment I felt as if the whole world belonged to me, that time stood still. That is the way I feel whenever I am in your arms," she said, lifting his head and gently kissing his eyes, his nose, his mouth.

"Natasha . . ."

She put her fingers over his mouth and did not let him finish. "I know my heart. But I am afraid of what I might find in yours," she whispered. "And I don't know what to do about it."

A split second later she dropped off the bench and

fled the greenhouse, disappearing into the darkness of the night.

An hour later Tony found him in the greenhouse, standing in the same spot, an uprooted tendril of ivy in his hand.

CHAPTER
❧ FIFTEEN ❧

Natasha awoke with a song in her heart and a smile on her face. She sprang from the bed and hurried to the windows, throwing back the shutters. Sunlight drenched her face.

She quickly dressed, choosing a high-waisted blue lawn gown. She washed her face and brushed her hair, then hurried downstairs to breakfast, hoping to catch sight of Trevor, but when she arrived, she learned Trevor had eaten much earlier and then departed for what he said would be a long ride.

After breakfast Natasha spent some time with Mrs. Mac, who was too busy dusting the cobwebs from the ceiling to spend much time talking. From there she wandered into the kitchen to watch Cook cut thick slabs of bacon into fat slices for frying, but like Mrs. Mac, Cook was too busy to give much thought to conversation.

Leaving the kitchen, she went in search of Luka and Pavel, finding her brothers were always underfoot when she wished they weren't, and were always gone when she wanted them. Unable to locate them or the dogs, she went to find Harry, but when she saw him talking to Ned, she decided to take a walk instead.

Two hours later, Trevor was on his way back to Marsham when he saw Natasha out of the corner of his eye, sitting on a stile that passed over a stone fence. He turned off the road and cut across the pasture, and as he drew near, he saw her arms were resting on top of her knees, her chin resting on top of them as she gazed out across the pasture, her mind obviously a thousand miles away. He smiled, wondering what she was thinking.

She noticed him when he rode across her line of vision. "I thought you were going to be gone a long time."

"It was my plan," he said, "but I found I couldn't stay away."

"Away from what?"

"You," he said, dismounting.

She gave him a startled look, and he could not help thinking of the beautiful girl he had come to seduce and how he had somehow lost track of that, finding deception was the last thing he had on his mind when he was around her.

Beneath his impassive gaze Natasha sat perfectly still, staring up into his face, every detail of her lovely face visible for him to see. No, it wasn't deception he thought of when he looked at her, or even seduction, but something more permanent. Something much more permanent.

He wanted her, that much was true—not just for a night, but for all time.

"What are you doing out here?" he asked.

"I was on my way to the lake, but it was so pretty here, I decided to stop for a while."

"Come on then," he said, offering her his hand. "I'll walk down to the lake with you."

"What about your horse?"

He released her hand when she came to her feet, and turning he began to unfasten the cinch, then pulled the saddle from the gelding's back. "I'll turn him out and send Ned back for the tack later," he said.

She watched him remove the saddle and hang it over the fence, then toss the bridle over that. The gelding whirled and ran a few feet before rolling in a low, loamy place. She watched him roll, then come to his feet, giving himself a good shake. Kicking and bucking, he loped across the pasture, and she found herself laughing. "Sometimes I envy them," she said. "They make life seem so simple."

"If all it takes to make life simple is a roll in the dirt, then go ahead. I won't tell anyone."

"It doesn't work," she said.

"How do you know?"

"Because I've tried it."

He was so astonished by what she said that he stopped a moment and stared at her. "You what?"

"I tried it," she said simply. "How else would one find out if it worked or not?"

"Good question," he said, unable to think of anything else at the moment, so distracted was he by the way the sunlight danced in her eyes.

"Don't worry," she said, giving him a playful shove, "there won't be the blood of such a frivolous sort running through the veins of your nieces and nephews. I have decided you were right. I was never in love with Tony, just as you said."

"What made you realize that?"

"Seeing him with Lady Cecilia. They are perfect together, you know. She is far better suited to Tony than I am."

"I am glad you are taking the discovery so well. Most women would be disenchanted to learn they had just let an earl slip through their fingers."

She didn't respond to that, for they had come to a fork in the path, and she pointed down the one that branched off to the left, saying, "This way."

He turned and walked beside her, down a narrow lane that went between a small copse of ancient yew trees, passing through a woodland of oaks, beeches, and holly before descending to a shallow valley of beech woods.

The scent of wet grasses and clover filled the air; a swarm of tiny insects hovered just ahead. He glanced down, where her skirt skimmed the grass as they walked, his gaze rising slowly to rest upon her profile. She felt his gaze upon her and looked down, where her bonnet dangled from her arm, tied with wide satin strings. It had become a flower basket, overflowing with the fruits of the woods and meadows, all stuffed into her bonnet in a jumbled manner that looked as if they fell in there by accident.

They walked on, neither of them saying anything as they hiked across quiet pastures bounded by dry stone walls covered with creeper—before cutting across a drowsy meadow where sheep grazed beneath the soft kiss of morning sunlight. When they came to a place where the path dipped into a dale full of mosses, ferns, and lichens all dappled with sunshine, she turned to look at him, wondering if he wished to go this way, but he did not look at her.

As they walked on, she thought about the expression

she had seen on his face, one that was pleasant but preoccupied. She wondered what he was thinking about. Probably the same things her brothers thought about when she had walked down here with them, she thought—whatever that was.

At the end of the path they came upon the glistening water of a lake, where beeches crowded the banks, mirrored in the tranquil waters. Just ahead of them, a shy fallow deer veiled in misty sunlight sniffed the air, then darted through the underbrush. Overhead, the *whirr* of a wood pigeon's wings seemed to drown out the rapid trilling of a nuthatch nearby.

He turned toward her. "This is a favorite place of yours," he said.

She nodded. "Yes, I love it here. There is something about this place that touches me."

She plucked a blade of grass as they walked along the fringe of the lake, where the water was languid and filled with water lilies. A green crescent of reeds covered one end of the lake where it was most narrow, not far from where a small island served as a home to coots, moorhens, and mallard ducks.

She dipped beneath a willow tree that spread far out over the water, the long, trailing branches skimming the surface. When she straightened, he looked at her and laughed, stopping her with a hand on her shoulder, turning her gently toward him. He was close enough now so that she could see the flecks in his eyes.

He reached for her, extracting a few twigs and leaves from her hair. "Even these flatter you," he murmured, and she wondered if she was falling more and more under his spell. His head lowered, and she went wobbly at the ankles. His face came closer, and she felt as if her stomach was filled with moths. The moment his lips were no more than a hair's breadth from hers, he drew his head back.

"If I start thinking about kissing you, we'll never make it to your lake," he said, shoving his hands into his pockets and walking on, just a little ahead of her. She frowned after him.

"I like kissing you," she said, noticing the way he jerked to a halt. She stopped as well.

His gaze was direct. "Sometimes your honesty slays me," he said.

"What do you want me to do? Lie?"

"Perhaps lies would not be so disarming," he said, and turned, walking quickly away.

When she caught up to him, he was standing beside a small boat turned on its side and half hidden in the reeds.

"Yours?" he asked.

"My brothers," she said, and smiled, remembering that boat, remembering the times she and her brothers had used it, Luka rowing them around the mirrored waters, Pavel trailing a fishing line from the back.

"I hate to see a good boat go to waste," he said. "Shall we?"

She looked up at his face, seeing the way he was looking at her, knowing, too, that he understood that she was praying he would ask her to go boating with him. It was the insightful little things he said and did that were, she decided, part of his magic. "Do you see the oars?" she asked.

He tromped around in the reeds, splashing and slopping water like a frisky pup, before he dropped down and came up grinning, holding two oars. He handed them to her and turned to clean out the debris mostly leaves and reeds—from the boat, slipping it into the water a moment later.

Without a word, he took the oars, and, putting them down, swept her into his arms and waded out into the water with her, lowering her into the boat before he reached for the oars and stepped inside to take the seat across from her. He rowed them, with slow, steady strokes, well away from the shore. She trailed a hand in the water, disturbing the water's green patina and leaving a whisper of a wake.

"Do you come out here with your brothers very often?"

"As often as they will allow," she said. "Luka and Pavel can only take small, infrequent doses of an older sister."

He watched her pull her hand inside the boat, laying it in her lap. She tipped her head back, so the sun could touch her face. "What is it about water?" she asked. "Why do I feel so drawn to it?"

"Perhaps you are really a water sprite and don't know it."

She smiled at that, but did not look at him. "My brothers frequently catch fish in here," she said. "Harry helps them with the cleaning, I help Cook fry them, and Mrs. MacDougal laughs and says she's gotten off scot-free, which is appropriate, her being a Scot and all."

"You never caught any fish yourself?"

"Once," she said, "but I felt so sorry for it when Pavel took it off the hook, I begged him to throw it back in."

"Did he?"

"No. So I grabbed and tossed it back myself. I decided then and there I would never go fishing again. There was something unnerving about taking an innocent creature from its natural place for such a trivial reason, forcing it into a world where it could not live."

Suddenly she did not feel like talking anymore. She

leaned further back into the boat. Settling herself into a reclining position, she closed her eyes, sensing the rhythm of the water beneath her, the warmth of the sun upon her face, and sensing, too, the meditative look on Trevor's face as he watched her.

When she opened her eyes some time later and glanced at him, he was still looking at her as if he was wondering what she was thinking. "What about you?" she asked. "Did you ever go fishing?"

"No. Tony did, but I was the firstborn, the heir, so my father was less charitable about allowing me to miss my studies."

"Are you saying Tony was the favored child?"

"Not favored, exactly. Tony, being the younger son, was allowed more freedom, more— My parents were simply a bit more indulgent where he was concerned."

She made a doubtful noise. "Somehow, I had the feeling that they were exceedingly indulgent with both of you."

He stopped rowing. Resting his elbows upon his knees, he looked out across the water, the expression on his face reflective. A moment later, he said, "I understand why you might think that, but then, things are not always what they seem. The same would apply to people, I think."

"Yes, I think it would. None of us really show the person we are on the inside to the world, I suppose, but I always thought men to be ... well, stronger—more certain of who they were ... more certain of themselves, of the future."

"A man is a contrivance driven by the never-ending need to prove himself to those about him. We are like pawns in a chess game. We are taught at an early age that being a man means you are moved by the things that will make you look like a man, not by feelings. Oh, we appear to be all those things you mentioned: strong; certain; in control. But it is all an illusion." He looked off again. "If we were honest with ourselves, I suppose we would all admit to being incomplete, of being afraid. We go through life blind—blind to who we are and what we are on the inside."

She felt an awareness she had never known before. It was as if her whole body had come alive. He had opened a door and had given her a glimpse of what was on the inside, and it frightened her. He was too appealing this way, too seductive, too desirable by half, and far too tempting.

"I never thought of it that way," she said. "I was more of the impression that being male and being the firstborn was a privilege, something to be envied."

He took up the oars again—and she knew then that he had revealed all of himself he was going to.

She felt something touch her hand; when she looked down, she was surprised to see it was wet. She was crying, for there came another tear to splash on the back of her hand.

"I don't want your pity," he said. "Don't burden me with that, as well."

She gave him a puzzled look. "Why," she asked. "What is wrong with pity? Would it be appropriate if I called it compassion? Empathy? Kindness?"

The oars clanked as he released them, his body leaning forward until a moment later he was lying beside her, his body half covering hers. Stroking back her hair, he took her in his arms. " 'If thou dost marry, I'll give thee this plague for thy dowry—be thou as chaste as ice, as pure as snow, thou shalt not escape calumny; get thee to a nunnery, go, farewell. . . . Or if thou wilt needs marry, marry a fool, for wise men know well enough what monsters you make of them: to a nunnery, go, and quickly too. . . .' "

She looked at him with surprise, her mouth slightly parted, her eyes as clear and purple as the violets that bloomed in the cool, sun-dappled shade of the woods that edged the lake.

"I should take you back," he whispered, nibbling and kissing the soft, tender flesh of her throat. "God help me, but I don't want to, nor do I think I can. I didn't intend for this to happen."

Too much, he thought. *Too much. Too fast. Too strong.* She was like an opium addiction. No matter how hard he tried, he could not stay away from her, could not keep his hands from touching her.

With a wrenching groan of despair, he kissed her, tenderly and long, with an intensity that he feared would be his undoing. *You are doing it again,* a mocking voice inside his head said. *Go ahead. Seduce her. Seduce her and see how she feels about you.*

The blood chilled in his veins. His heart seemed to stop beating. He felt frozen in place, with no emotion save despair, which seemed to flow into every corner of his body, crippling and disarming, making him feel more empty—more lost and more without hope than he had before.

It was wrong. Wrong to think he could make her fall in love with him. Wrong to think he could persuade her to marry him. Wrong to think he could make up for his transgressions, for the way he had come here with such dishonorable intentions. Despair touched him with icy fingers. Reality damned him. He wanted nothing more than to crush her against him, to take her here, in this boat, driving himself into the heat of her soft body, for only then would he forever banish what he was feeling in his own.

It was too late now, too late, and he knew it. Now he understood his reason for wanting to marry her. He wanted what he could never have. He wanted her to love him, wanted her to want him with the same driving, insane intensity that he felt for her.

He felt a stabbing pain in his head and wondered if he was on the brink of insanity. Is this what drove a man wild? This needing? This wanting? This ever-present denial?

He was not a rational man around her. He knew that and it frightened him. She held too much power. Too much power—and God help him if she ever discovered that.

If there had been any way he could have jumped up and left her, he would have. He would have run and kept on running until his heart burst. His heart was hammering now, each beat reminding him that he was a fool. Why had he allowed himself to fall in love with her? Why did he put himself into this lunatic situation? What made him think she could fall in love with him as easily as she had fallen in love with his brother? Why was he torturing himself with the impossible?

He pulled away from her and closed his eyes, willing his breathing to return to normal, undergoing a metamorphosis, changing himself from what he was to what he should be: in control.

Done. And when it was, he knew he could look at her again, knew that the fear, the despair, would be gone—knew, too, that he could be a man again.

He moved back to his seat, taking up the oars again. He looked at her young face, seeing the confusion written there. She swallowed, her mouth parted, her gaze soft upon his face.

"Don't look at me like that," he said. "If I did not know better, I could mistake it for something else."

The boat headed toward the low arch of a bridge where a willow tree had overgrown its bank. He watched her bend her body, his own body folding over as they passed beneath the bridge, the long, graceful branches of the willow catching in his hair.

They passed beneath the bridge and came out on the other side; he could not help wondering if that wasn't somehow symbolic. One glance at her told him that she was as composed as before, and he knew his own self-possession had returned.

Trailing her fingers through the water again, she glanced up at him. "The quote," she said. " 'Get thee to a nunnery. . . .' Where was it from?"

"*Hamlet,*" he replied.

"*Hamlet.* You surprise me again. I would have never taken you for a man who read Shakespeare."

"There are a lot of things you don't know about me," he said. *Like the way I think about you all the time; how I lie in bed at night, imagining the things I would do with you . . . if you loved me. . . .*

He did not look at her, but caught a glimpse of her out of the corner of his eye. She was watching him in that way she had, when he knew she was analyzing what he had said. *Analyze all you like,* he thought. *You will never know what I am thinking.*

He was so filled with love for her that he could not seem to think rationally. He studied her, his past staring back at him, and he wondered what it would be like to live his usual life again, his days marked by a few hours spent gambling at his club, or between the thighs of a woman who meant nothing more to him than a moment's passion, his world governed by the laws of nature and privateering, his heart touched by nothing more than spending his days sailing on the open sea.

"What are you thinking?" she asked, and he was startled by the interruption to his meditative silence.

"What?"

"Your thoughts ... What are they?"

He flashed her a smile and feared it was too wide, too quickly done. "I was thinking about food," he said lightly, "and wondering what Cook has prepared for lunch."

He saw the light fade from her eyes and thought he had never felt so alone—not since the time when he was six and his father locked him in the closet and forgot about him, leaving him there all day, in a world of darkness and quiet.

"Perhaps we should hurry back," she said softly, "or perhaps it would behoove you to pray for a little patience."

"Patience is a bitter plant," he said.

"Yes," she replied, "but I hear it has a sweet fruit."

CHAPTER
❧ SIXTEEN ❧

By four o'clock the next afternoon, Natasha decided that a day like yesterday made the one that followed seem unquestionably dull.

Tony had gone to Sally's to take Lady Cecilia riding. Cook announced early that the family would dine on a leftover joint of mutton, since she was busy putting a fresh crop of cucumbers to store in crocks of brine. Luka and Pavel were down at the pond catching frogs. Mrs. MacDougal arose in full spate at the crack of dawn, determined to go through the house like a mighty rushing wind, ready to blow every speck of dust, "clear to the Cotswolds." Trevor she had not seen, but she did overhear the twins say they had seen him ride out of the stables at a full gallop.

After lunching on the leftover joint of mutton, Natasha spent some time with Harry, watching him make mulch from wood shavings and chopped marrow, but she soon tired of that and returned to the house to spend some time in the morning room, taking uneven stitches in a basket of mending that always seemed to be overflowing.

Mending, not being an overly taxing enterprise, left

her mind free to wander. As her needle darted in and out of the hem of a muslin sheet, Natasha had a pensive expression on her face and trouble on her mind.

Pausing in thought from time to time, she would stare blankly at a crockery pot of daffodils on the marquetry table in front of the window, her thoughts on Trevor.

As far as she was concerned, her encounters with Trevor in the greenhouse and on the lake changed things between them. It mystified her, tormented her, and over the next few minutes she found her feelings for him too raw and too unexplored to confront. She was in love with him, but she was almost afraid to admit it, even to herself. After all, she had fancied herself in love with Tony a short while ago. True, she had never been in love with Tony, but still, it made her feel wary of her own confidence. Trevor, she assumed, went about his day-to-day life as if nothing had happened between them, while she tortured herself with tender new feelings that she neither desired nor understood. Confused, uncertain, full of self-doubt, she found herself lost in contemplation.

She was not so naive or foolish as to think she understood him, but her thoughts did lean toward trying to. In spite of being somewhat overwhelmed with the discovery that she had fallen in love with him, she was honest enough to admit she had no idea what she should do with either her newfound knowledge or her feelings. In her mind, deciding she was in love with Trevor changed precious little, save the way she felt around him.

She did know one thing: She was not ready for him to leave Marsham. She knew the moment he did, her life would somehow seem boring and dull. He had only come here to save Tony's bethrothal, and now that was done.

She sighed. He would not stay here forever, and the

awesome weight of that truth bore down upon her. It was times like these that she wished she were more knowledgeable about affairs of the heart.

What she knew of men in the romantic sense would not fill a thimble. While the old earl had been a devoted, loving parent-substitute, he had not been the ideal person to guide her in the ways of the heart. With a sharp sense of loss and longing, she found herself remembering vague snatches of her mother, wishing with all her heart she had lived longer. In all her life there had not been one married couple she could use as an example, and she had never felt the loss of that more than right now. Her parents were taken from her at a young age, the old earl was a bachelor, Harry and Cook had never married, and Mrs. MacDougal said herself that her husband had been dead so long she had forgotten what he looked like.

Realizing there was nothing in her past that she could draw upon, she shifted her thoughts to the here and now. Trevor was her focal point, and while she was certain of her feelings, she had not heard him speak of his own. He would, though, because she knew he cared for her. Why else would he pursue her as he had? Why else did he remain here at Marsham, when London was his home?

But caring is not the same as love . . .

She would not think about that. Trevor might not have told her he loved her, but Natasha was certain that he did—at least a little. She lay the sheet in her lap, and leaning back closed her eyes, conjuring up a perfect vision of herself and Trevor, seated before a roaring fire, he smoking a pipe and reading the London paper, she mending their children's socks as their little ones played about them on the floor. She imagined how he would lower the paper and look at her, and how she, feeling his gaze upon her, would lay down her mending to look back at him, catching the gleam of love and pride in his eyes. They would both smile and glance down at the children, knowing it would only be a matter of time until the babes were tucked in bed and they could . . .

Her eyes flew open and she wondered why these kinds of thoughts always ended just when she got to the best part. *Because, featherbrain, you don't know what happens next.* I do, she wanted to say. I live on a farm. I've seen animals breed. But, somehow, whenever she thought about that, she found it awkwardly disturbing to think of herself and Trevor in bed, her on all fours, Trevor mounting her from behind.

Something is missing here. She was certain of it.

If that wasn't sufficient to send her thoughts fleeing, she did not know what was. She glanced down at the sheet, thinking Mrs. MacDougal would be coming to fetch it in a little while, and as she always did, she would exclaim, "I dinna understand it . . ."

To which Natasha would ask her customary question, "And what is that?"

"How peculiar it is that the more sheets you darn, the slower you are at doing it."

She smiled, jabbing the needle through the muslin, thinking Trevor was such a complex man. *He loves me.* She smiled at the thought. *He really loves me. That extraordinary, handsome, sophisticated aristocrat is in love with me.*

Mrs. MacDougal burst into the room a moment later. "Whew! What a day! I have worked my fingers to the bone. Have you finished the mending?"

"I have," Natasha said, handing her the three sheets she had crookedly stitched.

"You finished all of them?" Mrs. MacDougal asked, looking disappointed, since it was a well-known fact that Mrs. Mac thrived on daily drama. "Well, I'll put them to immediate use," she said, tucking the sheets under her arm. Turning, she bustled from the room with the same burst of energy with which she had entered, winking at Natasha in the mirror on her way out.

After she left, Natasha found the quiet of the morning room a welcome retreat from Mrs. Mac's boisterous activities. Her mending done, Natasha lounged back in the big wing-back chair and propped her feet on the footstool, ready to get her thoughts back to Trevor.

She did not get very far, for any further thought on the subject was interrupted when her brothers came bounding into the house—asking her to come outside to look for nests in the gorse bushes.

She was about to say no, when Luka said, "I told you we shouldn't ask her. She never wants to play with us anymore."

If she wasn't already feeling a little guilty for ignoring Luka and Pavel as she had, Natasha might have sent them on their way without her, but Luka's words touched her. She went with them.

As it usually did, their interest waned after a short while—aided by the fact that they found no nests—and seeking a more interesting diversion, they hit upon the idea of playing hide-and-seek.

It was while hiding behind the feed bin in the stables that Natasha, hearing footsteps and thinking it one of her brothers, started to run, only to find herself face-to-face with Ned when she leapt out of her hiding place.

He grabbed her by the arm.

She jerked out of his grasp, taking a step back. "Oh," she said, her hand coming up to splay across her breast, "you frightened me." Her heart seemed frozen in icy fear, trapping the timid heartbeats within her chest.

"Where are you going in such a hurry?" he asked, his

eyes black and speaking of the things he would like to do, things that only their positions in life prevented him from doing.

Seeing her way blocked, Natasha stood still, uncertain as to what she should do. Suppose she refused to answer him? Suppose she gave him a dismissing look and started around him? What if he grabbed her? Fear ate at her now, and for the first time she felt a twinge of nausea. *Face up to him. He knows his place. He would not dare.* "My brothers are looking for me," she said, taking a step backward.

He took a step closer, his gaze moving insolently over her person, his cheek twitching with a tense muscle as he said in his surly way, "I seen you—you and that fancy brother of the earl's. Seen you in the greenhouse. Itching to give it away, weren't you?" He reached out one coarse hand to stroke her cheek. Natasha jerked her head away as she backed up, finding her path blocked by a stall door.

Ned was close enough now so that she could smell the horse and sweat on him, a smell she found quite pleasing on Trevor, but on him, she found it revolting. "Stay away from me," she said. "If you value your job—"

"You ain't gonna say nothing 'bout me, because you know if you do, I've got something to tell on you. So we can make a deal, me and you."

"I'm not making any deals with you," she said, feeling he could see and smell how terrified she was. "I have nothing to hide, and whatever I choose to do is none of your affair."

With swift calculations, her mind sorted through what was happening, weighing the facts. She knew she was in here with him alone. She could scream, but there was no certainty that anyone would hear her if she did. She could run, but what if he was faster?

Her gaze darted toward the door.

His gaze followed hers.

Looking back at him, seeing the leering grin, she knew he understood what she was thinking. She licked her lips, glancing at the door again, afraid to stay, afraid to run and give him a reason to put his hands on her again. She looked back at him.

He understood all right—understood and seemed to gain some perverse sort of pleasure from it. His breathing was heavier now. Lust glittered in his eyes. She knew she had no choice. She had to make a run for it. She had to try.

Just as she was about to break from him, Luka and Pavel picked that particular moment to dash into the stables, announcing to all the world that Natasha had been caught.

For a moment she was too overcome with relief to move. A shudder rippled across her. The rapid departure of the fear that held her in its grip left her feeling weak and wobbly-legged.

"We caught you," Pavel said. "It's our turn to hide."

Without another glance in Ned's direction, she darted around him, joining her brothers as the three of them ran outside. After her brothers left to hide, she prayed they would not pick the stables. She felt a tremendous desire not to penetrate that dark place again, having an uncanny feeling that if she did, she might not be so fortunate the second time.

As she ran in search of her brothers, she vowed to stay completely away from the stables from now on, but even then, something about her encounter with Ned did not sit right with her.

It was a feeling that plagued her throughout dinner:

somehow she did not feel that things between herself and Ned were over.

CHAPTER
❧ SEVENTEEN ❧

Trevor went to bed early that night, but he could not sleep. In her own room, Natasha was not faring much better.

She had been in bed for over an hour, but sleep eluded her. For some time now, her mind had been flitting back to the cause of her unrest—the figure of Ned lurking in the shadows of the stable. Over and over again, it flickered in her mind, a ghostly shadow cast across her life. No matter how hard she tried, she could not force the image from her consciousness. She tried thinking of Trevor—trying once again to picture the handsome planes of his face, yet all that rose up before her were the smoldering black eyes of the stable Gypsy.

Climbing out of bed, she turned up the bedside lamp and tried reading. After a few minutes, she found she was too restless, that the room was unbearably warm and stuffy.

As a last resort, she opened the window, letting in the cool night breeze, and went downstairs to warm a glass of milk.

She knew no one would be about at this late hour, so she went downstairs as she was, in her nightgown, with no slippers and no dressing gown, padding in barefoot silence through a sleeping house.

Once she was back in her room, she put the warm milk on the bedside table and leapt into the bed, falling back and laughing, feeling a bit exhilarated over doing something as daring as going to the kitchen barefoot and in her nightgown. *What would Trevor think if he had seen me?* Suffused with warmth at the thought, she lay there for a moment.

With a sudden burst of energy, she rolled to a sitting position, her feet dangling over the side of the bed as she took a healthy sip of milk, and, finding it scalding hot, dropped it.

The milk spilled down the front of her and splattered over her feet. With a yelp, she jumped up, jerking the gown over her head as she crossed the room.

Standing in front of the mirror, she looked down at the red skin where the milk had spilled across her stomach, deciding it did not look as bad as she'd thought it might. As she opened the door to her armoire and reached for a clean gown, she caught a glimpse of her body in the mirror. A thought, impure and immodest, flashed through her mind and she imagined Trevor seeing her like this. A flood of warmth spread slowly over her, touching her like a lover's hands, making her insides feel buttery and liquid.

She paused, the gown in her hand, thinking how strange it was to feel the same quickening of desire she felt only in his presence.

She dropped the gown onto a tufted stool and turned to stare at her naked reflection in the mirror, her gaze coming to rest on her breasts. Trevor had touched her there; she closed her eyes, recalling the pleasure of it.

She touched herself, as if by doing so she could understand something of what he had felt when he'd touched
her there. Did it give him the same pleasure it gave her?
The thought that it did was pleasing, and yet the sensation was different from when it had been his hand—not
altogether unpleasant, but different. Her hand traveled
lower, across the flat planes of her stomach, a ripple of
desire, nothing more than a trembling flutter, now a
wrenching stab of yearning, traveled downward, bringing a breathless dryness to her throat.

"A beautiful sight," came a voice from behind her,
"but an unbearable one. No man wants to see a lady
touching herself while he's about."

Trevor! Her eyes flew open. With a gasp, she
snatched her gown from the stool, and, holding it in
front of her, spun around to face him; he was standing
in the shadows across the room.

"What are you doing in here?" she whispered.

"I came to see you," he said, with a wolfish grin,
"never knowing my wish would be granted so literally
. . . or so liberally."

Leaning against the opposite wall, his arms crossed
across his chest, he regarded her with an amused twinkle in the depths of his deep blue eyes. It was a look
that heated her face; she knew it was, because she
blushed. There it was again, that same sensation she had
felt moments ago, only stronger and more pleasing.

"I hate to tell you this, yet I fear for my sanity if I
don't. There is something you should know, my little
modest one. While you have gone to great lengths to
cover the front of yourself, you have, I am afraid, quite
neglected the back. You are standing in front of a mirror, and I am having a damnably difficult time convincing myself to keep my hands off you."

Natasha gasped and leapt away from the mirror, but

Trevor went on, as if nothing unusual were happening here. "I have missed seeing you today, sweet Natasha. How have you been?"

Not bothering to answer him, Natasha dived into the bed and pulled the covers up to her chin. One look at his face and she thought, *Bad idea.*

"Wrong move, I'm afraid," he said, crossing the room and coming to stand beside her.

She looked up at him, her eyes growing wide, as if she knew instinctively what was about to happen.

"I'm afraid," she said in a voice so low he might have missed it.

"Of me?" he asked.

"No."

"Surely not yourself?"

"No," she whispered. "I am not afraid of you or me, but more of what happens when we are together."

"Dainty flower," he said as he began to remove his clothes, "what you have seen thus far has not even scratched the surface."

She blinked at that, watching him undo the buttons on his shirt, hearing herself swallow. "Why are you doing this?"

"Because I am bewitched by a violet-eyed Tartar who drives me to it," he said. "Because you want me to, and if what I saw a moment ago is any indication, you are quite ready for it."

Her eyes were huge and seemed frozen on him. She wanted to look away, but found she could not. What he said was true. She did want him, had wanted him for some time, yet her upbringing, her own sense of modesty, the fear of the unknown, made her put up a slight show of resistance. "You must take great delight in frightening inexperienced virgins."

He laughed. "By virtue of the name itself, a virgin

should be inexperienced—but alas, that is not always the case. Regardless, it may please you to know I have yet to have an inexperienced woman ... or, for that matter, a virgin."

She knew she was not his first woman, but the thought that she was his first virgin ... The thought pleased her, knowing she would be the first to give him that. As they looked at each other, the layers of pretense fell away. Even the room seemed quieter than it did before. Everything about them seemed to grow still and hushed, while the world faded away into nothingness. And then it came again, a tiny quiver of apprehension based on the fear of the unknown. Would it be painful?

She pulled the sheet higher, peering at him over the lace edging. His face was unsmiling, and yet she wasn't frightened because of it.

"I don't suppose you want to talk ... ?" she said.

"No, the time for talking is past."

"I—I'm not sure what you expect me to do."

"Don't fret over it. I will show you when the time comes," he said.

"You are going to force me, then?"

He smiled a mocking smile. "Force you?" He unfastened the buttons on his pants. "I think not. Didn't you say that you heard stories about me? All the way from London?"

She nodded weakly.

"Then you know I have never had to force myself on any woman."

It was strange that she had been so nervous about their conversation she had not noticed before now that he had no clothes on. It was a shock, but a minor one. For a moment she wondered what she should do— educate herself by allowing herself to look him over, or squeal with maidenly virtue and turn her head away and thus remain uneducated.

Education won out; she let her gaze roam over him at her leisure.

A man's body was truly a beautiful thing, she decided, and even the sight of the male part of him did not offend her. She was not ignorant. She knew what a man's phallus was for. She had seen farm animals bred. But angry and swollen as it looked, she found the sight of it neither frightened nor repulsed her. Looking at that part of him made her feel . . . Her gaze traveled quickly to his face.

How strange it was to learn that she could look at a man's privates and feel no shame, but the moment she looked at his face, she felt her face grow hot. Before she could think further upon it, he was in the bed with her.

She offered one weak yelp of surprise as his mouth came down upon hers, his hands going around her to hold her tightly against him. The shock of what was happening lasted only a moment, then she began to melt into a slow, languorous burn, the flame within her consuming all trepidation and fear.

Hot, confused, and trembling all over, she wanted something, and when he kissed her, his hand stroking her, she moaned, feeling the soft, secret place between her thighs grow warm and wet from his touch. His mouth traveled over her face and throat, pressing hot kisses as he murmured what he wanted to do to her, what he would do to her. She trembled with excitement as his mouth, hot and wet, closed over the stiff peak of her breast, his tongue teasing, taunting, until she writhed beneath him.

She cried out when he lifted his body from hers, sighing impatiently when she felt him against her again.

She opened herself to him, knowing she pleased him when he groaned, tangling his fingers into her long hair.

She would have liked to say that he forced her, to ease her conscience by saying he took her against her will, that he used her to his own selfish purpose, easing the violence of his own uncurbed passion with little or no regard for her youth, her innocence—that he callously took her virginity, leaving her helpless and in tears.

She would have liked to say that, but she could not.

Their joining was quick and fierce, for it took her no time to learn she wanted him every bit as much as he wanted her. The thought left her a little shaky, but so did the things he was doing to her. She felt exposed, naked, vulnerable. She also loved him, wanted him, and knew this would not be the last time.

The feel of a man's naked skin against her own nudity was alien to her and her body quivered in response. Yet there was a comforting familiarness, a reassurance that soothed her like the warm breadth of his palm, stoking her as one would a skittish horse.

"Lie still," he whispered. "I have so much I want to show you."

"Please," she said, not knowing what she meant.

She was vaguely conscious that she was in her room, surrounded by her things, things that were known to her, dear and familiar, but there was an element of the unknown here, a sensation that gripped her that was unexplored, unfamiliar. Yet she could not honestly say it was unwelcome. And then he was on top of her, pinning her to the bed, his knee coming between her thighs. In spite of herself, in spite of knowing she should refuse him, she felt her body respond, untutored, unsure, but responding nonetheless.

She felt herself opening to him, and wondered then if

she would find it odd later that the moment he thrust into her she was thinking that years of such strict upbringing and religious training were no match for raw instinct. Her mind might be telling her that he had no right to take her virginity without the sanction of holy wedlock, but her body seemed more than agreeable to giving it up.

There were two things that surprised her. One was the fact that he made love to her in a far better manner than she had imagined. How foolish she had been to say she had seen farm animals bred. She decided then and there that there was breeding and there was making love. She was ever so glad humans did it the other way. That surprise she kept to herself. She did, however, tell him about the other.

"It didn't hurt," she said.

He didn't say anything, as if he preferred to simply hold her, looking down into her face, waiting for her to go on. No, he did not say anything, but there was laughter in those eyes.

Her brow drew together. "Did we do something wrong?"

He chuckled. "It didn't feel wrong," he said. "At least not from my quarter." He drew a warm palm across her belly. "How about yours?"

"No," she said, feeling herself shudder at his touch, "it didn't feel wrong to me, either, but I was told it always hurt ... the first time."

"That is a generality, not a bare fact. There are no written rules when you make love."

"But why do you suppose it didn't hurt?"

He raised himself up on his elbows and looked down at her. "Because you were ready for me," he said.

At the sound of that, she smiled and sank back into

the bed. "Yes," she said, with much satisfaction, "I was, wasn't I?"

CHAPTER
❧ EIGHTEEN ❧

It occurred to Natasha some time later that Lady Cecilia had accomplished precisely what she'd set out to do. She had gained control of the situation and completely captivated Anthony in the process. The same wisdom that prompted her decision to snatch Tony from the jaws of defeat must have made her realize there was nothing to be served by having a lengthy engagement. As Cecilia told her, "If my father's wealth and influence can do anything, it can put on the most lavish wedding England has ever seen . . . and do it quickly."

Natasha decided her love for Trevor must be the real thing, considering she had almost no reaction to the news that Lady Cecilia and Tony had set a date for their wedding, save feeling a sense of tremendous relief and happiness to know Cecilia was going to marry the man of her dreams. She wondered if she would be likewise as fortunate.

Natasha sat at her desk, her watercolors in front of her as she put the finishing touches on a bunch of ox-eyed daisies she was painting. She dabbed her brush in the blue paint, and as she made the background a darker hue, she thought about the intense blue of Trevor's eyes.

Any further thought on the subject was interrupted, for at that moment Mrs. MacDougal burst energetically into the room in a cleaning frenzy, attacking the brass fender at the fireplace with a bottle of foul-smelling polish, a bit of flannel, and too much enthusiasm. When the polish fumes got the best of her, Natasha put her paints away and left the room.

She went outside to walk through the gardens, finding them especially lovely in the late afternoon. The dogs joined her, and she found herself wondering where Trevor was.

Inside the house, Trevor stood at the window, watching Natasha and the dogs walking along the garden path. As he had been doing of late, he was thinking. She was in love with him. He knew that, for it was so easy to see. He was also in love with her, but it hadn't been easy for him to see when it had happened.

As Natasha began to fall more deeply in love with him, he had fallen more easily into the role of lover, not realizing when he stopped playing the role and began living it. Loving her was such a natural thing—and so easy to do he had never stopped to consider that he was doing just that . . . falling in love with her.

He loved her, and she loved him. That should make him happy, but it didn't. Her love was based on trust. It was honest and pure.

He could not say those things about himself, about his own feelings, which had been based on deception and dishonesty. He had come here with a purpose in mind: to beguile her. There was no honesty, no purity, save in the feelings he had for her now.

She deserved more. Much more.

For days he had been cross and irritable, without knowing why. When talking to her only last night, he'd said, "It seems I am always waiting ... for no more than a smile, or the touch of your hand. I live with anxiety. Everything is solemn. I have no sense of proportion. It is as if I am in mourning. Perhaps in a way, I am."

Long before he had finished speaking, he realized he was not speaking from long practice or his preconceived plan for her seduction, but from his heart. He could not hide his feelings now, for his passion was made to be seen. It was love that sent him to her room that night—love, not some softer emotion. He knew that for certain, had known it since that day in the boat.

He loved her, and had loved her for quite some time. It was only natural then that it had happened, for when two people are in love, often the inevitable happens and they make love.

He looked away from the window, not moving, but simply staring off into space, remembering.

Since that night in her room, there had been other encounters, other beautiful times they'd spent together, other couplings. While he wasn't exactly proud that he had taken her without marriage, he could not in all honesty say he was sorry. And he did intend to do the right thing, for he knew he wanted to make her his wife.

Tony and Cecilia had made it so easy for him, for they were so enamored with each other and so involved in their wedding plans that they paid no heed to what was happening around them. For a few blissful days it had been a lovers' idyll, with him finding her to be more than he ever dreamed of.

But today something had happened to change all that, and he was feeling the melancholy of it, not understanding the cause. *Why? Why can I find no peace? I have*

done what I set out to do. I wanted her to fall in love
with me and she has.

With a wrenching in his stomach, he suddenly understood. He couldn't go any further with things until he
cleared his conscience. He could not offer her marriage
with the awful truth of why he had come here—and
what he had planned to do—standing between them. It
wasn't enough that he had decided not to follow
through with his plan to propose marriage, then send
her packing to Russia.

He understood now what caused this melancholy
feeling. Guilt. Profound, gut-wrenching guilt for what
he had set out to do.

He glanced out the window again, catching a glimpse
of her throwing a stick for the dogs to retrieve. She had
no way of discerning it, but it gave her a tremendous
innocence— not knowing the harm he had done her.
How ironic. He had set out to seduce her and had ended
up being seduced instead. He had started this thing with
no conscience, and now his conscience was making him
see himself in a new light.

He did not like what he saw.

With a softly sworn oath, he cursed himself, then
turned away from the window.

Over the next few days, the news of the upcoming
marriage of Lady Cecilia and the Earl of Marsham,
spreading rapidly throughout the tiny village and surrounding countryside, was expected.

The gossip about the earl's brother and his Russian
ward was not.

Mrs. MacDougal was the first to catch wind of a sor-
did bit of hearsay, and she quickly voiced her opinion
of those who repeated such prattle.

It was while standing on the steps of church on Sunday that she put Ella Evesham in her place. Ignoring the fact that Harry was standing beside her, Mrs. Mac said, "Ella Evesham, you should be ashamed of yourself . . . repeating gossip like that, right here on the steps of the church."

By the time Mrs. MacDougal finished with her, Ella promised not to say another word to anyone and dashed down the steps with the fear of the Lord in her.

"You sure set her straight," Harry said.

Mrs. Mac looked at him, her chest swelling proudly. " 'The wicked flee when no man pursueth: but the righteous are bold as a lion.' "

True to her promise, Ella breathed not a word, not one syllable to anyone . . . not even to her best friend, Millie Potsherd. Yet in spite of Ella's diligence, the news of Nathasha's abduction by the Earl of Marsham's brother, the Marquess of Haverleigh, was soon common knowledge about Applecore.

"I don't understand it. I put the fear of God into her," Mrs. MacDougal said to Cook. "Ella Evesham may be a lot of things, but fool is not among them."

"Well," Cook said, "if you put the fear of the Lord into her, surely it was not Ella who talked."

"Then who?" Mrs. MacDougal asked. "Who would have said those things about our dear Natasha? Who would do such a dastardly deed to someone the entire village holds with such fondness?"

"Perhaps it is just idle gossip," Cook offered.

Mrs. MacDougal shook her head. "No, the facts are all there, and now it has spread too far to be idle gossip."

"I don't know what we can do," said Cook, with a sad shake of her head. "What cannot be cured, must be endured."

"We are not going to endure anything. We will deny

it and keep on denying it—threatening any gossiping soul who repeats it within an inch of their life," said Mrs. MacDougal, and she meant it.

The merest reminder of the spreading rumors about himself and Natasha made Trevor realize what he had to do.

He would go to her and make things right. He had taken her virginity and ruined her name. He would offer her his name in return.

It wasn't a difficult decision to make, considering he had already thought about marriage, and considering how much he loved her. He had hoped for a little more time, wanting to woo her in true courting fashion, wanting her to have a proper engagement and a big wedding, but that option was closed to them now. Rumors were spreading as fast as a hay field afire, but he knew how to stop them. As soon as word of their betrothal was out, the rumors would cease.

He went to find Natasha, a proposal of marriage on his mind. He found her in the greenhouse, holding a clay pot in her hand.

"Lenten rose," she said, turning to look at him. "It blooms in March and April."

"It looks like a Christmas rose," he said, looking down at the pink blooms.

She smiled. "A close relation," she said. "And like its cousin, it is a poisonous plant. Your uncle loved poisonous plants."

"How well I remember."

"Oh . . . the ivy," she said, allowing her gaze to wander in the direction of that poisonous vine.

He looked at the rose. "It's a devilish plant. Why don't you destroy it?"

"Destroy it?" She glanced down at the innocent-looking rose. "It isn't the plants that are devilish, but the things man does with them. Take this one. In medieval times the black roots were thought to possess magic."

"As you seem to, whenever I am around you." He took a step closer, taking the pot from her and putting it down, then taking her hands in his, smudges and all, kissing each one in turn.

She was deliciously close, a fairy image dusted with muted shafts of sunshine passing through glass. He picked out the variation of color in her black, black hair, while the heavy weight of her skirts, caught against his legs, seemed to hold him trapped against her. About them, the heavy sweetness of flowers in bloom lent a drugging, moist warmth, and he was reminded of that drowsy, sated feeling that comes after making love.

He wanted her.

Now. Tomorrow. Forever. He knew that there would never be a point in his life when he would have enough of her. A lifetime with her was not long enough. Her thoughts filled his nights, her presence his days, and always the sound of her name was on his tongue like a litany. Natasha. Na-ta-sha. Warm. Exotic. Earthy. And soon to be his.

As if knowing his thoughts, she turned away from him, giving him her back; he wondered if it was shyness over what he was thinking that made her turn away.

He moved to stand behind her and gently placed his hands at her waist, pulling her back against him, feeling the shape of her body, inhaling the perfume of her as he nuzzled her neck.

Without really making a conscious decision to, he said, "When you are absent I live with the fear of being shut away from life. And then I see you and I breathe deeply, like Pluto emerging from his underground chambers, rediscovering life and the smell of roses." Turning her to face him, he looked down at the face that brought him so much delight. Taking her in his arms, he buried his face in her hair. "Forgive me, darling Natasha."

She laughed, her breath fanning across his neck. "Forgive you? For what? For loving me?"

He drew back, looking down into her lovely eyes. The trust in them twisted his insides. "Forgive me," he whispered again. "Forgive me for being something other than what I seem, for a hundred things I have said and done, not meaning any of them, only to find out that every deed, every word, brought me closer to you. I love you."

She tilted her head to one side, smiling tentatively, as if there was some element present that made her cautious. "Are you trying to confess something?"

He smiled at her. "Yes, and making a deuced sloppy job of it."

Her eyes seemed to sparkle. "What have you done? Burned the poison ivy? Snooped in my journal? Peeped at me while I was dressing?"

His heart cracked. How could he tell her? The way she looked at him tore his heart from his chest. She trusted him, and the love built on that trust shone in her eyes. Leaning his head back, he closed his eyes, praying for the right words. At last, when he opened them and looked down at her, he knew the moment had come.

Taking her in his arms, his thoughts were a tormented blur. His lips covered hers, a kiss as soft as the petals on the Lenten rose behind her. She looked like a vision before him, sunlight and innocence giving her skin an ethereal quality, the passion she felt for him tinting her cheeks a pale peach. She looked so young, so beautiful, and he would have told her, but he could not, for the only words that he could summon forth were, "I adore you . . . adore you . . . adore you . . ."

And then he broke her heart.

While she lay open to him like a bud in bloom, he told her the words he dreaded to say, how he had first come to Marsham, a man with a mission. "It was my goal from the very beginning to make you fall in love with me."

Trembling, she looked up at him, her voice strangely calm. "And then what? What were you going to do, Trevor, once I fell in love with you?"

His heart burned with remorse. How could he tell her? How could he not? If he owed her anything, he owed her the truth. Owed her his honesty. But how could he tell her that he planned on asking her to sail to Russia with him, so they could be married there, in her homeland. He didn't know how he could, but somehow he found the words, feeling the agony of each syllable, each word he uttered. "But I never had any intention of going with you."

Shocked and pale, she backed away from him, shaking her head in disbelief, her voice so low, he could barely hear her whisper, "I don't believe you."

"It's true, although I wish to God it was not."

He reached for her, but she scooted away from him. He knew how she hurt, knew it was all his fault. He wanted to hold her, to comfort her. How could he tell her his insides were bleeding as well? He had never loved before, and never had he bared his very soul to a woman like this, but knowing he could possibly lose her if she ever found out, he had done just that. Now he found himself opening his heart to her, telling her of his love, his feelings, asking her forgiveness, telling her, "I want you with me. Forever. I'm asking you to become my wife, my little love."

She stiffened, her voice one he did not recognize. "Your wife? Why? So you can insult me further by mocking me?"

"No mockery," he said. "No more lies. Only truth. Only the love I feel for you."

He knew her heart was beating as rapidly as his by the trembling in her voice. "And you expect me to believe you this time?" she asked.

"I love you," he said, taking her hand, wanting desperately to feel her forgiveness flowing from her hand into his, wanting to bask in her warm understanding. *Forgive me, my love. Forgive me . . .*

She jerked her hand back and slapped him. "I hope I never lay eyes upon you again," she said.

A moment later she was gone.

Trevor cursed his soul to damnation, then he picked up the Lenten rose, and, cursing, he hurled it through the glass.

CHAPTER
❧ NINETEEN ❧

Natasha ran from the greenhouse and kept on running.

Too deeply wounded to be moved by words spoken too late, she was not conscious of where she was going. She only knew she wanted to get away from him—far, far away.

She ran down the weedy path that led from the greenhouse, passing the duck pond, the orchard, not bothering to wave back at Harry when he saw her. She ran until she felt the heart within her would burst and the stitch in her side would rip her apart, yet even then she did not slow down. She only stopped running when her legs were numb and rubbery and her lungs felt on fire, when she could not run anymore.

Gasping for breath, she had the mare saddled. She burst from the stables in a full gallop. She rode far past the village of Applecore, intending at first to go all the way to London. But as she rode, her passions cooled and her reason began to return.

She could not abandon her brothers any more than she could leave Marsham. Where would she go? How would she care for them? Why should she punish her brothers for something that was her own fault—and she knew it was partly her fault, for whatever Trevor had done to her, she had given herself to him. Running away would only hurt those who were most innocent.

She pulled her horse up, seeing she was beside a tumbledown fence that edged an old graveyard. Dismounting, she found herself beside a grave with a marker in the shape of a Celtic cross, the words etched there written too long ago to be legible, but to her it did not matter. She hugged the cross and cried—not crying for the crumbling bones that lay beneath that stone, but crying because she hurt, because things would never be as they were. Was there anything as bitter as betrayal? She did not think so.

She knew not how long she cried, but when the hiccuping sobs had ended, when the last of her tears had dried, she knew that her weeping had dispersed her wrath. Now all that was left was emptiness, pain, and sorrow.

She found her horse grazing nearby, and mounting, turned up the road. It was late afternoon by the time she reached the road that led into Applecore, seeing as she passed a group of village boys, some older than herself, coming down the road, fishing poles and the day's catch in their hands.

As she approached them, they began to whisper, their jeers and cutting barbs becoming louder and louder, until one of the boys she knew to be a friend of Ned's taunted her, calling her, "The Earl of Marsham's whore."

"She ain't Marsham's whore, but his brother's," another boy said.

"Maybe she's Marsham's *resident* whore," another said. "Maybe she gives it to anybody that wants it."

"Maybe she's itching to spread her legs in Applecore," said another.

"Maybe we should give her a chance to do it right now."

She knew better than to say anything, to give them any indication that she had heard them, that their words had caused her pain. With her head held high, her riding crop in her hand, she nudged the mare into a faster gait.

As she rode past, one of them grabbed her horse by the bridle, jerking the reins so hard the bit gouged into the mare's tender mouth. The mare whinnied in pain and reared. Natasha felt a hand go around her boot and she lashed out against it with her whip, only to feel another pair of hands tugging at her arm. Losing her balance, she felt herself being pulled from her horse, just as the mare whinnied again and reared, throwing

Natasha from her back with such force that Natasha was hurled down an embankment.

There were no taunts now as the boys watched her limp body roll over and over until it reached the bottom. There were no jeering remarks when her head struck the twisted and bared roots of a massive tree. Not one boy from the village had the courage to call the still and twisted form that lay at the bottom of the hollow any names now.

Up the road, the village parson and his son were having a bit of trouble as well. Their horse had been clipping along the country lane at a smart pace when it threw a shoe. The parson, Mr. Potter, and his son climbed out of the buggy.

"Looks like the Almighty is urging us to walk the rest of the way," the parson said, taking hold of the halter and leading the poor beast on down the road.

The parson had to admit later that it had all happened from the glory of God, for if the horse had not happened to throw a shoe, forcing them to walk, they would not have seen the group of boys running from the hollow, nor discovered the bleeding unconscious body they had left behind.

While the parson saw to Natasha, his son went to catch her mare. A moment later they had the mare unsaddled and hitched to their buggy. Sending his son to Applecore for the doctor, the parson took Natasha back to Marsham.

When the doctor arrived at Marsham, Lady Cecilia took him to Natasha's room, where Tony stood at the foot of the bed and Trevor was seated beside her, holding her pale, lifeless hand.

The doctor looked at Trevor and Tony, then at Lady

Cecilia. "You," he said to Cecilia, "may stay. The rest of you . . . out!"

To Trevor, it seemed like an eternity until the doctor and Cecilia came downstairs. The moment Cecilia saw them, she burst into tears and ran into Tony's arms.

Agonizing fear shot through Trevor. She couldn't be dead. He grabbed the doctor by the arm. "What . . . ?"

"Calm down," the doctor said, prying Trevor's fingers away from his arm. "She has a nasty cut on the head, a cracked rib, and more bruises than a little lass ought to have, but she will be all right. I am sorry to say she lost the baby."

Lady Cecilia stopped crying and looked at Tony. "Oh, Tony! How c-could you?"

"What do you mean, how could I?"

"Y-you will have t-to marry her," she said, dissolving into tears again.

Tony looked astounded. He looked from the doctor to Trevor and back at Cecilia. "Marry her? But I never . . . I didn't— It isn't my baby," he said at last.

"The baby is mine," Trevor said, stepping forward, "and I have asked her to marry me already—although I didn't know about the child." He paused, his face pale and weary as he rubbed the back of his neck, considering something. At last, he said, "I don't think she knew about the child, either."

In that, Trevor was right. Learning she had been with child at the same time she learned she lost it made Trevor's duplicity even harder for Natasha to accept.

"There now, child," Mrs. MacDougal said, wiping her own eyes with a linen cloth. "Two barrels of tears will not heal a bruise. You are only making it harder on yourself. You are using up all your strength, and you need it to get well."

Natasha felt the hot trail of tears against her skin. "How can I face anyone? How can I face my brothers?"

"Those rapscallions? Why, they are the most forgiving lot, and rightly so, since it is forgiveness they always seem to need." She patted Natasha's hand. "You must not worry yourself about Luka and Pavel, love. They might drive a body to the gin bottle, but their love for you is steadfast."

The door opened, and Mrs. MacDougal looked up to see Trevor standing in the doorway.

"Leave us alone for a moment," he said, coming into the room.

Mrs. MacDougal nodded and started for the door.

"Please stay," Natasha said. "I have nothing to say to him."

Mrs. MacDougal paused, glancing from Natasha to Trevor, then Trevor gave her a look that sent her bustling from the room. Coming to Natasha's bedside, he sat down beside her, taking her hand in his. Weakly she tried to pull her hand away, but found she did not have the strength.

"Sometimes when we try the hardest to do what is right, things seem to work out for the worst," he said. "I know saying I am sorry is not what you want to hear, but I have to say it. If it would change anything, Natasha, I would give both of my legs to see this thing undone."

Her look was cold and full of vengeance. "I pray that God will not let you off so easily," she said, then turned her face to the wall.

"Then you should feel gratified to find that he has not. I have no bruises, but I hurt. I have no cuts, yet I bleed. It is all on the inside, where it does not show— where it takes so long to heal. I don't know what to say to ease your pain, and I know I cannot give you back what you have lost. I can only say that whatever pain you feel, I feel twofold; whatever you have lost, I have lost more. My heart has judged my guilt and the verdict is my punishment. That is where your satisfaction lies. You know my sins, my love, but you will never know the secrets of my heart. My conscience has a thousand tongues, and each one curses me for a fool. I desire forgiveness and peace above all earthly pride. I will spend my years yearning for a still and quiet conscience. I will not hurt you more by saying I love you. You know that I do. I will not cause you more suffering by asking you to let me spend the rest of my life making it up to you, although I would give all that I have for the chance. I can only humble myself and say, if you have anything to say to me, any sentiment to express, any feeling for me left at all, please—please say you forgive me."

Natasha turned toward him with hate in her heart. She saw the tears on his face and was glad he suffered. She heard the breaks in his voice that only agony can make and prayed it would continue. She had lost her baby without ever knowing it existed. That made her heart heavy, her grief great. Part of her wanted nothing more than to have him take her in his arms and hold her, while another part of her never wanted to see him again.

"I hate the sight of you," she said. "That is what I have to say." She turned her face to the wall. "Now, leave me alone."

"Will you at least let me . . . ?"

"Get out," was all she said.

He came to his feet, still holding her hand in his. When he kissed her palm, something inside her snapped. She jerked her hand back. "Get away from me, you murderer!" she screamed. "Haven't you done enough? What more do you want? My death as well?

Get out! Get out, do you hear me! Get out of my life!"
Her hysterical screams brought Mrs. MacDougal thundering into the room.

"It's the opium drops," she said to Trevor as she rushed past. "Out of her head, she is. Don't go blaming her for anything she said."

A second later Cecilia and Tony rushed in. Cecilia hurried to Natasha's side, taking her in her arms and talking in a soft, soothing voice. "There, there," she said. "Don't take on so."

Trevor looked at his brother, seeing the agonized pain that clouded his eyes, the look of fear and helplessness on his face. "I have lost her," Trevor said, looking bewildered and lost.

Tony threw his arm around his brother's shoulder and walked him from the room.

Trevor remained at Marsham for two weeks, until Natasha was doing better—at least physically. Daily he would seek her out, going into the garden or the room where she was sitting, her face pale, her eyes dull and lifeless. He would go to her, and on his knees, he would beg her to talk with him, pleading for her forgiveness, but each time he came, she would turn her face away, as if the moments of love and passion between them had never existed.

On the first morning of the third week, he did not come to see her, nor did she see him for the rest of the day. It was only that evening, when she was sitting in the conservatory having tea and she said to Mrs. Mac, "I hope this means he has given up," that she learned the truth.

"Och! I suppose it means that, seeing as how he left for London last night."

Natasha watched Mrs. Mac gather up the tray of tea and leave the room.

She closed her eyes and leaned her head back, feeling the warmth of tears on her face. "It is over and he is gone," she whispered, finding it painful that the reality did not comfort her as much as the thought.

"Though those that are betrayed
   Do feel the treason sharply,
Yet the traitor stands in worse case of woe."
                    —Shakespeare, *Cymbeline*

PART TWO

CHAPTER
❧ TWENTY ❧

Natasha opened her eyes and saw the sun pouring through the window, and then she remembered.

Trevor was gone.

At least Trevor in the flesh was gone, but the memory of him lingered.

Mrs. MacDougal came in and glanced at the untouched tray. "You are skin and bones, lass. You canna heal if you turn your back on food. You must eat."

"I'm not hungry," Natasha said. "Take it away."

With a sigh, Mrs. Mac picked up the tray and left the room.

When she walked into the kitchen, Cook took one look at the tray and said, "Did you ask her if there was anything else she would like?"

"It isn't the food," Mrs. Mac said. "She won't eat until she is ready."

"And when will that be?" asked Cook.

"I don't know, but from the looks of her, it better be soon. She isn't much bigger than a needle's shadow."

"What did the doctor say?"

"He said the same thing yesterday that he says every time he sees her, that she isn't doing well at all. He said she is young and healthy, but her body can't do without food forever. She's had a terrible shock and too many losses." Mrs. Mac shook her head. "She won't eat. She barely talks. She cries out in her sleep like the banshees are after her, and when she is awake she lies there staring at nothing."

"If you ask me, she's keeping all that grief and bitterness bottled up inside her. She needs to let it out."

"I know," Mrs. Mac said, "but what I don't know is how she will be able to."

"Or when," said Cook.

The days that followed passed in a murky haze. About the only thing that happened that she remembered vividly was the news that Mrs. MacDougal gave her when she walked into the kitchen one morning.

"Ned has disappeared," she said.

"And not likely to show his face around Marsham or Applecore ever again," said Harry.

"Good riddance, I say," was Cook's comment on the matter. "Never did trust that shifty-eyed Gypsy. In my opinion, he was working way above his station here. A groom, mind you, when he wasn't fit for nothing but a tinker."

"Or a scissor grinder," Mrs. MacDougal added.

Numb with pain and relief, his disappearance was welcome news to Natasha, but not even Ned's absence could ease the pain she felt. There was little doubt in her mind that it was Ned who spread the rumors about her in the first place, and it was common knowledge in the village that two of the boys who attacked her admitted it was Ned who taunted them and dared them to do it.

Well, he was gone now. The thought gave her little peace, for there was a part of her that refused to believe a man like Ned would give up that easily. There was something about the way he looked at her that went beyond mere attraction. He was a frightening man. Looking back on it all now, she realized she had made a mistake, and a big one, by not telling anyone about Ned's behavior toward her.

"You should have told us sooner," Mrs. MacDougal said. "He was a strange one, all right—enough to make a body shudder. Never did understand why the earl was so kind toward him. None of the dogs liked him, mind you, and any man a dog doesn't trust, I wouldn't give a tuppence for."

"Thank your lucky stars the man is gone," Cook said, offering her a ginger cookie.

"He'll stay gone if he knows what's good for him," said Harry.

The three of them hovered over her like guardian angels, watching her take her cup of tea outside to sit in the garden. The moment she sat down on the bench, she put her cup of tea beside her and buried her face in her hands and cried.

Back in the kitchen, Cook was standing at the window. "Poor little lambie. She is crying like her heart is broken."

"God knows she's had enough happen to her to break a grown man's heart, much less a wee lassie's," said Mrs. MacDougal.

"I wish I could get my hands on Ned," Harry said.

"Simply leaving here wasn't punishment enough," Cook said. "The man ought to be shot."

"He will get his due," Mrs. Mac said. "Mark my words, justice will be served."

"I only wish I was the one serving it," Harry said.

"Do you think there is any hope for them?" Cook asked. "Do you think Trevor will come back?"

"He might," Mrs. MacDougal said, "but I dinna think it will change things between them. She's a stubborn lass and young. In time she will see the truth of it, but it may be too late then. A man like Trevor won't stay single too long."

"How can you say that," Cook said, "when you know he is in love with her?"

"He loves her, but he will have to take a wife someday. He is the heir. He must marry and have children to secure his title. He may not marry for love, but he will marry."

"And Natasha? Will she marry without love?"

"She might, if the opportunity comes while her heart is grieving and unprotected."

Cook shook her head, noticing Harry had slipped from the room.

Mrs. Mac looked back at Natasha. Luka and Pavel were sitting beside her on the bench, one of them on each side of her, the dogs yapping and growling at their feet. Luka was holding her hand, while Pavel had his arm around her shoulders. "The boys are good for her," she said. "They seem to love her more fiercely now then they did before."

Lady Cecilia came often to Marsham for short visits, and each time she looked at the sad, hollow-eyed girl who was her dearest friend, she tried to involve her in the wedding plans. There were lists to compile and invitations to address, dresses to be fitted and parties to attend, and Natasha busied herself with many of these, and while she was as calm and dignified as the happiest of ladies, her eyes showed the ravages of grief.

"I don't suppose it would do any good to invite you to come to London for a visit?" Cecilia asked.

"No, it would not," Natasha said, with a weak smile.

"I do not feel up to that right now. I feel safer here at Marsham . . . safer and more secure. This is my home. My brothers are here. I need them both desperately now."

Cecilia put her hands upon Natasha's arm and gave it a loving squeeze, then she smiled. "I must return to London tomorrow. My mother is on the verge of apoplexy, fretting about all the arrangements."

"Of course you must go," Natasha said.

"But Tasha, I don't want to leave you."

"Dear Cecilia, do not worry for me. My life is not over," she said, "only sad."

"Are you certain—absolutely certain—that I cannot persuade you to come?"

"No, I need time to get over this. But I will get better. My father always said there would be a time for me, a time for roses. I know I shall get on, that things will improve, but I must follow my instincts. You understand, don't you?"

Lady Cecilia gave her arm a squeeze. "Of course I do, but that does not mean I won't miss you. You will come for the wedding, won't you?"

Natasha nodded, patting her friend's hand.

She might be heartsore, she might be the subject of ridicule and gossip, but she had a strength of spirit and the knowledge that her day would come.

She did not go to the wedding, but according to a week-old London *Times*, the marriage of the Earl of Marsham and Lady Cecilia Stanhope was as regal and lavish as any royal one.

Her feet tucked beneath a knitted throw, Natasha sat in the big chair in Marsham's library, warming the chill from her bones in front of a crackling fire. Occasionally she would sip a cup of tea, only to immerse herself in the three-page account of the marriage of the only daughter and heir of the rich and powerful Duke of Whybourn.

Natasha's gaze moved over the typeset account rather quickly, until she came to the part that mentioned the Earl of Marsham was the younger brother of Lord Trevor Hamilton, the Marquess of Haverleigh, and the future Duke of Hillsborough. There was no mention of any woman he might have been with, but there was some speculation as to whether the future Duke of Hillsborough would be taking a wife soon, if for no other reason than to secure the future of the title.

The reminder of Trevor sent tears spilling down her cheeks. The thought of him taking a wife caused her to double over and weep hysterically. She cried until she thought she was all cried out, and then she cried some more. When it was over and the tears subsided, she felt better.

She pulled the *Times* from her lap and tossed it on the floor. She did not feel like reading any more right now. She leaned back in the chair, closing her eyes. Winkum poked his cold nose against the palm of her hand, and she gave his head a good scratching. Blinkum was asleep on the rug beside the fender and Nod was nowhere in sight. Probably still looking for Luka and Pavel, she thought, and the reminder tore at her heart.

Luka and Pavel. She missed them terribly. Her thoughts ran backward, to the day Tony and Lady Cecilia had come to Marsham with a specific purpose in mind. She remembered how she had told them she had been thinking about taking her brothers and going back to Russia.

"To Russia!" Cecilia had exclaimed. "But *we* are your family now. You can't go back to Russia. Your place is with us, with those who love you. You told me yourself that you have no family left in Russia."

"There is no reason for you to go anywhere. Cecilia and I want you to live at Marsham for as long as you like," Tony said.

"But what about you?"

"My father has given us a town house in London, as well as the country estates that came with my mother's dowry," Cecilia said. "Tony and I would never suit in the country. We both love the excitement of London too much."

Before Natasha could tell them how speechless she was at their generosity, Tony said, "We want to send Luka and Pavel to Eton. My uncle stated in his will that he wanted them educated in the manner befitting the sons of a nobleman, and with that in mind, I think Eton is the only choice. Afterward, of course, there would be Cambridge or Oxford."

"Send them away to school?" Natasha said, her expression lost somewhere between sad and bewildered. *Send them away?* She had not thought about that. She despaired at the thought.

"You are displeased?" Tony asked.

"I—I just never thought of them going away so soon," she said, fighting back the tears. *Too many losses. There have been too many losses. I don't want to lose my brothers, too.* But as the thoughts slipped across her mind, she knew she would not be able to hold on to them forever, knew, as well, that it wasn't right to even think she wanted to. They had their own lives to live. Why should they be made to suffer because she had dealt unwisely with her own life?

"If they are to go to Oxford or Cambridge, then they must get a good education now," Tony was saying.

Natasha looked at him. "But, tutors . . ."

"Are not that reliable. And there are other advantages Eton offers besides intellectual ones. Your brothers would be going to school with the sons of the best families in England, forming friendships with future earls and dukes, friendships that would last a lifetime. To deny them an education at Eton would be to deny them a future," Tony said, and came to sit beside her, taking her hand in his. "I know how close you are to your brothers, and if there was any other way . . ."

She looked at him with a wan smile, returning the pat, then placing her hand in her lap. "I know. It—" Her voice broke and she tried again. "It isn't that I don't want all the things you mentioned for them, it is simply that I wish I did not have to lose them."

Lady Cecilia leaned over and slipped her arm through Natasha's. "There will be many opportunities for them to come home, and, of course, you must go visit them. Tony has ordered a new carriage for Marsham, and he has made arrangements for a solicitor in the village to handle all of your accounts."

"Accounts for what?"

"For Marsham. We thought you might want to oversee some repairs. God knows this place is positively creaking with age and badly in need of them. And then, there is the greenhouse, and the gardens. I know you have always taken an interest in the late earl's flowers and—"

"Cecilia, sweetheart. You are overwhelming Natasha with too many details. Suffice it to say there are ample funds on deposit for you to use to bring Marsham back to the grand state it once enjoyed."

"It is too much," Natasha said.

"Nonsense," Lady Cecilia said. "You will be doing us a great service just to stay here and oversee things. It is dreadfully difficult to find someone trustworthy for such a position. It is ever so much nicer when things of that nature are kept in the family."

Natasha sneezed, pulling her shawl more tightly about her, thinking that Tony and Lady Cecilia were now on their wedding trip to a sun-drenched villa in Italy.

And her brothers were off at Eton, engaged in mischief, no doubt. The thought of where Trevor might be flickered in her mind, but she dismissed it. About that time, Nod came padding into the library, looking as lost as a spring snow. He paused for a moment, then, as if he could not think of anything better to do, he came to sit beside Winkum, thrusting his nose in Natasha's lap as well.

Natasha sighed, looking down at the two dogs with their noses in her lap. Even the dogs felt lost without the twins.

"Well, we will simply have to find some things for us to do, won't we?" she said, giving the two beagles a pat on the head.

Fall was in full force now, a mighty November wind thrashing the countryside and catching the sleepy village of Applecore by surprise. Only a few weeks before the Michaelmas daisies were still in bloom, and the coral berries of bryony gave bright color to the dense foliage of the hedge. But now the wind was strong enough to blow slates from Marsham's roof, and Marsham, like many of its neighbors, lost a chimney pot or two. A stately row of ancient elms had always shaded the pathway down to the pond in the summertime, but in the cold November wind, they were no more than black silhouettes against a wintery-colored sky. During the night, two of the elms were uprooted and tossed on their sides.

"Elms got no more roots than a Gypsy peddler," Harry said, with a click of his false teeth. "If it were left to me, I would replace those two with something besides elms. Should have planted horse chestnuts in the first place, if you ask me. Horse chestnuts."

"Then we will plant horse chestnuts," Natasha said.

The next day the weather cleared and the wind died down. Natasha sent Harry into the village to hire someone to repair the slates on the roof, as well as a brick mason to replace the broken chimney pots. While he was gone, she went out into the garden, pulling up dead geraniums and the dried stalks of red and yellow chrysanthemums. In the rose garden dead purple flowers drooped from the bare branches of the bushes, the ground around swept bare of any leaves by the wind.

After depositing the dead roses in the trash bin, Natasha wandered back into the house, making her way into the kitchen for a cup of tea. She found Cook leaning over two steaming pots of water heating on the stove.

Natasha looked at the pots of water. Today was Thursday; Monday was wash day. It was too early to be heating water for a bath.

About that time, Cook looked up. "Wants to scrub down the stone floors, she does . . . in the middle of November."

"Scrub the floors? Mrs. Mac?"

"And who else? I tell you, since your brothers left that woman is past strange. Flies in and out of here like she has a hornet in her drawers, always buzzing—but she never lights. Now, I ask you, why do we have to scrub the stone floors in the middle of November? Why can't we scrub them once a year, in the summer, like any other Christian?"

Natasha was about to ask what being a Christian had to do with it, but the teakettle began whistling merrily, and Cook, clucking and shaking her head, began to make Natasha a cup of tea.

Taking her cup, Natasha left the kitchen, on her way to the library, for already she could smell the sweet aroma of burning apple wood coming from the fireplace. As she passed the old earl's study, something called out to her and made her stop. For a moment she simply stood there, staring at the closed door, wondering why she had the urge to open the door and go inside.

Giving in to the bedevilment that seemed to taunt her, she fished around in her pocket, locating her ring of keys; then poking the key in the lock, she opened the door.

A mellow shaft of sunlight streamed through the mullioned windows. Dust lay everywhere. She smiled as a memory came to her on the wings of an indrawn breath, a musty aroma, surely, but one she remembered so well—for the room still smelled of the earl's tobacco, and his pipe stand stood on the corner of his desk.

Moving around the room, she began to open one book after another, reading a note or two about this botanical garden or the other, or the latest expedition to some exotic place like Borneo. And then she found it: the earl's journal. Opening it, she read the last entry that had been added the day before he died.

Taking the journal with her, she moved to the creaky old leather chair in front of the window. She lit a small lamp and eased into the chair, losing herself in the earl's meticulously kept notes, finding an illustration or two that he had asked her to watercolor for him.

She read until it was dark outside and she heard Mrs. MacDougal moving about the house to light the lamps. Closing the journal, she came to her feet. She put the journal back in its place in the drawer, then gave the room a fond look before opening the door. One last look around, then she told herself she would be back.

There was something about this room . . . perhaps it was because it made her feel closer to her benefactor; perhaps it was because the old earl had been her last connection to her home in Russia; or perhaps it was simply because she was lonely—and while her brothers' rooms were positively stripped of all belongings when they went to Eton, the old earl's study was exactly as he left it.

She blew out the light, and taking the candle with her, she made her way upstairs. Once she was in her room, she removed her clothes and slipped into her dressing gown. She wrote a letter to her brothers, re-reading the last one she had received from them. Then putting her own letter aside, she made a mental note to give it to Harry to mail in the morning.

Leaning back in the chair at her desk, she looked around her room. The house seemed deathly quiet. Her gaze rested on her bed; she remembered a happier time, a time when the impassioned groans of Trevor had blended so perfectly with her own. As she stared at the bed, she was thinking that their child may have been conceived there, their child whose tiny body had been so callously ripped from her.

She came to her feet and blew out the lamp, removing her dressing gown, preferring to slip into her nightgown in the dark, as if by doing so, she could keep all the painful reminders of the past secreted away in the shadows.

She pulled her gown over her head, and, shivering,

climbed into her cold, empty bed. There was no warm body waiting for her there, no man to love her throughout the night and to keep the nightmares at bay.

No, Trevor was not here. But, oh, his memory was.

CHAPTER
❧ TWENTY-ONE ❧

Alone, her brothers gone, her life and her reputation in shambles, Natasha began to live a secluded life as the weather turned colder now, bringing to a new intensity fall's colors. Soon the creeper that climbed the back of the house flamed brightly, autumn's pale amber light fell across the reddening November trees, and down along the garden path a rambling bramble bush left a trail that was both prickly and sweet.

Wandering to the window, she looked out at the cold, brittle remainders of last year's garden. She studied the dark canopy of sky overhead, reading its forecast. There would be snow before morning, unless she missed her guess. Across the yellowed spikes of grass, a few leaves, lost some time ago from the lime tree, bounced across the yard like a curious robin. A sudden, furious gust of wind drove a pile of sycamore leaves along the flagstone path, their curved backs and bent points making them look like awkward crabs just learning to walk.

She stood staring out at the garden, turning a collection of thoughts over and over in her mind. Winter was upon them now, and that meant many lonely days spent indoors. What would she do with herself? How would she pass the time? Now that her brothers were gone, that meant fewer mouths to feed, and Cook would not need any help in the kitchen—and it was certain that Mrs. MacDougal did not need her help, either, for Mrs. Mac was going to enough extremes to find chores to keep herself busy.

She thought about finding work in the village, then reminded herself that she must not forget she was a fallen woman now, and still the topic of much discussion and speculation.

She would be accepted at church—with an air of Christian piety. She knew that was only because Mrs. Mac said the good parson had spent many Sundays since her accident delivering sermons on forgiveness, gossip, and casting the first stone. In spite of all the good sermons, she knew going to the village, let alone working there, was no longer a possibility for her. Just thinking about going made her remember the horrible way she had been treated the last time she was there: the holy looks from the village girls; the sly, suggestive looks from the young men.

It had not taken her long to realize she was not welcome in the village, and that the people there would be as slow to forgive as they were to forget.

When one is not welcome in the village, one learns to stay home. For that reason, it was here, at Marsham, among its lovely gardens, that Natasha began to heal, finding as well a purpose in her life. To her, Marsham was a place of peace, a shelter from ridicule and shame, a place where she could find herself, and she did that through the gardens and plants the old earl loved so well.

As winter set in, she began to look forward to spring, imagining herself pottering about Marsham's gardens, discussing with Harry the pruning of the rose beds or the draining of the water garden, or the best places to plant violets, and primroses, and cowslips, and wood anemones; not forgetting the lilac and laburnum, the asters, the jasmine, and the honeysuckle. As an afterthought, she added lilies of the valley, sweet peas, and the red pinks that she planned to plant around Harry's cottage come spring.

"Harry's cottage?" Mrs. Mac said when told of Tasha's plans. "Tasha, child. You would be wasting your time planting something as pretty as red pinks around his cottage. He won't take care of them. Mind what I say."

When Tasha gave her a questioning look, Mrs. Mac explained. "I had the misfortune of going inside Harry's cottage once—when he was sick and needed tending. It was a pigsty. You could not see the kitchen for the pile of dirty crockery, and the whole place reeked of a year's worth of past meals. It was enough to turn my stomach."

Tasha smiled at this, her gaze going to Mrs. Mac's rotund shape. Anything that would turn her stout stomach was foul, indeed.

Then Natasha hit upon a grand idea. "What would you think about our cleaning up the mess in his cottage and making it a real home for Harry?"

Mrs. Mac snorted her reply. "In a month's time it would be right back the way it was, looking like a pigsty and smelling like a garbage heap."

Tasha thought about that for a moment, remembering the tidy way Harry kept the garden shed, the orderly way he arranged his tools. "Has Harry ever been married?"

"That old fusspot? What woman would have him?"

Tasha took that for a *no*, then said, "I think Harry needs someone to show him how to take care of himself. If we set his cottage to rights, tidying it up for him . . . Well, what is the harm in that?"

Tasha was about to suggest that they give his place a bit more than a thorough cleaning—and a few instructions on how to care for it when they finished—when she saw those words would not be necessary. She stood silently, watching her thoughts chase one another across Mrs. Mac's round face. Already she seemed lost in speculation, her being a champion of lost causes and all.

At last she spoke. "No harm in that, I suppose," she said in a grudging manner. "Anything would be worth a try. I suppose it is our Christian duty, and all."

"Yes," Natasha said, fighting back the urge to break into a smile, "I suppose it is."

Early the next morning, Mrs. Mac was off, paying a visit to Harry's cottage—armed with a sturdy rush basket packed with a stiff scouring brush, a bottle of her own cleaning solution, a tin of wax, polish, and a few flannel cloths.

Natasha and Cook stood at the kitchen window, watching her go, Cook making some good-natured comments about Mrs. Mac going after dirt like some women went after a husband.

Natasha smiled, happy that Mrs. Mac had found a cause, something to put her efforts toward, but even as she felt happy for her, she couldn't help feeling just a little sorry for herself. If only she had a cause, something to put her mind to; something besides thoughts of Trevor. Always Trevor.

As the winter months that enveloped Marsham

Manor began to settle in, she found she no longer had to conform to anyone's standards but her own. She was free. Free of her obligations to the earl. Free of her responsibility to her brothers. Free, at last, of her adoration of Trevor.

She was her own person now, and she felt excited and effervescent, intoxicated even, with the musical lilt of her own voice, the dictates of her mind. She could be anything, do anything, go anywhere she wanted. Little did it matter that she had no specific destination in mind. That, she knew, would come in time. It was out there. She only had to find it, and she would, as one stumbles across an old bottle or belt buckle when taking a walk.

As Tony and Cecilia had hoped, Natasha began to busy herself with plans for the restoration of Marsham Manor. At first only the basic repairs were tackled: bird nests removed from the chimneys; broken windowpanes replaced; cracked molding and plaster repaired; leaky windows mended; rotting boards replaced in the stairway and floors—and when that was done, all the wood floors in Marsham received a loving polish from a crew of local girls, under the tutelage of Mrs. MacDougal.

"The old place fairly shines, it does," Mrs. Mac said, giving the gleaming brass finial on the banister another loving swipe. "Makes me wonder if losing a stone or two would do as much for me," she said.

Harry screwed up his face and gave her a surveying look. "A stone or two would make precious little difference," he said. "You might want to consider a bit more."

Natasha knew Harry meant well, but Mrs. Mac advanced upon the flinching gardener—to wave as brawny a Scot's finger as any stout woman ever had in his face.

Henry took a step backward, until the garden spade in his back pocket knocked over a marble bust of Mozart.

"*You,*" Mrs. Mac said, setting the statue of Mozart to right, "have about as much regard for greatness as you do for kindness."

"The truth is never gentle," Harry said.

Mrs. Mac swelled up to massive proportions. "As the Scots say, 'When you shoot an arrow of truth, dip its point in honey.' "

Natasha was about to tell Mrs. Mac it was the Arabs that coined that phrase, but Mrs. Mac looked formidable enough to take on the whole British fleet, so she saved it for another time.

As the days passed, she found she was reading more of the old earl's journals, curling in front of the fire in the evening with the dogs and a cup of tea, happily discovering that the earl had kept painstakingly detailed notes for some thirty-odd years.

It was about this point in time that she had what she thought of as a divine experience.

There were good days and bad days, but the bad days seemed more prevalent, where thoughts of Trevor never left her mind. Some days were worse than others. Once, when having a particularly distressful day, she sought sanctuary in the earl's study, which had become like a refuge to her. It was while she was there—studying the illustrations of the many plants he wrote about—that she began reflecting upon her past, laying bare the pain and anger in her heart and finding solace in prayer; she felt God urging her to make the gardens of Marsham even lovelier, to make them special and beautiful for others like herself, who needed nature's healing powers.

As she sat there, thinking about the lovely gardens the earl had made, she began to think of ways they could be improved, of particularly lovely plots of land that were now lying fallow—plots that seemed to scream for want of attention.

Problem was, while Natasha knew the locations that would lend themselves well to lush plantings, she had neither the experience nor the background to carry off such a task by herself.

For a brief moment she toyed with the idea of hiring someone to design more gardens for Marsham—there being more than enough money for this, due to Tony and Cecilia's generous support—but the more she thought about it, the more she realized she could never turn such a task over to someone else. Who else knew how beloved Marsham was to the earl?

She had been privileged to have the earl's confidence for several years and to have spent countless hours with him in the greenhouse and gardens, only to spend her evenings doing painstaking illustrations of the plants he wrote about in his journals. There was, she knew, no one who knew these things better than she, no one better to dedicate and devote themselves to making Marsham a botanical garden that would rival any to be found in England.

She set a task for herself. Before making any changes, she would familiarize herself with all of the books in the earl's study. As Cook said, "One does not learn to cook by tackling first a soufflé."

Coming to her feet, Natasha moved to the window and looked out, seeing the swirling gray clouds overhead. At that moment, the sun burst from behind a cloud; she could feel the brilliant rays hovering about her head like an aura.

Now some folks might have said this was simply the sun coming out from behind a cloud, but to Natasha, who felt guided by the very heart that throbbed within her, it was an omen—a sort of confirmation that God had not only given her a task to do, but that he had blessed her decision to carry it out by herself. After all, God himself had planted a garden.

Once she set her mind to it, a team of matched bays could not have pulled her off course. Industrious, smart, and a fast learner, she soon showed the staff at Marsham that she was also a woman with a tremendous amount of self-discipline. Immediately, she set upon the task of reading and familiarizing herself with the botanical books in the study. In the weeks that followed, she embarked upon that task with all the fervor and strength she possessed, memorizing many passages from Gerard's *Herbal*, and Pliny's thirty-seven books of *Historia Naturalis*.

During this period, she also began to order more books, laughing the day Mrs. Mac opened one and handed it to Cook. "Must be a cookbook," she said.

Cook took one look at it and said, "I would never cook something I cannot pronounce." She handed the book to Natasha. "Here, this must be for you.

Natasha took it, glancing at the title. *Historia Plantarum* and *Des Causis Plantarum*. "This is Aristotle's book," she said.

"Well, if it's his book, why did they send it to us?" asked Cook.

It was the first time anyone at Marsham Manor had heard Natasha laugh—really laugh—since the day Trevor left.

CHAPTER
❧ TWENTY-TWO ❧

It was a beautiful sunny morning when Natasha was in the garden cutting the dead blooms from the roses and had the most peculiar feeling that someone was staring at her, as if she were being spied upon. Turning around slowly, she scanned the perimeter of the garden, but saw nothing save the patches of sunlight that mottled the flowers and pathway.

I must be imagining things, she thought with a sigh, feeling a shiver of relief. She was just about to return to her cutting when she noticed the dark shadow of a man standing in the lime trees across the way. She brought her hand up to shade her face and strained her eyes, trying to make him out, but he was too far away to see clearly, and she was not completely certain she would recognize him even if he were closer.

A shudder passed over her and she chastised herself for her childish fright. The garden was close to the house and bathed in sunlight. A robin hopped about, poking here and there in the freshly troweled earth in search of a worm. The silver-gray foliage of the yarrow, the purple columbine, the blue cornflower—all spoke of the garden's innocence, yet she sensed the presence of something evil hovering nearby.

She was distracted for a moment when Beggar came whining around her feet and she looked down, giving his head a pat. But even then she could not shake the premonition that something was not quite right. She felt her body shudder, and for some reason, she had a vague, blurred vision of Ned.

When she glanced toward the man again, he was gone.

CHAPTER
❧ TWENTY-THREE ❧

The parson, Mr. Potter, happened by one afternoon when Natasha was closeted in the earl's study, reading. The fire in the hearth glowed with constant warmth, casting a mellow light on the richly-colored spines of the books on the bookshelves on each side of the hearth. The room was filled with the scent of bayberry candles, as Natasha sat curled up in a chair, the dogs forever at her side.

"What an unexpected pleasure," Natasha said. "Won't you sit down?"

The parson seated himself obediently while Natasha

put down her book and rang for Mrs. MacDougal to bring them some tea.

"How are your brothers doing?" he asked.

"They could not be happier," she said. "Each letter is filled with accounts of all the fun they are having. Even their studies are going well," she said. "I am looking forward to seeing them at Christmas."

"I hope to see them at church when they are home," he said.

Natasha looked a bit guilty, knowing her own attendance had come to an abrupt halt after her accident. "Perhaps they can go with Mrs. Mac," she said.

Mrs. MacDougal came in with a tray of tea and crumpets. The parson put a crumpet on a toasting fork and held it before the fire as he said, "You cannot hide yourself out here forever, Natasha. The sooner you come back into God's fold, the sooner the people of Applecore will forget all that has happened. They are a forgiving lot, and don't really mean you harm."

He burned two crumpets, and rammed a third on the fork. That one he got just right. As he ate it, Natasha told him about the earl's journals, her desire to turn Marsham into a botanical garden.

The parson encouraged her to do just that, offering his assistance. They chatted a few more minutes, then the parson left.

Natasha did not go to church that Sunday or the next Sunday, either, for that matter, so when he returned the following week, she thought it was to remind her of her continued absence from church. Before she could make her apologies, he told her the purpose of his visit. "I brought you something," he said, handing her a copy of John Parkinson's *Sole Paradisus Terrestris*.

Dumbfounded, Natasha looked down at the enormous book of 612 pages—110 of those being full-page botanical illustrations—and all she could think of to say was, "Thank you."

"I cannot take credit for the book," he said, "since the village folk took up donations to buy it for you, but I could be persuaded to admit to dropping a few hints here and there during my sermons."

"Would a cup of tea and a few crumpets be sufficient persuasion?"

The parson smiled. "Indeed it would."

As she had done with the other books, she devoured this one with a cup of tea in the evenings, before a crackling fire. The more she read and learned, the more her confidence and capabilities grew.

Christmas came, and Natasha's spirits seemed to lift the moment the twins came home. As holidays often are, this one proved to be too short, and before she knew it, it was time for them to return to school. At least this time she was able to hold back her tears until they left.

Soon after Luka and Pavel returned to Eton, she began her first task, choosing the cold winter months to rework the greenhouse with the help of Harry. Thankfully the worst of winter passed in gentlemanly fashion, and March was doing its blustery best. Natasha had just returned from a visit to Eton when Tony and Cecilia arrived. It was now toward the end of the month, and what little wind there was came from the west or southwest. The sun was gaining power daily, and Natasha now found it quite pleasant to be outside again after a long winter confinement.

She spent the afternoon in the kitchen garden, working in its mixed border of purple tradescantia, daylilies, sweet-scented lilac, phlox, and Michaelmas daisies, pausing to look at the lavender growing beside the gooseberry bush where Luka and Pavel liked to bury their treasures.

Cecilia was content to sit upon the stone garden bench and talk, wearing a lovely blue morning dress and one of those odd bonnets that Tony loved to refer to as ridiculous. She was telling Natasha all the latest London gossip and begging her to come back to London with them, if only for a short visit.

At first, all this talk about London set Natasha to thinking about Trevor, and she found her mood growing dark, but soon Cecilia's cheeriness began to creep over her, and she smiled and tossed a handful of weeds into the garden cart and sat back.

She pushed a trailing wisp of hair back from her face. "Come to London? Oh, my stars! I could never leave Marsham now. I would need an army to accomplish all I have set out to do as it is. If I were to be gone even for a fortnight, I would never finish my work in time. And poor Harry—he would be lost without me."

Cecilia's brows knitted together as she cast a speculative eye in Harry's direction. "Faith! The man looks lost anyway."

Natasha laughed at that.

"But you don't have to work all the time," Cecilia said.

The raucous cry of a rook overhead drew their attention away for a moment, then Cecilia leaned down and took the lid from a round box sitting on the ground beside her. Pushing back layers of tissue, she withdrew a beautiful lavender bonnet with purple satin ribbons and a curly feather that draped down one side.

Natasha studied the bonnet. It was far prettier than anything she had seen Cecilia wear before.

"I bet that cost a pretty penny," Natasha said.

Lady Cecilia shrugged. "I bought it for you."

The cheery expression on Natasha's face faded. "I have no use for a bonnet that fine," she said. "I never go anywhere. . . ."

"Then wear it to work in the garden. It is my gift to you. What you do with it is your own affair." With that, Cecilia thrust the bonnet back in the box and handed it to Natasha.

Natasha took the box. "But why?" she asked.

"Because you are my friend," Cecilia said, as if it were the most logical thing in the world, and looking at her, seeing the warmth in her eyes, Natasha supposed that it was.

Natasha looked at the bonnet, knowing she had never seen anything so fine in all her life—and just her color. "I do not know how to thank you," she said.

Cecilia smiled. "You don't have to. Your eyes do it for you."

That night, as they were coming down the stairs for dinner, Tony remarked to Cecilia, "It concerns me that Natasha has no one here to fraternize with save the staff. Observing her, one would think Harry to be her dearest uncle, and I am of the opinion that Cook and Mrs. Mac hover over her far too much."

"They are like family to her," Cecilia said. "She holds the lot of them in very high regard. I see no way that any harm could come from it. She seems happy."

"Regardless of her affections, it will not do for her to keep such close connections to the hired help once she begins to take her proper place in society. Any interested men of title would find her close association with the staff a great hindrance."

"From what she says, Tasha has no intentions of taking her proper place in society, or snagging herself a husband. She seems remarkably content doing what she is doing."

Tony chuckled at that. "She may be content, my love, but any man with an ounce of red blood that sees her will do his damnedest to change her mind."

"They may try," Cecilia said, with a smug countenance, "but Tasha will be a formidable opponent for one very important reason."

"And what is that?"

"She is still in love with your brother."

Tony seemed amazed by that. "In love with Trevor? Still? How do you know?"

Cecilia gave him an owlish look. "We women know these things," she said, shrieking when Tony grabbed her.

"Then come here and show me what else you know," he said, pulling her against him and silencing her astonished mouth with a long kiss.

Spring came, and the pace became hectic as Natasha worked the grounds by day and read her books and journals by night. Her hard work had its rewards, and these became days of endless wonder for her, days filled with learning and discovery.

As the renovation work around Marsham began to pile up, Tony and Cecilia sent temporary help from London, in the form of six additional gardeners—one of them having been in the employ of the Hamilton family for quite some time. "Since Trevor was in nappies," as he put it. Natasha took the reminder of Trevor without showing a flicker of emotion; the pain was all on the inside. That night, as she did every night, she wrote of him in her journal, releasing the pain in the only way she knew how.

It was while writing her thoughts of him late one

night that she hit upon an idea. For some time now, she had been thinking of making herself a hidden garden, and now she had the perfect reason: it would be a tribute, a reminder, a place of physical beauty to be erected, like a memorial plaque, to the memory of a love that was never to be.

There was a place not far from the water garden that lay in a secluded place, a tree-embowered grove with a quiet charm that had always spoken to her. She put the journal away and took out her sketching pad. The hidden garden would be small but beautifully executed, with room for only her most favorite plants. She drew the borders of shrubs, the May bloomers—lilacs, guelder rose, white broom, laburnum, *Malus floribunda*, and a shrub she found beautiful, which was too often ignored, *Exochorda racemosa*, or pearl bush, with its pearllike buds.

She closed her eyes, imagining the white flowers and feathery lilacs shedding light in the darkest corners of the garden, then she hit upon an idea. White. She would plant only the things that bloomed white. Absorbed now, she continued to draw the plan of her hidden garden, sketching in the plot for white broom, remembering its tendency to grow tall and leggy. She drew in the plots for white climbing roses, filling in with sturdy white irises and white tulips. She added *Magnolia stellata*, whose milk white flowers Luka and Pavel had tried to count once, only to give up when they reached a thousand. Next came the white narcissi, *Tresamble*, and daffodils, Madonna lilies—and of course no garden was complete without daisies.

Solomon's seal came next, and she remembered how the earl had written in his journal that it had derived its name from the markings on its stem, which when cut through are said to look like the seal of King Solomon.

She remembered something else, too, how the Tudor herbalists used it to cure bruises caused by "woman's willfulness in stumbling upon their nasty husband's fists."

Yes, she thought, no garden tribute to a man was complete without Solomon's seal.

She worked far into the night, but when she finished, she slept better than she could remember since Trevor had left.

She arose early the next morning, going to the secluded spot she had immortalized in her drawings the night before. Rolling out the plan, she secured it with four stones, then set to work, marking out each bed, each plot. She returned to the hidden garden every day, bringing a new bush or bulb to plant each time she came. It was only when she finished that she realized she had not only made the garden as a tribute to a love that would never be, but to her lost innocence as well, an innocence that she had so lovingly captured in a snowy display of white against a backdrop of glossy green.

Often she would come to the garden, thinking back upon the times she had spent with Trevor, not times spent in analyzing what happened, or might have happened, but finding herself content to merely think upon what did happen. While she could not bestow upon him the purity of a saint, she could not, in all fairness, wholly condemn him for what he had done. She could never trust him again, but felt she was past condemnation now.

And so, with all the devotion and enthusiasm of her young years, Natasha spent her time reading at night and executing what she had learned by day. She drew plans for garden after garden, plotting out ways to enhance the beauty of the mill pond, where the water tumbled over a cascade, or to build a rock garden where the land was rocky and had too much slope.

Soon Marsham began to flourish, and the moorhens nurtured their broods of black velvet chicks along the grassy lakeside, where the path curved through boscage and the light reflected a willow, low on the lake. Often she would sit there, beside the water in the evening, remembering how she and her brothers had disturbed the lake's gentle patina as they caught gudgeon with rods and nets and then ate them fried for tea.

The grounds of Marsham became an enchanted place, a place where great poplars thrust up from a tangle of underwood, alders, and lady ferns, where a curious green orchid called twayblade grew on the lake fringes and water forget-me-nots edged the slow-flowing stream above the lake; marsh marigolds studded the meadow, and when the summer drew to a close, ragged robin, meadowsweet, and marsh orchids bloomed in profusion. And so time passed, like the rhythmic undulation of flowers and leaves, and she wove their memories in her mind, like the delicate embroidery in colored silk she stitched in the evenings when she was too tired to draw or read.

Beating the very devil out of the parlor rug, Mrs. Mac paused with her arm in midair as she watched Natasha and the dogs coming up the path, Natasha's arms laden with a profusion of flowers, as they were every evening.

"It amazes me," she said to Cook, whose help she had enlisted, "that she seems to have grown even more beautiful during the winter."

"She is a woman now, and in full bloom," Cook said. "Sometimes I find myself thinking it would do my old heart proud to see *you-know-who* show his arse around here, just so I could take pleasure in kicking it—right after I treated myself to the pleasure of seeing his bloody face when he saw what he threw away. She was a beauty before. She is without rival now. Do you suppose he ever thinks of her anymore?"

Mrs. Mac did not have to think about that one wit. "Oh, I think he thinks of her more than any of us know."

CHAPTER
❧ TWENTY-FOUR ❧

"Are you up to this?" Tony asked his brother as he and Trevor made their way down the long hallway of Carlton House, en route to the ballroom. "Caro Lamb says Henrietta has announced her plans to marry you."

"Henrietta Oxford can go to hell," Trevor said. "Lord Byron has no idea how fortunate he is to have been forced into exile. I wish to God it were possible for me."

"Well, cheer up old chap," Tony said, clapping his brother on the back. "Lord Byron received his glorious exile when he signed the deeds of separation. If you want to marry so you can be divorced and sent into exile, then maybe Henrietta Oxford is the one for you."

"You can go to hell as well," Trevor said.

"That is precisely what Caro Lamb told me when I told her you had no desire to be married," Tony said.

"Caro Lamb would do good to mind her own marriage—which is in considerable peril, I might add—and leave the prospects of mine to me."

They stopped at the top of the stairs of that grandiose palace with its exquisitely ornate decor, Trevor's mind neither upon its costly furnishings nor its priceless art treasures. What he was thinking, as he often did, was about a violet-eyed beauty with hair as black as pitch and a heart-thundering accent.

In the first weeks and months after he had left her, he found it strange that the very thing that haunted his days and nights until the point of madness was also the very thing that helped him hang on to his sanity. The fact of losing her drove him mad. The thought of having her back gave him a reason to go on.

As the weeks became months, he began to fear he would never see his dream of having her back. When the pain of his loss became unbearable, he would force himself to think back, to relive each precious moment he had spent with her, pushing himself to concentrate upon the most minute details—the way her hair seemed to absorb the sunlight, the exact shade of the blue-violet depths of her exquisite eyes, the baby-soft feel of her skin, the milky fairness of it.

He remembered the way she had looked at him when he made love to her, the openness with which she gave herself to him, and as always, he remembered, to his own eternal damnation, the way he had cruelly driven that loving, adoring look from her eyes.

Somehow, by reliving the pain that was in his heart, he was able to alleviate the madness that lurked within his mind. But forever, there lurked the sound of her name. Natasha.

Before long, he began to find that remembering past times was not enough, and soon he began to dream, to imagine, to think of her in ways that never existed, to conjure up scenes and events that never happened, scenes that changed the terrible outcome of what occurred between them. But, as always, when the imaginings passed, he was left with only the bitterness, the pain, the residue of what might have been.

Christmas was the lowest point, when he wondered if he would ever find a purpose in his life without her, if he would ever have the chance to atone for what he had done.

Sometimes he had no difficulty enduring her absence and he would breathe easily, thinking, at last, he was again normal. Soon he would come awake, longing for the bodily presence that was too long denied him, as if each breath he drew was incomplete. *Pothos*. That is what it was. *Pothos*, desire for the absent being. It ate at him like a sickness. "Trop penser me font amours." He found himself remembering the old French song his nanny used to sing—"Love makes me think too much."

And if that was not enough, the Duke of Hillsborough died suddenly, and in his sleep. The moment word reached him, Trevor went to his parents' home to console his mother. The butler opened the door. "Good evening, Your Grace."

For a moment Trevor stood in the doorway, staring at the butler. He found it odd that before the news of his father's death became real to him, he found himself taking his father's place.

The Dowager Duchess of Hillsborough lifted her tear-stained face the moment her eldest son walked into the room. "The duke is dead," she said. "Long live the duke."

Trevor went to his mother, taking her in his arms. He was the Duke of Hillsborough now. How strange life could be. He never wanted to be a duke, and yet he was one, while the one thing he wanted above all others, he would never have.

Natasha. Natasha. Natasha.

When would the torment end?

CHAPTER
❦ TWENTY-FIVE ❦

Even before the gardens at Marsham were completed, Natasha knew, in spite of what others said, that it was more than a lonely woman's silliness, more than a bunch of youthful poppycock, more than a spinster woman's penchant for whimsy.

Uncanny as it might seem, there was something almost mystical about it—something within the realm of gardening that kindled her flourishing imagination and called her to nature—nature, neither understanding nor forgiving, but accepting with an equal mind.

The more she studied and learned, the more she saw how nature never overlooked, how she put beauty into every pathless forgotten wood, each weedy garden, struggling to give life to death. In her unfulfilled and fragmentary existence, she longed for the peace of nature. Nature who must love the incomplete, for what in nature was ever concluded?

She looked down at a handful of geranium seeds in her hand. "How small they are, and yet the mystery of beginnings is hidden within. Each tiny seed we plant, we plant in faith rather than understanding." She gave Harry an odd look. " 'If ye have faith of a grain of mustard seed' . . . Is that what faith is after all—obedience?"

Harry's weathered face turned a bit red, and she knew he felt cornered. " 'Tis, I think, what she teaches all of us . . . obedience to her ways. When you plant those seeds you have faith that they will grow, but you plant them out of obedience," he said, his face turning even redder. Then muttering his farewell, the gardener picked up the handles of his garden cart and pushed it toward the garden gate, leaving Natasha to stare after him, wondering what it was in life that made a man with such understanding become a simple gardener.

Here, at Marsham, Natasha had the space and resources to nurture her call to nature and her flourishing imagination. She never dreamed she would find such delight in draping a clematis swag, or making a miniscule composition of wild violets, the muted color of hellebores and bergenias, the contrast of the vivid yellow leaves of valerian in contrast to blue hyacinths and scillas. The world, in all its color, reached out to her, and she responded.

At the close of the day, when she was forced indoors, she would spend her evenings making color illustrations of many of the plants and plant associations she used in her gardens, or writing letters to those she corresponded with, enclosing as she always did a sprig of mistletoe—because she had read once that mistletoe was a warning to be cautious in love.

"Are you going to stay up all night? Even God rested between creations."

Natasha looked up to see the stout frame of Mrs. MacDougal filling the doorway. She noted that Mrs. Mac was watching her with a slight, knowing smile playing about her mouth.

"He rested, but only on the seventh day," Natasha said, putting her hands at the back of her waist and leaning back in the chair, hoping to stretch away the stiffness.

"Well then, if you aren't tired, would you mind writing out that recipe for salad you promised Cook?"

"The one from Mrs. Cherry," Natasha said as she searched through her correspondence. Mrs. Cherry was reputed to be the best cook in the Cotswolds, and after Natasha had sent her some anemone seed that she had written for—and as an extra treat enclosed a few seed for the great white OEnothera—Mrs. Cherry, in turn, sent Natasha her prized recipe for salad.

"I'm glad you reminded me," Natasha said. "I'm afraid I had forgotten." Locating the recipe, she took out pen and paper. Dipping her pen in ink, she began to faithfully copy Mrs. Cherry's recipe for salad.

Two slices of onion very thin
One apple
Six chilies
One rather large raw tomato sliced
Half a beetroot well boiled and cold before being sliced
Two tablespoonfuls of vinegar
Two tablespoonfuls of salt

After Mrs. Mac left, a suspicion of a smile touched Natasha's lips as she began to paint the red-orange blooms of lychnis and salvia, weakening the color and adding more yellow, matching to the exact shade the nasturtium by the back stoop that burst into bloom only yesterday.

How peculiar it was that the pain and despair of the darkest period in her life had been the very thing to prompt her to seek solace. She was now happy and fulfilled, her life spent out-of-doors, saturated with sunshine, color, and the perfume of flowers. Even the darkness was bursting with the fragrance of night-scented stocks.

She realized now that she had always put too much faith in others—her father, the old earl, her brothers, Lady Cecilia, and Tony, Trevor even—looking to them for the fulfillment in her life. And she had always been disappointed.

Things were going to change. From this moment on, and for the rest of her life, she, Natasha Alexandra Simonov, would rely on no one but herself. She was going to prove that she could carve out a place for herself, that she could do more than depend upon others to take care of her.

Like the old earl who adopted her, she was industrious and bound to self-education. Like the daughters of wealthy families, she was taught to draw and watercolor. To that she added her own diligence and self-discipline.

Many things had been taken from her, but the things she had been given—things that could not be taken away—these would see her through.

It was not long before she began corresponding with several of the most respected names in horticulture, writing to one, "No one can compete with nature by artificial planting, but one can learn from nature and use the knowledge of simplicity, reserve, and purpose to transpose a garden."

Before long, Natasha found she was beginning to cultivate a steadiness of purpose for the idea of design and layout, for planting and gardening, that was beginning to absorb her completely.

"One would have to visit Marsham to appreciate the grand scale of her accomplishments," Lady Cecilia wrote to her parents during a stay with Natasha.

Mother, you should see the rose garden, clotted with blooms. And please do clip the article she wrote for the Royal Botanical Society from the paper and save it for me. Save all your copies of the *Illustrated Gardener* as well, for it has just come to my attention that she is doing a series of twelve articles for them.

Although she still shied away from frequent visits to Applecore, Natasha's curiosity did take her beyond the boundaries of either Applecore or Marsham, and soon she began to visit nurseries, making a special trip to Loddiges at Hackney in order to see one of two *Wisteria sinensis* John Reeves brought back from China. She was instrumental in persuading Mr. Reeves to place the other wisteria in the horticulture society's garden at Chiswick.

By the time the gardens at Marsham were completed, her fame was spreading, and she knew she would not stop there. She was not so naive as to think it would be easy for her to botanize her way into the small, select group of world-renowned horticulturists. Well-known horticulturists were small in number, especially in England, and there were not many women among their ranks.

It was about this time that she formed a friendship

with Joseph Banks, a wealthy Lincolnshire landowner who was honorary director of the Royal Botanic Gardens at Kew. It was Joseph Banks who put her in touch with Humphrey Sibthorp, the professor of botany at Oxford, and Prof. John Martyn, professor of botany at Cambridge. Corresponding with these two men, she learned much.

In one of his letters to her, Joseph Banks invited Natasha to visit him at Kew Gardens. She went to Kew, and from that moment on, a whole new world opened up for her.

"You are going to be quite a famous lass," Mrs. Mac said one afternoon. "I can see it all now. Mark my words. Whatever you want is going to be yours."

Natasha forced a smile, not wanting Mrs. Mac to know how her words had cut to the heart of her.

Whatever you want is going to be yours . . .

Deep in her heart she knew that could never happen. Not really. Not if she were truly honest with herself. Trevor, she had wanted, but he was as lost to her as the babe they had created.

She knew then that many things would come to her in this life, but some things were never meant to be.

Trevor was one of them.

CHAPTER
❧ TWENTY-SIX ❧

While Natasha was using her artistic perception and botanical knowledge to make a name for herself, Trevor Hamilton, the Duke of Hillsborough, was becoming a powerful and respected figure in his own right.

Having distinguished himself during the war with Napoléon, he was almost as famous as his good friend . . . the Duke of Wellington.

There were no orators in the House of Lords of quite the same caliber as the Duke of Hillsborough, and he continued to grow in prominence and prestige, wielding the nation's power and purse. He counted among his friends the most influential in England, and among the ladies he was considered England's prime catch. The reality of having to take a wife had never hovered more heavily over his head.

Tony reminded him of that one afternoon when he stopped by Trevor's office. "Mother has been dropping hints of late. I think she would like for you to at least start considering the prospects for a wife."

Trevor gave Tony a weary look. "I know she would, but the time just isn't right."

"Will it ever be right, Trev?"

"I don't know. I came so close to marriage once," he told Tony, "so close that it is difficult for me to think of myself in any other fashion. In my mind, I know I am not married, but my heart sees it another way."

"Perhaps if you involved yourself more socially . . ."

Trevor gave Tony a derisive look. "Are you, in a roundabout way, speaking of social indiscretions?"

Tony's blue eyes studied his brother as his brows narrowed to a slight frown. "You are becoming quite cynical, Trev."

"You, dear brother, are absolutely right. I find I have a cynicism that would delight Byron. Strange as it may sound, I find myself agreeing with what he said: 'One must make love mechanically, as one swims. I was once very fond of both, but now, as I never swim unless I tumble in the water, I don't make love till almost obliged.' Like Byron, when the need presses down upon me, there are women one can go to without complications, without commitment."

"Have you considered taking a mistress?"

Trevor laughed. "I said without complications, without commitment. In some ways, one can become more entangled with a mistress than a wife." He turned to look at his brother, his eyes clouded with pain. 'I loved her . . . and I broke her heart. I understand why she turned me away. I deserved it. To this day, the guilt eats at me. I suffer, even now, but in many ways, it changes nothing. I loved her then. I love her now. To think of another woman—save for the biological urgings that press upon me from time to time . . ."

"I never knew your feelings for her went this deep," Tony said.

"They are not deep," Trevor said, "they are all-encompassing—to a depth and breadth even you would have trouble understanding. She is in me as much as the air I breathe, as much a part of me as my very bones. I am bound to eternal damnation by the dictates of my heart. I love, knowing I can never be loved in return. There are times when I think I will go mad with longing, times when I feel I could rip my own heart out with my bare hands, but even then, I know it would do no good. She is in my flesh, in the marrow of my bones. To even think of myself in love with another woman would be blasphemy. The memory of her lying in my arms oozes from my mind like knife wounds."

"And so you work."

"And so I work, and I will keep on working until I die—or I drive these demons that torment me from my mind."

"I'm sorry, Trev. I wish there was something I could do. Do you think it would do any good to see her, to talk to her?"

"No. I know what she thinks of me, what she would say. Coward that I am, I would spare myself that. There is no way in hell she would ever see me as anything but a liar, a scoundrel, and a cheat. She loved me. She trusted me. And I was only playing a game—hateful as the gates of hell. I hid one thing in my mind and said something else entirely, and now I pay."

Tony shook his head. "It is almost strange how the man who had so many women in love with him during his life can love only once," Tony said, picking up his hat and greatcoat and walking toward the door. He paused, then turned back toward his brother. "I don't suppose there is any way to interest you in coming to the theater with Cecilia and me on Thursday. Lady Barbara Kensington is our houseguest. She would be pleased, I know, to have you as her escort. She speaks very fondly of you."

A melancholy look passed over Trevor's face. "She

always has, and I of her," Trevor said, smiling sadly. He was remembering Lady Barbara was the first girl he had fancied himself in love with—when she was thirteen and he fifteen. She was the first girl he ever kissed.

Tony's voice sounded optimistic. "You will come, then?"

" 'Of all my loves the last, for hereafter I shall glow with passion for no other woman.' I cannot."

A helpless look crossed Tony's face. "I wish I could say I understood, but I do not." He shook his head. "I love Cecilia, but to love as you do . . . to be undone . . . The feeling escapes me." With forced lightness, he said, "Will I see you at Mother's for dinner on Sunday?"

"Sunday dinner at Mother's, as usual," Trevor said, his voice light and tinged with humor now. "For that, I can be regular as the changing of seasons."

"I wish your preoccupation with Natasha could change as easily as the seasons. It's been long enough, Trev. I would have thought you would have gotten over her by now."

"Don't worry about me. It will pass, I assure you. It may take a while, but it will pass," Trevor said.

Tony nodded, then said good-bye and ducked through the door. As he closed the door behind him, he paused a moment, then turned, staring at the door as if considering something. Then he shook his head, as a man would do who was saddened, or deeply regretted something.

It will pass . . .

"I wish to God I could believe that," he said, then slowly walked away.

The following Sunday, the Dowager Duchess of Hillsborough gazed at her two sons with a mother's fondness. She had lost weight since the death of her husband, but even that did little to detract from the slim and graceful woman, for in truth, it only seemed to add dignity to a face and figure that belonged on a much younger woman. Even in the black mourning dress she looked spectacular, and Trevor told her so.

"No one can look spectacular in black bombazine," the duchess said, "but I am hungry for compliments and I thank you for it."

"You are quite welcome, Mother."

As she studied the features of her firstborn, a worried frown crossed her brow.

It was apparent that Trevor had lost weight—and signs of strain and fatigue were quite noticeable on the face she knew so well. "I have never seen you looking so ravaged, Trevor. You are as pale as a gutted fish."

"Why, thank you, Mother. It's always nice to be around those who love you."

"You know I love you, Trevor, but if a mother cannot be honest, then who can?"

"Who indeed?" was Trevor's sarcastic reply.

A short while later, Trevor kissed his mother and made his departure. The moment he was gone, the duchess looked at Tony. "He needs a little prodding," she said. "See if you can't encourage him to get out more."

"I've been trying, Mother."

"Well, try harder, and give my love to Cecilia. Tell her to pay Dr. Harrison a visit. If she isn't with child, I'll eat my hat."

Tony's face brightened. "Do you really think so?"

"She has had far too many stomach ailments of late for it to be anything else. Of course, it should be her mother's place to tell her these things, but I'm not too certain that rattle-headed mother of hers knows any more than Cecilia does." The duchess paused in thought. "Perhaps that is why Cecilia was an only child. Well, enough of that. Now, come and kiss your mother, then go see how Cecilia is getting on. And don't forget to tell her about Dr. Harrison."

Tony kissed the duchess's cheek. "I'll tell her," he said, and started from the room.

"And don't forget about your brother," the duchess called after him.

Tony gave her a grin and a salute. "I won't."

True to his word, Tony kept a closer eye on Trevor in the days that followed, making it a point to get Trevor in the company of beautiful, well-born young women whenever he could. It became quite entertaining for Tony and Cecilia to observe from a distance as the women shamelessly flirted with Trevor, doing everything in their power to get his attention. But as far as Trevor was concerned, the women were all too eager, too available, and they tried too hard. There was only one woman out of the gaggle that seemed to cluster around Trevor who even came close to holding his attention for more than a few minutes.

There had been a time when Trevor had found Lady Jane Penworthy quite a sensuous beauty. Even now, he found her charming and witty; a woman who was able to get his mind off Natasha for a time. But Jane didn't have hair as black as a raven's wing, or eyes the color of violets, and whenever their eyes met there was never a jolt of desire.

"You could do a lot worse, Trev," Tony said. "Jane would make a perfect wife."

"Yes, she would—save for one thing."

"And what is that?"

"She isn't Natasha."

* * *

Cecilia went to see Dr. Harrison and was ecstatic to learn the dowager duchess had been right. But there was a gloomy veil of sadness over the Earl of Marsham's household a few weeks later when Cecilia lost the baby she and Tony so desperately wanted.

Natasha had been at Eton, visiting her brothers. When word reached her, she left immediately for London.

"I'm sorry to call you away from a visit with Luka and Pavel," Tony said when Natasha arrived late at night. "I thought it might help to have you here."

Natasha put her hand on Tony's arm. "I am glad you sent word to me. If it hadn't been for you and Cecilia when I lost—when I had my accident, I don't know what I would have done. There will be other times to visit my brothers."

Cecilia burst into tears the moment Natasha walked into the room. "There, there," Natasha said, rushing to Cecilia's side and sitting on the bed, then she took her in her arms. "You mustn't take on so."

"I wa-wanted th-this baby so badly," Cecilia said, sobbing. "Oh, Tasha. You of all people know how it feels."

"Yes," Natasha said, "and I, of all people, know that you will be able to get over it." She leaned back, and, taking Cecilia's handkerchief, she dried the tears from her face. Remembering her own loss, Natasha said, "Each day becomes easier than the day before, each hour passes faster than the last. It hurts now, but there will come a time when you can remember and not cry. Be thankful, Cici, that you have Tony. You cannot replace this child, but there will be others."

Cecilia took the handkerchief from Natasha and blew

her nose. She took a deep breath. "I knew you would understand," she said. "You are the first person who has come in here who hasn't told me not to cry. You don't expect me to act like nothing happened, that it doesn't hurt, because you, of all people, know how it feels."

"Yes," Natasha said, "I know how it feels."

CHAPTER TWENTY-SEVEN

Natasha returned to Marsham, but her stay in London had made her forget all about the strange occurrence that day she had seen the man standing in the trees. In truth, she wouldn't have thought about it again at all if it hadn't been for what happened shortly after she returned.

She had not expected trouble the afternoon she heard the dogs barking in the vicinity of the greenhouse and went there to see what the commotion was about. Feeling better than she had in many weeks, her step was light and her spirits lifted as she hurried down the path, calling the dogs by name, giving each of them a loving pat when they came to her: Winkum . . . Blinkum . . . and Nod . . .

Where was Beggar?

"There now," she said to the barking trio, "what is all

the ruckus about? Did you see a cat sneaking into the greenhouse?"

Nod seemed to shake his head, and she laughed. "You did? And you didn't try to stop him?"

She reached down to give Blinkum another pat when she saw it—a note tacked to the greenhouse door. It contained only one word, written in letters at least four inches tall.

WHORE

Her hands trembling, she snatched the paper from the door, tearing it to shreds. As if they were made of something she could not touch, she dropped the pieces of paper, the back of her hand coming up to cover her mouth as she whirled around. Preoccupied with her own grief and fear, she did not see Harry standing there, until he stepped forward with an apologetic look on his face.

"You saw it?" she asked, wiping the tears from her face and doing her best to compose herself.

"I heard the dogs," he replied. "I came to see what the barking was about. I'm sorry as can be that I didn't get here before you did."

"It doesn't matter," she said. "It doesn't take a note to tell me what people around here think of me."

CHAPTER
❧ TWENTY-EIGHT ❧

Luka and Pavel excelled at cricket their first year at Eton, so it was only natural that in each letter they wrote to Natasha, they reported their successes, giving her the score of each game, the high points in particular.

As their first year drew to a close, Natasha realized that although she had paid her brothers many visits to Eton, she had never watched them play. They gave her many demonstrations that summer when they were home, and after giving Natasha a few lessons, told her it was a real shame she had been born a girl. Her skills at cricket were, after all, passable.

When they returned to school after their first summer vacation and Tony heard Natasha had never seen them play—by way of a letter from Pavel—he promptly stuffed Lady Cecilia into the traveling coach and headed for Marsham. When they arrived there, he stuffed Natasha into the coach as well.

Almost before Natasha had settled herself, Tony was shouting to the driver, "Turn the team around and point their noses toward Oxford. Make haste, man! Make haste!"

In response to Tony's urging, the driver went at it like

a pickpocket at a fair, and in spite of being bounced and jostled about, Natasha managed to tie her bonnet more securely—after it was knocked askew for the fourth time—and settled herself back against the plush cushions of the coach.

She glanced up and almost laughed outright at the sight that greeted her, for sitting across from her, Lady Cecilia looked charmingly bewildered as Tony began to instruct the two of them in the finer points of cricket.

Natasha was within a minute of being talked to death when, miraculously, he finished.

The fat sausage curls under what Tony referred to as Lady Cecilia's ridiculous bonnet bounced adoringly against her flawless white skin as she brightened with laughter and clapped her hands together and said, "Oh, Tony! That was dashing good of you to explain it to us. You must know everything about cricket."

"And he told us every word of it," Natasha mumbled under her breath, fighting the urge to laugh at the way Tony's chest puffed out at Cecilia's words. It occurred to her at that moment just how well suited Cecilia and Tony were, for Cecilia was worshipful and adoring, and so blessedly easygoing that one found it quite relaxing to be around her, in spite of her incessant chatter.

Tony laughed, giving Cecilia an adoring look just before he dropped a kiss on her nose. "That is what I love about you, sweetheart," he said. "You would applaud an echo."

"If it was yours," Cecilia said.

The coach rattled on, and the three occupants settled down for a long ride, Tony interrupting the long stretch of silence only once, to say, "I consider it a jolly good stroke of luck that we are going to see the boys play."

He said the words *the boys* with such pride that it made Natasha wonder if they would be blessed with a child before long. That thought made her remember the child she had lost, and she found her mind going back to another time—and wondered if Trevor was as miserable as she.

Luka and Pavel were already on the lawn, along with the rest of the team, by the time they arrived. The moment she saw them, Natasha had a queer empty feeling inside.

A few months ago, when she had seen them last, they were gangly boys with too much leg and too little polish, but seeing them now, dressed in their cricket whites, she saw not two coltish boys but two very handsome young men.

How much they reminded her of their father. Tall, strapping, and fair, it was a delight to simply stare at them. She found it ironic that seeing her brothers would make her feel more lonely than she felt before, when they were with her at Marsham.

As she settled back in her chair to watch the game, she caught a glimpse of a man across the lawn. He was tall and of slender build, standing so that she only had a view of his side, but it was enough.

"*Trevor,*" she whispered.

It had been a year since she had seen him; a year since she had experienced that sweet pleasure, that delicious sensation she always felt around him.

She allowed her gaze to roam over him, refusing to believe what she was seeing. Her mind was simply playing a trick on her. *Surely not,* she thought. *It cannot be him.* But then, what other man could devastate her with nothing more than his presence? Who besides Trevor could create such mayhem with just the whispered memory of his name? *Trevor . . . Trevor . . . Trevor . . .*

She closed her eyes—and for a moment she allowed herself the luxury of going back and changing the events in their life that led up to that destructive day.

The sun was warm upon her face as she leaned back in her chair, her eyes still closed, and pictured him coming to her, kneeling before her and taking her hands in his, holding them to his breast and laying his head upon her lap. Memories came rushing back—a bittersweet remembrance. The thought of him—in his quietness, with his inward reflection, the very feel and shape of his shoulders, his buttocks so assertive only moments before, now so beautifully still—and as it always had, the tenderness of his nape touched something womanly within her. It was something she never fully understood—why the softness of the skin and hair there left her feeling compassionate, wondering at the defenselessness of a man's nape.

Her eyes flew open. She could not be feeling tenderness for him. She could not. She felt a rush of confusion. She could not care for him. She would not allow it.

He had almost destroyed her; the idea that she could still love the man she hated above everything was absurd. She gave a moan of dismay, feeling the color rise to her cheeks when Tony glanced her way.

Tony smiled at her, then gave his attention back to the game's preparations. Natasha found herself searching the fringe of crowd on the other side of the playing field, searching for confirmation, praying she would find none.

Then she saw him again, and for a moment she thought he might be coming her way. But a woman he must have known stopped him, and he dipped his head to listen to what she had to say—and she found the sight of him with another woman more painful than she wanted to admit. He laughed and lifted his head up, looking her way, and Natasha panicked, for she had no desire to see him, finding herself terrified at the prospect. A year was long enough to heal a broken heart, but the moment she saw him she realized it had not been long enough to subdue her feelings. Her heart pounding, her throat dry, she found herself thinking that in all her life, she had never seen a more magnificent man, nor one that she was more aware of, or that touched her in the same way.

Truly he was in splendid form with his tall height and perfect proportions, the aristocratic carriage, the aloofness she sensed in him, even from this distance.

For a moment she felt torn between her own emotions. Part of her wanted him to go away, to spare her the indignity of ever laying eyes upon him again, while another part of her wanted him to come closer. She told herself the latter was only a curious interest, and in a way it was. She found herself wondering if the dark blond hair still curled about his neck in a manner that made her feel nurturing, if his eyes were still the startling blue she remembered, if those hands . . . ahh, those hands.

She turned her head away at the memory. A moment later, when she looked back, he was gone. She did not see him again that day, and by the time the game started, she had successfully convinced herself that she had not really seen him at all.

The distracting reminder of her past out of her mind now, she gave her attention to the game, watching the players tromp to the field with a hearty send-off from those sitting behind the ropes. Her gaze drifted over the crowd, lighting for a moment upon the starry eyes of worshipful urchins and old duffers who told how it was in their day.

"Ah . . . cricket was cricket back then," she heard one of them say.

Once, she thought she caught another glimpse of the man she thought to be Trevor, but an explosion of the most deafening cheer pulled her attention away. Seeing his teammates hovering about Luka and clapping him on the back, Natasha shot to her feet, joining the other ladies in the crowd who were fluttering their handkerchiefs and waving their parasols.

After a hearty defeat, in which Luka and Pavel, agile and energetic as young puppies, had been instrumental in solidly trouncing the other team—Luka alone making five wickets for twelve runs—they began to enjoy their victory with no moderation.

This lack of moderation so enraged the captain of the other team—a capital bowler by the name of Tom Blewitt—that he flung the ball at Luka with an aim His Majesty's Lancers would have envied, and if Luka had not happened to see it coming and ducked, he would have been laid out for the coroner's inquest.

As for Tom Blewitt, he had let fly with such a vengeance that the cricket ball was looked for for over an hour before it was found, on the other side of the duck pond, embedded in the muddy bank. The umpire said the ball had sailed some four hundred yards before coming to rest in the embankment.

It was for that reason that Tony answered, "If they live long enough to finish Eton," when one of the bystanders said, "Those two young chaps of yours will have quite a bright future in cricket."

A moment later Tony grabbed Luka and Pavel, his arms going around them as he declared, with a hearty slap on each of their backs, "You remind me of the old days. I have not seen such playing since I was a student at Oxford. You play as well as I did."

"By Jove!" Luka said. "That is exactly what Trevor said."

"Trevor?" Natasha heard someone say, realizing it must have been her when Cecilia, her brothers, and Tony all turned to stare at her.

Tony was the first one to speak. "Natasha . . ."

Something inside her seemed to explode. "It was him. He *was* here, wasn't he?" she asked, her voice trembling, her knees feeling shaky and weary. Uncontrollable fury flamed in her breast that these people, who were closest and dearest to her, had all been a part of this deception. "Don't lie to me," she said. "Is that why you brought me here? To see me humiliated?"

Tony looked hurt as he stared at Natasha's pale face. "No," he said. "You know it isn't. I could never do anything so cruel to you. It pains me to think you believe I could. I have always tried to be your friend, Natasha. Always."

Natasha felt her anger dissolve when she heard the unmistakable sincerity in Tony's voice. He had been her friend. He and Cecilia both. She was about to tell him she was sorry for the outburst when Luka spoke up.

"Trev always comes to our games," he said, beaming.

"Gave us some good tips last year," Pavel added.

Natasha's heart slammed against her chest. "Last year . . . You mean he came last year as well?" she asked.

"It hasn't been that many times," Pavel said, and Luka nodded in agreement.

"Why didn't you tell me?" Natasha asked.

Luka and Pavel looked at each other as if each was waiting for the other to speak. At last, it was Pavel who spoke. "Because Trev said he thought it would be better if we kept it a secret."

"Oh, I'll just bet he said that," Natasha said, finding

her anger coming back all over again. Just the idea that her brothers would refer to that lying seducer as *Trev* instead of his whole beastly name sent a cold shudder over her. She had never felt so anguished, or so betrayed, and never would she have thought it could have wounded so deeply.

"Dear me," Cecilia said, trying her best to ease the situation. Glancing at Tony, she said, "I fear we have upset Natasha. Do let's change the subject, Tony." Then she began to babble with excitement about the Christmas holiday and how she hoped Luka and Pavel would spend some time with them in London.

Natasha was not listening to Cecilia. She was too busy sorting through her own emotions. She was somewhat angry, and, of course, hurt, but the biggest thing she felt was betrayed, and she did not know why. She supposed Trevor had a right to visit her brothers if he so desired. In all honesty, she remembered he had always enjoyed them and their pranks—save for the day that they broke the wheel on his carriage.

But they were *her* brothers, and for a moment she was not certain if she was more angry at Trevor for his visits to them, or at her brothers for their hearty acceptance of them.

By the time they left, Natasha had put the unpleasantness of this afternoon out of her mind, at least temporarily. When she told her brothers good-bye, she was resolved not to allow Trevor or any of his schemes to come between herself and her family.

Most of the coach trip home passed in silence—something that must not have sat too well with Cecilia, for it was apparent that Cecilia's heart went out to Natasha. With a serene disposition that could make the most of anything, Cecilia must have finally decided this silence had gone on long enough.

"When you last wrote, you said you might be coming to London," Cecilia said. "Do you know anything further? You know how much we've been wanting you to pay us a visit, but I cannot help wondering what it is that could bring you to London when Tony and I have been unable to."

"It is probably something botanical," Tony said.

Natasha looked at the earnest face of her dearest friend and smiled. "Mr. Banks presented my paper on bog gardens to the Royal Horticulture Society. I have just received an invitation from the secretary, inviting me to come to their next meeting, so that I might read the entire paper to their membership."

Cecilia took Natasha's hands in hers. "The Royal Horticulture Society? Why, Tasha, that is simply wonderful. Just think what an honor it is to be invited to one of their meetings—and here you have been invited to read your paper."

"When is the meeting?" Tony asked. "I should like to send a traveling coach for you."

"In three weeks, but I don't want you to go to that much trouble," Natasha said.

"Three weeks? Oh, that is perfect," Cecilia said. "I have it from the most reliable sources that a group of Russian dignitaries are coming to London. They should arrive about that time. It won't be as grand as when the czar and his sister came a few years back, of course, but all of London is buzzing with the news. It would be a perfect time for you to come to London. Just think of it, Tasha! You could meet some of your fellow countrymen. Oh, I do hope you have kept up with your Russian."

"Not as much as I should have," Natasha said, "but my French is passable."

Natasha had read that London was the most festive, the most elegant, and the most delightfully fashionable place in Europe, and once she arrived, she understood the truth of it. It did not take her long to realize it was a much different London she had briefly glimpsed when she had visited the ailing Cecilia or had been whisked aboard Trevor's ship.

This London seemed alive with a vitality—a liveliness of style enmeshed in a whirlwind of activity. As the Earl of Marsham's elegant traveling coach made its way through the crowded streets, Natasha had her face to the window, seeing stanhopes that seemed as tall as the buildings as they wove their way among one-horse tilburies, two-horse phaetons, tim-whiskies, curicles, and tandems. The walkways were as crowded as the streets, and there seemed to be no end to the legions of shops lined up like parading regiments in full-dress uniform.

As they passed the tree-fringed openness of Hyde Park, she thought she had never seen so many beautiful women, elegantly gowned and riding upon prancing, well-gaited mounts of thoroughbred breeding.

Looking down at her simple gown and knowing her bonnet was even less fashionable, she immediately felt out of place and longed for the sequestered confines of Marsham. For years she had managed to stay out of London. Why did she succumb to a bit of flattery now?

Oh, posh! I have come to London for more important things than prancing around the park in a fancy gown. Besides, she thought, giving the park a more serious study, *it could do with a few flourishes of its own. More flowers would do it a world of good.*

They turned down St. James's and she was reminded of how Byron and Samuel Rogers dined here on vinegar and potatoes, and how much things change—Lord Byron, once the darling of London society, was now held in contempt and living in exile.

She opened her much-read copy of *The Picture of London*, reading about shopkeeping and the bewildering number of goods to be found from one end of London to the other. She supposed she might do a little shopping, perhaps to buy herself a new gown to wear to the Royal Horticulture Society when she spoke.

The carriage pulled to a stop in front of Cecilia and Tony's town house, and Natasha put all thoughts of shopping behind her. The moment she stepped out of the carriage, Cecilia was running down the front steps, taking Natasha in her arms and telling her how delighted she was to see her.

"Welcome, dear friend, to London. Oh, Tasha! You have no idea how happy I am that you are here. You could not have picked a better time to come. *Everyone* is having a party. Why, you won't have a moment to yourself. Our ball to honor the Russians will be on Saturday." She tucked her arm through Natasha's and began walking toward the door. "I cannot tell you how relieved I am that you are here to help me with the menu selections. Faith! I have no idea what Russians like to eat."

"Neither do I," Natasha said, then she laughed and let Cecilia lead her into the house.

CHAPTER
❧ TWENTY-NINE ❧

By the time Trevor left his office in Westminster Hall and stepped out into the street, it was almost dusk. The weather was cooler than he expected. The dark lavender tinges of a forming cloud overhead was creeping further and further over the city.

He looked at the throng of people trying to hail a cab, and with another glance at the sky, decided he could make it to his town house before it started to rain. He did not hesitate, but turned straight toward home.

The street was jammed with late afternoon traffic, the walkways as well, with everyone seemingly in a hurry to get where they were going before the rains started.

He weaved his way through the throng of people, walking briskly down the street to the corner, where he paused for a moment beside a ragged old Gypsy woman, her long gray hair hanging limp and scraggly from beneath a straw hat bedecked with linen daisies and cornflowers which were as far past their prime as the peddler.

Normally Trevor took no notice of the people he passed, but as he paused beside this woman, she reached out and touched his arm, holding a bunch of violets toward him.

He declined with a shake of his head, knowing he had no one to give posies to. Just as he started to step past her and out into the street, he noticed the color of her eyes—such a deep, dark blue they appeared to be lavender. Only one other person he had ever known had eyes that color. He paused long enough to reach into his pocket and toss her a few coins, declining the nosegay.

A gusty draft of wind blew down the street, flinging a few hats into the air and swirling up a cloud of dirt and litter from the gutter. The skies overhead rumbled, and the first splattering drops of rain began to fall.

Ready to be on his way, he stepped into the street—anxious to cross to the other side—when he saw her. He was seized by a sort of panic, for he knew instantly that it was Natasha—knew even before his heart began to pound swiftly in his chest, before his throat went dry and his palms began to sweat.

It had been a long time since he had last seen her, a long time since he had seen her small, slender frame, the abundance of glossy, jet black hair, but for such a memory, time had no meaning, even though it had been such a long time since she had turned her face to the wall and told him to go away.

It was Natasha. He knew it, for he knew her as well as the face that stared back at him each morning when he looked into his mirror, knew her as well as he knew the exact number of days it had been since that fateful day when she had lost the child neither of them knew about—the day she turned him away and shattered his life.

The moment he recognized her, he broke into a run, weaving, pushing, shoving his way through the milling throng of people congesting the street ahead of him. He could not lose sight of her, not after all this time.

He was across the street now, running frantically after her, just as she rounded a corner a block ahead of him. He pushed himself harder, reaching the corner just as she crossed the street. He dashed into the street, frantic that he might lose her before he had the chance to really see her.

People shouted at him to look where he was going, but he was in such a panic—so afraid that he would lose sight of her—that he was not really aware that the shouts were for him, or of what they were saying. His feet seemed to be working independently, running ahead of the rest of his body. His chest felt as if it were about to explode. A deep, slicing pain began to pound in his head.

Suddenly he felt a new panic, a fear that he would lose sight of her. Something inhuman seized him and he pushed forward with a strength he did not know he possessed.

People around him began to curse and complain of being pushed and shoved out of the way. He felt a sharp kick to his shin, a sharp jab to his ribs, but something continued to drive him forward.

Just when he felt he had pushed himself beyond human endurance, the woman reached the other side of the street. She stopped, then turned. Trevor's heart plunged to his feet. The world began to whirl dizzily around him, blurring the faces of those who passed him, giving him strange looks, but he was mindful of nothing save the voice that roared loudly in his ears, the sound of his heart breaking.

Not her . . . not her . . . not her . . .

Someone shouted, and he heard the scream of horses, the vivid curse of a man. He looked up to see a swiftly moving coach bearing down rapidly upon him, the driver pulling frantically at the reins.

He only had time to bring his hand up, hoping to cover his face, when he felt the impact, felt his body hurling through the air. He felt as if the life were being crushed from him just as his body slammed against the street. Then the world around him turned as black as the silky filaments of Natasha Simonov's hair.

"Trevor? Can you hear me? Trev, come on old man. Don't put me through this. Open your eyes. Open them and tell me you are all right."

Trevor tried to open his eyes at the sound of Tony's voice, but they would not obey the command.

It was some time later, when he did open them, that the first thing he saw was his brother's concerned face.

"How do you feel?" Tony asked.

"Like I've been run over by a hay wagon."

"Close," Tony said. "It was a wagon belonging to Harding & Howell, Linen Drapers, over in Pall Mall." He paused a moment, looking at his brother. "What happened, Trev? What made you dash out into the street like that?"

Trevor started to shake his head, but a sharp, stabbing pain stopped him. He held his breath until the dizziness passed, feeling he had aged ten years since he'd left Westminster Hall—however many days ago that had been. His head hurt, his mouth felt like it was stuffed with cotton, and his face ached abominably. He looked at Tony and for a moment he considered telling him what had caused him to act so irrationally, but when he opened his mouth, it was not the truth that came out. "I was preoccupied," he said. "I've been working too much lately."

"I agree with that, but I don't believe for a moment

that's what happened. Now, are you going to tell me what really occurred, Trev?"

If his face hadn't hurt so much, Trevor would have laughed. "I never could lie to you worth a damn, could I?"

Tony chuckled. "Not any better than I could lie to you," he said. "Now, save us both a bit of time and tell me what—"

"Natasha," Trevor said, interrupting Tony. "I thought I saw her."

Tony did not look particularly amazed at his words, and that came as a bit of a surprise to Trevor.

"Perhaps you did see her," Tony said in a matter-of-fact way. "She *is* in London, you know."

Trevor's face grew pale. "No," he whispered, "I didn't know." He looked off. "It does not matter. The woman I saw . . . it wasn't her." His gaze was locked on Tony now. "I almost got myself killed and for what? A case of mistaken identity?"

"It could have been her, you know. Natasha isn't one you can keep at home. Cecilia swears she has been from one end of London to the other."

"It was not her. I saw the woman's face just before . . ."

". . . you got your own face rearranged by that draper's wagon?"

In spite of the pain, Trevor shook his head sadly. "I was so certain it was her," he whispered. "God, I've never had anything shake me up like that. It looked so much like her—right down to the same shade of blue-black hair."

"Well, I still say you could have been mistaken. You could have seen Natasha. After all, it happened so fast—and you did get the devil knocked out of you."

Trevor gave Tony a thoughtful look. "You aren't going to suggest amnesia, are you?"

Tony laughed. "No. You would never be so lucky. I am simply saying the blow you received could have blurred your memory for events that happened about the same time you were hit. Maybe you thought it wasn't her simply because you were hoping so much that it wasn't."

"Nothing could be further from the truth. You can't imagine how wrong you are, Tony. Don't you know how badly I wish it had been her? Do you have any idea what I would give to see her again—even from a distance? I cannot begin to count the number of times I have considered going to Marsham for the sole purpose of lurking around in the shadows, hoping for a glimpse of her, thinking that even if that was denied me, I would find some solace in just being close to her, knowing that I could touch the things she touched, and see the outpouring of her grief in the gardens she created there."

Tony sighed. "It is probably just as well that you did not go. It would have only taken you longer to get over her."

"It is not as simple as being a question of getting over her. I have known for some time that I will *never* get over her. She is with me each day. She is constantly in my thoughts. Her memory lingers in the back of my mind. She will be in my heart forever, and before you question that, I *know* it will be forever. You cannot rip out part of your life any easier than you can rip out part of your heart."

"I'm sorry," Tony said. "Sometimes I forget how it is with you . . . you hide your pain so well."

Trevor's hand came up to touch his cheek. "Not all of my pain," he said. "This, I don't mind telling you, hurts like the very devil."

"It should. The doctor said the entire side of your face was laid open. Twenty stitches, in case you're interested."

Trevor let his fingers move over his face, feeling around and identifying the stitches that ran from the corner of his eye to just below his mouth. He did his best to smile, but it hurt like hell. "This could be a blessing in disguise," he said. "Maybe this will move me down on the list of at least some of London's most desperate husband hunters."

"With your luck, it will make you decidedly more handsome to them—and consequently, more in demand. You know how women love to fawn and toady over heroes . . . and as much as it pains to say it, you do have that wounded-hero look that women seem to love."

Trevor looked at him for a moment. "I doubt that it pains you overly much," he said. "But, tell me, why is she here?"

"It is quite an honor for her, actually. She has been asked to read her paper before the general meeting of the Royal Horticulture Society next Tuesday."

"Her paper?"

Tony nodded. "Something botanical. She told Cecilia and me about it, of course, but you know how I have a memory for that sort of thing. Used to drive Father crazy, as I remember."

Trevor did his best to smile. "Yes, it did. I seem to recall his frequent disappointment over that. Being the second son, he did so want you to inherit his love for fluttery, flying things."

Tony laughed at that. "And all I inherited was his love for spending money."

"Well, that did not hurt you overmuch, and you've plenty of it to spend now," Trevor said. "How is she doing?"

"Are we back to Natasha?"

Trevor nodded. "Who else?"

"She is doing quite well, actually. Still misses her brothers, of course, but I think she has adjusted to their absence. Fortunately, for her, she stays quite busy with her gardening endeavors. You know, it is amazing for one so young, but bless me if she isn't receiving requests from some of England's most prestigious families. The Duke of Thistledown gave her complete charge of his gardens at Thistleton, and now her name is on everyone's tongue. First it was Byron and his poetry. Now the rage seems to be Natasha and her gardens."

Trevor smiled sadly. It did not surprise him, for the whole of society seemed dominated by their selfish pursuits of leisure, beauty, and pleasure. "Our Russian ladies seem to have a knack for taking the cream of England's society by storm," he said, thinking of Countess Lieven, the wife of the Russian ambassador, who introduced the scandalous waltz to London and seemed to have an infinite capacity for making mischief.

"If you are thinking of the Countess, Natasha still has a long way to go. Aside from her work, she rarely goes out—and when she does, it is for a legitimate reason, like when she went to Eton with us a fortnight ago to see the boys play."

Trevor looked surprised. "The last Eton game? I had no idea she would be there. Why didn't you tell me?"

"Because I knew you wouldn't go if I did. I know how much you enjoy seeing the boys and their games. I saw no reason to spoil your going."

"Spoil my going? Do you realize what could have happened if she had seen me, if we had, by some chance, come upon each other?"

Tony nodded. "I knew. She saw you, by the way, but there was no harm done."

"She saw me?"

"She thought she did, and when the twins mentioned you had come . . ."

". . . she was furious," Trevor finished.

Tony laughed. "Yes, furious would just about describe it, I think. By the way, Cecilia and I are entertaining the Russian dignitaries in our home on Saturday. Ordinarily, I would not expect you to come, knowing she was going to be there, but all of your friends will be there—Wellington, Castlereagh, Lord Palmerson, Canning."

"Canning!" Trevor said. "That charlatan! You know I cannot tolerate Canning."

Tony laughed. "It will be a large party. You need not see Canning . . . or Natasha, either, for that matter—if you so desire."

"I won't be attending," Trevor said.

"Why not?"

This time, Trevor gave his brother an honest answer. "Because I don't think I could see her again and be content to simply look."

"You are joking, of course."

"I have never been more serious in my life. After what happened to me the other day, I realize I can no longer trust myself around her. Right now, just knowing she is in London— It is all I can do to keep from rushing to her side and hauling her off with me, even if I had to shed every drop of my life's blood to do it . . . and had to drag her through it on my way out."

Tony looked concerned. "Trev, you must be careful who you say things like that around."

"Why? Because I sound mad? Because people will label me a lunatic? Perhaps I am mad, for the maddest thing I have ever done was allowing the two of us to be parted. I have relived that moment over and over in my mind. If I had the opportunity to do it over again, nothing short of the gates of hell could keep me away from her."

"My God, man. You were not simply pierced by Cupid's darts, you've nearly bled to death from them."

"There were times, during those first few months when I would have gladly welcomed the prospect," Trevor said, closing his eyes against the pain of remembering.

Tony stood, picking up his coat, the drops of rain still clinging to it. "I have exhausted you," he said. "I will give you some time to rest. I will check on you tomorrow."

Trevor did not open his eyes, but he nodded. It did not matter that she had been gone for a year now. During the night, she was always with him, in his heart. Perhaps it would always be so. The love he carried for her was all encompassing, all that made him go on.

That night, as every night, he was alone. The shadows that lay across his bed were hollow memories, the emptiness within his arms the only true reality. Curse the darkness as he would, cry as he might, dream as he always did, when the morning came, she would still be gone from him. Gone, and never to return.

He rolled over, not caring that a deep, slicing pain cut across his face as he buried it into the pillow. Since the day he left her, his life had been nothing but pain and eternal damnation.

And now, she was here.

You are here, in London, going on about your life, giving your talks, planting your flowers ... But how? How, Natasha? How can there be flowers when I must live without you?

CHAPTER
❧ THIRTY ❧

Four days before Tony and Cecilia's ball, Natasha was to read her paper on bog gardens to the Royal Horticulture Society.

The afternoon of her reading, she left Cecilia calmly sorting through the responses to the ball—something she had done every day for the past week.

As Natasha departed the grand salon, she paused in the doorway for a moment, watching the calm, sedate manner in which Cecilia opened each note and listed the name of the sender under one of two columns: ACCEPT or DECLINE.

Natasha shook her head. Giving anything for four hundred people would have her on the verge of a fit about now. Giving a ball for four hundred of the cream of English society would have sent her straight to Bedlam. She smiled at the sight and turned away, going up the stairs and thinking as she did that it had to be divine intervention that had Cecilia giving a ball for the visiting Russian dignitaries and herself reading a paper on bog gardens to the Royal Horticulture Society.

She went to her room and dismissed the maid, preferring to dress herself as she always did. Next she went to her wardrobe and extracted her brown silk, which was the better of two dresses she wore to church each Sunday, reminding herself that she had intended to purchase a new gown.

Laying the dress across the bed, she had a vision of how lovely Cecilia had looked downstairs, the swirling skirts of her rose-colored silk dress spilling across the floor, the fashionable lines, the crackling rustle of new fabric. She looked at her brown silk, its stingy skirts, the out-of-fashion style, and the limpness of fabric worn too much. For an instant she thought about wearing the emerald silk Cecilia and Tony had given her upon her arrival. She went back to the wardrobe, and, removing the gown, placed it on the bed next to the worn brown silk.

Deciding the green was far too stylish and too revealing for such a group as the members of the Royal Horticulture Society, she replaced it in the wardrobe and put on the brown silk. She stood before the mirror, satisfied with her choice. She was reading a paper on the creation and beautification of bog gardens, not on self-ornamentation. The brown gown, in her estimation, gave credence to what she was about.

She brushed out her hair and plaited it into two long braids, which she wound like a wreath over her head. To add a bit of importance to the occasion, she pulled a piece of cream velvet ribbon from her old cape and wove it among the braids, pinned a brooch in the froth of lace at her throat, and decided the small diamond earrings she always wore would do.

Tony and Cecilia accompanied her to the Royal Assembly on King Street, a Gothic edifice with a vast columned entry and steps coming up from the street on two sides. The Assembly Hall was much like a theater, with comfortable cushioned seats and a raised dais. She had been forewarned that the hall was rarely filled for meetings of the horticulture society—something that did not bother Natasha in the least. It was an honor to be invited to speak, but by no stretch of the imagination was Natasha looking forward to standing on the speaker's platform and addressing an audience of several hundred people. For this reason, when she learned there would be in the neighborhood of two hundred present, she was relieved.

Natasha was seated next to the society's president, to the left of the speaker's platform. Looking around the hall, she saw the audience was, as she had previously suspected, mostly male, but there were several women, some sitting in groups, which made her think they were not simply wives who accompanied their husbands.

She gazed out into the hall, seeing an abundance of faces, finding she was unable to discern any particular individuals due to the distance and dim lighting in the hall. She was able to pick out Cecilia and Tony, only because she knew where they were seated. She took three deep breaths, exhaling slowly, then cleared her throat, glad the hall was buzzing with the low drone of voices speaking in hushed conversation.

The president of the society came to his feet; when he reached the podium, the conversation died away. She listened to his steady, confident voice as he spoke, noticing his speech never wavered, nor did he wring his hands.

Immediately she separated her hands, thankful she had her sheaf of papers in her lap, which gave her something to hold.

When she was introduced, she rose to her feet, feeling suddenly uncertain of her choice of gowns, for the brown silk, she feared, made her difficult to see against a backdrop of dark paneling. Her paper rattled a bit as she approached the lectern and she prayed she would not embarrass herself by becoming the laughingstock of the society. She glanced briefly at Cecilia and Tony, knowing they smiled at her, even though she could not see their faces clearly, then placed her papers on the lectern, thanked the president, Mr. Templewhite, and the distinguished members of the society for extending to her such a kind invitation.

Before she began reading her paper, she announced she would like to dedicate this occasion to the memory of her late benefactor, a man well known to all of them, the late William Weatherby, the Earl of Marsham.

"He was a kind man who opened not only his heart to three Russian orphans but his home as well," she said. "It was from the earl and his love for botany that I acquired my gardener's thumb, coming to love Marsham, its gardens and plants, as much as he did. But, if I am to be perfectly honest, I will have to say there was one plant he nurtured that I did not share his fondness for. If anyone present has knowledge of someone interested in the cultivation of *Rhus radicans*, a deciduous climber native to North America, known as poison ivy, please inform them that I have several plants I am *itching* to give away."

The hall erupted with laughter, and she closed her eyes for a moment, breathing deeply, feeling the tension ease out of her. When the laughter died away, she began to read her paper, issuing a challenge to plant a bog garden in any place that water occurred naturally, if they would only bear in mind that it was a garden of water plants that could not tolerate deep immersion.

It was at this point that she began to explain her preference for choosing plants that looked well in a natural design rather than the more formal look that spoke of intentional planting.

She lost her place once—when explaining that many bog plants spread easily, and to prevent this, one should use only clumping plants—but found it quickly enough so that no harm was done. As she read, she sensed the interest of her audience and began to feel the same excitement she felt when planning a garden or doing the actual planting.

She ended by reading the description of the plants she found to be excellent for the bog garden, starting with the weeping willow, which, "serves as a backdrop with its fountainlike cascade reflecting in the water—the cattail, *Typha laxmannii*, the waterlily, pickerel rush, the many varieties of iris."

When her talk was finished, she unveiled a large watercolor she had done of her own bog garden at Marsham.

The applause was deafening.

Mr. Templewhite came to his feet and joined her at the lectern, and the energy coming from the audience grew louder. Natasha stood smiling out at the faces she could not make out, feeling she was born for this.

Fifty rows back, sitting in the darkness at the rear of the auditorium, a man was thinking she was born for something, but it wasn't for pretty speeches about bog gardens.

Trevor had come here, hoping for a glimpse of her, getting far more than his original desire. She had changed. Even from here, he could see that. She was a confident, poised woman now, a woman who was making a place for herself, a place that did not include him. If it were possible, she was even more beautiful than he remembered—in spite of the severe hairdo, the dowdy dress, the professional, tutorlike attitude.

The healing gash in his cheek throbbed as he watched

her, his mind absorbed with the revelation that this articulate, self-possessed woman was the same girl he had fallen in love with, the same girl with the tumble of raven black hair and luscious violet eyes, the one whose heart-thumping accent haunted him still.

Warm and loving, virtuous, protective of those she loved, she loved as deeply as she hated, but when he had made love to her, it was in love that she opened her heart to him, in love that she had taken him into the heat of her, in love that she had conceived their child.

And it was in love that he cleansed his heart of all the wretchedness, the lying, the deceit, in love that he confessed his transgressions to her, in love that he asked her to be his wife. The memory threatened. God, her hatred had been as blind as her love, and it had left him in darkness, a confused man with a paralyzed life, a wily lunatic obsessed with one thing: to have her again.

He watched her, knowing when she lost her place, knowing and understanding, for he, too, had lost his. And when she finished and was deafened by praise, he wanted to tear away the pretense, to stand up and scream out her name, to tell them that he remembered her naked breasts looking as beautiful as the wildflowers dotting the turf on the hilltop, that he had made love to her among the sweet grasses of midsummer and laced her ebony hair with gillyflowers and daisies, that he had hoisted her up on half-tumbled walls and sought the warmth of her, easing his fingers into her as their breaths mingled and he thought he would go mad with the pleasure of it.

What would she think then, this prim gardener, this chaste speaker on bog gardens? What would she think if he leapt to his feet and came dashing toward her, taking her right there, on the lighted stage in front of God and the righteous Royal Horticulture Society? How long would she fight him before she fluttered like a wounded bird, opening herself to him, sighing and melting against him, surrounding him with her moist heat?

God, to be inside her again . . .

Would it bother her? Would she be disturbed? Good. *Let her be disturbed as I have been disturbed, night and day since I saw her last. Let her know . . .*

He noticed that people were leaving. His heart pounded. His face felt hot. His hair clung to his forehead, wet with perspiration. His gaze was fixed on the dais, on the woman in somber brown who spoke to a circle of admirers. He clenched his jaw, his brows drawing together. His expression was grim, an almost painful appearance, one that warned of trouble or spoke of mental tension.

He had seen her.

He stared straight ahead, feeling both the pleasure and pain of it in the most exquisite of extremes, an anguished expression on his face that also spoke of rapture. He broke the silence with a deep groan, mumbling her name coupled with a wild term of endearment, speaking as he would to a child that was dying, his words coming low and heartfelt, wrung from the very depths of his soul. With an anguished cry, he wiped his forehead and rose slowly to his feet.

A passing woman looked at her husband. "The poor fool must be mad."

Mad?

Yes, he *was* mad. Mad with longing. Mad with wanting. Mad with constant denial. But it was over now. And that made him maddest of all.

He had seen her. At last, he had seen her. Would this be the end of it then? Would the sight of her, the sound of her voice, be the thing he sought, the elements he needed to purge the memory of losing her? Would this, then, put an end to his slow, agonizing death?

It was a strange way to kill himself, not by his own hand, not by the swiftness of a knife to his breast, but by fragments and hairbreadths, by maintained silence, the agony of never seeing, the nerve-stretching tension of never knowing.

Turning away from his seat and into the aisle, he made his way out of the hall, pushing and shoving his way through the departing throng, as desperate to get away from her as he had been to come.

At last, he broke through the doors that led out to the street, hearing as he hurried through them the ironic mumblings of someone he passed.

"The man is a lunatic."

The violent rumbling of his wild laughter followed him out and onto the street.

CHAPTER
❧ THIRTY-ONE ❧

The day started off well, with an elated Cecilia coming home to tell Tony she was expecting again. Tony's first reaction was to cancel the ball.

"Oh, don't be silly," Cecilia said. "I am perfectly

healthy—the doctor said so—and he could find no reason why I shouldn't carry this baby until it's born."

A veil of happiness seemed to settle over the household after that. But by the night of the ball, Natasha had become so miserable and so tense at the prospect of seeing Trevor again, that Tony volunteered to write in blood that Trevor was not coming.

"Are you certain?" she asked.

"Yes," he replied.

"You invited him?"

"Of course I invited him—he's my brother. But you needn't worry about him coming. He declined."

She felt a rush of emotions, conflicting feelings of relief and disappointment. She frowned, biting her lip. "But what if he shows up unexpectedly?"

Tony looked about ready to throw up his hands. "Believe me when I say this, Tasha. Trevor has no more desire to see you than you have to see him. He wouldn't come if ordered here by the king himself."

That only made her feel worse. How dare he hate her as much as she hated him! How bloody unfair. She would have gone on, allowing her thoughts to flow along the lines of self-persecution, feeling the luxury of wallowing in it for a bit, but Tony must have sensed this.

"Now, cheer up, puss," he said, giving her a cuff under the chin and handing her the cup of tea Cecilia had just poured. "Cici tells me you have the most exquisite gown in all of London to wear tonight." He came to his feet. "I am going up now. If I am to companion two lovely ladies, then I must start making myself presentable. I don't want to miss your arrival. I have already decided to be the first man in line at the bottom of the stairs when you come down."

He started to leave—until Cecilia cleared her throat

and gave him a look. When he glanced at her, she nodded toward Natasha, who was still looking uncertain.

"Now, give us a smile," he said, "or I'll never get out of here."

Natasha could not help smiling at that, but it was a forced smile, one that was pasted on her face instead of flowing out of her heart.

Natasha wished Cook and Mrs. Mac were here to see her as she came down the stairs that night in an abundance of heavy violet satin encrusted with a fortune in pearls, amethysts, and fiery diamonds that edged the low-cut bodice and capped sleeves of her gown. Her hair was braided into a coronet, surrounded by a diamond-and-pearl tiara that Cecilia insisted she wear. She wore no other jewelry.

"Are you certain?" Cecilia had asked when Natasha declined to wear any of the numerous jewels she offered her.

Natasha nodded. "Faith! I look like a bloody jeweler's daughter."

And now Cecilia and Tony stood at the bottom of the stairs, both of them smiling up at her as she descended, both of them taking her by the arm the moment she reached the last step.

She knew they were happy to have her here, that they were looking forward to introducing her to their friends. She knew, too, that they were hoping to flame a little romance into being, if at all possible. Feeling like an unsuspecting lamb, she was led around the room, so she could smile and offer her hand when introduced.

"Are you nervous?" Cecilia asked.

"Very," was Natasha's response.

"Don't be," Tony said. "You are the envy of every woman here."

"That's why she's nervous," Cecilia said, and the three of them laughed.

Their cheeriness came to a sudden halt when they caught sight of Lady Blessingame—not that the urge to laugh heartily was not there, for Lady Blessingame did make quite a spectacle. At least ninety, she was wearing what appeared to be a young girl's frilly white dress. Her hair was shockingly red, her eyebrows an uncompromising jet black. Her décolletage was indecently low, and she wore a wreath of pink roses on her head. For all the world, Lady Blessingame looked to Natasha as if she had stepped out of a confectioner's dream—the kind children had when they ate too many sweets.

The ballroom glittered like a sparkling jewel, the lights of a thousand candles reflecting in the mirrored walls. Catching a glimpse of the mirrors as they passed, Natasha nervously glanced at herself, finding she was surprised at the woman who stared back. She found she looked much more in control than she was.

"You are going to be the darling of London after tonight," Cecilia said. "Just you wait and see."

Natasha did not think she would be the darling of anything, and certainly not London. There was no way the cream of English society would find her bumbling country ways adorable, or enchanting, or any of the other dozen or so words Cecilia had used in the past week to describe them. The people in this room seemed as bright and as polished as the mirrors in the room.

She glanced up at Tony, who looked as if he were about to say something, when Cecilia declared they must hurry on toward their honored guests. Natasha felt her face heat up at the reminder, she shot Cecilia a helpless look.

Cecilia smiled and patted her arm. "You look lovely. You don't have a thing to worry about."

That, in Natasha's mind, was a gross understatement. Nothing to worry about? With herself on the verge of being presented to some of the Czar of Russia's closest confidants—and she had nothing to worry about?

"Natasha," Tony said, his voice vibrating with humor, "If you don't stop looking at your feet, you will find that the ladies present will take that for timidity and they will delight in digging their claws into your unsuspecting flesh. Now, raise your head and look every inch the regal daughter of a noble Russian count."

Natasha's head shot up. Her chin went up, and her spirits along with it. She heard Tony's soft chuckle. Not giving her more time to think upon it, they crossed the room with Natasha in tow, making their way toward a group of distinguished men in uniform. She kept her gaze fastened upon them as they threaded their way through the watchful crowd.

As they passed, the Duchess of Gainsboro laughed and said, "Cecilia, I have not seen you since I returned from Italy," She put a restraining hand upon Cecilia's arm, detaining her for a moment.

Cecilia looked at Tony and then at Natasha, and, smiling, waved them on. "I will join you in a moment," she said.

Natasha smiled, giving her a quick nod before affixing her gaze in the opposite direction, where the group of men stood talking. As she looked, she noticed one of the men who was taller than the others smiled at her, nodding his head in the slightest mocking bow.

Her face flooding with color, she realized she had been staring, and that the handsome blond giant had been blatantly staring back. She was so disturbed by this that she almost ran into Tony when he paused to speak to someone.

While Tony exchanged greetings, she stole another

look at the group. One look at the white uniforms, trimmed with red and gold—that reminded her so much of her father's own uniform—and there was little doubt in Natasha's mind that these were the Russians Cecilia and Tony had spoken about. The honored emissaries of the czar.

In truth, they were splendidly dressed in what she knew to be full-court uniforms—with many medals pinned on their chests, gleaming gold epaulets, and bright red sashes draped from shoulder to waist. For a moment she simply stared at them, remembering a time when her father had looked as dashing.

Three of the five men were dark-haired and of average build. But the one who had smiled at her so arrogantly was tall and very blond, quite the most elegant and handsome man she had ever seen.

It was to this blond-haired giant that Natasha was first introduced.

"Natasha, may I present Count Nikolay Rostov," Tony said.

Count Rostov's blue-eyed gaze moved over her at leisure. "I have often been told English women were beautiful, but I did not believe it until now," he said, bowing and giving Natasha's hand a kiss.

Tony went on, enthusiastically telling the Russian count that Natasha, "is regrettably not the daughter of an Englishman. She is one of your own country . . . the daughter of a Russian nobleman."

Count Rostov's brows raised with surprise. "You are Russian, mademoiselle?"

Natasha nodded. "I am."

"And your last name?"

"Simonov," Tony said. "Natasha Simonov."

If he was surprised by that, Count Rostov gave no hint of it. "And your father was . . . ?"

"Count Alexi Simonov," she answered.

Count Rostov gave her a warm smile and said, "Meeting such a beautiful flower from my homeland has indeed made this trip worthwhile."

Before Natasha knew what was happening, Count Rostov took her arm. "Mademoiselle Simonov, I cannot allow such music to pass without taking a beautiful daughter of Mother Russia into my arms."

Count Rostov guided her toward the dance floor, and Natasha found her nervousness vanish the moment he took her into his arms.

"What brings you to London?" she asked.

He answered her in French. "I have accompanied a group of the czar's men, but I must confess my real purpose in coming lies in the country."

She found her French reply coming easily to her lips. "Really? You are going to visit the English country-side?"

He smiled down at her, a lazy grin sweeping across his tanned face. "Although I must say you will probably find the purpose of my visit quite dull and boring. I have a strange pastime," he said.

She laughed. "It cannot be any stranger than mine," she replied. "But tell me, what is this strange pastime of yours?"

"I abhor the thought of telling you," he said, a smile lighting his blue eyes. "I am here to purchase plant specimens to take back to Russia."

She felt chilled, as if a cold wind had suddenly swept down from the steppe and into the room. She looked up at the count. Their eyes met. "I cannot believe it," she said.

"I told you it was boring and dull," he said in a teasing tone. "Please say you won't allow my interests to sway your judgment of me."

"Oh, that is not what I meant at all. It is simply that I am so astonished, for you see that is my area of interest as well. I have a greenhouse and gardens at my home—and I spend my time puttering among flowerpots and plant clippings."

He gazed down into her violet eyes and chuckled. "And far outshine the flowers, I would think. I should love to see the gardens of such a charming lady. Would it be terribly improper for me to invite myself?"

She smiled at him. "It wouldn't be improper at all if *I* invited you."

"You wouldn't dare," he choked out, laughing. "What would the proper English think?"

"Consider it done," she said, then whispered for his ears only, "and the English be damned."

He threw back his golden head and laughed. "Mademoiselle Simonov, has anyone ever told you that you are enchanting?"

"No," she said, smiling up at him, "but there is always a first time."

For an intense moment, his gaze locked with hers, then it began to move slowly over her face. "You are making it damnably difficult for me to continue with my plans to visit Kew Gardens on the morrow," he said.

"And why is that?"

"Because I find I want to accept your invitation to see your gardens instead."

She smiled up at him. "Go to Kew Gardens on the morrow," she said, "and then you may visit Marsham. I won't be returning there until later in the week. There will be enough time to pay us a visit after your business at Kew is finished."

Lady Cecilia made a sudden appearance—and seemed bent upon drawing Natasha away. Looping her gloved hand through Natasha's arm, she cooed, "My dear Count. I do hope you will excuse us, but this is our darling Natasha's first official visit to London and there are so many people dying to meet her."

The count nodded. "I understand, but I must say it is difficult to hand over such a beauty from my own country to the English."

Lady Cecilia laughed and tapped him on the arm with her fan. "Perhaps you should give the English some of the credit for how lovely she looks, for you can see she has been well cared for."

Count Rostov looked Natasha over at his leisure, his gaze resting upon the jewels that glittered at her breasts, seeming to ignore those at her sleeves. "*Very* well cared for," he said, and Natasha wasn't certain if he was referring to the jewels or to her bosom.

Without wasting a moment, Cecilia whisked Natasha away.

Natasha did not have time to think much more about Count Rostov, for the young dandies in the room seemed to be waiting for Tony and Cecilia to finish their introductions. The moment they stopped, Natasha was surrounded with offers to dance.

At the conclusion of what had to be at least a dozen dances, Natasha thanked her partner, Lord Wittingly, for the dance, declining another by declaring she needed to rest. A moment later she made her way up to her room, powdered her nose, adjusted her gloves, and went back downstairs.

Count Rostov was waiting at the bottom of the stairs, and Natasha felt warmed by his look.

"I have been looking for you, mademoiselle."

She stopped one step above him, but even that did not make them more equal in height. She looked at him and her heart thumped against her chest. For the life of her she could not think of anything to say or do, save to raise her fan. She was in the process of deciding if she should smile and be on her way, or make an attempt at conversation, when Count Rostov asked her to dance.

"May I?" he asked, taking her by the hand and leading her out onto the dance floor when the orchestra began the next song. She wondered why he bothered to ask, since his possessiveness in leading her along did not seem to hinge upon her reply. But she thought no more about it, for he was charming and witty and her countryman—and he spoke French, made her remember all the things she'd missed since leaving Russia, and made her forget the pain of losing Trevor, if only for the night.

Count Rostov glanced over her shoulder. "I see the wolves are slavering in the background, awaiting the end of this dance so they may make a dash for you. Do you wish to dance more, or would you like a glass of champagne and a quick turn about the terrace?"

"A glass of champagne sounds wonderful," she replied.

With a fluid move, he caught her more firmly against him and gazed down into her face. "And the other?" he asked.

"That, too," she said, finding she felt young for the first time in many, many months.

The count looked as if he was about to say something else when someone tapped him on the shoulder to cut in.

"I believe this dance was promised to me?" a deep voice said.

Count Rostov nodded politely and released her. "Another time, mademoiselle," he said, then left.

Whirling around, Natasha stared into the cold blue eyes of the Duke of Hillsborough.

"Trevor," she whispered as he took her hand and placed it on his arm.

She froze.

He was here, standing in front of her, looking as handsome as ever, gazing at her as if the long months, the pain and betrayal that separated them, had never existed.

Unable to do anything except breathe wildly, she searched her mind for some clue as to what she should do. He was here . . .

He couldn't be here. Tony said he wouldn't come.

But he had.

Suddenly she noticed the red scar that cut across his face, but purposefully she ignored it. She did not want him to think she gave him any consideration at all. There was little doubt in her mind that he had come for the sole purpose of seeing her—more than likely to humiliate her, to toy with her again. Did he have friends in the wings waiting and watching, friends he had placed bets with, friends who speculated whether she would melt in his arms or slap his lying face?

She wanted to scream. She wanted to slap him and keep on slapping him until she was too exhausted to move. She could think of nothing, save hurting him and humbling him, as he had hurt and humbled her. She had thought time had eased her anger and her pain. She had been wrong. The time that had passed had not been enough to erase the damage, the memory of what he'd callously taken from her.

Fury, as intense as the humiliation she felt, seemed to motivate her. This was her chance. Her chance to give him the same degrading treatment he had given her. Her chance to get even. Her chance to show him and all of London how much she despised him.

Oh, she knew what she wanted to do, all right. What she should do. So why didn't she?

She closed her eyes, feeling the agony of indecision. She felt her lungs tighten, felt the breath trapped in her body. *God, help me,* she thought. *I don't know what to do.*

Trevor leaned forward, whispering, "If you don't want to be the talk of London tomorrow, I suggest you smile at me and move your feet to the music."

She glanced around, seeing dozens of gazes fastened upon them. She gave him a wooden smile, following his lead when he took her in his arms.

He held her close—too close—and she could do nothing, save to remain stiffly impassive. He did not speak, and for the life of her she could not think of anything to say. She only knew that she felt more alive than she had since he'd held her last—knew, too, that this was the man who had taken her virginity and gotten her with child, while knowing all the while she was nothing to him.

Yet in spite of all those reminders, she knew deep in her heart that it was only her pride—her noble, violated, hardheaded, resolute, damaged pride—that kept her from melting against him.

She knew this man, knew the scent of him, knew the graceful, magnetic pull of his body, knew, too, the power of him. He whirled her around the room, shattering the peace she thought she had found—sending too many reminders of what it had been like to lie with him into her troubled mind.

She might have made it . . .

If the dance had not been so long. If Trevor had not been so devastatingly familiar. If her heart did not bid her to reconsider. If her mind did not sense her weakening, telling her that he was playing her for a fool a second time.

It was too much. Her body jerked to a halt.

Without a word, she gave him a look that said all the horrible things she felt for him—and then she did something unthinkable. She turned and walked away, leaving the Duke of Hillsborough standing in the middle of the dance floor.

Alone.

With a few swift steps, Trevor caught up to her, and, taking her by the arm, he led her through the gaping throng, thrusting her ahead of him and through the doorway just beyond.

Once they were outside, she whirled around. "How dare—"

In one quick move, his hand came up to clamp over her mouth. Jerking her against him, he stared down into her face with cold eyes, his voice throbbing and low, almost hissing with anger. "I thought I knew you, but I see I was mistaken. You are nothing but a fool."

Pulling his hand away, she said, "I don't know how you can say that, since I am the one who walked off and left *you* standing on the dance floor. If that makes me a fool, then it makes you pathetic." The moment she said it, she wanted to take the words back.

For the briefest moment she thought he might strike her. Suddenly he released her with such fury, she staggered backward, losing her balance. She caught herself, and, regaining her poise, looked up at him, recoiling from what she saw in his eyes. Her hand came out, as if reaching out to him in silent entreaty. "Trevor, I—"

"There will come a time, Miss Simonov, when you may find you need me. For your sake, I pray that day never comes."

Even in this darkness, she could see the fury that

throbbed against his temples. Good, she thought. *Let him be angry. Let him suffer as I have suffered.* "Are you saying you would refuse me?"

"No, but you might find the price I ask too high to pay."

She shrugged. "It does not matter. You are the last person on earth I would ever ask for help."

"I will remember you said that," he said. "For your sake, I hope you never have need of me, for if you do . . . God help you, but I *will* remember."

CHAPTER
❧ THIRTY-TWO ❧

Trevor . . .

As soon as she opened her eyes she remembered what had happened between them last night; she rolled over in the bed, burying her face in the pillow, and cried.

An hour later she was standing in her dressing gown, staring out the window with a drowsy sort of ennui, the dull sort of malaise that comes when one is not really sleepy or tired, but simply caught in a nebulous state of being dormant.

She was not relaxed, nor was she self-composed, but neither was she troubled. If she had to choose a word to describe herself, it would be *passive*—a state of inactivity where the best she could do was to simply exist.

She felt different here, in London, in a place so dramatically different from Marsham and Applecore. Like a cut flower in a glass vase, she felt isolated and out of her element, knowing that she still looked the same, but knowing, too, that each day that passed, each minute, each hour, was taking its toll upon her. It was only a matter of time until she, like the flower, began to deteriorate.

There was something corrupt here, something tainted about life in this place, where extravagance and passion saturated everything, whether it was gambling, love, dancing ... even architecture. People here seemed to live on pure lust for life, with little sleep, a lot of drinking, and the general squandering away of their lives. Everything was gaiety, fashion, and frivolity. There was no substance. Nothing she could take root in, let alone flourish. She felt stagnant here, withering.

She wanted to go home, back to Marsham, where the soil was rich and nourishing and the soft sunlight of a hazy morning mellowed the patchwork fields.

Every morning in London seemed the same—damp and foggy—and nowhere she looked would she find the pointed wings and fanned tail of the kestrel that hovered over the moorland slopes.

The maid fluttered into the room, and, by the time Natasha turned away from the window, she was already laying out her morning gown.

Natasha frowned. Morning gowns, day dresses, walking gowns, riding outfits, carriage dresses, ball gowns ... It was too much.

What was wrong with getting up in the morning and putting on one sensible dress to wear for the duration of the day? She glanced at the dress, imagining it after a morning in the greenhouse. Lifting her hands up, she examined her nails, finding she missed even the dirty smudges that were usually there.

The maid looked at the dress she had spread across the bed, then glanced at Natasha. "Will the rose muslin be all right, miss?"

Natasha looked at the frilly rose-colored dress, feeling it was far too lavish for her needs; she had no plans to go out today. But then she looked at the expectant face of the maid and nodded. "The rose will be fine, Nelly," she said.

Her spirits in steady decline, Natasha dressed, catching an occasional glimpse of the London fog through the window, longing for the sun-drenched walls of Marsham. She missed the large, airy rooms, the quiet tranquillity, the smell of dinner warming on the hob. She found herself longing for the place where the spindle berries grew at the edge of the copse; where the lime trees echoed the busy murmur of bees; the cool stretches of silent, leafy roads; the yellow fields of rape, where lambs bleated beside the winding country road that led to Applecore.

She fastened the buttons at her sleeves, finding that even the clothes smelled different in London. At Marsham, her clothes were hung on lines out-of-doors to air in the warm currents of sun-heated breezes. She closed her eyes, remembering the scent of clover and roses, of sunshine and pollen.

"I don't belong here," she whispered.

"Beg pardon, miss?" Nelly said, turning away from where she was putting Natasha's things away in the wardrobe.

Natasha smiled. "Nothing. I was just talking to myself."

Nelly smiled. "Do that a lot myself."

A moment later, Natasha made her way downstairs, wishing that she had not promised Cecilia that she would stay until Wednesday. More days in London—when she was so anxious to return home. What would she do with herself in the meantime?

The days passed quickly, in spite of her doubting they would. Soon Wednesday morning dawned, without rain, without fog, and Natasha took that to be a good sign. "Nice traveling weather," she told Cecilia at breakfast.

"You are ready to go home, aren't you?"

Natasha nodded. "I have enjoyed my visit with you and Tony, but truthfully, I cannot wait to put London behind me. If this trip has taught me anything, it has taught me that I am a country lass at heart."

Cecilia sighed and looked wistfully out the window. "I suppose there is a bit of the country lass in all of us at times," she said. "Perhaps I should consider having my baby in the country."

At Natasha's swift intake of breath, Cecilia looked horrified. "Oh, Natasha," she said, placing her hand on Natasha's arm. "I didn't mean to remind you . . ."

"I know you didn't," Natasha said.

They finished breakfast and were about to leave the dining room when the butler appeared and announced Natasha had a visitor, presenting the caller's card on a silver tray.

Natasha took the card. "Count Rostov," she said. "I thought he was going to Kew Gardens."

"That was before he met you," Cecilia said, smiling. "He is a divinely handsome man, don't you think?"

Natasha didn't seem to hear, for there were other thoughts on her mind. "I wonder why he changed his mind about going?"

Cecilia took her by the arm. "I have no idea, but I do know a good way to find out would be to ask him."

Natasha smiled, and Cecilia accompanied her to the grand salon, where Count Rostov waited. He was alone, dressed splendidly in a uniform, one that was not as ornate as he wore the night of the ball, but his carriage, his aristocratic and authoritative stance, made her think he was every bit as handsome as she had found him then. After her humiliating scene with Trevor, she found his presence quite welcome.

Bowing low when they entered, he greeted each of them, kissing their hands with such eloquence. He exchanged a few trivialities with Lady Cecilia prior to her excusing herself, leaving Natasha and the count alone.

For some time he seemed content to simply stare at her. Not to be outdone, she returned his gaze. After what seemed to be an eternity, he smiled and dipped his head. "Touché, mademoiselle. Your nobility shows, even in the simple dress of a country girl."

The simple dress of a country girl? Natasha almost snorted at that. *What would he think if he saw me at Marsham?* she wondered. *Would he find me so noble in my faded muslin with dirt smudges on my face and loam under my fingernails?* For the oddest reason, she found herself thinking that he would.

Count Rostov moved away from her then, taking up a position before the window, where he stood, military straight, his hands folded behind his back as he rocked back and forth from the balls of his feet to his heels. "I am at a loss for words," he said. "Something quite unusual for me." He turned to look at her. "I was supposed to go to Kew Gardens today, but I found I could not go without seeing you again."

"I am glad you came," she said. "Would you care to sit down?"

He smiled at her. "Mademoiselle, I would care to do a great deal more than that."

His frankness delighted her, and she found herself laughing. "Well, a chair is all I am in a position to offer you at the moment," she said, returning his teasing smile.

"At the moment?" he asked.

She nodded.

"Then I shall have to see to it that I am around when you are in a position to offer me more. Am I still invited to visit you at Marsham?"

Natasha did not answer right away, for she was thinking of the impropriety of the situation, something she did not think of the night of the ball.

As if aware of her thoughts, Count Rostov said, "I do hope you will say yes, for I did mention my interest in seeing your gardens to the Earl of Marwood. As it turned out, he and his charming wife, the Lady Sarah Mayfield, have invited me to visit them in the country. When they told me it was riding distance from Marsham, I took the liberty of accepting. Do you know them, by chance?"

"Only slightly," Natasha said. "Lady Sarah Mayfield is a cousin of Lady Cecilia's."

"So she informed me. And the invitation?"

"Still stands," Natasha said.

Count Rostov flashed her a smile. "You have made my day, mademoiselle. I am now off to Kew Gardens. I count the days until I see you again at Marsham."

He crossed the room and took her hand in his, bringing it to his lips. "Until then," he said, pressing his mouth to her hand much longer than was proper.

"Until then," Natasha said, drawing her hand away.

CHAPTER
❧ THIRTY-THREE ❧

Natasha returned to Marsham and to her work, doing her best to forget about Trevor, concentrating instead on Count Rostov's promise to visit.

She wasn't as fortunate as she had hoped, for when it came to thoughts of Trevor, she found it was never as simple to remove him from her heart as it had been to get him out of her life.

Two days after her return, Natasha arose early, the sound of the dogs' ferocious barking pulling her from a long, dream-filled sleep.

After dressing, she went downstairs, finding neither Cook nor Mrs. Mac were up and about. It was still dark outside, with the first gray-pink streaks of dawn spreading across the horizon. She felt strange today, restless, full of anxiety, when she knew there was nothing to be anxious about. She had a fleeting memory of seeing the man in the trees the day she found that horrid note tacked to the greenhouse door. She wondered what it all meant.

Were Cook and Mrs. Mac right? Was it simply some pathetic person from town with nothing better to do than to cause a body misery? *Lord, don't they know I've had more than my share already?*

She started to make herself a cup of tea, realizing the stove had not yet been started. She began pacing the floor, trying to decide if she should remain downstairs or go back to her room. She glanced out the window again, seeing the sun peeking over the meadows in the distance.

Feeling too restless to remain indoors, she went upstairs to change into her riding clothes, thinking an early morning ride would do her good. She needed to get out of the house, knowing that she had been reluctant to do so since the day she found that note on the greenhouse door.

You cannot stay inside forever, you know.

Whoever it was that was trying to frighten her would grow tired and give up eventually. Until then, she would go about her life as she always did.

Walking toward the stables, she could feel her heart thumping in her chest. She did not know why, but she felt miserably tense. Part of her said it was because she had not been out of the house for two days. Another part said it was because she feared something was about to happen.

That's it. Start jumping at your shadow. Start seeing things where there is nothing. Next thing you know, you'll be hearing things. Who knows, you might even start talking to them.

She opened the stable door, leaving it open to give her more light. It was still early, and although she knew Harry would be up, she thought it was still too early for him to have fed the horses. She had a flashing memory of Ned, feeling sorry that Harry was having to take over his duties until a new groom could be found.

Stopping by the feed bin, she lit a lamp, then scooped

up a portion of oats to feed her mare before their ride. The interior of the stable was dim and quiet, all the horses, save her own, having been turned out to pasture until the new groom arrived.

She made her way across the damp humus floor, reaching the stall where her mare, Lady Gray, was kept. She placed the lamp on the hook, the sudden glow of light flowing through the open stall door illuminating the bloody gore that lay inside. For a split second Natasha stood there, looking down at the butchered body of her mare, seeing instantly that her throat had been cut, and not too long ago, for her blood was still oozing out and drenching the straw. Blood . . . It was everywhere. Soaking into the straw. Splattered on the stall walls.

She did not even know she was screaming until she heard the dogs' barking frenzy and felt Harry's arm go around her shoulders.

"Come on," he said. "This is no place for you."

She tried to speak, but she was sobbing too hard. By the time Cook and Mrs. Mac arrived, hastily tying their robes, their nightcaps flapping, she could only blubber repeatedly, "Lady Gray . . . Why would anyone want to kill Lady Gray?"

She never mentioned the incident again, not that she forgot it, but because she had secreted it away in a place where it could not touch her.

Some time later, when Harry suggested going into the village to get her another horse, she said, "I don't want one. I never want another one," and the thought of it made her sick.

CHAPTER
❧ THIRTY-FOUR ❧

In answer to his mother's summons, Tony left his town house early and made his way to her residence in Hyde Park.

"Good morning, Mother," he said, coming into the salon and greeting the dowager duchess with a kiss.

"Good morning, Tony. Will you have tea?"

"No, I had mine earlier with Cecilia."

"And how is she feeling?"

"Wonderful. I've never seen her so radiant or so happy."

The duchess smiled and nodded her head. "Giving birth is a happy occasion, the fulfillment of womanhood. I always knew Cecilia would make a perfect wife and mother."

"I agree with you, Mother, but I know you did not call me over here to discuss how Cecilia and our unborn child are faring."

The duchess smiled. "You are right, of course. I called you here, Tony, because I want to discuss Trevor."

"Then shouldn't you be talking to Trevor?"

"I would if I thought it would do any good. I want

you to talk to him." She paused a moment, as if waiting for some disagreement from her son, but Tony remained passively silent. "It is time Trevor took a wife. He is the duke now, and it is imperative that he secure the title. He must have an heir."

"Why don't you tell Trev all of this?"

"Because I want *you* to talk to him, Tony. Anything I say to him goes right through him like water through a sieve. You're his brother. He will listen to you."

"Mother, I don't like meddling in Trevor's affairs— besides, it isn't simply a matter of persuading Trevor to marry. It's a matter of convincing him that there will never be a possibility of having Natasha back in his life."

"Then go to him. Convince him. Tony, Trevor must realize that this cannot go on. If something isn't done, it could become an obsession with him . . . if it hasn't already. He needs to be jolted out of his lethargy. If that happens, his interest in other women will come around."

"And how do you suggest I give him a jolt? By tying his coattails to a kite during a thunderstorm?"

"Have him pay her a visit. He has to face up to what has happened and settle this thing between them once and for all."

"I thought it was settled when she sent him away from Marsham."

"Oh piffle! The girl was hurt, and with good reason, I might add. No woman worth her salt is going to go running after a man who has betrayed her, no matter how much she loves him."

"And you think things will work out between them? You think Natasha will believe anything he has to say?"

"I do not know, but even if she doesn't and sends him packing a second time, it may be what is necessary to make him realize it is time to get on with his life. It is either going to work out between them or it isn't. It's been over a year now, and I get the feeling we are at a complete stalemate. Trevor needs a little prodding. He should either right things between himself and the girl or he should get on with finding himself a suitable wife."

"You are thinking about Lady Jane Penworthy, I'll wager."

"And if I am? You know yourself that she would be perfect for him, and of all the women who have thrown themselves at him, she is the only one Trevor seems comfortable around."

"He may be comfortable around Jane, but he won't ever love anyone like he loves Natasha, Mother. You know that."

"I never said he had to fall in love. I said he had to marry. Once he does that, he can do as he likes. Will you talk to him?"

Tony grinned. "When have I ever refused you anything?"

"Quite recently, if my memory serves me right."

"Mother, it isn't that I object to naming the baby after your father, it is simply that I cannot abide the name Percival. Besides, it might be a girl."

"But we don't know what it will be, and since you won't name your son Percy, then you will have to pacify me and talk to your brother."

"I am on my way, and a thankful man at that."

"Thankful?"

"That you did not name me Percival," he said, ducking through the door before he could hear his mother's retort.

A short while later Tony had the carriage stop on King Street, half a block from Westminster Hall, where the houses of Parliament met and Trevor kept an office.

Walking up the street now, he thought about his visit with their mother. She was right, of course. It was time for Trevor to take a wife—and time for him to lay this thing to rest between himself and Natasha. Lady Jane Penworthy was a good choice, and Trevor did show some interest, however slight, in her. Maybe it was a good idea for him to pay Natasha a visit, to confront the ghost from his past.

The street was lined with buildings, traffic bustled in the street, and all about him the walk was crowded with milling people. When he reached Westminster, he hurried up the stone steps that led inside.

The building was terribly old and quite gloomy, the chambers and hallways lined with uncomfortable-looking wooden benches that someone had painted crimson. He shuddered, thankful that Trevor was the firstborn and the one who had to inherit all this luxury of serving in Parliament. Ignoring the crowd of lawyers, he made his way toward Trevor's office.

Opening the door, Tony went inside. Trevor was writing something, but he looked up as Tony stepped inside.

"Well, this is certainly a surprise. I thought you had an aversion to houses of Parliament," Trevor said.

"I do, and believe me only the gravest of matters would bring me inside the hallowed doors." Tony paused and looked around. "Egads, this place never ceases to give me a shudder. How ever can you stand it? It is positively creeping with age."

Trevor scowled. "You didn't come here to tell me that," he said.

"No, I didn't. I came here to talk some sense into your head. I think it is time you straightened this mess out between yourself and Natasha."

"I agree."

"I think it might be a good idea for you to go to Marsham to see her."

"I agree."

"I think that is the only way you will ever know for certain just how . . ." He stopped talking and looked at Trevor strangely. "What did you say?"

"I said I agree with what you are saying."

"You do?" Tony asked, dropping into a chair across the desk from Trevor. "What brought on this change of heart?"

"I'm not certain. Perhaps it was the shock of seeing her again. Perhaps it is simply because this has gone on long enough. I know Mother is anxious for me to secure the title, and I know that her concern is legitimate."

"This change of heart wouldn't have anything to do with Lady Jane Penworthy, would it?"

"I don't love her, Tony. But I could be reasonably happy with her."

"So you are going to Marsham?"

"I am."

"And what are you going to do when you get there?"

Trevor smiled. "Don't worry. I'm not going to shoot her. I am going to ask her to marry me."

"And you think there's a chance that she will?"

"There is always a chance," Trevor said, coming to his feet and turning to stare out the window at the traffic in the street below.

"Well," Tony said, coming to his feet, "that wipes out my plans for the next two hours."

"What plans are those?" Trevor asked, turning back to look at his brother.

"I had envisioned a rougher time of it," Tony said. "Now I find I have time on my hands."

Trevor came around his desk and slapped his brother

on the back. "Then let me buy you lunch," he said, "for good luck."

"I will," Tony said, "because you are going to need it."

Immediately after their lunch, Trevor departed for Marsham. It was time to settle this thing once and for all.

It was late when he arrived, but late or not, he was determined to see Natasha tonight. As the trip from London had progressed, Trevor had become more and more agitated with each mile he traveled. In vain he'd tried to find something to calm his jittery nerves, to ease the growing knot of anticipation from his stomach. Nothing seemed to help, and by the time the coach came to a stop in front of the massive doors of Marsham Manor, Trevor knew nothing would.

Nothing except seeing Natasha again.

"I would like to see her," he told an astonished Mrs. Mac. "Now."

"Now, Your Grace?"

Trevor made no motion to hide his irritation. "Has she gone to bed?"

"No, Your Grace. She was just going up."

"Then I will see her now, if you please. I will wait for her in the library."

And with that, he turned down the hall.

A few minutes later Natasha walked into the library, feeling a sense of escalating panic fill her. What was he doing here? What did he want with her?

Stopping just inside the door, she took in the sight of him, a tall, dark figure standing rather majestically at the fireplace, his long cape swirling about him and his hair still damp and windblown from his long ride.

He was prodding the fire with a poker when she entered. A moment later he put the poker on the stand and turned to look at her. "I have come to see you," he said.

She did not reply.

He went on. "I have some things I want to say to you, and I hope you will be gracious enough to listen. Perhaps you should sit down."

Still saying nothing, she came closer to the fire and dropped into a chair. She saw the way his jaw worked as he reached for his glass of port, then he turned and stood looking at her for a moment. Holding her breath, she returned his look, as if by doing so she could see in his eyes the reason that forced him to come.

"Would you like a glass of port?" he asked.

Sucking a breath of air into her starving lungs, she gave him a direct look. She could not believe he was here. He had swallowed his ducal pride and had come to her. This was her chance to repay him . . . by throwing him out of her life a second time. "No thank you. I think I am strong enough to hear whatever it is that you have to say without the help of spirits."

He gave her a mocking nod and removed his cape, tossing it over a nearby chair, then he took a drink of port, placing the glass on the mantel. When he finished, he turned toward her. "I suppose you're wondering why I've come."

"I've a certain amount of curiosity about it," she said. She was not going to make this easy for him. Why should she?

For what seemed an eternity, she sat perfectly still, feeling the tension that consumed her, wanting so desperately to appear calm and in control.

"It has been over a year since I left here," he said, "and during that time I have had more than enough time to think back over things."

"As I have," she said. He was so controlled. What if he had come to tell her that there was someone else? That he was going to marry? She remembered seeing him laughing with a woman that day at Eton, feeling her heart begin to pound. For a moment she closed her eyes, allowing the agony of that thought to dissipate. She groped for control, and when she felt she had some semblance of mastery over her rampaging emotions, she opened her eyes. For a moment she simply stared at his face, then she allowed her gaze to roam over him at will.

Standing across from her he looked huge and wild and completely foreboding. He did not say anything, but simply stood there looking at her as if he were remembering something, something that was better forgotten. The words she wanted to say—the hurting, biting comments she had long rehearsed for this moment—were suddenly gone from her mind and she could only look across the short distance that separated them, staring into his eyes, searching his face for some sign—some clue—as to why he was here at all.

To her dismay, she could find no hint of an answer. Then she noticed the scar on his face.

She studied it, remembering that she had seen it on the night of the ball and how she had ignored it. The scar was still red, speaking for the newness of it. She wondered how it happened, but she made no mention of it to him.

"Well," she said at last, "are you having some difficulty remembering why you came?"

"Yes," he said, "I am. I find this is not as easy as I had imagined."

He moved to a chair across from her and sat down, leaning forward, his elbows resting on his knees. He stared at her for some time, seemingly in no hurry to speak, and then, without saying a word, leaned his head back to rest against the chair.

Her gaze never left his face. The scar. It changed him. Made him look more cynical—and yet, in a way it made him more handsome than before, for it added a ruthless, rugged quality to his features. Her eyes drank in the sight of him, noticing other changes—and there were many—for he was different now, different everywhere except the eyes.

She felt herself growing pale with annoyance. Just how bloody long was he going to sit here looking at her, playing cat and mouse?

"So, you have come to Marsham?" she said at last, hoping to stir some response from him.

"Yes."

She gave him a wary look. "And *why* have you come?"

"I have come to ask you to become the Duchess of Hillsborough," he replied.

He said it so simply, with such smoothness, such restraint, that she did not for a moment comprehend.

As if understanding that, he broke it down into simple terms. "I am asking you to become my wife."

She comprehended that well enough. His words came back to her in a rush. He was asking her to be his wife. Just like that. And of course, since he was the powerful and mighty Duke of Hillsborough, he naturally assumed she would jump at the chance, since he was obviously accustomed to getting his way.

"Why? Why are you asking me? Is it because you find it time for you to take a wife? Do you need heirs? Have you someone else in mind, in case I don't accept?"

He came to his feet and stood silently studying her,

as if amazed that she could hit so close to the truth. Did it bother him that she made it sound cold and callous?

He opened his mouth, as if he were going to explain. Perhaps he was going to tell her he loved her, that she was and always would be first in his heart, but when he spoke, all he said was, "Yes."

His reply jolted her. She sprang to her feet. "You vile—You—you must be insane!"

He smiled. "You are absolutely right there, my love, for I have been insane since the day you sent me away from here."

"Then you can remain insane, for I do not want you here now."

"I am not leaving, not until I have laid things between us to rest, regardless of the outcome. I want to do the honorable thing."

She snorted at that, finding little relief, for in truth, she wanted to throw something at him. "Since when has it been important to you to do the honorable thing?"

His look softened, and she saw it, but refused to acknowledge the pain she saw in his eyes.

"Since I made a mistake that will haunt me for the rest of my life," he replied.

He always knew what to say. She would hand him that much. It had always been one of his strongest assets. It was little wonder to her that he was so successful in the House of Lords, that he was considered to be such an outstanding statesman. Everyone knew the devil was a master at beguiling. Problem was, no one understood that Trevor was nothing more than the devil in disguise.

Once beguiled, twice wise, she thought. He would not dupe her a second time. Did he really think she would be flattered to hear she was his first choice? Why? Because she had already proven she could conceive a child? Was he that presumptuous? Yes, she thought. He was.

Their eyes met and held. They stared at each other for a suspended moment, each of them unable to look away, intense blue eyes gazing into vivid violet. For a moment she felt as if she was gazing into his soul, and the anger and pain seemed to go out of her; she knew she was seeing him now, not with her mind, but with her heart. She cursed herself for being weak, for caring when she should not, and she knew, too, that he saw the flush rise to her face. She couldn't help wondering if his heart pounded as furiously as did hers.

Obviously well aware that she could see the adoration, the yearning, in his eyes, he moved swiftly. He crossed the room, coming to stand before her. He reached out, taking her hand in his, and looking down, began to stroke the finger that he must have thought he would soon be placing his ring upon.

"I know I haven't given you any reason to trust me, but I am asking that of you now. I want things to work out for us. I want the chance to show you what is in my heart. All I am asking for is a second chance."

She snatched her hand back. "I may have fallen for your lies once," she said, "but that doesn't mean I will do so again. I could never trust you again, Trevor. Never."

"But you will," he said softly. "If it takes me the rest of my life . . . if it takes every shilling I possess. Even if I go to my grave in order to prove it to you, someday, someway, somehow, you will know."

She closed her eyes, fear, anguish, and abandonment all seeping into her very soul. She felt the heat of a tear slipping down her cheek and she turned away from him. There was nothing she could do to salvage her pitifully thin remnant of pride, for he demanded even that from her. He had her in his snare as much as he had before, only this time, if she gave in to his beguiling, there would be no escape.

Her heart wrenched with a feeling of hopelessness. She had never felt so afraid of him, so terrified that he might do this time what he had been unable to do before: destroy her.

She was afraid. More afraid than she had ever been. This man held too much power over her, and that, if anything, was the cause of her hopelessness. While she knew she could not trust anything he said, what really made her feel so helpless was knowing that she was still as big a fool as she had ever been.

She cared for him. God, even now, in the moment of such deep despair, she was acutely aware of his nearness, the way his very presence seemed to fill a room.

Her emotions on a rampage, she studied the face of the man who had asked her to marry him, the man who said he wanted nothing more than to become her husband.

Her husband . . .

The words snagged at her heart. She regarded him silently, this pensive, beautiful man she had loved with all her heart—loved and loved still. But he would never know, she vowed. He would never, never, never know.

Some time ago, Natasha had decided that she was unlucky as far as men were concerned. They either died when she needed them, hurt her, turned against her, or they deceived her. She had loved him, but even then he had been guilty of pain and deception. She had thought she would be stronger, but she realized now that he was a threat to her—that he would always be a threat to her.

Her life, her love, her emotions belonged to her now, and that was the way she wanted it. She could not risk caring for him again; she did not want to go through that emotional calamity once more. Loving hurt too much. It demanded too much. It extracted too great a price. She could not go through that anymore. She would not care for him again. She wouldn't. She couldn't.

Loving him had almost destroyed her once. She might not be so fortunate a second time. The fear, the anxiety, the repercussions of it all began to weigh her down.

She felt her shoulders shake with the sobs she could no longer hold back. She had never expected much out of life, had never complained about the many misfortunes that had come her way. *But why?* she wondered. *Why is it written somewhere that I cannot be happy? Why can't I go on with my simple life at Marsham? Why can't I spend the rest of my life designing gardens? Why? Why? Why?*

She felt the warmth of his hands as they grasped her shoulders, pulling her back against him; felt, too, the weight of his chin resting upon the top of her head, the slow, steady beat of his heart—and the way her own body stiffened in readiness to resist.

He sighed. "I am a bloody fool," he said slowly. "I always was where you were concerned. I have been far too presumptuous and I apologize for it."

She made a move to pull away, but he only held her more firmly. "Give me a chance," he whispered. He relaxed his hold a bit and began running his hands up and down her arms. "I'll make it up to you." His words were low, throbbing. "Give me a chance."

He loosed his hold upon her—just enough to turn her in his arms—and in a way she was glad. She wanted to see those lips that spoke to her with such tenderness, that face that looked at her with such emotion, those eyes that mirrored his soul. Oh, yes. She wanted to see

those things, to see them as she had seen them once before . . . to see and remember, because then, and only
then, could she harden her heart.

She stared at him. She remembered, all right, remembered and grew wiser. She thought of him now, the sincerity, the earnestness in his voice. The perfect picture
of a broken man.

She looked into that face, into those intense blue eyes
she remembered so well, and she saw the expectation,
the hope there. Oh, yes. He was all sincerity now,
whether out of revenge or guilt, she did not know—not
that it mattered now, for either reason was a flimsy
foundation for a marriage.

He made a soft sound, deep in his throat, and pulled
her against him, his mouth near, and nearer still, until
he brushed his lips over hers, so light, so brief that it
was no more than a whisper, a warm caress, a touch
that came and went before she could draw in a breath to
protest.

He smiled down at her, drawing the curve of his finger along the line of her lips. His smile was bittersweet,
inviting, his eyes even more so. It was an expression
she had never been able to completely get out of her
mind, an expression that made her feel as if she could
not make sense of anything now.

She pulled back, but he held her firm. "Don't go," he
said. "Just let me hold you for a moment."

She was torn—torn between staying with him and escaping to the security of her own room, to a place she
knew would be safe. His presence, his soft words, that
smile, those eyes . . . They gave her no peace now. She
wondered just how long it would be before she looked
at him with her heart twisting within her.

Her whole body tensed in anticipation. He looked
tempting like this. Even the way the candlelight touched

his hair made him seem too adored, too golden, too perfect, and then she remembered that even Satan could disguise himself as the angel of light.

Don't do this to me, her heart cried. *Don't come to me now, speaking soft words . . . touching me in a way that makes me ache . . . looking at me with your heart in your eyes. I know what it feels like to be touched by you—to feel the warmth of your breath upon my throat . . . to know the sweet heavy weight of your body pressing upon mine. I know these things and the recall causes me pain. I know, too, the consequences of trusting you, and the memory of that is more than I can bear.*

She stared at him, her resentment spilling over into a quiet rage. His words did not soften her, nor did his apologies. He *had* been presumptuous, assuming too much. Did he really think that he could come in here whispering a few words of endearment and have her writhing in his arms? Did he really think her that naive, that gullible?

Yes, she thought, *he does. And why wouldn't he?*

Her mind spun back, far, far back, to another time, another place. She had been another girl then, young, innocent, trusting, believing in him and everything he said.

"*Poor innocent Natasha. So confused. So afraid. You want me, but you don't want to.*"

"*No,*" she whispered. "*It's not true. It's Tony I want. Not you.*"

"*You can lie to me all you want to, but you can't lie to yourself. You aren't in love with Tony any more than Mrs. MacDougal is. What you felt was nothing more than infatuation. Even now, that is wearing pitifully thin.*"

"You are wrong. I do love him."

"So you say, but words don't mean very much. It's your face that tells me the truth. It isn't love for Tony you're feeling right now, but desire for me. No matter what you do. No matter how hard you try. You won't be able to hide your feelings for long. I bother you, sweet Natasha, and we both know it."

She found the memory painful, but what hurt the most was knowing it was all still true. He did bother her, and he had as much as told her he knew it by the way he had come swaggering in here today. He saw her as nothing more than an old melody he decided to hum again; a second verse to an old, old song.

Her spirits plummeted. She felt the color fade from her face. Her fingers grew cold. The sound of her too-rapid heartbeat hammered in her ears. No, her heart cried. Not again.

Her face was deathly white now. She stared at him with tortured violet eyes. She started to speak, then gestured helplessly, finding the words too agonizing to say. With an anguished cry, she wrenched herself away from him. Her hand came up to cover her mouth—and with another cry, she fled the room.

CHAPTER
❧ THIRTY-FIVE ❧

He was waiting for her the next morning when she came out of the greenhouse.

She saw him standing there, just outside the door, with his leg propped up against a garden cart. She drew to an abrupt halt.

"Back again?" she asked.

"As you can see."

"Why?"

He took a step toward her, then stopped. "I told you last night."

"Last night you said you came here to talk and we talked. So, why are you here now?"

"We talked, Natasha, but we did not say anything."

"I don't know about you, but I said plenty. Perhaps the problem is simply that you refuse to hear what it is that I said."

He gave her a steady look, seeing the disappointment, the heaviness that seemed to shroud her. He wanted to hold her, to tell her it would work for them, that he was strong enough—determined enough—to see that it did, that he had enough love to carry them both if need be, at least until she knew her own heart.

He wanted to tell her those things, but he did not. *I only want your love,* he thought, and wondered why it was that a man who was considered to be one of the finest orators in the House of Lords found it so difficult to express himself, to articulate even the most simple phrases. *I love you,* his heart seemed to pound out with each painful throb. *I love you.* Couldn't she see it written in his eyes? *I love you*—three simple words he could not speak.

His eyes moved over her, seeing the outline of her body more clearly than he had last night. Then he saw the way she looked at him and his body went numb. She was small and uncertain, like a little girl, and he found himself wanting to take her in his arms and tell her it would be all right, that nothing could harm her so long as he drew a breath.

Then why didn't he? For a moment, panic filled him and he feared he would not be able to speak. Just the sound of her voice was a lyrical transport back to another time, and he fought against the pain of it, the pain of remembering his loss. What would her final answer be? Was he going to lose her again?

She was looking at him in that odd little way she had of tilting her head to one side. Still the silence stretched between them. *Idiot! Say something. Don't give her this. Don't let her know what her presence does to you. Don't let her know what power she has over you.*

He hardened himself against such feelings. What had brought him here in the first place? Had he really been so foolish as to think she would feel any differently toward him? Well, he had his answer now. She had refused him and slammed the door in his face once. . . . What was he waiting for?

For her to do it again?

Before he could think of a way to tell her what he was feeling, she turned away and started walking.

"I don't have time to talk to you right now," she said. "I need to change."

He watched her go, wondering if this was the way it would always be with them: her walking away and him standing alone and watching her go.

He did not see her again until later that afternoon, when he returned from hunting with the dogs. He dropped three pheasants off in the kitchen for Cook to prepare, then he left, going upstairs to change his clothes.

As he passed the library, he glanced inside and saw her. She was standing quietly by the window, her face bathed in light which gave her an angelic quality. She was as beautiful as she had ever been, with the milky fairness of her skin in such contrast with the blackness of her hair. He did not know why that pose struck such a chord of memory, but it did; he felt a gush of sensation flow into his heart. He remembered the first time he had seen her clipping down the tree-shaded lane that led to Marsham, riding a prancing horse and wearing her best blueberry riding suit.

God, how far they had come. How far they had to go. The thought of it wearied him, and he found himself doubting what he was about for the first time.

A soft breeze drifted through the open window, fluttering the leaves of a book she had been reading and left lying open on the table beside her. For a moment his attention was distracted by the ruffling of the pages; he felt as if a great portion of his life had passed in much the same way.

He stepped into the room. Without looking at him, she said, "I saw you coming with the dogs."

"They need to be hunted with more often. They are getting fat and lazy."

"There is no one here to hunt with them, save when Luka and Pavel are home."

He heard the way her voice seemed sadder when she spoke of her brothers. "Is it hard for you, having them away?"

"It is the most painful thing I've ever experienced, save when you—" She caught herself. "Of course I miss them. They're my brothers. They're all I have."

Trevor came closer, stopping just in front of her, turning toward her, grasping her shoulders, for in truth, he would not have been surprised if she had bolted. He looked down into her face. Sunlight caressed her cheek, highlighting the curve and giving it a luminous quality. There was no contempt in the eyes that looked up at him now, only apprehension and a sort of resignation, and perhaps—perhaps fear.

There were so many things he wanted to tell her, so many wounds he wanted to heal. He felt awkward and clumsy—a quaking, bumble-headed fool. How would he ever make her understand? How would she ever know what was in his heart? He did not know, but he knew he had to try.

"Natasha," he whispered, unable to say more, for a sharp, swelling pain in his heart prevented him. His gaze never left her face, and it seemed to him that she was slightly befuddled, as if she were feeling just a little lost. He prayed she could read the assurance he so wanted to give her in his eyes. Understand me. Know what this is about. *I loved you then. I love you now.*

He lowered his head. His lips were warm when he kissed her, but hers were stone-cold. He saw the sorrow, the defeat in her eyes, and despite the pain in his own heart, sympathy welled up within him. He knew he loved her, that he had never stopped loving her, knew, too, that he had her best welfare at heart.

She looked up at him through misty eyes that were fever-bright. "Are you going to force me or deceive me this time?"

His heart shattered. *Neither, his heart cried. Not this time. This time it will be different. I won't hurt you again,* he thought. *I won't force you.* He knew at that moment that what he thought was true.

He would not force her. He had caused her enough grief. He glanced at her again, his heart cracking at the way she looked at him through dulled eyes. *If you want me, you will have to come to me. I deceived you once. I seduced you, knowing all the while what I was about, but no more.*

He stood there, watching her, then, at last, he spoke. "I think I have some idea of what you are feeling. The eyes, as they say, cannot lie, and your eyes, sweet Natasha, say that it would delight you if you never had to lay your gaze upon me again. Whatever the reasons you think I came here, I did it out of love for you—you must believe that. I am as aware as you of the things that passed between us in the past, of the sins I committed against you—sins that I must tell you did not go unpunished. I have begged your forgiveness, and I do so again."

He saw a curl lifted by the breeze settle over her shoulder and he reached to take it in his hand, intending to put it in its proper place. He jerked to a halt when he saw the way her eyes widened, saw, too, the way she backed away from him.

"Don't be afraid of me," he said. "Anything but that." With an agonized groan, he stopped and looked off, his gaze going down the long, gleaming hallway to where an elegant hall clock slowly ticked. "You need not fear that I am going to be the ogre you've imagined me to be. I have no intention of forcing you to do anything."

He turned back to look at her and fell silent. She was watching him. She did not understand what he was saying to her. He could see that in her eyes. He wondered now if she ever would.

He watched her, seeing the helpless way she was looking at him. He felt the strength go out of him. He was tired. He didn't want to fight with her. He didn't want to see the wariness in her eyes. He had said what was in his heart, but it did not seem to move her. What had he expected? A standing ovation? He had told himself he would give her plenty of room, more than enough time. Perhaps it was best if it started now.

He knew she could see the look of anguish upon his face, but he also knew she had no way of knowing of the sense of aching loss. He was a man, he thought, and a man was a capable being. A man did not weep, or show his emotion. A man did not pour out his soul. No, a man did none of those things, but Trevor feared he might. At length, without saying a word, he turned and left the house.

It was half past three in the morning when he came home. It took him almost a bloody hour to get his key into the lock, and then when he finally made it inside, he knocked over the umbrella stand. Umbrellas went clattering across the floor.

A moment later a light appeared at the top of the stairs. He stumbled to the bottom of the staircase, grabbing the newel post for support as he looked up. He saw three Natashas, and all of them looked angry. He blinked.

She came down the stairs, stopping two or three

stairs above him. She made a face, as if she smelled something she didn't like.

"You've been drinking," she said.

"My dear, I have not been drinking. I have been getting myself inebriated—soaked, top-heavy, raddled, soused, lit, crocked, corned, three sheets to the wind, blind drunk—and at last, and blessedly so, passed out." He hiccuped and gave her a watery smile.

"What did you do? Drink away the last of your senses?" She came off the bottom step.

He gave her a low, sweeping bow. "That, my violet-eyed duchess, was my intent." He stepped around her and made his way into the library, going to the decanter and taking off the lid. He poured himself another drink.

She followed him, putting the lamp down on the desk as she entered the room. "Don't you think you've had enough?"

"Enough what? Enough humiliation? Enough of begging a woman with a heart of stone? Enough of loving a woman who cannot abide the sight of me? Enough misery? Enough suffering?" He looked at her sadly. "Sweet Natasha, I've had enough of many things— things you know nothing about, but I could never have enough of what I want."

She said nothing.

He dipped his head as if acknowledging her right to ignore all of this. "Bottoms up," he said, tipping the drink back and downing the contents.

"Why are you doing this?" she asked.

He looked at her, a smile slowly appearing on his face. "Are you so certain you want to know?"

She nodded.

"You won't like it," he said. "Perhaps I shouldn't tell you."

She stood there, looking at him. *The vine bears three*

kinds of grapes: the first of pleasure, the next of intoxication, the third of disgust. She wondered if it was true.

She felt his gaze upon her, and when she glanced up, his eyes were blue-black and watching her intently. She did not know why, but it was a look that sent a shiver of awareness over her. Even in this inebriated state, he cut a fine figure. She knew she should go back to bed, that she should ignore him while he was in this drunken state.

He staggered to a leather-covered chair, stumbled over the footstool, and almost went sprawling. She found it strange that she could feel both amusement and anger.

"You angry?" he asked. When she didn't say anything, he added, "You are."

"How do you know what I feel?"

"You look upset."

"And you look like you tried to outdrink an elephant."

He leaned his dark blond head back and gave her a look that half the women in London would have fainted over. "I have spent my evening in lightsome mirth, mingling with the Muses, and now I'm ready for the splendid gifts of Aphrodite."

Any humor she felt vanished. "Why have you done this? What purpose does it serve?"

"What purpose does it serve? My dear Natasha; a man when he drinks takes a pause from thinking."

"Come on," she said, crossing the room to where he lay sprawled in the chair. "You can talk about this in the morning. Let me help you to bed."

"Why?" he asked, laughing as he made a grab for her. "Why would you want to help me?"

"I wish I knew," she said.

* * *

She bypassed his reaching for her easily enough, thinking she had never seen him looking more relaxed, more like a young boy.

"You are, as you so eloquently put it, blind drunk. I doubt you can get out of the chair by yourself," she said, finding herself distracted by how truly handsome he was.

"Then, if I cannot get up, you can join me," he said, laughing as he made another grab for her.

Because she had allowed herself to be distracted by him, he managed to get his arm around her waist. Before she could do more than yelp, he was yanking her into his lap.

Startled, she looked up into his face, which was mere inches from hers. The laughter disappeared from his lips; the humor drained from his face. She made a small sound of distress. He was holding her so hard against him that she could barely breathe.

The light from the lamp gleamed golden, catching the glints in his hair, making it easy to see the fire in his eyes. When he lowered his head toward her, she could see his lashes were long and straight.

What was it about him that weakened her? Why this man and no other? She felt dazed, as if a sleepy sort of drowsiness had taken hold of her. She watched his gaze wander, from her shoulder to her throat to her breasts. She remembered that she had been asleep when he had returned, that she had quickly thrown her wrapper over her gown, tying it loosely. She looked down, seeing the wrapper had parted, exposing her gown, making the fullness of her breasts quite visible where they pressed against his chest.

Her gaze flew up to meet his. "Trevor, I . . ." Desire dried the words of denial in her throat.

He studied her face. "What is it about that face that has caused me so much torment?" he asked.

"I don't . . ." She drew in a long breath; all thought faded away.

His finger traced the outline of her mouth, and she remembered the first time he had kissed her. Such a long time ago. *Too long,* she thought, knowing she wanted him to kiss her again. She closed her eyes and felt his lips brush her cheek. Frustration curled her hands into fists.

"Sweet, innocent Natasha," he said, his lips in her hair, his breath coming warm and caressing against her ear. "I wonder what it would be like to make love to you again."

She could feel the pounding of her heart in her throat and wondered what strange longing drove them both to the point of desperation and denial. She closed her eyes, remembering the sweet taste of his mouth, the sounds of passion that came from deep in his throat when he kissed her. *Please,* she heard her mind begging. *Please . . .*

She did not utter a word, simply stared up at him, her mouth parted, her breathing shallow and rapid. His gaze moved over her, touching her, warming her like the palm of his hand. She wanted to shake him, to pound him with her fists, to drive him as insane for her as he was driving her. The need, the intenseness of it, was like an aching tightness in her chest. She had thought herself immune to him, and perhaps she was . . . when he was sober.

He was not sober now, and the thought of him being just a little out of control, the knowledge that he did not have the fine edge of mastery over himself that he always had . . . it was as powerful as anything she had experienced.

"I . . ."

"You what?" he whispered.

She shook her head and looked away. "Nothing."

His hand came up to take her face, turning it so that she was compelled to look at him. "What is it?" he asked, his voice low, his words so softly spoken.

She would have looked away again, but he stopped the motion with his mouth. With a low moan, his lips covered hers, and she felt herself go weak. The tightness in her chest intensified. Her body grew pliant and warm. His tongue touched hers, and she felt as drunk as he.

He groaned again, a deeper, more throaty sound, and threw his leg over her, trapping her there. His breathing was ragged, now, his hands moving over her like they had a will of their own.

He caressed her hips, her waist, his hands spreading warmly across her ribs; then his hand was molding itself to her breast.

Reality hit her like a slap to her face, but it must have hit him sooner—for before her body could react, before she could stiffen in his arms and push herself away, before she could tell him to stop, he broke the kiss and jerked his head back as if she had doused him with a bucket of cold water.

She felt wild, cheated, angry, full of desire—and incensed because she did. Her breathing coming in rapid pants, she stared up at him, unable to believe it had all been so easy, that she had wanted this every bit as much as he had. She saw a flash of something in his eyes and wondered what he thought he had seen in hers, for suddenly his body stiffened and all traces of emotion were wiped, clean as a slate, from his face.

"If you don't want to be taken like a trollop on the library carpet, I suggest you take to wearing more clothes when you are around me. . . . Especially if I have been drinking—which is something I plan to do a great deal of before I go."

She came to her feet, pulling the edges of her wrapper together. The desire she felt for him had not completely subsided, yet the anger over his bitter words was seeping into her befuddled brain. She felt dazed, uncertain, and just a little put out with herself, knowing her face was red with humiliation. The only thing she could think of was to get away from him.

Turning away, she hurried to the door, stopping briefly when she heard the sound of her name being called.

"Natasha."

She looked back at him.

"Don't worry. I probably won't remember this in the morning," he said.

"No, but I will," she replied, and hurried out of the room.

He awoke the next morning with his head swollen from the wine of yesterday. He opened his eyes and remembered last night; his heart was filled with regret. He had sworn to leave her alone, to keep his hands off her, and he hadn't even made it through the first day.

Mrs. MacDougal came into the room about that time and threw the draperies back as if she enjoyed it, sending brilliant shafts of sunlight spilling into the room.

"Good morning, Your Grace," she said.

"Out," Trevor said, groaning. "And close those bloody drapes."

"Had a bad night, did we?"

Trevor groaned again and lifted his head from the pillow. "When I want to talk, Mrs. MacDougal, I will let you know."

Mrs. Mac looked at him as if she was on the verge of breaking into a smile, but she managed to control the impulse. "Very well, Your Grace. Will there be anything else?"

"Out," Trevor said. "Now."

"As you wish, Your Grace."

Trevor pulled the pillow over his head, hearing Mrs. MacDougal's footsteps, then a pause.

"Ahem . . ."

"Yes?" The sound was muffled through the pillow.

"Sorry, Your Grace. I thought it prudent of me to disturb you once more."

He lifted the edge of the pillow slightly as he spoke. "Mrs. MacDougal, you have always had the infernal habit of disturbing me—even when it is not prudent. What the deuce is it this time?"

"I thought . . . That is . . ." Mrs. Mac stiffened and spoke to the ceiling. "Would you like me to get you something for your headache, Your Grace?"

The pillow was jerked away; Trevor looked at her with a scowling face. "And what makes you think I have a headache?"

"Your disposition, Your Grace."

"My disposition?"

"Yes, Your Grace."

"I don't need anything for my headache but a little peace and quiet."

"Very well, Your Grace. I shall see that you get it." She turned away, closing the door behind him.

Trevor rolled over and closed his eyes. There were too many servants here, too many distractions—and then he remembered he had just proposed to another distraction the day before. He groaned, remembering that it wasn't too many steps from his room to Natasha's.

He looked at the door that led out into the hall. *Only a few steps to her room. What would she do,* he wondered, *if I went barging through that door right now, not wearing anything, save a scowl caused by this bloody headache?*

Hearing no reply, he glanced at the clock on the mantel. Half past ten? Good God! He hadn't slept this long since he was at Oxford.

He made one attempt to sit up, but the slicing pain to his brain made him reconsider and he fell back into the bed. He thought about last night, remembering fuzzy details, seeing a blurred vision or two, mostly of Natasha standing at the top of the stairs in a white silk robe with her black hair hanging in a long braid down her back, her face as pale as her gown as she held the lamp aloft, staring down at him with an accusatory look. Not that he could blame her. He had been completely soused.

He remembered going into the library, remembered, too, the drowsy, warm weight of her in his arms. He felt himself getting hard. He recalled kissing her, too, feeling an immediate arousal at the memory of it. And then he remembered the way she had looked at him just before she left the room.

He sighed and lifted the sheet and looked down at himself. As far as getting rid of an arousal, remembering that look was an excellent way to do it.

CHAPTER
❧ THIRTY-SIX ❧

Trevor found her the next morning, sitting in the kitchen garden, near the overgrown herb beds, her feet propped on an old lead planter. With her was the dog he remembered as Beggar.

He stopped for a moment, watching him sniff among the cabbages, his tail curled over his back. Natasha, he saw, had her sketching pad in her lap and was drawing rutabagas.

"You mean that dog is still here?" he asked.

She looked up over the top of her sketch pad. "Gypsy?" she asked.

He paused and looked at the dog. "Gypsy? I remembered his name to be Beggar."

"Oh, Beggar," she said, looking fondly at the shaggy gray mutt she had called Gypsy. "Beggar has been gone a long time now."

"Gone? You mean he died?"

"I don't know. He just disappeared one day and never came back. Gypsy is his son." She laughed. "At least we think he is. Mrs. Pickle came marching up to our kitchen door one fine spring morning with a wicker basket on her arm. 'I believe this belongs to you,' she said, putting the basket down on the stoop and walking away. A moment later, Gypsy poked his head out. Harry went into town a few days later and learned Mrs. Pickle's dog had puppies. Five of them were exactly like the mother—but one was a disgrace to the litter. That one . . ."

" . . . was the disgrace," he finished.

She laughed. "Yes, that was Gypsy."

"Gypsy," he said. "Not Beggar." He shook his head. "There have been a lot of changes around here."

The laughter went out of her eyes. "Yes, there have been," she said, forcing herself not to think back to those terrible dark days, the weeks and months after he had gone.

Gypsy must have heard his name called, for he lifted his nose out of the cabbages, looked at Trevor, then moved on to the asparagus.

"He has located the trail of a rabbit I chased out of the garden this morning," she said, suddenly noticing that Trevor was dressed for riding.

"I was on my way into town. I have some papers to post to my barrister in London." He paused a moment, looking at her. "Would you like to come along?"

"No," she said. "I—I have too many things here that I need to attend to."

He nodded and started to turn away, but caught himself. "I just thought of something," he said, looking at her oddly. "I remember how much you always loved to ride . . . and yet I have not seen you on a horse since I arrived. Have you given up riding, or are you afraid I'll ask to come along?"

Her expression froze. A hundred bloody memories came rushing into her mind and she felt her face grow warm, her heart hammer in her chest. A twinge of nausea struck. "I don't ride anymore," she said.

"Why not?" he asked. But before she could think of an answer, he looked thoughtful for a moment, then said, "How foolish of me. I just realized I haven't seen a horse suitable for riding around here." He gave her a good-humored smile. "A lady such as yourself cannot be seen clopping around on a plow horse with feet as big as a wagon wheel."

"It does not matter. I haven't time for riding," she said in a tone she hoped would dismiss the subject.

"I could take the carriage," he said, "if you'd like to come into the village with me."

There was such power in him, such persuasion. She looked at him towering over her like a sheltering tree. He looked infinitely patient to her, standing there like a conquering pirate—strong, invincible. "No, I really must get back to my work."

"I see," he said.

No, you don't see. You don't see at all.

Suddenly he seemed restless, as if he were anxious to be away, and she decided he must have been, for he said, "Well, if I cannot charm you into coming, then I'll be off."

She was repotting a chrysanthemum cutting in the greenhouse when Trevor walked in. Hearing him approach, she looked up. "You're back early," she said.

"Am I? It is half past six."

"That late?" she said. "I had no idea. The time has escaped me."

He looked at her dirty hands, the smudges on her apron, and smiled. "You must be having a good time."

Her smile was hesitant. "I find the work relaxing. It keeps my mind off—other things."

"What kind of *other* things?"

"Things I shouldn't be thinking about," she said, giving him a secretive look. "And *that* is all I am going to tell you."

He laughed. "Well then, come along with me . . . if it won't disturb your potting. I have something for you."

She looked wary. "Something for me?"

"Yes, and that is all I am going to tell you."

She laughed at his good-natured mood, wiping her hands on her apron as she went with him, walking down the path toward the stables.

"Has the cow had her calf?"

"Not that I know of," he said.

"Do we have a visitor?"

"If we do, I know nothing about it."

"Has a letter come for me?"

"I don't know. You better ask Mrs. MacDougal."

"Then where are we going?"

"Right here," he said, giving a loud knock at the stable door.

She looked up at him, standing beside her, his face painfully close, the fading sunlight picking out his features and making the blue of his eyes much lighter.

A moment later the stable door opened, and John Fletcher, the new stable boy, led out a dainty chestnut mare.

All the life and animation seemed to drain out of her and her face turned a deathly pale. "A horse," she whispered.

He looked at her oddly, not understanding her reaction. His expression said he knew there was something strange happening here, something that he did not comprehend. "Yes, it's a horse," he said, as if telling himself that perhaps she was simply upset by his gesture, uncertain as to how to accept a gift from him. "At least they told me in town that it was a horse."

Her body felt cold. Her hands were starting to get numb. She had never seen such a beautiful horse, but whenever she looked at her, it sickened her. Everything seemed to be in slow motion. She saw Trevor looking at her oddly. She could see the gentle motion of his lips as he spoke to her, but she could not hear what he was saying. All she seemed to hear was the sound of her own screams that day as she stood looking down at her mare. Blood. So much blood. Everywhere.

She wasn't aware he had touched her until she felt him gently shake her. "Natasha, are you all right?"

She looked up at him, feeling dizzy and cold. "I am fine," she said. "I just don't want the horse."

His glance went from her to John Fletcher and he seemed to catch himself. "Take her away," he said, his voice sounding angry and gruff.

John led the mare inside and closed the stable door. For a moment Trevor stood there, looking down at her with a look of angry panic on his face, as if she had suddenly spoken some foreign language or given way to some mad ravings.

She took a deep breath and released it, feeling the warmth flow back into her body. "I'm sorry," she said. "I did not mean to sound ungrateful. It's just that—"

"You don't want a horse," he said, looking at her as if he was trying to understand. "If I had known . . ."

"Please," she said, "it isn't your fault. The problem lies with me. I had no right to be rude. I'm sorry. Please forgive me."

He looked as if he were considering it, and she saw the warring emotions in the depths of his eyes, knowing when she had won. "No harm done," he said, giving her a boyish smile that made her realize that he, too, in spite of being a man, in spite of being tall and well proportioned, in spite of being a wealthy, powerful duke, was vulnerable.

The knowledge of it cut to the heart of her. He could disarm her so easily, she thought. He was a devil in disguise, as warm and tempting as a summer breeze, touching her like flower petals, turning her anger, her indifference, to desire—with nothing more than a teasing smile, or the sight of laughter in his eyes.

This wasn't the Trevor she remembered. He was so different from what he was before. Now he seemed unsure of himself, more prone to moodiness and sullen departures. It occurred to her that this might be just as difficult for him as it was for her.

"Trevor," she said, reaching out her hand to touch his sleeve, but she grasped only thin, empty air. She realized suddenly that he was walking away.

She wanted to go to him. She wanted to tell him what it was that made her behave this way. She wanted to ask him to hold her, to understand her, to help her heal her wounds.

But she said nothing, standing there instead, watching his retreating back, feeling as if suddenly the world about her had gone dark.

He didn't understand her, but then she saw no reason why he should. She didn't understand herself. Not anymore.

CHAPTER
❦ THIRTY-SEVEN ❦

As Trevor walked off, he caught a glimpse of the bent figure of Harry moving about the garden. With a sudden impulse, he turned into the garden and made his way over to where the man was cleaning the prongs of his garden rake.

"Natasha . . . You are very fond of her, aren't you?" he asked.

Harry went on cleaning the prongs of his rake and did not look up. "Fond as I would be of any child of my own, I guess."

"Then help me to understand her. Help me to know what she suffered, what she went through while I was gone."

Harry looked at him, his blue eyes faded but full of life. "Why?"

"Because I love her. Because I want to make it better for her. Because I don't know how."

Harry ran the rake over the flower bed a few times. "What do you want to know?" he asked.

"Everything. How life was for her. How she adapted. Why she was so upset when I gave her a horse."

Harry's head snapped up. "A horse? You gave her a horse?"

"Tried to," Trevor said, shaking his head and ramming his hands deep into his pockets. "She wanted no part of it. Looked for a moment like she was going to faint."

"She doesn't ride anymore," Harry said.

"Why? She always loved riding. What made her change?"

The old gardener stiffened in resistance, giving Trevor a suspicious look that made him think Harry had not as yet decided to trust him.

"I am the only one who can help her," Trevor said, "the only one who can heal the hurt. And I will do it, with or without your help—the primary difference being that with your help, I can reach my goal much quicker."

"What goal is that?"

"To make her happy. To give her what she wants."

"Even if it means giving her her freedom?"

Trevor's heart lurched. "Even that."

"How do I know I can trust you?"

"You don't, but you care for her, and I'm gambling on that being reason enough for you to gamble as well."

"I find it hard to trust someone who brought her nothing but heartbreak."

"It may interest you to know that my own heart hasn't fared any better," Trevor said. "Now, if you care for her as much as you say you do, then tell me what I need to know. Why did she stop riding?"

"Because *he* killed her horse."

"Who killed her horse?"

"That Gypsy boy, the one what told all those stories about her and put the boys in the village up to doing her harm."

"Ned," Trevor said. "You are talking about the groom, Ned?"

"Aye. Ned," Harry said.

"You saw him do it?"

"No, but I didn't need to. We all know it was him. It wasn't too long after you left that things started happening. First there were the notes."

"What notes?"

"The notes he left around here. I found most of them before anyone saw them, but one note she found before I did."

"What did the notes say?"

"Horrible things. One said 'Russian harlot, go home.' The one she saw was tacked to the greenhouse door. 'Whore' was all it said."

"My God," Trevor said, feeling his heart wrench. It was all he could do to force himself to stay here and ask Harry to go on, so badly did he want to go to her.

"I found that little dog. Beggar, his name was. Found him in the rain barrel." He paused, giving Trevor a threatening look. "I never told her about those other notes, and I never told her about the dog."

Trevor nodded. "I understand," he said. "Was it possible that the dog fell in the rain barrel?"

"And put the lid on?"

Trevor grimaced. "Go on."

"The worst was the day I heard her screaming and found her in the stables. He slit her horse's throat, and when I found her, she was standing there, in the doorway of the stall, screaming."

Rage welled up within Trevor. He could never remember having the urge to murder someone as much as he felt it now. "And so, she has never ridden again," he whispered.

"Won't have nothing to do with horses."

"I wish I knew where that bastard was," Trevor said. "I would give half of all I own just to get my hands on him."

"What good would it do if you found him? It wouldn't change anything."

"No, but I would make damn certain that he never harmed her again."

CHAPTER
❧ THIRTY-EIGHT ❧

Natasha did not see Trevor until that evening. When dinner was announced, he was not in the dining room when she entered, so she took her place at the table and sat there, staring at a bunch of grapes sitting on the top of a bowl of fruit. She wondered where he was, thinking it strange that his presence seemed to be in here with her, even when he was not. She picked up her napkin. She wasn't about to let herself become accustomed to having him around.

For some time she sat there, wondering if he would seek her out, or at least come to dinner. She thought about all that had happened between them and wondered why she was not at least willing to try.

She allowed her mind to dwell upon his fine features, taking them one by one. She was sitting there, doing just that, with her elbows resting rudely upon the table, a dazed look upon her face, when suddenly it occurred to her that it was no image of Trevor she was seeing, but the living, breathing reality of him.

"Oh," she said. "You startled me."

He smiled. "Did I? I was beginning to wonder if you were going to notice me at all."

Oh, I notice you all right . . . She felt her face grow warm and she looked down. "Well, I was thinking about something," she said.

He looked interested. "It must have been something pleasant," he said, "judging from the look on your face."

"I was thinking about mucking out the stables," she said, not yet willing to give him any advantage over her.

That seemed to put an end to his curiosity, at least for now, for he said nothing more, but simply took his place at the table across from her. When he was seated, he sighed and looked rather helpless as he glanced around the room as if he didn't know what to do. She found it strange that it did not please her as much as she thought it would.

There was something about seeing a man of his stature, his strength, looking helpless that touched her. For a moment she wondered what they had started here, wondering, too, if they would ever be able to bring it to a resolution without one or both of them being hurt. She remembered riding her father's horse once, and when she had urged the beast into a run, he had gotten the bit between his teeth, and she had not been able to bring him under control. This was how she felt now: like she had started something and now it was out of control.

She glanced at him, seeing the puzzled look on his face. She gave him a half smile and did her best to look pleasant. She did not want him to know what she felt inside. Feelings and thoughts in the wrong hands became weapons. Being around him like this hurt her enough. She did not want to give him more ammunition.

She cocked her head to one side and fixed him with an earnest, inquiring gaze. She felt her heart pounding and she had an inkling her face was flushed. He seemed not to notice. Only his eyes glittered, resting for a disturbing moment on her mouth.

She looked into those blue, blue eyes and knew instantly she had made a mistake. Looking at him unnerved her, made her think like a woman in love instead of a woman scorned. She knew what he was thinking, why he was here. So, he thought they would be together like two halves of an apple? Just like that . . . She wanted to laugh. She savored the thought, savored, too, her redress.

As Mrs. Mac served them, he began to engage her in polite conversation, but she knew he was keeping the subjects light, holding himself back.

"You have done wonders with the gardens here," he said. "I can see why your work is so important to you."

She looked down at the roast duck that Cook had labored over, feeling nausea rise in her throat. It wasn't supposed to be like this, she thought, but even as she thought it, she knew she was getting exactly what she told him she wanted from him—nothing.

"I am glad my love for it shows, for that is precisely what it was . . . a labor of love."

He gave her an odd look, his gaze fastened on her mouth as she said the word *love*, but he made no comment about it. "And you have plans to do other gardens?"

She nodded. "As many as I can work in between my illustrations and working in the greenhouse."

"In the greenhouse," he said. "And what do you do there?"

"It is where I keep many of the garden plants during cold weather—the rare, exotic species, of course, stay there year-around. I have a few plants I am experimenting with. I have been most fascinated with pollen. It is all very interesting, you know. Sometimes I go out to sit in the garden with my notepad, just to think about it. Your uncle was most intrigued with it as well."

"Pollen," he said. "You like to think about pollen."

She nodded, thinking the way he said it sounded like he thought it was a new word. "The Greeks and Romans knew about pollen," she added, feeling suddenly self-conscious from the way he was looking at her.

"Greeks and Romans . . ." He stared at her for a moment, his gaze wandering over her face.

Her face grew warm. Instinct told her it was best to ignore him and his hot looks, but in her frustration, she started talking. "Yes, the Greeks and Romans. Theophrastus did many experiments with the date palm. He is the one who discovered when the male palm was in flower, if he cut off the spathe and shook the bloom and dust over the fruit of the female, it retained its fruit and did not shed it."

"The male palm . . . and the female," he said, his look a combination of intrigue and sensual heat.

She felt her heartbeat escalate. *If he does not stop looking at me like that, I am going to leave,* she thought, wondering if she had said it aloud, for almost immediately he seemed to give himself a mental shake.

Disappointment shadowed his features, but his voice was light, teasing. "Mercy," he said. "What an exciting life you lead, and I dared to think I could drag you away from it?"

"I find it exciting," she said, cursing the quaver she heard in her voice. "And safe."

It was the first spark of real interest she had seen in the deep blue depths of his eyes. "Safe?" he asked, giving her an amused look. "I wonder why I am intrigued by that? What do you mean, exactly, by safe?"

"You always know what to expect with plants," she said. "They follow a preordained plan. We may not know everything about them, but we do know they are predictable. Roses always bloom in the springtime. The chestnut tree never bears walnuts. There is order."

"And you find that safe?"

"Safer than most people," she said, seeing the warmth fade from his eyes. A quiet, unreadable but tense emotion passed over his face. His expression turned stone-cold. The moment it did, she was sorry, for she liked him ever so much better the other way.

"Then I shall take care to see that I do not follow *my* preordained plan," he said.

Her benumbed brain did not seem to comprehend the implication of his words. "Not follow it?"

He gave her a nasty smile. "Of course, for if I did what was ordained, I would throw you over my shoulder in a flash and carry you upstairs to make love to you, wouldn't I?"

A fine edge of panic gripped her throat. She glanced from him to the door, then back to him. "You may anyway," she said. "You almost did the other night."

He gave her a look she could only call a smirk. It irritated her, but she knew that was probably his intent.

"Is that what you think?" he said. "I hate to disappoint you, sweetheart, but in spite of my inebriated condition, I was completely in control. One has to feel overwhelming desire in order to lose one's head like that, and so far, that has not been a problem around you."

Before she could register her shock, her anger, he shoved back his chair and stood up, throwing his napkin back into his plate. "I'm going out into the garden for a smoke. I will see you at breakfast."

He gave her a curt nod. A moment later he was gone.

She looked down at the duck, lying cold and uneaten in her plate. Her vision began to blur and she wondered if all she was destined to do around him was cry . . . and be miserable.

A moment later she tossed her napkin in her plate and went upstairs.

It was becoming a habit for her, eating dinner alone.

Natasha looked down at the boiled mutton and cabbage and lost her appetite—not because the food was not good, for it was, but the more she thought about Trevor, the more her emotional hunger superseded her physical one.

And she was hungry. Hungry for a clue as to why he had really come here, how long he was going to stay.

She pushed her chair back from the table and came to her feet, leaving the dining room. The pressure of having him about was beginning to drain her. She was becoming preoccupied and on edge, and winding its way through those two sentiments was a hint of sadness. She knew things between them had never been more broken, but what hurt the most was knowing that she wasn't certain that she wanted to fix it.

"You not eating dinner again tonight?" Mrs. MacDougal asked, coming out of a doorway and almost crashing into her.

"I find I'm not as hungry as I thought."

"He isn't hungry, either, I take it?"

"I don't know if he is or not," Natasha said. "I have not seen him."

Mrs. MacDougal shook her head and started off down the hall, mumbling to herself something about wasting food and there being "plenty of people going hungry in the world tonight; a body ought to be ashamed of wasting perfectly good food."

Natasha went to the library and poured herself a glass of brandy, took a sip, then decided anyone that went through that much punishment to put their mind at rest needed a lot more than just a drink.

She took a few more sips, just to be certain it tasted as bad as she'd first thought, and when she decided it did, she poured what she did not drink back in the decanter—remembering Mrs. MacDougal's sermons on thrift. She put the lid on the decanter and wandered aimlessly around the room, seeing Trevor in so many places.

It was amazing, really, how a place could take on the personality of another. She glanced at his chair . . . and immediately thought it odd that she was already—in such a short time—thinking of the old earl's chair as Trevor's. She remembered the way he looked sitting there, the latest newspaper in from London spread before him, his very presence filling the room.

With a sad sigh, she gave the room one last, long look, then departed, going down the long hallway. She passed the music room, then stopped. She went inside and lit the lamp, going to the piano. She stood in front of the keyboard, thinking back over the few days he had been here.

She played a note, then two, picking out a slow, melancholy tune with one finger.

Was he never going to leave? What was he waiting

for? Hadn't she made her resistance clear enough? She did not trust him, could not look at him without remembering. She knew that she could perhaps, in time, find it in her heart to forgive him, but she would never be able to forget. Never could she love him the way she had once loved him. Never.

Oh, he could stir this heart of hers and make her knees go weak with just one look, but that wasn't love. She could stand at the window and watch him stride to the stables, remembering that purposeful way he had of moving, the way his mouth could break into a lazy grin, but that wasn't love. And sometimes she could feel his eyes upon her and would turn to find him watching her, standing there looking very tall, very handsome, and an agonizing pain would pierce her chest and she had to resist the urge to go to him, but that wasn't love.

But, there were times . . . times when his blue eyes were warm with laughter, times when the gentle movement of his hands brought back a rush of memory, times when nothing more than the strength of his physical image made her want to know what it would be like to lie in his arms once more.

Once and only once, she told herself. One time and no more.

She thought about that for a moment, her finger still picking out the sad, melancholy song. *It's a good thing he isn't here,* she thought. *I don't think I could trust myself tonight.*

She sensed his presence even before she saw him. Her finger stilled; the last mournful note faded and drifted away. She turned around. He stood in the doorway, one arm braced against the jamb. He was watching her with the hooded gaze and inscrutable face he affected so well.

She lifted her chin and stared at him, her breath

trapped in her throat, her heartbeat hammering painfully in her chest. There was something sentimental about the moment, as if they both knew that things were not going to work out for them, that this would be their last time together. He was giving up, and she was too stubborn to give in.

He pushed away from the doorway and stepped further into the room, pausing only long enough to close the door behind him and turn the key in the lock. Without taking his eyes from her, he began walking toward her with steps that were both slow and sure.

"No," she whispered. "No," she whispered again, knowing even as she did that there would be no stopping him—knowing, too, that she did not wish to stop him, and that somehow he knew that, knew the kinds of thoughts that had been going through her mind. *It's been so long . . . so very long. Hold me, Trevor. Touch me and make me forget. Touch me like you used to.*

She wanted him, there was no denying that, but it surprised her to feel the intensity of it. She had thought herself stronger than this. Discovering the opposite was true filled her with anguish. She lifted her hand to the piano, picking out the haunting melody of "The Lover's Waltz."

He stepped closer, moving directly behind her before he stopped. She could feel the warmth of his breath upon her neck, the heat radiating from his body. There was a certain smell that she always associated with him, an earthy smell that spoke of masculine things—of tobacco and horses and leather.

His hands grasped her shoulders, rubbing them lightly, from the top, down to her elbows, and back up again.

Her hand trembled and she paused, the lone solitary

note fading, and she found she was too weak to play anymore. She could not turn to look at him, nor could she move. Her throat was dry and she drew a deep, shuddering breath.

"Don't stop," he whispered against her ear.

Weakly she played the notes while he disarmed her with his hands. Touching, caressing, then grasping her more firmly, he pulled her back against him, pressing his body against hers.

She came to the end of the song, and he whispered, "Again."

She hit a wrong note, then picked out the melody, going too slowly.

His arms came around her to undo the buttons of her dress, slipping the small pearl ovals through the buttonholes until he had her dress opened from her throat to past her waist. As he pushed it away from her body, she felt a cool caress of air as the bodice fell about her hips, catching on the fullness of her petticoats and hanging there, riding the swell of her hips.

The shock of his warm hands against the coolness of her breasts brought a gasp of surprise to her lips; she found herself closing her eyes and leaning her head back against him.

His hands moved over her, touching her with infinite slowness and patience, driving her senses wild, making her body scream out against the methodical touch that stretched her nerves to tautness and made her muscles go limp.

He turned her in his arms then, and she whispered his name impatiently.

"Trevor . . ."

"Shh," he said. "We do better when we don't talk." His mouth covered hers, and she found herself thinking he was right. They did do better when they did not talk.

He kissed her and touched her and kept on touching her until she was as breathless as he. Then he pushed her dress down, pulling the tabs on her petticoats and undergarments as he did so, until she was standing there in nothing but her stockings and her shoes, her clothes puddled about her feet.

She sucked in her breath sharply at the feel of having her body exposed, warmed only by the touch of his hands.

"What's the matter?" he whispered. "Are you afraid I'll make love to you? Or are you afraid I won't?"

"Neither," she whispered, feeling herself going weak at the knees.

He supported her lightly, allowing her body to drop to the floor. He came with her, pushing her back against her discarded clothes. She felt him leave her for a moment and knew he was removing his clothes. When he came back to her, his body rolled over hers, and she opened to him willingly. He kissed her, touching her with his mouth until she thought she would scream from the agony of it. He kissed the hollow of her neck, her shoulders, her breasts and the smooth valley between, his thumbs working her nipples into hard points. Her body felt as if it was on fire and her mind felt splintered—fragmented into too many pieces to collect.

Their coupling was wild and violent, just like their time together had been. When it was over and sanity began to creep into her brain, she opened her eyes and realized they were under the piano. A smile curled across her mouth and she turned slightly toward him, lifting her head in order to see if he had noticed it.

He had.

"I have a feeling it won't be as easy getting out," he

said, his words light and humorous, but the look in his eyes cut through to her very soul.

"No," she said, "the way out is never as easy as the way in."

"Will it always be that way?" he asked.

Her head fell back to rest against his shoulder. "I don't know. Some things are difficult to alter," she said. "The world changes and we change with it."

"You make it sound like a verdict that must be accepted, but there is something about it, something in the agony of change that seems to be more than even a man can bear. Unhappiness remembering happiness. I am learning the words to a new song, but the old melody keeps playing in my heart."

She looked up, seeing the inner workings of the piano, wishing it were as easy to see inside herself. There was an uncomfortableness that stretched between them, and she longed for a way to say the many things that needed to be said.

Speak to me. Tell me what you are thinking. We came so close. Don't let it end this way. Don't let it slip away. She waited for him to say something, anything, so they could pick up and go on from here.

He said nothing, and she felt the burning of tears behind her eyes. She knew by his silence that it was time to leave, that it would never work for them—even though neither was certain where they wanted to go from here.

He looked at her lying there, pale and desolate, drawn inward, like one of her flowers that closed itself into a tight bud when darkness came. She was near him, lying with her face bathed in the warm glow of candlelight, but there was something ethereal about her, as if she were a bodiless form with no more substance and color than a specter. The reality of her struck a thread of remembrance; he recalled the day of her accident, when she had turned him away. Tony had come to him, and he had said the pain seemed to blot all else. Tony had remained silent for a moment, then said, "That is because an hour of pain seems as long as a day of pleasure."

It was over . . . and he knew it.

That aspect was the only blemish on a pure and noble feeling. It felt good to know he had done the right thing, that he had come to her and he had tried, and now he would give her what she wanted, her freedom. But it hurt like the eternal fires of hell to lose her. If he had to say he had learned a lesson out of all this, it would be that one has to suffer in order to think. It did not seem right, but he knew it was true. One has to suffer to grow better.

CHAPTER
❧ THIRTY-NINE ❧

Trevor arose early and packed his bags.

It had been his intention to leave without saying anything further to her. He thought about the things Harry told him. For a moment he wondered if he should stay here, if for no other reason than a desire to protect her, but then he remembered the way it had been between them last night and decided there was nothing worse than trying to hold on to something that was already gone.

He picked up his bag, then put it back down. Something in him just wouldn't give up.

One more time, his heart cried out. Go to her just one more time.

With a resigned sigh, he closed the last of his bags. *One more time,* he told himself. *One more time and no more.*

Leaving his room, he made his way down the stairs, hearing voices coming from the library as he made his descent. He recognized Natasha's voice, and thinking she was more than likely talking to Mrs. Mac, he headed in that direction.

He thought of how she might look, standing there as beautiful as he had ever seen her. For some ridiculous reason, he imagined her as she had been so long ago, in a lemony yellow dress that made the black of her hair more vivid, looking at him with her heart full of love. Her cheeks were tinted the color of blowsy roses, making him want to kiss her until her mouth was as red as ripe cherries.

He still wanted to kiss her—until she ached and cried out his name and forgot all about her bloody plants and her foolish Russian pride. But he only looked at her, knowing she had filled his world with roses and brought to earth the stars, knowing, too, that she despised the very sight of him.

He stepped through the door and froze.

His gaze traveled from Natasha to the man standing beside her. Count Rostov.

His heart shattered, and something within him withered and died. Of all the reasons he had imagined she

would reject him, the thought that it might be for another man never entered his mind.

At that moment Natasha saw him; she looked
stricken. "This is Count Rostov," she said.

Trevor nodded. "The count and I met in London," he
said, "but I had no idea I would be seeing him here."

"Mademoiselle Simonov was kind enough to invite
me to view her gardens here at Marsham."

The room suddenly grew as silent as a tomb while
Trevor's gaze riveted on Natasha. Without ever taking
his eyes off her, he said to the count, "Then I hope your
visit here is more rewarding than was mine." Without
another word, Trevor turned and walked through the
door.

Natasha ran after him. "Trevor . . . wait. I can explain."

He turned. "I am certain you can, but then, there is
nothing to explain, is there? Whatever was between us
was over a long time ago. It just took me longer than it
did you to realize it."

"I can't help the way you feel, but I want you to
know it isn't the way you think."

"Are you trying to tell me, Natasha, that you didn't
know the count was coming, that the knowledge that he
would be here any day did not weigh heavily on your
mind while I was here making a fool out of myself?"

"I knew he was coming, but—"

"Please, spare me the gritty details. Obviously, I
helped you make up your mind. Tell me—what did it
for you? Didn't my lovemaking measure up to his?"

He saw the color drain from her face and heard her
shocked gasp, but he perversely went on. He was hurting so badly that nothing could have stopped him.
Nothing. The thought of her with another man drove
him to say things he should never say, made him want

to hurt her as he was hurting. "I have only one bit of advice to offer you—and that is if you decide you want to get rid of him, find another way to do it besides making love to him under the piano. For you, I think a feather bed and satin sheets would be more appropriate."

"I never thought it would end like this, with you being so cruel," she said.

A deep, aching sadness rose up within him as he stroked the velvety softness of her cheek. "Darling Natasha. You are still such a child. Don't you know nothing ever turns out the way we plan?"

He stepped around her, and a moment later he was gone.

He stopped by the kitchen long enough to tell Mrs. MacDougal that he would send someone for his bags, then he made his way toward the stables thinking: *What comes from the heart, goes to the heart. When the heart is broken, all bridges are burned.*

It was the end of happiness. He could only pray it would be the beginning of peace.

A moment later he was off, riding toward London, the dust billowing behind him, the road before him lying as straight and smooth as the satin ribbon in Natasha's long black hair.

CHAPTER
❧ FORTY ❧

In the first week that followed, Natasha did her best to fulfill her role as a hostess whenever Count Rostov came over, but thoughts of Trevor were never far from her mind. Gradually, as the first week turned into two, Natasha found her spirits lifting somewhat, for it was difficult to be gloomy around someone as charming as Niki.

As the days turned into weeks their friendship grew, and Natasha began to open up to him. One afternoon as they walked in the garden, she told him about her past, beginning with losing the baby.

"I am not what you think I am. Although I have never been married, I have known a man and conceived his child."

His gaze dropped to the slimness of her waist.

She turned away and began walking again. "I was set upon by some village ruffians and I lost the babe ... before I even knew it existed."

"Is there no hope of marriage?"

"No."

"Your choice or his?"

"Mine," she said, and stopped, waiting for him to make his excuses and depart.

"It was him . . . the Duke of Hillsborough?"

"Yes," she said, pausing.

"Are you tired?" he asked.

"No, I simply thought you would want to turn back now."

He smiled down at her and the effect of it warmed her. "You have been around the English too long, sweet Natasha. I judge you by what I see, not by what I hear. Your heart is pure."

She gave a mocking laugh. "As pure as snow—until I drifted."

He stopped, turning toward her and taking her in his arms. "I have a confession to make," he said.

She said nothing, but stood there in his embrace, gazing up at his face.

"I have drifted more than once."

She looked at him and could not help smiling. She shook her head and started to say something about how that did not matter, for it was perfectly acceptable, expected even, for a man, but before she could form the words, his fingers came up to swear her lips to silence.

"Are we even?" he asked, his look expectant.

She studied the steady strength in his eyes, seeing the sincerity, the open admiration, the honesty. She found comfort in his nearness, which seemed to surround her like a beloved old blanket. So much about him was as familiar as the French they spoke, yet there was the aspect of newness that made her aware of him as a man.

"Even," she said, basking in his smile.

Perhaps this is what I needed, she thought. *God doesn't always give us what we want, but what we need.* She looked steadily into his eyes. *Are you what I need, Count Rostov?*

He did not answer her, of course, but strong hands drew her closer as the warm vapor of his breath caressed her lips. Here, among nature's bounty, he seemed more real to her than he had in a London town house. His mouth touched hers with heart-stopping tenderness, his gaze holding hers until the gold-tipped lashes drifted closed. She could feel her heart hammering in her throat, could feel, too, the strength and desire of him pressing against her belly. But even then, she could not control the word that seemed to steal across her mind: *Trevor . . .*

He pulled back from her, his soft gaze wandering over her face, his eyes bright and searching, his mouth soft and damp from their kiss. "Natasha Simonov, from the land of my birth— You aren't going to make this easy for me, are you?"

As she searched her mind for some reply, he took her arm in a jovial way and turned their steps back toward the house. "By the way, Lady Sarah Mayfield said to give you her love. She wants you to come for dinner on Saturday. Will you come?"

She nodded. "How long will you be staying with the Earl of Marwood?"

He smiled and picked up their pace. "As long as it takes." Something about her startled expression must have amused him, for he laughed. "Mademoiselle Simonov, I have gone to great lengths to provide myself the opportunity to botanize with you."

"Put that way, you make it sound positively lethal."

"That," he said, "is my fondest hope." With a sweeping bow, he said, "Lead on, fair lady. I have a journal screaming to be filled with horticultural notes."

"Where would you like to start?"

He laughed. "With tea."

The bubbling sound of her laughter joined his, and she went with him up the path.

Later, they were in the library, where Niki was making drawings of an exotic orchid they had carried in from the greenhouse. "I cannot get these blasted petals right," he said. "They look like fingers."

"Here, let me show you," Natasha said, coming to his side. She burst out laughing. "I think you were being kind when you said they look like fingers," she said, and with that, she leaned over his arm and took the pen in her hand.

A few strokes and she had the exact curve of the lower petal. "There," she said, handing the pen back to him. "Now, you try."

He placed the pen on the table, and, taking her hand, drew her against him as he rose to his feet. "I have been," he said, "for weeks."

She looked up into his face, his steady gaze locking with hers, holding her frozen in place.

"I didn't know you needed help," she said. "You should have told me. I would have been happy to draw them for you."

"You misunderstand me," Niki said. "I want you to marry me, Natasha. Marry me . . . and let me take you back to Russia, where you belong."

"I could never leave here. My brothers—"

"They can come with us. They, even more than you, belong there. They have titles waiting for them, and lives of promise. What have they to look forward to here? More charity?"

"I can't marry you, Niki."

"Why? Because you don't love me?"

"I—I care for you a great deal. You know that. But I don't think that is enough for marriage."

"Not even if I said it didn't matter to me? Not even if I said I had enough love for both of us? Not even if I said the thought of not having you at all was more devastating than having you and knowing you didn't love me?"

"It's wrong."

"What could possibly be wrong about something so right? I'm offering you a chance for yourself and your brothers, a chance to go home. A chance to get away from all the pain and suffering you have known since coming to England. This isn't the place for you, Tasha, and you know it. We have so much more than so many others have when they marry. We get on well together, and we enjoy the same interests. What are you waiting for? Do you think your brothers will come home and everything will be as it was before? Well, it won't be. Luka and Pavel are growing up. You aren't the center of their universe anymore. Now is the time to think about yourself, about having a family of your own to fill your life. You cannot hold your brothers any more than you can hold to the memory of a man who wronged you. Marry me. Marry me and let me take you away from all of this."

"I can't," she said, and before he could say anything more, she had run from the room.

A few days later, Natasha sat in the dining room, picking at her breakfast as she read the letter from her brothers that had just arrived. There wasn't much in the note that she had not read before, for Luka and Pavel did have a tendency to report to great lengths about some activities such as cricket and to skim over others such as academics, but she was always happy to have a letter from them and continued to enjoy each one, re-reading it time and time again, until the next one came.

It never bothered her that she wrote to them far more than they wrote to her. She knew what an aversion her brothers had for anything academic.

When she finished the letter, she folded it and placed it in her pocket, returning to the sideboard for a second cup of tea. As she poured, she caught a glimpse of Niki riding up; she laughed at the sight of him carrying a potted palm on horseback.

A moment later she was holding the front door as he wrestled the palm inside. "Beware of strangers bearing gifts," she said, laughing and wondering what the palm was for, especially since it was rather sickly looking.

"Lady Sarah sends this with her fondest hopes that you can nurse it back to vivid green health."

Natasha eyed the palm. "I suspect Lady Sarah is killing it with kindness. It looks dreadfully like it has been overwatered. What do you think?"

"Exactly the same thing," he said. "And I told her so."

Natasha raised a brow. "And what did she say?"

"She said to bring it to you anyway, that two opinions were always better than one."

"Well, come on then. We'll take it to the greenhouse. I have something there I want to show you anyway."

"Oh? Is one of your man-eating plants hungry?"

"If it was, I would never allow you around it. You are becoming as necessary to my well-being as fresh country air."

He stopped dead, and she turned to look at him gazing at her through drooping palm fronds, with that heart-thumping grin and pure affection in his eyes. "I hope you mean that," he said.

"I do, but we had best not stand here cooing at each other like two doves while you hold that ridiculous palm. Is that your back I hear cracking?"

He grinned. "No, it's the fetters of my heart."

"You'd better be glad your interest lies in horticulture and not poetry."

"I have never been happier over that fact than I am right now," he said. "Lead on, fair damsel, before my arms give out."

In the dining room, Mrs. Mac was clearing the dishes from the sideboard as she watched Count Rostov and Natasha walk toward the greenhouse.

The door opened, and Cook walked in. "I was coming to see what was holding you up," she said, her gaze drifting in the same direction Mrs. Mac's had taken a moment ago. "They make a handsome couple, don't they?"

Turning from the window and picking up a silver butter dish, Mrs. Mac smiled at Cook's words. "Yes, they do. But it is what he is doing for Natasha's confidence that endears him to me."

"You think we have a romance blooming?" Cook asked.

"If it isn't in bloom yet, it soon will be, I'll wager."

"I wonder what *he* will think about that if he gets wind of what's happening here?"

"I doubt it will make him any happier than losing her did. I canna judge the poor man too harshly. He did love her. No one could ever convince me otherwise."

"Yes, he did, but sometimes that isn't enough."

"No," Mrs. Mac said, "sometimes it isn't."

Cook picked up the egg platter and a stack of teacups. "What do you think will happen? Do you think the count is serious about her?"

"He appears to be," Mrs. Mac said, following Cook out of the dining room and into the kitchen.

"Do you think they will wed?"

Mrs. Mac put the dishes down. "You know, I have thought about that, but there is something about all of this that makes me uneasy. Perhaps it is nothing more than my Scots' superstition, but I have an uncanny feeling that something is about to upset the applecart."

"I hope you are wrong," Cook said.

"So do I," said Mrs. Mac. "It is one time I would love to be wrong."

CHAPTER
❧ FORTY-ONE ❧

It was late one afternoon that she ventured outside, walking for a time with the dogs. When she reached the barn, she climbed the ladder to the top of the hayrick to see if she could catch a glimpse of Harry, who was bringing up another load of hay for winter from the meadow beyond. She sat on the rounded mound of hay and looked out over the patchwork of meadows, where the last crop of spring lambs ran close to their mothers' sides. The hay smelled damp from last night's dew, and the air about her was cool and filled with the songs of many birds.

She closed her eyes and leaned her face back, feeling the healing power of the sun striking her face. *Go inside*, she thought, *and burn away the pain and ugliness.*

Fill my head with sunny thoughts and make me whole again.

She opened her eyes, catching a glimpse of the tall, heaping burden of the hay wagon creeping across the meadow, recognizing Harry as he headed the team toward home. He would be here in a few minutes, and thirsty.

She decided to go inside to dip him a cool glass of water from the stoneware crock in the kitchen.

Instead of taking the ladder, she slid down the opposite side of the hayrick, landing in a heap of loose hay at the bottom. Coming to her feet, she began picking bits of hay from her hair, dusting the chaff from her skirts as she stepped through the hay to cleaner ground.

Giving her skirts another shake, she looked up and saw him.

Ned Hughes.

She felt herself trembling, felt dryness sucking at her throat. She saw a vision of her horse lying in a bed of straw and blood, and she knew her instincts had been right. "You," she whispered. "It *was* you."

He seemed nervous, his eyes flicking first in one direction, then another, as if he wanted to make certain no one else was about. "It don't take you long, does it? You change lovers like some women change drawers."

"He isn't my lover," she said.

He took a step toward her. "You shouldn't have let him hang around you like that. It was my turn."

She started to respond, then thought better of it. Perhaps if she ignored him he would go away. She thought of all the things this man had taken from her, things he had stolen as surely as if he had been a thief. Her legs felt cold and quivering, but rage seemed to burn her face. She thought of her baby, of Trevor and Lady Gray, and her stomach turned. *All of this for what? For one man's perversion, his twisted mind? Why? Why? Why? . . .* She wanted to cry. She wanted to gouge out his eyes and make him suffer as he had caused her to do. But she could do nothing save stare at him and watch his expression change from nervous tenseness to contempt, then to a twisted, savage smile.

"You got no cause to be uppity with me. I know what you like . . . and I know you ain't particular who gives it to you."

The blood pounded in her ears so loudly she could hardly hear what he said. She began backing away from him. "Stay away from me," she said, frantically looking around for something to protect herself with, when she saw a pitchfork sticking in the hay.

She grabbed it, holding it out in front of her. "Come any closer and I'll run you through," she said.

"You ain't gonna do nothing like that, 'cause if you stick me I'll bleed—and I know how the sight of blood upsets you." He took another step, and then another.

She kept backing away from him, keeping the pitchfork between them, when her foot caught on something and she lost her balance, falling backward just as Ned made a grab for her.

He lunged forward at the same moment she lost her balance, which must have made him lose his, for he pitched forward; Natasha screamed, thinking he was going to fall on top of her.

A second before she screamed she saw fear and terror flare in his eyes, then he screamed, recoiling and throwing up his arms just as he fell against the pitchfork.

She hit the ground, then rolled to her side and scrambled to her feet, her body trembling, her knees weak as she looked down at him sprawling in the hay, seeing the three puncture marks on his chest, the blood-smeared pitchfork lying at his side, the slow-spreading bloodstain that spread across his chest like guilty fingers pointing at her.

For a timeless moment she stood there, and in the still, humid hush of the late summer evening every insignificant sound and smell seemed heightened—the rapid hammering of her heart, the mild rustling of the wind in the chestnut trees, the far-off shrieking cry of a falcon, and the sweet, sticky smell of blood.

She had killed a man, she who had never killed anything; she who couldn't bear to catch a fish and always begged her brothers to toss theirs back. She had killed a man.

I've killed him, she thought dully. *I've committed murder. God, help me . . . Please help me.*

This couldn't be happening to her. It couldn't be. But it was. Her gaze returned to the body sprawled before her, the leering, contemptuous smile now gone from his face. Suddenly she was glad—glad she had rid the world of this monster, of this man with a mind so twisted that he would kill and destroy lives for his own selfish pleasure.

It was then that she started screaming; she kept on screaming until she reached the house.

Just as Natasha reached the house, Niki rode up. Seeing Ned's body sprawled in the hay, he dismounted quickly, dropping down beside the body. The man, whoever he was, was dead. A moment later he saw the hay wagon roll into the yard. Harry pulled the team of horses to a stop, set the brake, and jumped down just as Niki walked up to him.

"Who is he?" Niki asked.

They crossed to where the body lay. Harry looked down. "I'm glad the bastard is dead," he said. "It's him. The one who killed her horse and the little dog. A man like that don't deserve to live, but I hate to think what it will do to her."

"She doesn't have to know," Niki said. He stood and picked up Ned's feet. "Help me move him," he said.

"Where to?"

Niki looked around, his gaze resting on the wagon. "In the hay," he said, "and hurry. We haven't much time."

"Bloody bastard," Harry said, looking at Ned with contempt, then rising to his feet. He grabbed Ned's arms, and the two of them carried the body toward the hay wagon.

"The only reason I'm sorry she killed him is she kept me from doing it," Harry said.

When they reached the wagon, they hollowed out a place and heaved the body into the back, covering it with hay.

They had just started toward the house when Natasha came out the door with Cook and Mrs. MacDougal in tow.

"Natasha, what's wrong?" Niki asked.

"What's all the commotion about?" Harry said at the same time.

"I killed him," Natasha said, her face gray, her voice trembling and weak.

"Killed who?" Niki asked.

Mrs. MacDougal responded. "Ned. She said he tried to grab her and she picked up the pitchfork to protect herself."

"I tripped," she said, tears starting to fall faster now, "and he kept on coming, like he was falling. He just fell against it," she said, sobbing. "I didn't mean to kill him. I didn't."

"You sure he's dead?" asked Harry.

"I know he's dead. He didn't move. I killed him."

"Where did all this happen?" asked Niki.

"There," Natasha said, pointing toward the hayrick, the expression on her face suddenly changing. "It was there, by the hayrick." She ran to the hayrick and began looking wildly around.

"There ain't no body," Mrs. MacDougal said. "Are you certain it was here?"

"It was here. *He* was here," Natasha said. She pointed at the pitchfork. "You see? There's blood on it. That proves I killed him."

"That proves you gave him a good poke," Cook said.

Mrs. MacDougal looked at Niki and then at Cook. "Well, if you killed him he must have been mystically transported to the bad place, because there ain't no body here now," she said.

"Either that or he wasn't dead—and when Natasha came into the house he high-tailed it," Cook added.

"What do you make of all this?" Mrs. MacDougal asked, looking at Niki and then at Harry.

"Must have been like Cook said," Harry said.

"Perhaps you just wounded him and after you left he ran off," Niki said.

"There was so much blood . . . and he was lying so still . . . I don't see how he could have gotten up," Natasha said.

"Only the good die young, Tasha," Mrs. MacDougal said. "Now, why don't you come on in the house and let Cook give you a nice cup of tea. Whatever happened to that reprobate, I don't think he will be showing his leering face around here again."

"Right," said Cook. "And it serves him right, too." She looked at Natasha. "If he was struck as bad as you think, then he will think twice before coming back." She looked at Niki. "Don't you agree?"

Niki nodded. "If he comes back," he said, "it will be a miracle."

CHAPTER
❦ FORTY-TWO ❦

A little while later, Niki walked into the library. Natasha was sitting there, staring at the cold grate, a cup of tea sitting on the table beside her untouched. Visions of Ned Hughes's body lying in the hay swam before her eyes.

She heard a sound beside her. A warm, comforting arm came around her shoulders as Niki's weight sank down into the cushion beside her. She turned her face against his shirtfront and cried.

"Don't think about it anymore," he said. "I won't let anything happen to you."

"I'm glad you're here," she said, pressing her face against the starchy smoothness of his shirt and finding comfort in the warm, living smell of him. She had seen too much of death.

"Cry," he said. "Get rid of it. Let me take care of you." His arms held her with sympathetic tenderness and he kissed the top of her head.

As if seeing herself from a distance, she saw the way he held her, the concern for her etched across his handsome features. She saw herself clinging to him, wetting his shirt.

Her tears subsided at last, giving way to hiccuping sobs, and after a while she felt warm and cozy, not really aware that she had drifted off to sleep. A while later, she opened her eyes.

"Feel better?"

She nodded, feeling groggy but better. His hands were stroking her hair, the sound of his voice low and throbbing and infinitely dear. There was no pain associated with this man, no suffering, no fear. She gave herself up to the comfort of it.

After a while he pulled back, his hand coming down to cup her chin as he lifted her face to look into her eyes. "You cannot stay here—you know that, don't you?"

"He might come back," she said, knowing what he had said was true. She could not stay here. Her first thought was for her brothers. They would be coming home to visit soon. She could not risk anything happening to them.

"Come home with me, Natasha. Back to Russia, where you will be loved and safe. Let me provide a life for you and your brothers. We will get your lands back and their titles. They will have a life there they could never have here. You're Russian. You don't belong in England any more than I do."

He kissed her softly. "I'm a patient man. I can wait for you to care for me."

"I care for you now, Niki. You know I do."

"But not as you cared for him."

"No," she said, feeling sadness well up within her. "Not as I cared for him."

"It doesn't matter. I can protect you and your brothers. That is something he cannot do. Say you'll come. Say it."

Deep in her heart she knew the things he said were true. They would be safe in Russia. Her brothers would never have to know about the terrible things that had happened here. She would never lie awake at night wondering if Ned would return, wondering if he would harm her brothers. "I'll come," she said. "As soon as we can get my brothers here." She looked into his face and saw his eyes had become warm, the irises bright and shining. The edges of his mouth curved upward and he leaned forward and kissed her.

"You won't regret it," he said. He came to his feet, drawing her up with him. He turned toward her, his arms going around her. "I'll start making arrangements tomorrow." He leaned down and kissed her mouth softly. "Soon," he said, "soon all this pain will be behind you."

"We're going to Russia?" Pavel asked, and Luka let out a jubilant cry that Mrs. MacDougal said would make a banshee shudder.

"Yes," Natasha said. "We're going home."

"Yahoo!" Luka shouted. "We're going to visit Russia."

Natasha frowned. "We are not going for a visit," she said. "We are going home to live."

Luka and Pavel exchanged glances. It was Luka who spoke. "To live? In our old home?"

Natasha glanced at Niki. "Perhaps, in time," she said, noticing Pavel did not seem to be taking this as well as Luka.

It was Pavel who spoke next. "Will we ever come back home ... to England, I mean?"

Natasha shook her head. "I don't think so."

"Your sister and I are going to be married," Niki said. "Our home will be in Russia, as will yours. It has always been your home."

Pavel glanced at Luka. "England is our home now," Pavel said, "not Russia."

"Don't you want to go back?" Luka asked.

"Not forever."

There was something about the way Pavel said the word *forever* that had such a foreboding sound it made Natasha uneasy. She glanced quickly at Niki.

He looked at her, she could see his blue eyes were steady and clear. She took this as a positive sign he would be there, that he would always be there, yet his face showed lines of obvious concern—concern for the way Pavel was taking the news, and the effect he knew it must have upon her.

He smiled at her, a smile of reassurance, then reaching for her hand, he gave it a supportive squeeze. She felt remorse that she did not love him in the way she had loved before, but looking at the bright gold waves of his hair about his face, she knew there were some things as lasting, as enriching, as love.

There was strength in him, where Trevor had failed her. She trusted him. She could depend upon him. His words were grounded in truth. These were the bedrock of a good marriage. Love would surely come. She was certain of it.

Further thought was interrupted when Pavel spoke. "When are we leaving?" he asked.

"Tomorrow," Niki said.

Luka tipped his head to one side and looked at Niki. "Do they play cricket in Russia?"

Niki smiled and ruffled Luka's hair, which closely

matched the color of his own. "They will if you teach them to," he said.

Pavel remained stubbornly silent.

Two days later, Natasha, Luka, Pavel, and Count Nikolay Rostov boarded a ship riding gently on the waves of the Thames. As the ropes were cast off, Natasha wondered why she felt no sense of elation knowing this ship was bound for Russia. She glanced over the towering spires and shingled rooftops of London and found she held them as dear as the memory of Russia's onion-shaped domes.

Two countries. Two men. Had she made the right choice?

Swift decisions are not sure.

The ship began to pull away from the dock. A sense of panic filled her breast. Thoughts of Trevor crowded her mind and his words came back to haunt her. *Darling Natasha. You are still such a child. Don't you know nothing ever turns out the way we plan?*

She had made the right choice. She was certain of it. *Then why do you feel more regret over what you have left behind than pleasure over what you have chosen?*

As if sensing what she felt, Niki stroked her cheek. "Everything passes, *chérie*, even regret."

She turned her head away, seeing a young, ragged boy standing on the dock just a few feet away. He was selling copies of the *Times*. Niki tossed him a coin, and the boy grinned, catching the coin in one grimy hand. A second later he tossed Niki a paper.

Niki caught it and gave the grinning youth a salute. Then he turned to Natasha. "Here," he said, handing her the paper. "Every woman likes to have a keepsake."

Natasha took the paper, thankful for the understanding she sensed in him, for the considerate things he always did. "Thank you." A moment later she opened the paper. An article in the middle of the page caught her eye.

THE DUKE OF HILLSBOROUGH TO WED LADY JANE PENWORTHY.

Her hands trembled, her heart began to pound, yet her lungs seemed incapable of function. The color drained from her face and she was suffused with warmth.

Niki glanced down at her. "Are you all right, *chérie*? Does sailing make you ill?"

Natasha could not speak. She simply stood there, her gaze riveted on nine simple words that left her shattered.

His gaze followed hers. "I'm sorry," he said, "I didn't know. But perhaps it is better this way. Now you know the truth. Now you can have no regrets."

Blinking to hold back tears, she looked at him and attempted a smile. "I have no regrets," she said, but in her heart she knew that saying does not always make it so.

Niki reached and took the paper from her hands, as if by doing so he could remove the memory and the pain. Why did the news shatter her so? she wondered. What did she expect? He had come to her, hadn't he? He had asked her to marry him. And she had sent him away. Wasn't that what she wanted?

Yes, of course it was. But even as she thought it, she couldn't hold back the tears that rolled down her cheek. Nor could she stop the pain that lodged in her heart as she watched the newspaper sink beneath the murky waters of the Thames.

"Absence doth nurse the fire
Which starves and feeds desire
With sweet delays."
—Fulke Grenville, *Absence and Presence*

PART THREE

CHAPTER
❧ FORTY-THREE ❧

No one can enter Russia from the west and not be struck by the beauty of St. Petersburg bathed in the splendor of northern light against a backdrop of snow.

As the ship drew closer, the Greek steeples and gilded cupolas of convents appeared, then the colonnades of palaces, which bordered the quays of granite along the Neva River. All about her the world seemed frozen and silent, the golden image of buildings and spires standing in stark contrast to the blue of the river and the sky above.

"It is so cold here, when it is already spring in England," Natasha said to Niki.

"Spring will come here, too, only later."

Soon they were speeding down Nevsky Prospect, a single esplanade where dandies and their ladies paraded along the fashionable avenue in much the same manner as they did in London, and she wondered how she could have forgotten the magic of a troika ride through a snowscaped city, the sound of the three-horse sleigh gliding over snow mingling with the jingle of harness bells, or what it felt like to have her muff and eyebrows frosted with ice.

Looking down at Natasha, Niki pulled the fur robes more closely about her. "Are you cold?"

"Numb would be a better word," she said, unable to stop the chattering of her teeth. "I had forgotten it could be so cold."

He laughed. "This is springtime. It can get colder."

Natasha glanced up ahead, where the troika that carried her brothers sped ahead of them. She could not see her brothers, but Niki said, "They are there, little grandmother. Never fear."

Niki's brother-in-law, Prince Speransky, must be a powerful man, Natasha thought when she caught her first glimpse of the palace. Built in the classical style, with a curved facade faced with columns and niches filled with statues, it far surpassed anything she had seen in London. But it was the interior, with its pink marble walls and white columns, which surrounded a magnificent staircase, that left her gaping in the light of a hundred crystal chandeliers.

"Is this where the czar lives?" Luka asked.

"No," Niki said, "but his Winter Palace isn't very far away."

When a tall, slender man in a uniform approached them, Niki turned to Natasha. "This is Count Dolokhof. He will show you to your quarters."

A moment later Niki was excusing himself. "I need to see my brother-in-law," he said. "I think you will find your rooms comfortable. You must be tired. This will give you a chance to rest. I will see you at dinner, unless the prince desires to meet you before then." With a low bow and a reassuring smile, he turned and was gone.

Natasha followed the slender count who showed them upstairs, expressing some concern—which was basically ignored—when they were met by another man who was only introduced as Petya. It was Petya who took her brothers down a different hallway.

"Where is he taking my brothers?"

"They will join you at dinner, mademoiselle," Count Dolokhof replied in a tone that said the subject was closed.

Natasha was ushered into an elaborate chamber of three rooms, all decorated in various shades of blue and richly detailed with gold. The outer chamber was dimly lit, but the light of a northern winter streaked through the panes of tall, elegant windows flanked by long and heavy damask draperies, sagging in puddles on the floor. The furniture was graceful, richly carved, with inlay and much gilding. The ormolu clock on the marble mantel was twenty minutes off by her timepiece, and in a world of absolute perfection, she found that small discovery reassuring. She thought about changing the time on the clock, then decided to leave it as it was, as a reminder that nothing in this world was perfect, no matter how much it appeared to be.

Across the room, an ornate silver inkwell stood with a wide-legged stance on the top of an escritoire, where a stack of writing paper and quill seemed to call out to her. She smiled inwardly, remembering how she never could pass up the opportunity to write letters, recalling how many she posted to her brothers and Cecilia. Nearby, a grand piano sprawled in the corner, with heavy carved legs that seemed to smile at her with perfect white teeth. Looking at the piano, she recalled a small pianoforte her father had brought her from Italy, and closing her eyes, the sound of mazurkas called out to her from the past.

She opened her eyes and went into the bedroom, thinking she had no idea where in the enormous palace Niki resided, or where her brothers had been taken.

Removing her muff and cape and tossing them across the bed, she moved to the dressing table to take off her hat, seeing the melting snow had left portions of her hair wet. She turned, staring at the bed for a moment, then decided she was not tired enough to sleep, so she took a chair close to the fire, and, holding her hands out over the flames, began to wait.

She glanced at the clock twice—each time adding twenty minutes—finding time seemed to pass much more slowly in Russia than it did in England. Coming to her feet, she crossed the room, pausing before the windows as she looked out on a world of winter white.

All about her was silence and brilliance, where trees creaked with the cold and rooftops had grown fat with snow over the winter. Cold, crystalline, and brilliant, St. Petersburg was like a bishop's vestments, a royal robe of purest white, embroidered with silver and encrusted with diamonds and pearls. How different it looked from the patchwork of English countryside snuggled down under a blanket of snow.

There was a sensation of numbness about her, and she placed her hand on the cold pane of glass, willing herself to feel. She felt lost, disjointed, as if a part of her body had been cut off and she had not, as yet, learned to live without it. This was her home, and yet she felt alien here. She was Russian, and yet she was also English. She was both. She was neither. She was two halves that came together and did not fit.

Who was she? Softly she began to sing the old melody from her past.

> *But what am I?*
> *An infant crying in the night?*
> *An infant crying for the light:*
> *And with no language but a cry.*

At half past eight, she was summoned to meet the prince. When she arrived in the small salon, her brothers were already there. Seeing the relaxed atmosphere, she had an inkling Luka and Pavel had been there for some time.

Robust, intelligent, charismatic, Prince Speransky's six feet, eight inches towered over Natasha, who on her tiptoes barely reached five feet. He was a man of enormous proportions, with hair as black as Natasha's own. Splendidly dressed in a manner that much resembled the uniform Niki had worn to Tony and Cecilia's ball, the prince had a great many more medals pinned on his chest than Niki had, and his gleaming gold epaulets were larger and more grand, while the sash that draped from shoulder to waist was not red, but blue. As blue as the Neva.

Giving her a warm smile, Niki stepped forward and said, "Natasha, may I present Prince Speransky."

Prince Speransky's black-eyed gaze moved over her at leisure, and Natasha took advantage of the lull to look him over a bit as well. Then she looked off, thinking he reminded her of the days of the great cossacks, when they thumbed their noses at czar and sultan alike, carrying around the heads of their enemies on the points of their pikes, taking the spoils of war and the women they wanted.

Prince Speransky did not look very many generations removed from those cossacks.

Suddenly she felt cold, as if someone had opened a window and filled the room with a flurry of snow. She looked up at the prince. Their eyes met and held. For all his attempts to look impassive, she knew there was something lurking in the back of his mind, knew, too, that he understood she knew this—and that he was enjoying her knowledge of it. He was a man of intrigue and mystery, and it did not take her long to understand that the prince was a man to be reckoned with.

When he spoke to her brothers, Natasha noticed Prince Speransky was much more cordial toward them. That irritated her, of course, and she attributed it to the fact that they were males and obviously held in much higher esteem by him.

Before she could make any more observations, dinner was announced. She was thankful when Niki took her arm to walk with her. How different this felt from the dinners at Marsham, or even the more formal dinners at Cecilia and Tony's town house. *Time. You will adjust to it in time.* But even as she thought it, she wondered if it would ever be true.

Her brothers walked ahead of them, in the company of the prince. They were wearing military uniforms, the kind schoolboys sometimes wear, and Natasha was reminded of how tall they were, of what dashing young men they were becoming. With them being identical and difficult for the unpracticed eye to tell apart, she wondered how the young women would ever be able to decide which one they liked. Then she remembered how very different they were—how Luka was chatty, outgoing, the lover of fun and adventure, while Pavel was sensitive and studious, the one who meticulously thought things through. The one with such good judgment. She remembered, too, that it was Pavel who did not want to come to Russia to live.

Soon they reached the enormous dining hall, where four massive chandeliers reflected their magnificence onto a polished table below. Luka and Pavel were seated at the head of the table, to the right and left of Prince Speransky, while Natasha was further down the table, sitting between Niki and Grand Duke Bezukhof, an old war-horse with a propensity toward repeating the same story about driving Napoléon out of Russia and falling asleep during the meal.

She glanced at her brothers, seeing they seemed relaxed enough, for they were chatting with the prince—or at least, Luka was doing most of the chatting—and she could tell by his animated gestures that he was talking about the love of their lives, cricket.

She turned her head to look at Niki, who flashed her a smile, but it was a bit too quick and a tad too wide to be real. It occurred to her that the Niki she met in England and the one she saw here were two different people. In England he had been more jovial and relaxed. While she could not exactly pinpoint the difference, or its cause, she was aware that there was a fine edge of reserve about him now, a consciousness that would not allow him to completely be himself.

The Countess Maria, sitting next to Niki, spoke to him, and Niki turned toward her. It gave Natasha the opportunity to observe him engaging in polite conversation with the countess. She could hear only snatches of what they were saying, and it came to her that she had not known him very long.

She did not get to think more about it, for Grand Duke Bezukhof awoke from his nap with a snort, driving further thought from her mind.

But later that night, as she lay in her bed looking at the ceiling, her eyes burning with unshed tears, her heart beating fast, she thought, once again, that she really did not know much about Count Nikolay Rostov at all.

Seeing little of Niki, and even less of her brothers, became sort of a pattern over the next two weeks, with Natasha spending a great deal of time alone. Besides feeling lonely, she began to harbor a certain feeling of resentment over her isolation. When she complained of this to Niki at dinner one evening, he placed his hand over hers, giving it a pat, and assured her he would see what he could do.

"It isn't intentional, *chérie*, but merely an oversight. There is much going on in the palace. These are times of political unrest, and there are matters that need our attention."

"What kind of political unrest?" she asked, feeling some alarm. She did not want to be in Russia during another war.

She saw Niki's gaze go from her to Prince Speransky, whose black eyes were fastened sharply upon Natasha. "Are you unhappy here, mademoiselle?" the prince asked.

"I have no life here," Natasha said. "I am unaccustomed to being idle. There are many things I miss."

"What things, for instance?" the prince asked.

"I miss my brothers."

"Who were away at school a great deal in England, and therefore were not with you much of the time," the prince said.

"There are other ways of communication," she said in her defense. "My brothers and I corresponded frequently, and I visited them whenever I could."

"And you found that more satisfactory than your present set of circumstances?" he asked.

"I find it ironic that I know less about Luka's and Pavel's lives now, when I am living in the same palace with them, than I did in England when we were miles apart."

Apparently the discussion about her brothers was terminated, for the prince gave her a contemptuous black stare and abruptly changed the subject. "And what else do you miss, mademoiselle?"

"My friends, my work."

He leaned back in his chair, folding his hands into a tent over his stomach, a posture that said to all those present that he had her in his snare now and would soon make light of it. "Ah, yes. Your gardening," Speransky said in a way that evoked a snicker from many of those present.

Incensed that he would deliberately underrate her botanical endeavors and the recognition she had gleaned in the horticultural field, she spoke more harshly than she intended. "My work went far beyond the boundaries of simple gardening," she said. "Perhaps those who informed you did not know of the extent of my work with plants and garden designs."

He gave her a cold smile. "Perhaps I speak out of ignorance," he said, and the muted flow of conversation about the table faded to uncomfortable silence.

She steeled herself, determined not to back down. There was much more at stake here than a simple discussion of the difference between gardening and horticulture. "I have often heard that those who know the least about a subject presume the most."

He was looking at her now, with eyes too fathomless and black to read. "And do you regret coming to Russia?" he asked.

"I regret the circumstances I find myself in," she said, glancing at Niki and sensing his reluctance to speak.

Thankfully the Countess Maria, sitting across the table from them, apparently harbored no such reservations about speaking in front of the prince, for she nodded her gray head and smoothly returned the discussion to its former topic. "Do not be overly concerned with the mention of the political unrest here," she said. "There is nothing for you to worry about, child. Czar Alexander is simply a perplexing man and difficult to understand."

"In what way?" asked Natasha.

"He is more concerned with being the peacemaker of Europe than the Czar of Russia," the countess said.

As if taking his cue from the countess, Niki said, "Alexander is a man of ambitious plans and idealistic programs, which he announces with great fervor and then abandons. His inconsistency has caused much concern. He now seems to be interested only in religion, and many find him too distrustful of the change that comes from liberal ideas. His advisor, Arakcheyev, is taking much of the blame for now, but who knows? It could change in the twinkling of an eye. Rulers have been overthrown for less."

Was it as he said? Had she and her brothers simply come at a busy time, and, like a few scattered crumbs, had fallen into the cracks? She felt some of her resentment dissolving. She didn't suppose she should solely blame Niki, for she could see it was not entirely his fault. Possibly it was nothing more than an oversight. She had the feeling that he was not much happier about their lack of time together than she was. He never said anything, of course, but she was a woman, after all, and one with a good deal of women's intuition, and she had a suspicion that whatever the cause of the odd arrangement of their lives, it wasn't really Niki's doing. Her intuition also gave her a pretty good idea just who it was that was responsible.

She glanced at the prince, who was watching her in that infuriating way that made her think he was privy to her thoughts. She made a mental note to talk to Niki the next time they were alone.

* * *

She saw him for a few minutes the next afternoon, in the salon where she joined him for tea.

"What is Prince Speransky to you?" she asked him, noting how the muscle in his jaw worked at the mention of the prince's name.

"He is my brother-in-law—or rather, he was . . . since my sister died in childbirth two years ago."

"I'm sorry. Was she your only relative?"

"Yes."

"And you live here, in this palace, with the prince?"

"Officially yes, but I spend most of my time in the country, at my hunting lodge."

"A hunting lodge!" she exclaimed, with excitement. "Do you think we could go there sometime? My brothers and I love the country and—"

He laughed, and she noticed the way the corners of his eyes crinkled. "I *know* how much you love the country, *chérie*."

She smiled back at him, feeling relaxed for the first time in days. This was the old Niki. But he wasn't to stay with her for very long, for at that moment, Count Dolokhof interrupted them with a message that the prince wanted to see him.

The teasing glint went out of his eyes. "I will be there in a moment," Niki said.

"The prince said it was urgent," the count said.

Niki kissed her good-bye. "Take Mademoiselle Simonov to see her brothers," he said.

"They are doing their studies."

"I am aware of that, but they are her brothers; I doubt a few minutes with them will interrupt things overly long. If there are any problems, I will take full responsibility."

"Very well," the count said, with a bow. "If you will come this way, mademoiselle."

* * *

While Natasha was sequestered with her brothers in their schoolroom—listening to them state their preference for an education at Eton rather than in the stuffy schoolroom with uncompromising tutors—Niki was with the prince.

"I think we should move faster with the plans for the wedding," the prince said. "Our little nightingale seems to be having a great deal of difficulty deciding if she is Russian or English."

"If they were allowed out more it would make it easier," Niki said.

"You know why we must keep them here, why we don't want too many people knowing her brothers are twins. Once one of them is on the throne, we will have to keep the other one under tight security. Another heir in the wrong hands could— Well, never mind all that. The sister is our problem right now. She grows restless. It is obvious she is not adjusting well."

"You haven't exactly given her any help in that quarter. She is virtually a prisoner here . . . and I grow weary of having my own life manipulated as well."

"You knew what you were getting into when you went to England, but I feel the problem here isn't that you resent my meddling in your life, it is because you have fallen in love with her."

"Which should make things much easier," Niki said.

"Not if she decides she wants to go home. It is your responsibility to see that she is happy with her lot in life, that she is willing to sacrifice a few things to see one of her brothers on the throne. That is why you went to England, is it not?"

"I went to bring her back, yes, but I had thought at the time that because she was Russian she would welcome the opportunity to return. I fear now that I might have been wrong. There are times when I wonder if Natasha could ever be happy here."

"And you would be willing to let her go, even if it meant losing the woman you love?"

Niki opened his mouth to answer that when Prince Speransky cut him off. "Think carefully before you answer that, Niki. You are either with us in this or you are against us."

Niki must have seen what he could do about her spending more time with Luka and Pavel, for the following week Niki came to her apartment to take her for a ride with her brothers in a fashionable four-horse sleigh. Spring would be coming, she thought, for it was one of those rare occasions when the sun was out and the weather was not so bitterly cold.

On the outskirts of St. Petersburg, they stopped for a while and let Luka and Pavel try their luck with a richly decorated wooden sled.

After a few successful runs, they called to her to join them, and Natasha gave the sled a try. She ended up in a snowdrift, her brothers doubled over with laughter and Niki giving her unmentionables a frank look, then making a comment about her trim ankles.

Giving him a hot glare, she slapped her skirts down, and, refusing his help, crawled to her feet by herself. "I'll get the hang of it in a minute," she said, and was ready to give it another try when Niki took her by the arm.

"Let your brothers do the sledding. I'd rather have you with me."

"I would have never guessed," she said, not trying to muffle her hostile tone.

He stopped, taking both of her hands in his.

"Have you missed me, *chérie*?"

"How could I miss you? I hardly remember you."

"Are you angry with me?"

She sighed. She wasn't angry with him. Not really. It was just that— "I am miserable here, Niki. There is nothing for me to do. I rarely see you or my brothers. I have no friends here, and the servants act as if they are afraid of me. Even the land seems inhospitable, for there are no gardens for me to visit, no greenhouses. For someone who spent her entire day working with plants, it is difficult to be in a place where I rarely see a plant at all." She shook her head. "Oh, I don't know. It's just that this is nothing like I imagined it would be."

He took her in his arms. "I know it's hard on you, but it won't be long, I promise."

The talk about gardens reminded her; she looked at him and said, "Whatever happened to the plants you came to England to find? Are there greenhouses nearby? Where do you keep your work?"

For a split second she thought she saw a rather helpless expression on his face, but it was soon replaced by one of sincerity. "I have a confession to make to you, *chérie*. I was selected to go to England to gather plants because of my political connections, *not* because of my botanical knowledge. In that regard, I am less than a novice."

She gave him a puzzled look. "But when I first met you, you wanted to see my gardens at Marsham."

He smiled, the expression in his eyes soft and adoring. "What I wanted, darling Natasha, was to be near you. I was smitten from the start."

Surprise registered on her face. "You were?"

"I was. Completely and with much determination. And wisely, too, I might add, for here we are in St. Petersburg—with the prince in the midst of plans to give a grand ball to introduce you to Russian society and to announce our betrothal."

She ignored what he said about the ball, her mind on graver matters. "But why am I kept from my brothers?"

"The prince is quite concerned about their education. They spend most of their time with tutors. There is much about their heritage that they have not learned, nor are they proficient in French or Russian. Their understanding of Russian history is almost nonexistent. And then there are military matters they must be familiar with . . . if they are to live the kind of lives your father intended."

She could not help thinking: *My father or the prince?*

A few days later, Niki came to see her, followed by three servants carrying botanical books, sketch books, and a box of paints, and these things occupied her for a time. But soon she found they only made her more homesick, for they reminded her more and more of what she had left behind.

The next time she saw Niki was when he took her brothers ice fishing. As they returned from the country, Natasha told him of her feelings. The moment she began to tell him there were so many things she missed and how out of place she felt here, Luka and Pavel began to parrot the things she said.

"It's no fun here," Luka said. "Everyone is old. Can't we live somewhere else? Why can't we go to school with boys our own age?"

"Why can't we go back to Eton?" Pavel asked.

"Yes," Luka agreed, "why can't we?"

Pavel's discontent did not surprise her, since he was not overly thrilled with the prospect of coming to Russia in the first place, but Luka's readiness to return home seemed to her like an omen. After much discussion, both boys expressed their dissatisfaction with almost everything Russian, while still expressing an overwhelming desire to return to Eton.

When they arrived back at the palace, Luka and Pavel were still grumbling as they started up the stairs. When Natasha started after them, Niki took her by the arm. "Join me for tea," he said, and nodding, she went with him into one of the many salons.

A servant brought tea, placing the silver tray on a table between two chairs near the fire.

"Would you like me to pour?" the woman asked.

"No," Niki said. "We can manage."

The woman looked at Natasha, then with a nod, she departed.

Natasha picked up the teapot and reached for a cup when Niki's hand came out to stop her. "None for me," he said.

"But that is— I thought you wanted tea."

"What I wanted was a moment alone with you," he said.

She looked into his eyes and saw that something was troubling him. "What is it?" she asked.

He smiled. "Nothing, sweet Natasha. Must there be a problem for me to desire your company?"

She continued to stare at him for a moment, then she poured herself a cup of tea.

"I know you are displeased with the way things are going," he said after a long lapse of silence. "And you have a right to be. I know most women would feel the same way."

"I am not most women," she said, "and I think you are wrong. Most women would relish the opportunity to live so lavishly, to be pampered by so many servants and to have their wardrobes stuffed with dozens of opulent gowns. But I do not think *any* woman would be thrilled over virtual confinement, loneliness, and boredom. Or a man, either, for that matter. Do you know that I actually *enjoy* wearing my old dresses now? Can you believe that some days I take *two* baths ... out of utter boredom?"

He laughed. "So that's where all that hot water is going."

"I am not the kind of woman to live a life such as this. I have enjoyed my freedom far too long. I miss my work. I miss digging in the dirt and taking long walks with the dogs. I miss the companionship of servants who aren't really servants but are more like my friends. Where I once spent my days learning, I now count how many panes of glass there are in the windows of my chambers, or the exact dimensions of each room. I long for something mentally stimulating, for a challenge. Anything, except this eternal boredom. Do you have any idea what it is like to be caged?"

"You are not locked in your room, Natasha. You are, and always have been, free to come and go at your leisure."

"Where? Where would I go? And with whom? In England the dogs are friendlier to me than the servants are here." She sighed and stared at the fire. "There are only so many solitary tours I can take of a palace, only so many unfriendly looks I can tolerate from those I pass. After a while my rooms began to look better to me than the outside, and that is when I knew it was time to go."

His face fell. "Go? What do you mean, go?"

She leaned forward and put her hand on his. "It won't work, Niki. I should have never come. My brothers are not happy here; they long to return home. I am not happy here. We don't belong. I was wrong to come here, wrong to tell you I could marry you, wrong to let it go this far without telling you I can't go through with it. I want you to speak to the prince. I want to stop the plans for the ball."

"Why?"

"Because I can't marry you."

"You just need time to adjust. Of course you belong here. This is your home."

"No. This is my history, Niki, my past. But my future and that of my brothers lies in England. I know that now."

"Things will get better, Natasha. Spring is here and—"

She shook her head. "I made a decision to come here without thinking things through, without looking toward the end. I was acting on impulse, reacting—overreacting really—to things going on around me, without any thought for the future. I gave in to one set of influences without giving much consideration to the others. It was my own weakness that made me decide between alternatives that I did not choose for myself. So many things had happened I felt pressed—desperate to decide. In my desperation, I saw only two alternatives—to live in fear for the rest of my life or to come to Russia with you."

"Natasha, you are simply confused."

"No, I am not. I see things much more clearly than I did before. I see there were always more alternatives for me than I thought. I did not have to come to Russia. I chose to come without thinking things through, without forethought."

She looked at him to see how he was taking this, and her heart went out to him. He looked so lost, so helpless, and the sight of it wrenched her heart. She knew what agony felt like, knew what it felt like to have your hopes and dreams shattered. But all the while she was feeling compassion for Niki, she could not help thinking of another. *Is this how Trevor felt when I sent him away?*

The sound of Niki's voice jerked her thoughts back. "It was forethought—concern for your future—that brought you here, or have you forgotten that your life was in danger?" he asked.

The shattering desperation she heard in his words flooded her with regret. Was she destined to go through life hurting people? For some reason, as she looked at Niki, seeing the suffering in his eyes, she could not help thinking she had seen an even deeper pain in Trevor's eyes. *I hurt him. Terribly. And now it's too late. Too late to tell him how sorry I am. Too late to tell him how much I still care. Too late to tell him I was wrong—so terribly wrong—to send him away. Too late to beg him to forgive me, to ask for another chance.*

"Natasha, have you forgotten those things?" he asked. "Have you?"

"No, I haven't forgotten," she said softly. She didn't want him to beg. She didn't want to carry that burden as well. Trevor had come to her a second time. Trevor had begged. Yes, and the burden of it was too great; the agony of it ate at her still. "Oh Niki. I haven't forgotten any of those things. It is simply that I realize there are other ways to deal with danger besides running away. I'm sorry for what I've put you through, sorry for any embarrassment this might cause you, but it's better this way. I know it. It is far, far better to have a small regret now than a bigger one later on."

"Now or later," he said, "the hurt is the same."

She sighed, feeling tired, drained. She didn't know what to do. She felt so helpless. "I find it strange that we make decisions that we cannot change based on things that do." She took his hands in hers. "Oh Niki.

Don't you see? It isn't too late. I can change what has happened. I can go back. But it must be now."

He pulled his hands away, cutting to the heart of her with a cold, cold look. "Is it because of *him*? Is that why?"

She shook her head. "No, Trevor isn't the reason why. I know it is too late for that. I know now that I was wrong, that it was my fault this has happened. Too late, I realize what a mistake I made. I should have listened to him instead of my wounded pride. I should have followed my heart's desire, instead of listening to my mind cry out for retribution. I wanted to make him pay, to see him suffer. But I never knew that when I struck him, I would be the one to bleed."

"What will you do . . . if you return?"

She looked down at her hands, noticing how soft and white they had become since coming here. "Other than returning to Marsham and resuming my work, I don't know. I only know I must go back, that I could never be happy with anyone else."

"I don't think you believe it's over. I think you still think there is a chance to get him back."

She shook her head. "No. Trevor is one of those things in my life that cannot be changed. He is probably married by now, and even if he isn't, he would never come back to me. Not after what I did, after the way I treated him."

"Then why go back? There is nothing for you there. At least I love you and want to marry you."

"I care too much for you to give you half a marriage, Niki. I couldn't do that to you any more than I could ever be happy here. I find that by coming here I have tied a knot that cannot be untied. The only way out is to cut it. I cannot marry you, Niki. I just can't. I want to go home. I want to return to England."

He stood, coming to where she sat, and took her hands, then drew her up to stand in front of him, drawing her into his arms. Her body stiffened in resistance. He kissed her forehead, feather-light and gentle, and all she felt was regret. He held her tightly, as if by doing so he could prevent her from going.

She could feel the impress of his uniform buttons, as well as the steady rhythm of his heart. He was kind and gentle, his body was long and lean. His face was molded perfection. A man who would be any woman's dream. But she did not love him—and she knew now that she never could.

He kissed her, and there was a bittersweet flavor to it, a kiss given neither in love nor hate, but one that dwelled in a midmost point, much like the way she had felt when she first came here, feeling neither English nor Russian, but lost somewhere in between.

She was no longer lost. She was past that now, and she realized she had suddenly grown up. She did not look at things the same way she did before, with everything based on sentiment. Now she could look at reason. Now she understood. The rashness of youth was behind her. She was like a piece of fruit, not knowing she was ripe until she had fallen from the tree. Hitting the ground had been especially painful, but she had discovered herself, and the core of strength within. She knew that the ability to survive was there.

She was a woman now. She could live with fear and not be afraid. Whatever awaited her in England she would face it. Fear and apprehension would no longer control her life. Everything was in sharper focus. The road before her was no longer crooked, but straight. Although her blood was Russian, the heart that pumped it was English to the core.

She was going home.

She didn't know how or when, but she knew it with an assurance she had never felt before. With a sense of peace that comes with making a decision, she pulled away from him, dropping her forehead to rest against his chest. He had become so dear to her, a friend that she could never replace. There were many, many things that she felt, but "I'm so sorry," was all she could seem to say.

He released her, and she felt herself go weak at the knees. She dropped back into the chair, uncertain as to what she should say next. She only knew it was best to finish what she had started, to put things in motion as quickly as she could. "I think it would be best if we left as soon as possible."

He didn't say anything, and she had difficulty reading what she saw in his eyes. There was sadness there, and regret, but there was something else, something that seemed to hover between fear and dread. Without speaking or even looking at her again, he turned to stand in front of the fire, his hands clasped behind him as he stared down into the flames.

"It isn't that easy, Natasha. There are reasons ... Things that have been put into motion ... Things that cannot be changed."

Her heart clattered in her chest. "What kinds of things, Niki? What are you trying to say?"

He didn't say anything, and she felt herself getting angry.

"Answer me," she said. "I have a right to know."

He turned to look at her, but she refused to look into his eyes. She didn't want what she saw there to soften her. She didn't want to back down now.

"I don't know how to tell you this, but leaving here now is impossible," he said. "You will have to stay."

She stared at him in disbelief. Her heart began to

pound. Her hands gripped the arms of the chair until her knuckles turned white. Had she heard him right? "Impossible?" she said. "I—I don't understand. You mean because of the weather?"

"I mean because of things you have no knowledge of. There are reasons, Natasha . . . Things you know nothing about."

She sprang to her feet, ignoring the warning signals he was sending out. She didn't care if he seemed afraid to tell her very much, nor was she concerned as to why. She had never felt so angry, nor more consumed with the need to know what he was keeping from her. "What kinds of things? What reasons?" she shouted. "Tell me, damn you! What are you talking about?"

He looked at her, and she found herself thinking it was a look she would carry to her grave. She had never known the eyes could express such anguish, such despair. He was torn. God, she could see that now, and it wrenched her heart to see just how much. Was it because of her? Because of her wanting to leave. *No,* she thought. *It isn't that. There is more . . . much more . . . Speransky.*

She closed her eyes, seeing Speransky's cold, black stare. What did he stand to gain from all of this? For an instant she felt as if she and the prince were locked in a battle of wills—and somehow, Niki had gotten himself trapped in the middle. She opened her eyes and looked into his. She had never known more than at that moment just how very much he loved her. "Tell me, Niki. Please . . ."

"I wish I could tell you," he said, "but I cannot."

A coldness settled into the marrow of her bones. Tears burned at the back of her nose. "Then I *am* a prisoner here."

His composure slipped. "You aren't a prisoner!" he

shouted, then gaining control of himself, his voice turned softer. "You aren't a prisoner, Natasha. You cannot leave, but they aren't the same thing. Please, don't look at it that way."

She gave a mocking laugh. "They aren't the same thing? How convenient for you to be able to see them in such a light. Tell me, does it ease your conscience to do so? Or do you simply think me too big a fool to know the difference?"

"Natasha . . . *chérie* . . ."

Trapped . . . She glanced around the room, feeling the walls closing in on her. Would she ever leave this place? Anger stiffened her resolve. The look she gave him could have been carved from stone. Her words were cold and detached. "Do not call me that again . . . ever!"

He sighed, rubbing the back of his neck. "If you would only be reasonable; if you would trust me just a little longer, I will explain everything."

"How much longer? After the betrothal ball? After I am forced to marry? When will you tell me? When it is too late? I am not a fool, Niki. I know there is more here than I am being told, and I know that somehow my brothers are involved. I don't know how big a part you play in all of this, or why Prince Speransky has such an interest in it. I only know one thing: I want to go home. You won't allow it. If I am not free to go as I please, then I am a prisoner."

He started to speak, but she cut him off.

"I will tell you one thing, and one thing only. You will come to regret this. That much I promise you."

"Darling Natasha. I regret it already."

CHAPTER
❦ FORTY-FOUR ❦

Natasha refused to go down for dinner that night. A short while later, she received what she supposed would be called a royal summons, delivered by Count Dolokhof.

Minutes later, she was escorted into a small, private study she had never seen before, where only Prince Speransky and Niki awaited her.

"Come in, my dear." Prince Speransky took Natasha's hand in his, a gesture that made her wonder if he thought this made him appear fatherly.

It did not.

He escorted her to a chair. "This may take awhile," he said. "Perhaps you should sit down."

She looked at Niki, but his expression was an unreadable mask. She looked back at the prince. "I will stand, thank you."

"Sit down, mademoiselle," the prince said in a manner that made her think she should do as he asked.

Natasha, wearing one of the plain dresses she had brought from England, dropped into the chair with a swish of silk, her gaze affixed on Prince Speransky's face. For a moment he simply returned her stare, as if he were waiting for her to demurely look away, giving him the edge over her. She remained steadfast, her gaze locked upon him, her stare unwavering.

Prince Speransky moved away from her then, taking up a position before the window, where he stood, military straight, his hands folded behind his back as he rocked back and forth from the balls of his feet to his heels. "I have received some information that distresses me."

Her gaze flicked to Niki, but his gaze was fastened upon the prince. "If you are referring to my desire to return—"

"I will do the talking, mademoiselle, if you please."

Natasha snapped her mouth shut.

"Hundreds of years ago . . ." he began.

Natasha groaned. Was this going to be a Russian history lesson, then?

The prince went on. ". . . clans led by Scandinavian princes made many raids into what is now Russia. These Scandinavian princes were known as Varangians, and one of their raiding clans was led by Rurik of Jutland."

"They were Vikings. I remember him from my studies," Natasha said, hoping to speed things along. "Rurik of Jutland became the progenitor of a dynasty that ruled portions of Russia until it died out in . . ."

". . . 1598," the prince finished, taking control of the conversation once again. He went on to tell her that back in the year 1598, Ivan the Terrible had killed his eldest son, Ivan. "In a fit of rage, leaving only his idiot son Fyodor to rule. Understandably, the dynasty died out with Fyodor."

Natasha squirmed in her seat. She was beginning to get a headache. She saw no point in all of this. All she wanted was to return home, and so far, she hadn't heard one reason why she couldn't. What, for goodness sake, did some Russian czar who had been dead for hundreds of years have to do with her? She wanted this conversation to be over. She wanted out of here. The prince, in spite of his attempts to be somewhat fatherly in his approach, made her nervous. "Why are you telling me all of this?" she finally asked.

Prince Speransky turned, raised his brows, and looked at her. "I see you have acquired the English habit of getting directly to the point."

"I do not mean to appear rude, but I would like to return to England, and so far, I have not heard one good reason why that is such a difficult request."

He gave her a cold smile. "Of course you may return to England, if that is your wish."

Quickly she looked at Niki, whose stunned expression said he was as surprised at this as she was. Natasha rose to her feet. "Thank you for being so gracious. My brothers and I do not wish to appear rude, but we are most anxious to return. I would like a moment with them, so that I might tell them the good news."

She glanced toward the door—and was about to start in that direction—when the prince's voice stopped her cold.

"*You* may return to England, Mademoiselle Simonov, but your brothers may not."

She gasped, whirling to face him. "What do you mean?"

"I mean exactly what I said. You may remain in Russia or you may return to England, but your brothers, Luka and Pavel, are to remain in St. Petersburg."

"For how long?"

"Forever, mademoiselle."

"Forever? But why? Why must they stay here? Why are you doing this? What are my brothers to you?"

"Now, would you like me to finish my story?"

Natasha swallowed, trying to ease the dryness in her throat. She nodded her head.

"Then return to your seat."

Natasha did as she was told.

"Several years ago some ancient documents were discovered. One of the documents proves Ivan the Terrible's son fathered a son before his father killed him in that rage of anger. We now have proof that your father was a descendant of Ivan the Terrible's—through his murdered son, Ivan, and the son he fathered before his death. Because of your father's death and the consequent fire, we thought there were no more living descendants of Ivan's son, that the dynasty died out when your brothers and you were killed in the fire. It was not until recently that I discovered, by chance, that you and your brothers were alive and living in England. Can you imagine what that bit of news meant to us? Do you not understand what will happen when the people of Russia, who are so dissatisfied with the czar, find this out? The line of Ivan the Terrible did not die out. It continues."

There were a lot of people Natasha would rather be related to than Ivan the Terrible, but she did not tell the prince that. Instead, she simply said, "I am sorry, but I still don't understand."

"Then understand this. Your brothers are the only known heirs to the dynasty begun by the Rurik princes."

She gave him a blank look. "But the czar . . . The Romanovs have ruled Russia for some time now."

"They are imposters. Theirs is not the true line. One of your brothers should be on the throne."

She could not have been more astonished if he had told her she would be crowned Queen of England. For a moment she sat there in stunned silence. *One of my brothers? One?* "All my brothers want is to return to England."

Prince Speransky's face grew dark red. The veins on his neck stood out. He took a threatening step toward her, and Natasha found herself sitting further back in the chair.

"You misunderstand me, mademoiselle. I have not taken the time, and gone to so much trouble, to bring you and your brothers to Russia only to have you treat it so callously. Your brothers are the true heirs to the Russian throne. That may not seem important to you, but to the Russian people, it could be a godsend. For that reason, it is imperative that they *must* claim what is rightfully theirs." He paused a moment, the anger in his face lessening, his tone turning condescending once more. "As their sister, you would be a princess."

A princess? Me? Natasha frowned at the thought, then felt the compunction to laugh outright. She had a perfect picture of that—a noble Russian princess with twigs and leaves caught in the fine gold lace that edged her skirts, her face smudged with dirt, bits of moss dangling from her hair.

"I have no desire to be a princess, and I am certain being a prince is the last thing running through Luka's and Pavel's minds. My brothers and I have no desire to live in Russia. England is our home now. We are happy with the lives we had there."

She finished speaking, and then it hit her . . . something the prince said.

I have not taken the time, and gone to so much trouble, to bring you and your brothers to Russia only to have you treat it so callously . . .

She came to her feet, and turning to face Niki, she said, "How could you?" Her voice faltered and she feared she might cry. "Oh, God! I trusted you! I believed in you—and all the while you were only—"

"Don't say it," he said softly, "because it isn't true."

"You were sent to England, weren't you? To find us; to bring us back. It was all part of a plan. You were sent there for a purpose, were you not?" She turned and began pacing. "Oh, God. I made it so easy for you. All you had to do was ask. Fool that I was, I believed you. I trusted you. You never had any intention of marrying me. It wasn't me you wanted. You only wanted my brothers."

"I may be guilty of many of the things you said, but as for loving you, that much was the truth. I had every intention of marrying you," Niki said. "I *still* want to marry you."

"Liar!"

"No lie," he said, "but the truth. Shall I prove it. Shall we be married now?"

"I would rather be dead."

Prince Speransky stepped between them. "I think enough has been said for now. I will give you both time to think about what has been said here tonight." Then to Natasha, he said, "Mademoiselle, we will speak of this another time, when your passions are not so hot."

"There is nothing to speak of. Time will not change our minds. If anything, it will only make us more determined. My brothers and I want to go home, and you won't allow it. Well, let me warn you now: I will not give up. You cannot keep us here forever. Do you hear me? I will try—and keep on trying—until I find a way."

That seemed to amuse the prince; a slow, curving smile stretched across his face. "You are welcome to try, mademoiselle. It should be amusing, I think, to play with you as the cat with the mouse."

CHAPTER
❧ FORTY-FIVE ❧

Natasha sat up most of the night, unable to believe this had happened again. First, Trevor betrayed her. Now Niki.

Not again. Please don't let it be true again.

It was true, and she knew it. He had been sent to England to dupe her—and he had succeeded. The knowledge of that hurt, but what hurt deeper still, was knowing that he had not been the first.

How different Trevor was from Niki, and yet how very much they were alike. They had both come to her with an intent to deceive, and they had both succeeded. There were other similarities, too. Both had come with the intention of convincing her of their love, then sworn later that it was true. Both had offered marriage. But there, too, they differed. While Trevor had offered marriage in the beginning with no intention of ever going through with it, Niki, at least, planned to fulfill his promise before they left England. She was certain of that. However, the thought did little to make her feel better. Was there no one she could trust?

* * *

All her talk with Prince Speransky did was get the date for her wedding to Count Nikolay Rostov moved forward and the time she was allowed to be with her brothers moved back to where it had been in the beginning, which meant she saw them hardly at all.

On one of the rare occasions they were allowed to be together, she told them everything, finding they were not surprised when she told them one of them was to become czar if the prince's plan was carried out.

"It's Luka," Pavel said, "because he was born before me."

"You shouldn't have told them," she said.

"The prince said we couldn't see you anymore if we didn't tell him which of us was born first," Pavel said.

Natasha realized then what a precarious position they were in and how the prince would use one of them to get what he wanted from the others.

"I don't want to be czar," Luka said. "I wish they'd picked Pavel."

"I don't want it, either," Pavel said. "I want to go home."

"We are going home," Natasha said.

The boys' faces brightened and they said in unison, "We are?"

Natasha nodded.

"How?" Pavel asked.

"I—I don't know yet," she said, seeing how their faces fell.

"She's just talking to make us feel better," Pavel said. "She knows we can't get out of here."

"No, I'm not. I have a plan. I just haven't worked out the details yet."

"What kind of plan?" Pavel asked.

"You have been told, I am sure, that the prince has

moved the date for my wedding forward and that he is giving a big ball to announce our engagement."

The boys nodded. "We know all that," Luka said.

"Well, what you don't know is that there is to be a special guest here that night, an Italian opera singer by the name of Adrianna Luciano. She is on tour and the prince has asked her to give a small performance here that night, in honor of our betrothal."

"So?" Pavel said. "Are we going to hide under her skirts when she leaves?"

Natasha smiled. "No, I am going to ask her to take a message to Tony."

"And Tony will come after us," Luka said.

"He had better," said Natasha.

"If he doesn't, Cecilia will make him," Luka said.

Natasha laughed at that. "Yes, she probably would."

"I thought you said she is from Italy," Pavel said. "How is she going to tell Tony?"

"She is on tour. The prince doesn't know it, but I saw a leaflet telling about her tour. After she leaves St. Petersburg she goes to Moscow . . . and then she goes to London."

"What if she won't help us?" Luka said.

"That is the chance we have to take."

"What if they won't let you talk to her?" Pavel asked.

"Then we will have to find another way," she said. "We cannot stay here. Do you understand why they haven't allowed us to go out except to remote places?"

The boys looked at each other and then back at her. They shook their heads.

"They don't want anyone to know there are two of you—that you are twins. They won't allow both of you to attend the ball. They will keep one of you locked away, just to make certain the rest of us do as we are told. They know that by keeping us apart they have a better chance of controlling us. I don't know if I'll be allowed to see you again, that's why I'm telling you all of this now."

As Natasha had feared, Luka and Pavel did not see their sister again before the night of the ball.

Two hours before it was to begin, Count Dolokhof instructed both Luka and Pavel to dress for the ball. "Only Luka will be going to the ball," he said, "but I think it best if you are both dressed alike."

He started from the room, then paused, turning back. "One more thing," he said. "Prince Speransky would like you to present a bouquet of flowers to Adrianna Luciano. You are to write a short note, thanking her for honoring us with her appearance. I will come after you when it is time. Have the note written when I return, Luka," he said, his gaze going from one twin to the other, as if he was uncertain as to which was which. "I will look at it then."

After the count left, Luka and Pavel looked at each other. "I have an idea," Pavel said. "We can write the note to the singer, but instead of thanking her, we'll ask her to contact Tony when she goes to London."

"But the count said he would read the note," Luka said.

The boys looked at each other, then Pavel smiled. "We'll both write notes," he said. "The count can't tell us apart. I'll pretend I'm you. I'll show him the thank-you note. You can have the note asking for help in your pocket. It's simple. When he comes back, he will ask to see the note. After he reads it, we'll switch places."

With that, the two of them put their heads together and began to plot their scheme, in the same manner they had done many times before at Marsham Manor.

* * *

Natasha dressed for the ball in an emerald green gown that Catherine the Great would have coveted. Her hair was piled on top of her head with a fortune in jewels woven into her braid. When she was dressed, Count Dolokhof brought an emerald-and-diamond necklace and earrings, instructing her that they were hers to wear.

"And if I refuse?"

"Prince Speransky would find a way to persuade you, mademoiselle."

"I am sure he would," Natasha said, "and I know the two boys he would use to do it."

"You will wear the jewels then?"

"Do I have a choice?"

The count dipped his head. "I will tell the prince you have acted wisely."

"Tell him anything you like. You will anyway."

When Niki came for her later, he entered the room, a commanding figure with sure strides, wearing a uniform of pure white, set off with ornately fringed epaulets and a heavily braided golden cord that had been looped and tasseled over one shoulder. There was a fortune in gold in the buttons of his coat, while a magnificent diamond cross hung from his neck with a silk ribbon of azure blue. A saber with a handle of inlay and jewels brushed against the golden stripe down the leg of his perfectly creased trousers.

She looked him over and said coldly, "Well, it would seem that our loving prince expects us to put on quite a dashing good show tonight. Tell me, are there any jewels left in the coffers?"

Taking her in his arms, Niki ignored what she said; instead, he simply told her she looked stunning.

She pulled away from him, turning back to face her mirror. "I do not feel stunning, Niki. I feel wretched."

"I know, but you might as well try to enjoy yourself. Feeling wretched won't change anything. Prince Speransky will keep one of your brothers away from the ball, just to make certain you behave yourself."

She didn't bother to tell him she had figured that much out for herself already. She simply turned away from the mirror and picked up her fan, giving him a direct look. "Oh? Does he think we are going to tell Adrianna Luciano everything? That we are going to beg her to take us with her? Or does he think we'll try to hide in her wardrobe?"

"He expects you might try something, and for that reason we will be closely watched."

"Even though he knows I won't do anything, simply because of what would happen to my brother if I did?"

"I must warn you, Natasha. Don't try anything foolish. It is too dangerous. Prince Speransky isn't like me. He would have no qualms about doing away with any one of you if it suited his purpose."

"I know that," she said. Then with an impersonal tone, she added, "Well, shall we go and get this over with?"

Much later, as Natasha and Niki sat listening to Adrianna Luciano sing, Count Dolokhof walked into her brothers' suite. Luka and Pavel, in identical full-dress uniforms, sat on the small settee near the fire.

"Luka?" the count asked, still not certain which twin was which.

Pavel nodded.

"Have you written the note?"

Pavel nodded.

"Good." The count carried in his arms a large bouquet of flowers, which he placed on a table near the door. He crossed the room and came to stand before Pavel. "Let me see the note," he said.

Pavel stood, removing a small cream-colored envelope from his pocket. He handed the note to the count.

Opening it, the count read the note. He nodded. "Very good," he said, and handed the note back to Pavel, who returned the note to his pocket. Then to Luka the count said, "Pavel, you understand that it is not possible for you to go the ball, but you must not change out of your uniform."

"Why?" Luka asked.

"It is only a precaution—in case Luka took ill and we needed to exchange you."

The count looked back at Pavel. "I'll carry the flowers," he said. "You keep the note in your pocket, Luka, until time to present them, then place the card in the flowers. Do you understand?"

Pavel nodded.

"Good. I'll be there with you, so there is nothing to worry about. I'll remind you when it is time to put the note in the flowers." He turned toward the door. "Well, it is time to be off. Come with me."

As the count started for the door, Luka stood up and Pavel sat down in the place Luka had just occupied. When Luka reached the door, the count looked down at him and smiled. "Be careful that you do not lose the note," he said.

"I won't," Luka said.

Because Natasha and her brother had behaved themselves at the ball, Prince Speransky felt generous. He instructed Count Dolokhof to bring Luka and Pavel to Natasha's room the next afternoon.

Not even the news that her brothers were coming to

see her could cheer Natasha. All she could think of was that she had been so closely guarded all evening she had not been given a chance to say anything more than "Hello" to Adrianna Luciano. It was only a setback, she kept telling herself. *She would think of another way.* Yet she feared she might have missed her only chance.

Her brothers were escorted into her room, and, with a click of his heels, Count Dolokhof departed. As soon as the count left, the boys began laughing. Natasha, having seen her brothers' mischief before, turned to them and said, "What have you done?"

"We have rescued us," Pavel said.

Natasha's heart hammered. "How?"

"The flowers," Luka said. "The ones I gave the opera singer last night. There was a note in it," he said proudly.

The boys went on to explain what they had done.

When they finished, Natasha's hand flew to her chest. "You mean the note for help that was in Luka's pocket was the note Adrianna Luciano received?"

"Yes," Pavel said, "because I pretended to be Luka at first, so the count read the note in my pocket."

"Oh my God! What if she tells the prince?"

"She won't," Luka said.

"How do you know?" asked Natasha.

"Because she opened the note and read it while I was standing there," Luka said.

"What did she do?" Natasha asked.

She kissed me and said, " 'What a love you are. Darling, I shall tell *everyone* I meet about zee touching note you have given me. *Everyone*, do you hear?' And then she looked at Count Dolokhof and stuffed the note down her bosom."

Luka said the words with such a high-pitched feminine voice and such a convincing Italian accent that she and Pavel doubled over with laughter.

"Darling," Natasha said a moment later, "I do not care if she tells *everyone* in zee world, as long as she tells Tony."

Then she hugged both of her brothers, and, kissing each of them, she said, "You are wonderful. I will never, ever say anything about your pranks again."

"I liked being hugged by Adrianna better," Luka said, with a teasing laugh. "She has a bigger bosom."

Natasha looked at both of them, unable to decide if she was happy because they were growing up or sad because they had.

CHAPTER
❧ FORTY-SIX ❧

Trevor looked at his brother, who had come barging into his office only minutes before, with the most bizarre story he had ever been privy to.

"What do you mean *I'll* have to rescue them?" Trevor said to Tony, with cold, ruthless fury. "They sent word to *you*, didn't they?"

Tony looked at his brother. "Trev, you know I can't go. Cecilia is due to have her baby any day now . . . and after what happened last time—"

"Then let them stay there. It's what they wanted, isn't it? I have been ordered out of Miss Simonov's life one time too many. A herd of elephants could not drag me back in."

"Trevor . . ."

"Tony, there is just so much rejection a man can take."

Tony's look softened. "I know, and I know you've had more than your share, but they need help."

"Then let them get it elsewhere. Or better yet, let them stay where they are. I find it ever so much more peaceful now that the Simonov clan is back where they belong."

"You don't mean that, Trev. You can't leave them there. They're prisoners."

Trevor gave him a cold look. "I can leave them and I *will* leave them. I have my own life to lead now, and in case you have forgotten, I am to be married in less than three weeks."

"If you aren't back in time, the wedding can be postponed."

"Not *this* wedding," Trevor said. "My feet are cold enough as it is."

Tony opened his mouth to speak.

"No," Trevor said. "I am not going. What Natasha does is none of my affair. If she needs rescuing, you'll have to find someone else to do it . . . or leave her there."

"You're the only one who can get them out and you know it. It won't be a problem for you, you can sail right into St. Petersburg. You've got your own ship."

"I am not going, Tony. Don't ask me again."

"Very well," Tony said, turning away and going to the door. He opened it, then turned back for one last look. "I guess I was mistaken. I thought you loved her," he said, shutting the door behind him.

Trevor picked up the blotter on his desk and threw it against the wall. "I do love her, goddammit, and it's almost destroyed my life!"

The next day Tony was sitting in his study thinking about Natasha and the twins when Trevor walked in.

Tony looked up. "Good God! You look terrible."

"Thank you, brother dear. Would you like me to tell you it is all your fault?"

"What happened?"

"I have wrecked my life—what little there was left of it, thanks to you."

"What do you mean?"

"After you left your guilt-ridden little burden on my stooped shoulders, I went home to get myself roaring drunk, and then I had the misfortune to pay my ex-fiancée, Lady Jane Penworthy, a visit."

"Your ex-fiancée? What happened?"

"What do you mean, what happened?" Trevor shouted. "What would you expect to happen?"

"I would expect that you told her Natasha was in trouble and that you had to go after her," Tony said.

"Yes," Trevor said, "and that is exactly what I told her."

"And?"

"And she told me if I went after her, the wedding was off . . . for good."

"What are you going to do?"

Trevor sighed and ran his hands through his hair, then he glanced at Tony with a look that laid him bare. "What else can I do? I'm going after her."

"When are you leaving?"

"Now."

* * *

A week after the ball Niki came to Natasha with some bad news. "I have to go away for a while."

"You're leaving? When?"

"I am leaving tonight," he said.

"Where are you going?"

"North," he said, "almost to the Finnish border—to a monastery near a place called Vyborg."

"Vyborg? Why are you going there?"

"I am taking the document there for safekeeping . . . the one that proves your family's connection to Ivan the Terrible."

"But why? Isn't it safe enough here?"

"The prince is concerned. He wants it in a place no one would think of looking. Although the people here in the palace are in his employ, he does not trust them all. He deems it best to have no one but the two of us knowing where the document and your brothers are."

"My brothers?"

"I'm taking Luka and Pavel there as well."

The color drained from her face, but the news did not shock her as much as she would have thought. Perhaps it was because she was becoming accustomed to shocks by now. "Why? Because the prince wants to guarantee they are in a remote place as well?"

He nodded.

She wanted to cry. "When—when will I see them again?"

"Not until after the wedding. I'm sorry."

She shook her head sadly. "Another measure to make certain I go through with it," she said.

"Is it so bad?" he asked. "Is the thought of marrying me so repugnant to you?"

"No, it isn't that. We've been over all of this before.

It's wrong. You know that as well as I. There are too many lies, too many deceptions between us now."

He nodded. "I would like to think that we are at least still friends."

One tear rolled down her cheek. Then there were two. She gave him a melancholy smile. "Oh, Niki. We *are* friends," she said, "but we are also enemies."

CHAPTER
❧ FORTY-SEVEN ❧

I will not cry. I will not cry. I will not cry.

You're too big to cry, and you know it won't do any good anyway. Natasha reminded herself of this, wondering when she had ever listened to good advice.

Sitting cross-legged on the bed, she could not help brooding, for there was no way she could get over the cloud of gloom that seemed to hover about her. Her brothers and Niki had been gone one week when this depression seemed to grip her, a lowness of spirit she could not seem to shake. She wanted to see her brothers. She wished Niki was here, so she could talk to him. She found herself wondering if Adrianna had gotten word to Tony. Was Trevor married? Had Cecilia had her baby? Then she remembered her own lost baby.

Too much, she thought, putting her palms to her temples and giving her head a squeeze. There were too many thoughts, too many memories, all of them causing her pain.

She could not think about the past, for she was reminded of Trevor and her loss. Yet whenever she tried to pull her thoughts from yesterday and focus on tomorrow, she was reminded that the future did not look much brighter. She felt trapped—trapped in the meaningless void of the present, unable to recall her past without pain, afraid to think about the future without apprehension.

Maybe crying wasn't such a bad idea after all.

A tear rolled down her cheek. Then two. Before long she was crying like a baby. Once she started crying she could not seem to stop.

Falling across her bed, she cried for the loss of her brothers and for her own shortcomings that had caused it. She cried for the loss of her unborn child, and the hatefulness of her turning away from its father. She cried for the weariness she had seen in Niki's eyes, and for the uncertainty of her own future. But once she started crying, she found what she cried for the most was thinking of Trevor wed to another.

Tears soaked the satin coverlet. Sobs choked her throat. She groped blindly for her handkerchief, and burying her face in it she cried brokenly for having lost the only man she'd ever loved. She tried to muffle the heart-wrenching sobs of acute loneliness that gripped her, but nothing would stop the agony.

Trevor . . .

It was unfair that she realized only too late she could not live without him. She, who had thought herself so strong, so capable. Well, she had dished up something she could not swallow this time. She closed her eyes in agony, the choking, overwhelming grief consuming her once more.

For days she had not been able to eat. She slept in only fitful snatches before the dreams began to haunt her—dreams of what might have been. And now she had started to cry, finding she could not stop. "Trevor," she whispered. "I'm so sorry."

Something scraped outside her window. A scuffling sound—quick, and faint, then silence. She raised her head, listening, then hearing nothing, she turned to look toward the window, unable to see anything. *Well, what did you expect, three floors up?*

She was about to turn her head away when she heard a thump, then a scraping noise. Her heart hammering in her throat, she watched as the window slowly opened.

Her heart skipped a beat, then seemed to lodge in her throat. What happened next was undoubtedly the greatest shock of her life.

A booted foot came through the window. Another foot. Then two legs. A moment later Trevor stood before her. Shock drained the color from her face, seeming to take away all feeling. She felt as if she had been struck dumb.

"You were expecting someone else?" he asked.

She had no idea how he had come to be here. She only knew that he had come, that he was here, magically appearing out of nowhere, when he was the last person in all of the world she would have ever expected to see.

For a moment she could not speak, nor could she move. She could only sit there, staring at him as if he were some sort of apparition. She heard herself shudder, and she realized she had stopped crying.

"However do you manage to get yourself into such scrapes?"

Trevor . . . So dear, so beloved, so lost to her—and yet he was here.

He couldn't be.

But he was. Trevor, standing in the shadows, his face bathed in moonlight. Trevor looking as tall and beloved as she had ever seen him.

Three floors up?

She must be dreaming, she thought. She had to be dreaming. She blinked her eyes.

"I'm no apparition—just a fool fruitlessly searching for someone more stupid than himself."

Her heart cracked. "You have found her," she whispered as she studied every detail of his cherished face. "Oh, Trevor, I am so glad to see you."

His look, while not cold, showed no signs that he was moved or touched in any way by what she said. "Are you now?"

She nodded. "Yes."

His expression was one she could only call detached and impersonal. What could she expect?

He stepped toward her, and she saw the open window behind him, reminding her of what had just happened. "How did you manage it?" she asked, still not believing what she had seen. "This room . . . it is three floors up."

"Only one floor, if you come from the roof of the other wing." He went to the lamp and turned it up, then he turned back to look at her, and she could well imagine what he saw—a whimpering woman with her face red and swollen, her hair in disarray, sitting on a rumpled bed in her dressing gown. Not that it mattered, for he did not seem to notice, but what really hurt was knowing there was no reason why he should. Twice he had begged her forgiveness. Twice she had sent him away.

"How did you know I was here, in this room?" she asked.

"I brought my spy glass from the ship. I like you in that shade of blue, by the way."

Her mouth gaped open as she remembered the aquamarine blue gown she had worn earlier. "You watched me change my clothes?"

"I had to be certain it was you."

She was too stunned to speak, but he was having no trouble. "You're too thin," he said. "What are they trying to do, starve you to death?"

"The choice not to eat was mine," she said, noticing how his gaze went to the tray of food sitting untouched on the table by the bed.

"Get dressed," he said curtly.

She could not believe he was here. "Why you?" she asked, not realizing she had said it aloud.

He gave her a cold look. "Why indeed?"

"I didn't mean—"

He cut her off. "Obviously, I have come for you, which should come as no surprise, fool that I am."

"My brothers said they sent word to Tony."

"Who could not come. But if you are dissatisfied with me . . . Want me to leave?"

"No!" she said, scrambling off the bed, her gown riding high on her leg and exposing a naked hip.

She heard him groan; the sound of it warmed her, but the look in his eyes sent a chill to drive the warmth away. "I can't believe you are here," she said, more from nervousness than anything else.

"They say stupidity saves a man from going mad. Hurry up," he said then. "Where are your brothers?"

"Gone. They've been taken to a monastery up north."

"More problems. Just what I wanted to hear." He reached for a roll on her tray, and coming to her, stuffed it in her mouth. "Eat," he said. "I don't have time to coddle a weakling. Do you have any idea where this monastery is or what it is called?"

She pulled the roll out of her mouth long enough to say, "I only know it is north of here, close to the Finnish border, near a place called Vyborg."

"It is near the sea then?"

She nodded. "You came in your ship?"

"And prefer to leave by the same way," he said, shoving the roll back into her mouth. "Dress warmly."

"Mmmmph," she said, stepping behind the open door of her armoire, knowing he could see her legs beneath the door, but too happy to care. A moment later she stepped out. "How are we going to get out of here?" she asked, praying he would not say by the window.

He looked as if he were about to smile, but he didn't. "I prefer to use doors whenever possible," he said. "Getting out is always more difficult than getting in."

"Yes," she said, thinking that rule could apply to other things as well.

They moved toward the door: opening it slightly, Trevor looked out. "Come on," he said. "How far is it to the stairs?"

"Not far," she said, slipping out behind him. "Down the hallway and to the left."

Keeping against the wall, they hurried down the hallway, making the turn, seeing the stairs just ahead.

Somewhere a door closed. They ignored the sound of it, jerking to a halt when they heard the approaching sound of feet.

A moment later two guards came up the stairs. Seeing them, one of the guards shouted as they broke into a run.

Turning swiftly, Natasha and Trevor ran back down the hallway. Behind them, the guards gave another shout. She heard the sound of running feet and knew the guards were drawing closer.

They reached her room, slipping quickly through the door. Trevor slammed it behind them, turning the key in the lock. The lock was small and fragile, made for privacy, not to keep an armed guard out. She knew it would not buy them much time.

"Hurry," he said. "We have no choice now. We'll have to take the window."

She swallowed but didn't argue. She would just as soon tumble to her death from three floors up with Trevor as starve to death in the solitary confinement of her room, or be run through with a saber belonging to one of the guards.

"Blow out the lamp," he said, moving to the window. She turned the lamp down, the light in the room growing dim, until they were sealed in darkness. Gradually her eyes became adjusted to the loss of light; glancing toward the window, she could see a dim light.

She came to the window, then glanced at him, thankful the room was dark, so he would not see the fear on her face.

"It isn't as difficult as it seems," he said, as if climbing out a window on the third floor was something he did every night before going to bed.

He went out first, disappearing into the darkness just as she heard the pounding on the door. She leaned out over the casement, seeing a knotted rope swinging next to the window. She looked up, thinking it must be fastened to the roof overhead. She looked down, unable to see him or the end of the rope, which was swallowed up in the darkness below. "Trevor?" she whispered.

"Down here," he said. "Don't try to climb down the rope. Drop. I'll catch you."

"I wouldn't blame you if you didn't," she said.

"What do you think—that I came all this way to drop you on your bum?"

"It would serve me right."

"Yes," he said, "it would. But I am feeling charitable tonight. Come on. Hurry."

The lock on the door rattled, then came the sound of heavy pounding.

"I'm afraid," she said. "I can't see you."

"But you can hear me," he said, "so you know I'm here. Hurry, Natasha. We haven't all day."

Something heavy hit the door; it rattled on its hinges. She climbed out the window, hind side first. A moment later she was hanging by her hands, feeling the burning scrapes on her arms, but too terrified to let go.

The door rattled again. The lock gave, and the door swung open, hitting the wall with a thud. She heard a shout, the hurried tread of feet.

"Drop," he said. "I've got you."

She wanted to, but her hands seemed frozen.

"Natasha, for God's sakes! You're going to have to trust someone sometime, and it might as well start with me. Now, let go!"

She closed her eyes and took a swallow. Then she let go, feeling herself falling through nothing but empty black space.

"Oooph!" she said, hitting something warm and solid. Her arms went around his neck.

"Don't go getting all warm and cuddly on me now," he said. "I didn't come here for that."

It was a harsh reminder—and an effective one. She didn't have time to think more, for he dropped her on her feet.

"I heard shots. Are you all right?" a voice asked from somewhere behind them, and Natasha whirled around to see Farnsworth, the first mate from the *Mischief Maker*, a gun in his hand.

"We're fine," Trevor said, "but I thought you were going to meet me back at the quay."

"I decided to wait around a bit, just in case."

"Your wait is over," Trevor said. "They're right behind us. Let's go."

She heard voices overhead, then shouts. Trevor grabbed her hand and led her across the roof to where a ladder waited.

This time, she went first. When they reached the bottom, he said, "Now, where in the hell is Vyborg?"

Two shots rang out, and she started running. "I don't know," she said, "but can't we find out on the way?"

"I like the sound of that," Farnsworth said, running along beside her.

"Take her with you," Trevor said. "I'll cover you from back here."

She turned her head to see Trevor drop back, running a few feet behind them. Farnsworth took her by the hand and began to pull her along with him. She ran toward the river in a blind panic, amazed that her feet could move with such swiftness when her mind went so slow.

They seemed to run forever, and she wondered if he had decided to run all the way to Vyborg. She had almost decided that he had, when at last they reached the quay. She looked back once more, seeing a mounted guard coming up behind them, their torches tiny pinpricks of light glowing in the darkness. Turning back, the sound of horses approaching quickly reminded her that they would be upon them in a minute.

A shot rang out. Then another.

Behind her, Trevor swore. She pulled away from

Farnsworth, then turned, seeing Trevor jerk to a halt, his hand going down to grab the top of his leg.

"My God! Farnsworth, he's been shot." More shots rang out. A red hole seemed to explode across his leg.

Farnsworth ran back, his arm going around Trevor's shoulders. "It's not as bad as it looks," Trevor said as the two of them hurried toward her.

"There it is," Trevor said a moment later, and she looked up. She saw the black outline of his ship riding the waves of the Neva.

They went down a series of steps, to where a dingy waited, with two men to help them row. They had just pushed away from the quay when she saw the reflection of torches upon the water, heard the report of a gun.

Trevor shoved her down in front of him, leaning low over her, covering her body with his. She couldn't see anything, but she could hear the steady rhythm of his breathing, the splash of the oars cutting through the water. Another shot rang out, then another. She heard one whistle overhead, then hit the water with a plop. More shots rang out, but she did not hear any of them come as close as the one moments before.

It seemed like an eternity before he said, "You can sit up now. We're out of range."

She raised her head, looking down at the red stain on his thigh. "How is your leg?"

"I'll live," he said.

She did not have the opportunity to say more, for at that moment the dingy scraped—then thumped—against the side of the *Mischief Maker*.

She had never been so happy to see anything in her life. Taking her hand, Trevor helped her to the ladder. Just as she started up the rope, she turned back to him. "I'll never say anything about the name of your ship again," she said.

"Don't make any rash promises. We're not out of this yet," was all he said.

Once they were aboard his ship and underway, Natasha sat on the corner of the desk in Trevor's cabin, watching Farnsworth tend to Trevor's leg.

"You're lucky at least," Farnsworth said. "The bullet went clean through." She watched Farnsworth cut away the leg on Trevor's pants, saw, too, the muscled expanse of leg. A smile curved across her mouth.

Trevor gave her a curious stare.

"I was remembering the time you removed your trousers in Tony's dressing room, and the look on Cecilia's face when she opened the door and saw you standing there in your drawers. She looked positively enslaved. That," she said, "was when I realized I loved you."

"It was a long time ago," he said, "and doesn't have much bearing on the problems that face us now."

"Not on your problems, perhaps."

He looked at her strangely, but he did not respond to that, not that it mattered. She knew him well enough to know he had not ignored her words as easily as he would like her to think. Somewhere, deep inside of her, she felt the first stirring of promise, the first faint glimmer of hope.

"Have you married?"

His head jerked up. "What?"

"I saw the announcement of your betrothal in the paper. I was just wondering . . . Oh, never mind."

"I'm not married," he said gruffly. "You didn't give me enough time."

"I'm sorry," she said.

He changed the subject by asking several questions about her time in St. Petersburg. She told him about it, about Prince Speransky and the way they had sent the note with Adrianna Luciano. Then she told him about their family tie to Ivan the Terrible.

"Ivan the Terrible," she said. "Can you believe it?"

"Yes," he said. "With ease."

It was still dark when they reached the monastery at Vyborg, and Natasha found herself wishing it was daylight, for there was something about the place that made her shudder.

Trevor, at first, told her to wait on board, but she would have none of it. After a few minutes of arguing, he relented. "Only because we don't have much time. When word reaches this Speransky, I'm sure it won't be any problem for him to figure out where we are headed."

"How much time do you think we have?" she asked.

"I don't know. Probably not much. Unlike us, they know where they are going, and will make better time."

The moon was hanging low in the sky, spreading mellow light and long, stretching shadows across the ground as she and Trevor made their way through the iron fence that surrounded the monastery. It would be dawn soon, and with the prince's men close behind, they would have to find her brothers quickly.

"Oh, Lord," she said, feeling quite weak as she tried to wiggle through the opening Trevor made in the bars of the fence. She noticed he went over the top and wondered if she shouldn't have tried that way as well. Her legs felt so rubbery by the time she squeezed herself through that she crumpled. He grabbed her by the arm before she fell.

"I'm not too steady on my feet," she said.

"That's because you almost starved yourself to death. Why don't you—?"

"I am not going to wait here alone," she said. "This place frightens me." She looked around her. "I prefer to be with you." She inched closer, feeling his gaze locked upon her, finding she was unable to look at him, for shame ate at her still.

"Then keep well behind me, and if anything goes wrong, run," he whispered. "Speransky's men won't have any qualms about shooting me, but they won't risk shooting you."

They approached the crumbling old monastery from the back, staying to the thick overgrowth that edged the fencing that encircled it. From every angle, the place looked haunted, shimmering in the moonlight, a mere mist before her eyes that brought to memory direful tales she'd heard as a child, tales that made her whimper and hide under the covers. She could understand why Prince Speransky had chosen this place. No one in their right mind would ever suspect anything of value or anyone of sound mind would be here.

They left the screen of trees and shrubbery and ran across a barren expanse, treading upon ground that was still damp from the recent melting of snow. Somewhere in the distance a dog barked, but around them, all was silent. There were no signs of life, no smoke coming from the chimney, no lights—nothing, save the reassurance that Trevor was near and the sound of her own heart beating.

They crossed what had at one time been a garden, passing an old sundial before they reached a weathered door. "Wait here," Trevor whispered, and breaking the lock, he slipped inside.

It seemed an eternity before he returned, but she knew it had not been all that long. "Come on," he said. "I think I've found their room."

Natasha nodded when he motioned for her to be quiet.

She followed him down two long, winding corridors,

holding her breath when he stopped at a door. "What makes you think they are in there?" she whispered.

He put his ear to the door. "Because I can hear them talking. At least, I pray it's them," he said, opening the door.

"Trevor!" they said in unison, scrambling off their beds.

Natasha ran to them, taking each of them in her arms. "Are you all right?" she asked, giving each of them the once-over.

"We're fine," Luka said, turning his face up to hers, and she felt her heart thud at the dear sight of his tousled golden head. "A dashing good bit of adventure it was, too."

Natasha boxed his ears. "Adventure? You almost got yourself killed."

"We may yet," Trevor said. He ruffled the hair on Pavel's head and said, "Come on. We need to get out of here. It's almost daylight."

They'd started for the door, when Natasha said, "Wait!"

Trevor stopped and turned, giving her an exasperated look. "Now what?"

"The document," she said. "The one that proves our lineage to Ivan—"

"Natasha, we don't have time to go hunting for keepsakes. Why in God's good name would you want proof of that?"

"I don't want proof for myself," she whispered. "I want to destroy it, so they won't have a reason to come after us again. I don't know about you, but I could live the rest of my life without another adventure. Without proof—"

"You're right," he said harshly, cutting her off.

"If only we knew where this document was," Natasha

said, sticking her head through the door and looking down the corridor.

"I know where it is," Pavel said. "I saw it on the desk in Niki's room this afternoon."

"Are you sure it was the document?" Natasha asked.

"He showed it to me," Pavel said.

"Where is his room?" Trevor asked.

"I'll show you," said Luka.

They crossed the hall, going to Niki's room, which wasn't too far away, and was, thankfully, empty. Once they were inside, Trevor lit a candle, placing it on the table beside the bed.

The room was much larger than her brothers' room, and looked to be some sort of library, for volumes of ancient books and manuscripts lined the walls and the large desk was cluttered with maps and old documents.

They had almost reached the desk when they heard a noise and turned, seeing the door open as Niki came into the room, a gun in his hand.

Niki looked from Trevor to Natasha, then to where her brothers stood behind them. "Somehow this doesn't surprise me," he said. "I had the feeling that you would come, even before Speransky's men arrived with the news."

"Speransky's men . . . They are here?" she asked.

He nodded. "I have the whole of five minutes to persuade you to give up this madness and to return to St. Petersburg."

"And my brothers?"

"Nothing has changed for them, I am afraid."

"Then we cannot return."

"Nor can I let you go."

She looked at Trevor. His face was tense, his jaw clenched. Her gaze went from him to Niki and then to the desk, resting on the scattered papers lying there. She hoped Trevor would divert him by talking, to give her time to locate the document. Perhaps she could grab it and rip it to pieces before Niki could stop her. That, at least, should throw a cog in the prince's well-laid plans.

"It isn't there," Niki said.

Natasha's head jerked up. She felt the color drain from her face. *So close,* she thought. They had come so close. Her gaze locked with Niki's; for a moment the two of them stood there, as if each was remembering another time, another place.

After what seemed an eternity, Niki picked up the candle and moved behind the desk. Placing the candle on the corner of the desk, he turned slightly, and while keeping the gun aimed at them, he used one hand to remove a few books from the shelf behind the desk, extracting a small chest that was secreted away.

"Pavel," he said, "come here."

Pavel went to stand beside him as Niki withdrew a key from his pocket. "Unlock it," he said, handing Pavel the key.

Pavel unlocked the chest.

"No, don't open it," Niki said.

He motioned for Pavel to return to where he had been; when he was standing beside Luka once more, Niki opened the chest and withdrew a yellowed sheet of parchment. Even from where she stood, Natasha could tell it was very old.

"I believe this is what you were looking for," he said.

Natasha's gaze never left his face. Their eyes locked, and as they had done before, they stared at each other. The distance and the things between them stretched beyond imagining, and Natasha could not help wondering if this was the end. Consumed in the paralysis of fear, she could only let her eyes say what the rest of her could not. There was too much goodness in him. She knew there was. But then she had trusted him, as she had trusted Trevor, and like Trevor, he had deceived her.

She saw the muscle in his jaw clench, and for just a moment, her gaze dropped down to the gun in his hand.

His knuckles were white.

She knew the battle that went on inside him, knew that she had to try something. "Come with us, Niki," she said. "You aren't part of this. I know that."

Looking back at his face, she saw the beads of perspiration on his forehead, knew the struggle went on still. *Please . . . You are our only hope . . . If not for me, then at least for my brothers . . . Please . . .*

"Come to England with us," she said again.

Suddenly she saw something in his eyes and her gaze dropped down to the sheet of parchment in his hand. Slowly he lifted his hand and brought the paper to rest over the candle. It ignited with a *woosh*, the paper crackling and curling up at the edges. He dropped it on the floor, and the five of them stood in silence, listening to the crackling sound of their one link to history going up in smoke.

When it was nothing more than a pile of blackened ash, Natasha looked back at Niki's face. "Go on," he said, not looking at her but at Trevor. "Take them—all of them. Get out of here before I change my mind."

Oh, God, he was giving them their freedom. Suddenly it struck her, just what that meant. He would have to come with them, for if he didn't . . . Natasha took a step toward him, ready to beg him to come, if necessary. "Niki—"

"Go on," he said, waving the gun at Trevor, his voice sounding more harsh this time. "Get her out of here. Get them all out of here."

She looked at him, trying to find some understanding of this in his eyes. Why was he doing this, when it would have been so simple for him to come?

"Go quickly," he said, his voice harsh, "before it's too late."

Trevor took Natasha by the arm; they hurried toward the door. Just as they reached it, Natasha jerked her arm away and turned back to look at him one last time.

"I did love you," he said. "I never lied about that."

"I know," she said.

A moment later the four of them hurried through the door.

Standing alone in the room, Niki stared at the open door. " 'Our hours in love have wings,' " he whispered, " 'and second thoughts were ever wiser.' Go in love, little Natasha. Go, and don't look back."

A moment later he put the gun to his head.

CHAPTER
❧ FORTY-EIGHT ❧

Natasha looked at the exhausted faces of her brothers, asleep in their cabin. They were young men now, and she felt a sense of loss. Is this how it felt to be a mother? To tuck your babes to bed one night and have them wake up grown? She covered them with a blanket and went to find Trevor, who had been avoiding her since they set sail for home.

They were off the coast of England now, and she knew the time had come.

She found him in his cabin. The room was dark, and she could see only the outline of his body as he stood before the window, his back to her. Beyond him the water was a backdrop of moonlit spangles upon a pitch-black sea.

She closed the door with a click, but he did not turn around. "I knew you would come," he said.

"Yes," she said, "you always seemed to know me better than I knew myself."

"There was a time when I thought I knew you; a time when I realized I did not. Still," he said, turning and offering her a salute with the glass in his hand, "I had a damnable time purging you from my mind."

"And were you successful?"

"Reasonably so. As long as I didn't remember what it was like."

"And was it difficult . . . not remembering?"

"What do you think?"

"I think it was the most difficult thing you have ever done."

"And why do you say that?"

"Because remembering is like a woman. If you don't chase her, she will follow you on her own."

"And does she finally follow on her own?"

"With her heart in her hands," she said, going to stand before him.

He looked down at her, seeing the path of tears on her face, and he reached out to wipe them away with his thumbs, his hands slipping down to cup her face, lifting it into the moon's full light. "Natasha, Natasha," he said. "How this face has haunted me. You belonged to me. I think that is why it hurt so much. You were mine, and I damn well knew it. That made me begrudge everyone—everything—that kept us apart."

A wave of anguish shot through her, so sharp and stabbing that she made a small moaning sound, swaying on her feet.

The look he gave her was bittersweet. " 'Flesh of my flesh and blood of my blood,' it was always those little sounds you made that were my undoing. When I heard you had gone . . . with him . . . I remembered the way you felt when I touched you, the sounds you made. The thought of someone else touching you like that—"

He threw back his head with an anguished cry. "God, to love like that and be defeated."

She was crying now. "I love you," she said. Then "No. What I feel—it is so much more. Whatever I have done, whatever pain I have inflicted, I can only tell you I have felt it so much more. I love you, Trevor. I have always loved you."

His arms came around her, drawing her against him, and she closed her eyes, laying her head against his chest, her arms going around his middle. She could hear the secret sound of his heart beating an ancient song of strength and endurance. In a rush of feeling, she felt the spirit of her homeland, a thousand years of history, a collection of memories as ancient as faith coming out of a frozen haze. The shadows of snow in October, a czar's garden in spring, the dull lilac of a winter morning, the glint of crimson sun on an ancient dome. She knew now that she would never leave Russia—she was Russia.

She saw herself in a twilit forest, a place where she had been before. He was there waiting for her, amid the yellow fields of rape and pastures green. . . .

She was home.

ELAINE
COFFMAN

Published by Fawcett Books.
Available at your local bookstore.